FATHOMS

OF

FORGIVENESS

Book Two of the

Sacred Breath

Series

By Nadia Scrieva

ISBN-13: 978-1475065688
ISBN-10: 147506568X

For Melody Bernal. Your enthusiasm is my rocket fuel.

TABLE OF CONTENTS

Full fathom five thy father lies;
Of his bones are coral made;
Those are pearls that were his eyes;
Nothing of him that doth fade,
But doth suffer a sea-change
Into something rich and strange.
- Shakespeare, The Tempest

Chapter 1: Tremendously Effective Threatening

"If you ever attempt to harm her, I swear on the souls of my Viking ancestors that I will not hesitate to shoot you again."

He swallowed. "I believe you… grandma."

Visola snorted at being called this. She moved her slender fingers up to fiddle with the barrel of the rifle on her back. "Young man," she almost sneered. "Don't you dare think that just because I'm now aware that you're my grandson anything is going to change between us. I have been Aazuria's defender for five hundred years, and she is more than a job to me. She is my friend, she is my mentor, she is my monarch, and she is at the top of my list of females I would totally experiment with if I ever happen to develop lesbian curiosities. The last time I shot you? Consider it a warning spank on the bottom. Next time I won't be so forgiving."

Trevain lifted a hand to scratch under his ear sheepishly. This encounter was not going as smoothly as he had hoped. He glanced at Aazuria, who only gave him half of a shrug (one of her shoulders had been badly injured) and a half-encouraging smile. He still was not accustomed to the changed appearance of his fiancée. Aazuria's snowy-white hair had been garnished with dozens of strands of freshwater pearls, and gathered into a stylish side-ponytail which hung over her good shoulder. He could not look into her newly cerulean eyes without feeling a small jolt of electricity travel through him. It was silly and superficial that the melanin draining from her body would have such a profound effect on him, but it was what they represented that thrilled him most: her true self was bared to him, all her secrets exposed in her new skin.

They would be married soon, but not soon enough for

his liking.

He realized that he felt a bit jealous of his grandmother; he wished he could have been at Aazuria's side for five hundred years. The loyal bond between the women was so fierce that he could hardly understand or relate to it. He had never loved anyone that hard, or for that long. There was his younger brother Callder whom he had taken care of for most of his life, but that relationship had been strained even at its best. As Trevain beheld Aazuria's stately posture he realized he was hoping to learn what it was like to be devoted to someone for centuries. He was only a normal almost-fifty-year-old man, and not too long ago he had considered himself elderly. How quickly everything had changed.

Aazuria sent him a puzzled smile, and he realized that he had been staring at her, lost in thought. He cleared his throat before turning back to Visola. "I'm very sorry to have stolen your woman, grandma." He was lying. He was not really sorry.

"Okay, cool it with the 'grandma' shtick. It's making me uncomfortable. Just call me 'General' for now." Visola grimaced. It was a peculiar situation, because the red-haired warrior woman still looked like she was in her twenties. "For the record," she said, "I'm completely straight, and so is Aazuria, but I was just trying to demonstrate the unparalleled breadth and intensity of my love for her. She is as close to me as my own sister—and my own sister is my *identical twin*, in case you haven't noticed!"

"I noticed," Trevain said, glancing at the other green-eyed redhead in the room. The quiet doppelganger was leaning against a wall with her arms crossed, rolling her eyes at her sister's temper and unobtrusively observing the conversation. He feared having to deal with another overbearing and aggressive matriarch like Visola. (One was truly enough.) However, his curiosity and politeness won out, and he extended his hand in greeting to the woman in the shadows. "We haven't been introduced."

2

The woman straightened and moved towards him to accept his greeting. "I am Sionna," she said simply. He was immediately surprised by the difference in her demeanor. Although she was a duplicate of Visola, her expression was infinitely calmer, and her voice was infinitely more tranquil. It was impossible that anyone would confuse the two sisters after a few seconds of hearing each of them speak. Once Sionna clasped his hand, she seemed to realize that it was not affectionate enough, and she smiled and gave him a gentle hug. "I'm delighted to meet you. Aazuria has told us great things, but some of us did not believe them." She glanced at her sister dryly as she said this, momentarily forgetting that she had been just as suspicious and disapproving.

"Should I have believed her, Sio?" Visola immediately snapped. "He did try to hurt her. Several times. If I hadn't been there..."

"I doubt he really meant to... but it does not matter. The past is in the past," Sionna said to her sister. She turned back to Trevain with a warm smile. "Don't bother calling me great-aunt. That would be strange. Technically I have the same DNA as your grandmother, so I could be considered—oh, never mind. I sometimes ramble on and on about everything biology-related, so just stop me if I get boring. You may call me Auntie Sio if you like. That's what your mum used to call me when she was a wee thing."

Trevain was a bit surprised at the thought of his mother being young; he had never known anyone from his mother's side of the family. Now that he was in Adlivun, he could fill in the pieces of his life that had always been missing. "It's great to meet you, Auntie Sio."

Visola frowned. "Don't get too cozy with him, sis. He may have our blood, but he was not raised among us. We have no idea what large, crucial fragments of common sense he's lacking. He put my little girl in an insane asylum for forty years!"

"Psychiatric hospital," he corrected, but he had lowered

his voice and head shamefully.

Aazuria stepped in then, seeing his discomfort. She slipped her arm around him gently. "This has been a rather touching family reunion. Thank you both for so warmly welcoming Trevain."

"Welcoming?" he asked her in an undertone. "Warmly?"

"Darn, I forgot to pop a fruitcake in the oven." Visola said, snapping her fingers. "I was too busy winning a war." When Trevain sent Aazuria an awkward look, Visola cheerfully took her rifle off her back and pointed it at Trevain. "Hey, grandson, do you want to see how my underwater assault rifle works?"

"No, thank you." He rubbed his arm, remembering the impact of the previous bullet which she had shot between the bones of his forearm. The wound had not completely healed, but he knew that he had deserved that bullet. Long after the scar had faded, it would still be depressing to remember his own actions which had earned him the sniping from his grandmother.

"She's just bluffing," Sionna informed him. "That particular gun fires a heavy tungsten dart and it's only meant for shooting underwater—it doesn't aim as well in the air due to different dynamics."

"Don't tell him that!" Visola hissed at her sister. She moved forward, placing the muzzle directly in front of his face. "Can't miss from this range. I will shoot you, kid. I will shoot you in a much more painful location than before." As she said this, she glanced down at his nether regions and wiggled her eyebrows menacingly. Visola's threatening stare had been expertly honed over several generations of threatening, and it was tremendously effective.

"Uh, I…" Trevain took a step back warily.

Aazuria could not hold back a chuckle. She gently elbowed her husband-to-be. "Do not worry so. Your grandmother is the most terrifying thing in all of Adlivun.

That is why she is my undefeated general."

"She still has a gun pointed at my face," Trevain said matter-of-factly.

"Oh, sweetie. Forgive my impolite sister," Sionna said, putting her hand on the weapon's barrel and lowering it. "She's just very, very new to being a grandmother. Just give her some time, Trevain, and she will warm up to you."

"I'm warming up to him already," Visola said with a frosty smile.

"I can see that," Trevain muttered.

"Dear, how about we check on your mother and Callder?" Aazuria asked, trying to ease the tension in the air. "Sionna will give you a tour of the infirmary."

"Sounds great," Trevain said. His head had jerked towards Aazuria at the mention of his younger brother, and he was fairly confident that if he had been a dog his ears would have perked up in recognition of a word that he was particularly fond of. Trevain had not seen his brother in weeks, and he had missed the drunken lout much more than he thought he ever would.

Poor Callder. The Coast Guard had declared him dead months ago.

Chapter 2: My Boat Exploded

"When you said that the commoners lived in 'volcanic caves' I imagined... well, I imagined plain old caves," Trevain said, looking around in awe as they navigated the ornate corridors.

"They are caves, are they not?" Aazuria asked in confusion.

"Yes, but they're..." he looked around, trying to find the words. "They're..."

"Did you think we lived in primitive Neolithic dwellings with stick figures decorating the walls?" she asked him with amusement. Her indigo eyes and silvery hair glistened in the firelight of the gilded candelabras they passed.

"I just didn't imagine *this!* I feel like I'm walking through the hallways of the Palace of Versailles."

Aazuria nodded once, not missing a beat in her brisk stride. "That structure is exactly what our designs are based on. My family moved here from Europe around the same time that Versailles was being expanded. It was the popular palatial style, and Papa was partial to it."

Trevain shook his head, smiling. "I have to admit that when your sisters first told me about your underwater world, I didn't expect such a high quality of life. Libraries, schools, mines, marketplaces and hospitals. You're pretty much self-subsistent. Growing acres of mushrooms and farming huge pools of fish and domesticated manatees—which, by the way, are delicious."

"We even have a natural reserve for a tame, lovable creature that humans hunted to extinction everywhere else.

Have you heard of Steller's sea-cow?" Aazuria asked him. When he shook his head, she smiled. "Of course, like land-dwellers, our people still fish and hunt for sport and for delicacies, but we try to respect the purity of the Arctic waters and sustainability of life here. We are a very independent people, with hardly any trade or commerce between the various undersea nations."

"This is all so mind-blowing. I have always fished so close to these islands, and I had no clue all of this was under here," he said with wonder. He turned to glance at her again, observing the proud silhouette of her nose and chin. "If I had known that such treasures existed, I would have gone hunting for them in my youth."

"Do not even begin lamenting your youth again. You are but one twelfth of my age!" she said, shaking her head. "Your own home is of comparable grandeur, just with a modern layout. Besides, you know that what is mine is now yours to share." She glanced at him, and saw that he was looking at her with admiration. She had misunderstood. He did not mean the treasures of her kingdom. She felt her cheeks flush with heat—she knew that her blush was exponentially more visible through her now-pale cheeks.

"I just wish I had met you sooner," he said softly.

A smile came to her lips. "Each meeting occurs at the precise moment for which it was meant. Usually, when it will have the greatest impact on our lives."

"We're here," Sionna called out to the couple. She and her sister had been walking ahead of them and conversing quietly. The candlelit corridor extended out into the infirmary. "We have unusually high numbers of wounded at the moment due to the recent battle…"

"And it was only the first wave," Visola added with a frown. "We have to get everyone healed and start preparing immediately for the next. It could be at any time."

Sionna nodded. "The infirmary isn't usually this chaotic and crowded, but we have some of our allies from Japan here as well. The Clan of the Ningyo."

"Ningyo?" Trevain asked curiously as he followed the twins. "Like the weird fish-people from the folklore?"

Sionna regarded the ceiling with exasperation. "Please, Trevain. You're an intelligent young man. Just forget everything you know about sea mythology. They're exactly like us: just people, no tails."

"They have incredible fighting skill though," Visola said. "Many of them trained with the samurai. They still follow the code and teach it to their young. So be respectful when you run into them. *Especially* Queen Amabie! You want to bow deeply when you greet her. She was known and feared by the samurai—speaking of which, her millennial is coming up in a few years, and we're going to have a huge bash. I have no idea what to get her... what do you get for the queen who has everything?"

"Her millennial?" Trevain asked in disbelief.

"Her thousandth birthday," Aazuria explained to him. His face registered surprise. How could he possibly bow deeply enough to honor a thousand-year-old samurai queen?

"Intensive care is through those doors," Sionna said, pointing. "If you ever need me and I'm not at the palace, this is usually where you will be able to find me. There are a few other wings over there, but Callder is in... hey! Zuri, get back here."

As soon as Sionna had turned away from the intensive care wing, Aazuria had tried to slip away from them. She paused and turned back to face Sionna with a distressed look on her face. "I need to see her," she whispered. "I held Elandria while she almost died in my arms."

Trevain understood her position, having recently gone through the experience of believing his own brother dead as well. He still urgently needed to see Callder's face for confirmation that it had all been a lie. He moved to Aazuria's side and slipped a hand around her waist comfortingly. She sighed and leaned her head against his shoulder. It was her injured sister, Elandria, who had helped him to cope with his loss, however blissfully false it had ended up being. Elandria was a quiet girl who never spoke with her voice, but only used sign language—despite having the angelic voice of a professionally trained opera singer. He loved her like she was already his own sister, and he could not imagine life without her. She had to pull through, or Aazuria would be inconsolable and he would be devastated.

Sionna frowned. "Elandria only just got out of surgery. Her right ventricle was damaged. She has all kinds of tubes placed in her, and an apparatus helping her breathe. We need to allow her to rest, and I won't allow any contaminates in the water. She lost a lot of blood, and she can't risk infection. Aazuria, trust me. Just be patient for now."

Aazuria closed her eyes and nodded. "Fine. Take us to Callder."

The twins began moving through the infirmary, and Trevain followed with his arm still around Aazuria. He observed as many women in simple green dresses rushed around, carrying various implements. It was the strangest hospital he had ever seen; it looked more like an exotic luxury spa. Picturesque hot springs were scattered throughout the massive candlelit room with mossy paths between them.

"Where are all the patients?" Trevain asked in confusion.

"Submerged," Sionna explained. "In individual 'pods' of water. The minerals have healing properties that expedite recovery. That's not hogwash either, it's fact. By the way, Aazuria should be soaking her shoulder."

"This little stab wound?" Aazuria asked, trying to be flippant. Her tight grip on Trevain's arm betrayed to him that underneath her carefree words she was rather tense. "Why bother healing it up when I will surely just get impaled in the same spot again as soon as it is better?"

"That was hilarious," Visola said with a grin. "Stabbed

twice by the same enemy! We should name the whole battle after that. 'The Shoulder Skirmish.' Or perhaps 'Shoulder Scuffle' sounds better. "

"Wonderful. I shall be mocked for this mistake for the rest of my breathing life," Aazuria said. She lifted a hand to absentmindedly prod the bandages around her wound. Talking about it seemed to make it hurt more.

"Adding insult to injury is my sister's specialty," Sionna said. "We're here." She turned into a corridor and threw another set of double doors open.

An unexpected sight greeted them. Callder was bare-chested, with bandages wrapping much of his chest and midsection, while two nurses fawned over him. One had her lips attached to his, while the other sat in his lap with her dress hiked up around her waist.

"For Sedna's sake!" Sionna shouted, throwing her hands into the air. "Both of you! Who authorized coitus with the patients? You're both fired!"

The nurses immediately ripped themselves away from Callder and arranged their clothing before facing Sionna shamefully.

"Please, Doctor Ramaris… he is just a lonely war hero…"

Sionna extended an incredulous finger towards Callder. "Him? A war hero? Is that what he's been telling you?"

The other nurse turned to Aazuria, curtseying deeply. "My dear Princess!" she pleaded, knowing that Aazuria had a reputation for being far more merciful than the Ramaris twins. "Take pity on us! He was so charming…"

"No. There are *dozens* of war victims in need of assistance," Aazuria said evenly. She did not raise her voice, but it was laced with authority. "This is no time for dallying. You both will go at once to aid the other nurses. Once the volume of patients is reduced, your employment here is terminated."

"Yes, Princess," they both said softly.

"And your employment with me begins," Visola added with a gleeful nod. "You both have been recruited to Adlivun's military. Yay! Now get back to work."

The two nurses scurried from the room, their heads lowered in embarrassment. Aazuria felt a small pang of remorse for them—there were hardly any men in Adlivun, thanks to the destructive impact of her father's long reign as king. She observed Callder's state of undress and she had to conceal a smirk. She found him as handsome as his older brother, but decidedly more coarse and jagged around the edges; both men were almost impossible to resist.

"Now why'd you all have to go and do that?" Callder complained, pointing at his bandages with a pout. "Can't you see I'm in need of some serious sexual healin'? Those ladies were just..." Callder trailed off when he saw his fourth visitor. He slowly raised himself from where he was seated. He took several shaky steps forward, with his hand clutching his bandaged chest. "Big brother?"

Trevain felt tears prick the back of his eyes. He shook his head and cleared his throat gruffly. He did not know what to say. It was true; the Coast Guard had been wrong. The death certificate needed to be ripped up into tiny shreds and cheerfully trampled. His little brother was really alive and well. Very well. He looked at Callder affectionately, trying to think of the appropriate greeting for this situation. He uttered the first three tender words which came to mind.

"You whoring buffoon!"

Callder crossed the room as quickly as he could, and ignoring his injury, he seized his brother in a manly embrace. "I'm so sorry, Trevain. I should have listened to you. I'm so sorry."

Trevain hugged him back strongly, needing to feel that he was really made of flesh and blood. "You fool," he said, trying to fight back his tears. "Callder, you foolish... fool!"

"I love you too," Callder said earnestly. He winced, but did not complain that Trevain's arms were crushing his still-healing ribs.

Sionna and Visola exchanged small smiles with each other. Aazuria looked at them, and she could see that they both were thrilled about the newest additions to their family. Although the Ramaris twins were tough on the exterior, they were the most loving siblings that she knew underneath their crass manner. She turned back to the embracing men, and felt emotion brim up inside of her. It seemed that the bond between Ramaris siblings had stayed strong throughout the generations, even though the Murphy brothers had a different name and overseas upbringing. How uncanny it was that the relationship between Trevain and Callder was so similar to that between Visola and Sionna, even though they had not grown up around them to be influenced. *Nature is powerful,* Aazuria thought to herself. *Nurture is important in determining the path we take, but nature is what defines us, and defines exactly how we will traverse that path...*

"Where's mom?" Trevain asked Callder. "I thought she'd be here with you."

"She's sleeping in the hot springs," Callder said, gesturing to the pool. He punched Trevain in the arm and grinned. "Hey, did you know we can breathe underwater? How cool is that? And all this time you had mom locked up because you thought she was crazy..."

"Callder, my boat exploded."

"What?" Callder frowned. "How? Well, that's no big deal, right? You have insurance."

Trevain closed his eyes.

"Hey, what's wrong big brother?" Callder hit him again playfully. "We'll just get a new boat with a better name than the stupid *Fishin' Magician*. You know what would be epic? Let's call it *The Master Baiter*."

A burst of laughter shot out of Visola's throat. Aazuria bit her lip to conceal the giggle that was threatening to erupt; she knew that this was no time for laughter. Sionna's eyes had widened. "Whoa. This is unbelievable; he has Viso's sense of humor. It skipped a generation."

Trevain opened his eyes. "Callder, the boat exploded with the *whole crew aboard*."

"No." Callder's face darkened. He took a step back from his brother, and looked him squarely in the eyes. "No. No! You'd better not be saying what I think you're saying. Were you on the boat when it happened? Is... is everyone okay?"

Trevain shook his head. His fists clenched and unclenched. "Only Brynne survived."

"Thank God!" Callder said, throwing his head back in relief. He exhaled a huge gush of wind. Then he realized how callous his words sounded and he cleared his throat. "I mean... that's horrible. It really is horrible, but I am just so, so glad Brynne is okay..."

"Leander. Arnav. Doughlas. Edwin. Ujarak. The Wade brothers." Trevain slowly listed the names between breaths, gritting his teeth. "They're all gone."

Callder shook his head, swallowing. "I guess we're way past decimation now, huh? I wonder if Arnav would say we've been obliterated or annihilated. Which one would be more correct?"

"Neither," Visola said firmly. "You are alive, young man. You were pitted against a mighty enemy, and you survived. You joined with us, your mother's people, and what you are is *victorious*. We have succeeded in defending ourselves, despite suffering losses—the first wave of the Clan of Zalcan has fallen."

Callder was carefully observing the woman who had spoken. Captivated by the gorgeous redhead, he cleared his throat and tried to put on his best charming smile. "Victorious, huh? Well, I can assure you of one thing, you beautiful sex goddess. Although I may have been harpooned like the wild animal that I am, every part of my body is still fully functioning. I'm just as virile as ever—and I can take you (and your lovely sister if she's interested) to heights of pleasure you've never imagined! So if you're looking to do a little celebratin' of this great victory…"

Both of Visola's eyebrows lifted in amusement. Aazuria placed a hand on her bandaged shoulder, looking around a bit awkwardly. Sionna screwed up her face and made a gagging noise.

"Callder…" Trevain said with a sigh, placing a palm against his forehead. "You're not going to believe this, but that woman you're shamelessly trying to get into bed with is actually our grandmother."

"*What?*" Callder erupted in laughter. "Yeah, 'cause I have a grandma who's younger than I am with the juiciest pair of tits and tightest little ass…"

A small gray-haired and wrinkled woman had just shakily raised herself out of the hot spring in time to hear her son speak these words. She immediately wanted to sink back down and bury her face in the sand. "Ugh," Alcyone said, cringing in horror. "Callder, that's disgusting! That's my mother you're speaking to. Mama, please forgive him, he doesn't know. Apologize this instant, Callder!"

"Are you kidding?" Callder saw that the expression on Alcyone's wrinkled face was humorless. He looked from his mother to his brother in disbelief and confusion. "You're both joking… how is it possible?"

"It's okay, kid," said Visola winking at Callder. She approached him and lightly slapped him on the bottom. "I'd rather be called 'sex goddess' than 'grandma' any day. I'm way more accustomed to it. I didn't even know I was a grandmother until a few days ago, but I've known I was a sex goddess for a few centuries."

"Mama!" Alcyone complained in a dismayed whine. "Stop flirting with my son!"

"Sorry, Alcie. He started it." Visola looked at Callder curiously before poking his cheek. "Hey, I like this one. He's got spunk. A bit slouchy though…"

"What? I have no clue what the hell is going on here,"

Callder admitted blankly, "but I do gather that I've done something wrong, which is a familiar and comforting feeling."

"Straighten yourself!" Visola commanded in her General-voice. Callder found himself following her command without really intending to. Visola walked around Callder slowly, sizing him up. "I'm going to train both of you boys to be warriors in the Ramaris tradition. Callder will shadow Elandria's personal guard once she is healed."

"Warrior? Sounds like fun," Callder said. "I know how to use a sword—mom signed me and Trevain up for fencing lessons when we were little."

"Aw, really?" Visola asked her daughter. "That's so smart of you, baby." Although Alcyone looked like an elderly woman, Visola still spoke to her as though she was younger—which she was.

"He's always had a passion for it," Alcyone explained. "He is quite skilled and relaxed with a sword in his hand."

"It's because I've had so much practice," Callder joked.

"Okay, Callder. You're going to have to cool it with the masturbation jokes," Trevain cautioned in a fatherly tone of voice. "You're in the presence of a princess."

Callder turned to the white haired woman who had remained rather quiet throughout the conversation. He studied her face, and thought that she looked vaguely familiar. "That's right, those pretty nurses called you 'Princess' and begged you for mercy. Mom explained to me that this was a different type of place with an old-fashioned monarchy. I just want you to know how awesome I think it is that you're powerful and stuff. People respect you." He approached her, taking her hand and kissing it while bowing. "You're also ravishingly lovely, Miss Princess of Adlivun—are you single?"

Aazuria smiled. "I am engaged to your brother."

"*What?*" Callder exclaimed. "Oh, snap! Trevain is boinking a princess!"

"Boinking?" Alcyone shrieked, pointing a wrinkled finger at her son. "Callder! Show some respect."

Sionna had brought a hand up to her neck in horror. "Good Sedna, preserve me. He speaks exactly like Visola. I may be forced to slice my own head off if I must listen to more blasphemous vocabulary."

A deep blush had come to Aazuria's cheeks, but she kept smiling. Trevain had been studying this exchange angrily—he did not like the way his brother held Aazuria's hand a little too long. He also felt a pang of jealousy at the amused look on his fiancée's face. She was normally so stern and impassive, but when it came to his brother's antics she always became too lenient and forgiving.

"When did this happen?" Callder asked eagerly. "Jeez, how long was I unconscious? Tell me everything! How did you two meet?"

"I should thank *you* for that, Callder," she responded warmly. "It was you who introduced me to Trevain. I am Aazuria Vellamo—do you not remember me?"

"No way," he said, stumbling backwards. "The... the stripper? Undina? But... that's impossible. You don't look anything like her. She had black hair and dark eyes... but your face! Yes, your face is exactly the same. You're Undina. You were a princess going incognito?"

"I chose the stage name Undina because it was my mother's name," Aazuria said softly. "She was the descendant of a Celtic warrior clan."

"Wow." Callder's brow furrowed as he turned to his brother. "If this is true, Trevain, then you owe me big time for making you talk to her. Imagine that I hadn't forced you to get off your lazy, antisocial ass and talk to the pretty girl? You would have been miserable and alone forever. Say it. Say that I'm your hero!"

When Trevain frowned and his lips parted to protest, Visola jumped in. "No way! It was all my idea," she said with a grin. "I needed money for weapons and I chose to work in that bar. Who knew that a little strip club in Soldotna would reunite long lost relatives? Regardless, I should get the credit for this."

"I give all my gratitude to Princess Aazuria," Alcyone said softly, dipping into a solemn curtsy. "Zuri killed her own father to make Adlivun safe for us. She freed me from my white-walled prison and brought me back to my family and my best friend. While Callder was unconscious I had a chance to catch up with Corallyn, and it just reduced me to tears. I hadn't spoken to her in sixty years, but it was like not a single day had passed. This is where I belong. This is where I need to be."

"Corallyn?" Callder asked. "Aazuria's little kid sister who wasn't even a pre-teen? I'm so confused. Mom spent all of yesterday just explaining to me where we are and why I woke up underwater. It took her hours to convince me that I wasn't dreaming or dead. This is a lot of information to take in all at once."

Trevain put a hand on his brother's shoulder. "Vikings, Samurai, and Celts. I know it seems outrageous, but let's just go with it."

"My boys need to learn sign language so they can communicate with us in the water," Alcyone said.

"We'll assign them private tutors," Sionna said. "They'll be fine."

Visola nodded. "I hate to have to leave my two favorite new grandsons," she said, "but I have an important meeting at the palace. Are you coming, Aazuria?"

"Of course. We have serious matters at hand, and thousands of bodies to dispose of."

Chapter 3: Napoleon of the Undersea

"...And he implied that in exchange for his help getting those guns off the black market, he wanted me to sleep with him," Visola said, taking a long swig of the warm sake, "so I did."

"No!" Queen Amabie gasped. "Earnestly, Visola?"

"Why would I lie to you? You're my hero," Visola said. She exhaled ecstatically. "I just can't believe that in all the mayhem of battle you managed to remember to bring my drink!"

Aazuria had left the war council seven beverages ago. Once the conversation had gone from concerning the good of the nation to drunkenly catching up on the gossip of the last fifty years, she had excused herself to see to other affairs. She knew that her general had a special fondness for Queen Amabie, and she thought that the two women should have some alone time.

"What are allies for, good friend? Besides, you know I only brought my army to help defend your nation because I wanted a rematch. I need to prove that I *can* win against you in a drinking competition. You have wiped the floor with me in days of yore, but it shall not happen again, General."

"My power is constant like the waves," Visola boasted with a smirk.

Amabie frowned and leaned forward keenly. "Truly, Visola. How could you sell yourself like that? Is it not difficult for a weapons master to do such a thing? You are so connected to your body."

"Why would be difficult for me?" Visola asked, with a halfhearted smile "Over the years I have come to see my body as little more than a weapon. An inadequate one at that! If I can sell the temporary access to one inadequate weapon and use the proceeds to purchase ownership of more effective weapons which will protect the lives of innocent people and their innocent bodies, then I think that's a great deal."

"Your logic is as flawless as your firearms are mighty." Queen Amabie studied her friend's face carefully. "This is about Vachlan, is it not? Everything you do has always been about him, Visola."

Visola suddenly found the floor very fascinating. Her fingers played nervously with the unicorn trident attached to her hip. After several seconds of silence, she reached for her sake, and doused her throat with it. The warmth of the drink was comforting. It even inspired a creative response.

"If what you mean by that is I went to extra, possibly unnecessary measures because I thought he might be the one attacking us, then you are correct. He might have sent a first wave led by that crazy woman, Atargatis, but he almost certainly knew she would fail. He was behind this all along—he sells his loyalties to the highest bidder, and now he is Zalcan's little bitch. Shouldn't even a mercenary have morals? That's the textbook definition of a whore!"

"It is all okay, Visola…"

"I do all I have ever done for Adlivun, for Aazuria, and my daughter. I would do anything to stop him! Anything; whatever it took to defeat him. I would do much worse than anything I have ever done. So, yes. It's all about Vachlan"

"That is not what I mean, dear," Amabie said kindly. "I am not speaking to the warrior in you. I am speaking to the woman."

"Then you are speaking to no one at all." Visola looked up at her friend with vacant eyes. "Not much of that remains."

"I saw her yesterday," Amabie said, reaching out to stroke her friend's wild red hair. "You knew that we were supposed to have a formal, public execution for the leader of the enemy forces. It is hallowed tradition, the formal drowning in blood. Yet all Atargatis had to do was mention that she had slept with your husband, and you threw a knife into her eye. Do you not think that was a tiny bit impatient of you, Visola?"

Visola slowly nodded. "I'm sorry, Queen Amabie. I know. I know it was rash. I'm so sorry… I just lost it and I couldn't control…"

"You were just being a woman."

"I always am when I make my greatest mistakes!" Visola said fiercely. "I mustn't allow it any longer." Her eyes narrowed with focus as she declared, "I am a warrior, first and foremost. I cannot afford to make any more foolish decisions based on my heart."

Amabie observed her for a moment before responding. "We may be the fortunate ones with the gift of dual breath," she said gently, "but yet we are human. We cannot sacrifice all that we are by nature to fill the artificial roles society has created for us."

"Oh, it's not artificial," Visola said, shaking her head. "I refuse to believe that. If my position at the head of Adlivun's army were completely arbitrary; if my birth into a warrior family was merely coincidence; if my heritage and destiny were not somehow intricately linked… who would I be?"

"You would be Visola."

"No! I would be nothing. I am only what I am, and nothing more! You—you were meant to be the Queen of the Ningyo. There is no one more suited to that role than you. It is in your blood and your spirit… just as Aazuria is meant to be our leader. We can all be only what we are."

"Darling, you are burying yourself in your job and sacrificing your identity. The only reason that you are at odds with yourself as a woman is because you keep shutting that part of you down and pushing it away. It is not healthy. You are building up all this anxiety and tension…"

"Oh, don't be silly, Queen Amabie!" Visola said with a carefree shrug and smile. "I'm perfectly fine…"

"You have not been fine since Vachlan left you."

Visola's shoulders slumped suddenly forward, as though the puppeteer who had been controlling her had dropped the strings. "Did you hear what Atargatis said? Vachlan thinks that I cheated on him. That's why he left when I was pregnant with Alcie. He thought… but *why* would he think that? How *dare* he think that?"

"King Kyrosed Vellamo planted a lot of strange ideas into people's heads," Amabie answered. "He was a manipulative bastard. Do not blame yourself for this. It is not Vachlan's fault either…"

"Two hundred years apart. Two hundred years he has been my sworn enemy. He has joined forces with the Clan of Zalcan, the worst brutes who breathe beneath! He has killed thousands, he has destroyed nations. He commands legions, and intends to throw them all against me… all because of a lie told by Kyrosed?"

"It is almost sweet in a way," Queen Amabie said pensively.

"What?" Visola asked in confusion. "My husband wiped out a whole kingdom under the Bermuda Triangle. He tried to do the same thing to you in the Dragon's Triangle. Now he's coming here, to finish what he's started. He's been practicing a systematic methodology. Now he's ready to ruin Adlivun too—he's ready to crush me. How is that sweet?"

"It demonstrates how much he loves you. Your betrayal, although only a false idea, was so intolerable and unspeakable to him that it drove him to insanity."

"Very sweet indeed," Visola said, gripping her ceramic cup tightly as she ingested more sake.

"Truly, Visola. No man or woman dedicates their life to a vendetta of revenge upon the object of their affection *unless* that affection was once so great that it was the crimson burning sun of their whole existence."

Visola paused for a moment. "That's it? That's the silver lining? That's your positive spin on things? You think telling me you believe that he is raising hell because he *loves me* is going to make me look on the bright side and gain perspective?"

"Is it working?" Amabie asked, lifting a thin, arched brow.

"Damn you!" Visola said, furiously. "Of course it's working! But only because you have gotten me exceptionally drunk."

"I told you I would win one of our drinking contests someday," Amabie said cheerfully.

"I am easy to defeat when I am overemotional," Visola admitted. "That is why Vachlan has been two steps ahead of me this whole time. I am fairly certain he is going to kick my well-toned and rather shapely ass."

"No! I do not appreciate the tone in your voice," Amabie said sternly. "You almost sound like you feel you deserve his wrath. You sound like you are welcoming this!"

"Perhaps I am," Visola grumbled softly. "I do deserve it. Remember my father? He always used to make these jokes about being psychic... having this great mystical intuition. When Vachlan and I travelled to Bimini to inform my father of our engagement, my father told us that he could not approve. He said he saw only heartache in the future for us. Our marriage would not last; he said I needed a man who would follow me, not one who would compete with me for control. Vachlan was too strong."

"It is necessary for a man to be powerful in his own right, yet to always honor his wife's decisions. My husband was like this."

"Your husband was a marvelous man," Visola said mournfully. "He was always right beside you, always helping and supporting you. He would never do the dishonorable things Vachlan did; he would never have left you when you were *pregnant*. When he vanished, I nearly lost my mind... Aazuria took care of me, and she probably saved my life. She told me that my baby would love me more than Vachlan ever had, and more than anyone ever could; because that was the way a child loved their mother. She was right. Having Alcie made everything better, and made everything worth it. I spent years searching her face for signs of Vachlan. I would see his ghost in her expressions when she was happiest. When she smiled so wide that her cheeks dimpled. Those proud high cheekbones of hers, and her angular jaw. It was like having a little part of him still with me, you know? My little Alcie... everything was fine until I lost her too."

"You have found her once more, Visola. As mothers, we all must deal with the pain of separation from our children. Most men do not feel this connection to their young as strongly. Pain can either break you down, or give you great strength."

"I'm not sure whether I experienced the former or latter." Visola gave her friend a small smile before taking another drink of sake.

"You wonder this?" Amabie asked with a laugh. "Ask anyone whether you are strong, Visola. Ask anyone whether they know anyone stronger than you. Then you shall know."

"Maybe. I really wish I were more like my sister," Visola said. "When we were little, I used to lie in bed beside her for hours before we fell asleep. I would look at her, and think about how strange it was that she looked exactly like me. I would put my hands and feet beside hers and search for the slightest differences." Visola stared off at the wall, lost in remembrance. "Most of all though, I would wonder if her thoughts were the same as mine. If her dreams were the same as mine. I had no way of knowing. Did we both have the same aches and pains at the same time, the same pleasures and joys?" Visola refilled their cups. "Now I know we don't. Sionna has all the light inside of her, and I have the darkness.

She has all the purity, and I have the dirt. She likes to talk about how we were once both the same cell. Well, when that cell cleaved itself in half, it may have resulted in identical chromosomes, but the soul... the very soul of that cell did not separate identically. She got all the good stuff. She's a fucking paragon, and I am a... parasite."

"No, dear friend. Sionna may be a paragon, but if so, you are a *paradigm*. You are the quintessence of everything a victorious general, friend, and mother should be..."

"Mother!" Visola barked. "I ruined my daughter's life! Because of me she was in a mental institution for forty years..."

"And because of you she fell in love and gave birth to two strong sons. Both of whom are now in training to carry on your family's great tradition! Everything happens for a reason, Visola. You cannot deny this. Every decision you make cannot be the right one, but as long as the positive repercussions balance with or outnumber the negative ones, you are making progress. Progress is all we can hope for, and it is what you are best at achieving."

"You are just saying that..."

"No!" Queen Amabie said, standing up and raising herself to her full height. She swayed slightly on her feet, indicating that she was a bit tipsy. "You are like the great Empress Jingū!"

"Who?" Visola asked curiously.

"Empress Jingū was a great Japanese warrior who conquered Korea after her husband died! Legend has it that she battled for three years while carrying her husband's unborn child—she waited until she was victorious before giving birth."

"Impressive," Visola mumbled.

"Cheer up! You, my friend are the Boudicca of the Deep! Our Joan of Arc, our Tomyris..."

"Only as good as the women," Visola lamented.

"No! You are the Napoleon of the Undersea!"

"Not a big fan of Napoleon," Visola said as she fumbled to pour herself more sake.

Queen Amabie's eyebrows creased in thought. "Alexander the Great. Gilgamesh. Genghis Khan. Attila the Hun! Name the warrior, and you are his very equal, his aquatic counterpart."

"Okay. Now I'm feeling a bit better," Visola said with a sniffle. "Not fair. You know how to stroke my ego better than anyone."

"You need to acknowledge your own brilliance. I am lucky to have you as my ally, for I would not want to ever be pitted against you."

"Dawwww... I love you, Queen Amabie," Visola said with a sleepy smile. "I wish it changed the fact that Vachlan is going to defeat me."

"Oh, darling. That's the sake talking."

"No, I mean it. I do not have the will or energy anymore. If I could just cast aside all of my memories, I could take him on. If he were anyone else but my husband, I would wipe the floor with him and make him eat his own shit while laughing condescendingly. I would carve my name into his flesh. I would jump rope with his intestines, or wear them as necklaces and bracelets while asking him casually how they looked. I would dance upon..."

"Then do it," Amabie said. "Cast aside your doubt and do it."

Visola reached out and placed her hand on Amabie's hand. She would normally never be so familiar with the woman, but due to her drinking, the lines of courtesy were blurring along with her vision. She blinked and squinted in order to see more clearly, but this only led to the realization that it was her mind which was clouded more than anything. She sighed.

"I can't beat him, Amabie."

Both women were startled when Aazuria burst into the room, dripping wet, her feet pounding the carpet. "Queen

Amabie, General Ramaris—have either of you seen Corallyn?"

"Not since yesterday when I killed her evil mother," Visola slurred. "Why?"

"I cannot find her anywhere," Aazuria said, brushing locks of wet, white hair out of her face. Corallyn was her youngest sister, whose body was of childlike proportions, although she was nearing a hundred years in age. "I had the guards sweep the whole palace. She is not in her quarters, nor anywhere else..."

Visola frowned. "Have you checked intensive care? She probably snuck in to see if Elandria was better."

"That was the first place I looked!" Aazuria reached up and grasped her wounded shoulder, battling a bout of pain. Blood was seeping through the bandage due to her vigorous exercise. She was evidently distressed and frustrated by her missing sibling. "What if she ran away? What if she was angry with us?"

"She's probably just sulking in a corner because of the stuff with Atargatis," Visola spoke with a slight slur. "When your mother shows up out of the blue and kills a whole bunch of people, it's never easy to deal with."

Queen Amabie lowered herself carefully to her chair. "Princess Aazuria, some of my elite warriors said that they were heading to your Mirrored Caves for festivities... to celebrate vanquishing our common enemy. Perhaps your little sister is amongst them?"

"I do not think Corallyn would be celebrating the death of her mother," Aazuria said with a deep frown. There was terror in her eyes. "I feel within me that something is gravely wrong."

Chapter 4: Elegant Crimson Calligraphy

It seemed that all of Adlivun and all of their Ningyo allies were in the Mirrored Caves, dancing, chatting, and enjoying themselves in the water. They had changed out of their armor, and they all wore brightly colored flowing fabrics which floated in the water behind them like the swirling ribbons of rhythmic gymnasts. The Alaskans wore their malachite green while the Japanese wore bright red or white, depending on their rank.

Aazuria swam through the cavernous rooms, frantically searching for her little sister.

Although many of the people in the room did not share the same spoken language, it did not matter. Everyone communicated with their hands in the universal sign language. Speech was a garbled, incoherent burble underwater. The only thing easily discernible was laughter. The sound of distorted, joyous murmurs reached Aazuria's ears from every part of the Mirrored Caves. Her shoulder throbbed as her bone rotated in the joint, swimming quickly through the rooms. Lights bounced off the mirrors, and she was frequently met with her own troubled reflection. She tried to remember the last words she had exchanged with Corallyn, for any clue to where she might be.

"Well, that's just peachy," Corallyn said with her hands on her hips. "My biological mother tries to kill everyone I love and I'm not allowed to execute her? Why is Visola allowed to do anything she wants?"

"Hush, Corallyn," Aazuria answered firmly. "It was for the best that it happened this way. Believe me."

"Whatever, big sis. Your mother was some majestic

lady, so you don't know what it's like..."

Aazuria placed her hands on her sister's shoulders. "I killed Papa. Now I have to live with that. I do not wish the same for you."

"He deserved it. He was a..."

"Coral, your mother was not always like this. When I first met her, she was an ambitious, dedicated young performer. The worst villains are created from the kindest people when bad things happen to them."

"So it's all Papa's fault," Corallyn said quietly.

"No. Your mother's actions were her own."

"My actions would have been my own as well!"

"I cannot allow you to make mistakes that you will greatly regret."

Corallyn gritted her teeth. "Fine. Damn you! Go make more smoochies with 'Uncle Trevain.' Damn Visola too! I'm going to sulk in a corner."

Now, which corner could she possibly be sulking in?

Many of the people Aazuria passed, both warriors and civilians, bowed deeply to her and saluted across their chests before congratulating her bravery and sympathy for her shoulder. They offered condolences and wished Elandria a rapid recovery. Aazuria's hands automatically formed the gracious signs necessary to acknowledge all of their kindnesses and pleasantries. Her head nodded, and her mouth smiled, but her eyes remained unsettled and anxious.

Whenever she was engaged by someone who might have known Corallyn, she asked if they had seen her. She described the girl's appearance and small stature to many of the Ningyo warriors, who shook their heads, profusely apologizing and bowing. Aazuria was growing increasingly agitated, and the swarm of celebrating sea-people only added to her frustration. She turned to exit the Mirrored Caves, and found herself swimming directly into someone.

Caring green eyes assessed her hysterical state with concern. She felt a small wave of relief run through her because of his understanding gaze. Aazuria reached out and placed a hand on his arm, as if trying to draw strength from him.

"*Did you find her yet?*" he asked, slowly and carefully forming the words in sign language. He did not yet have much confidence in speaking with his hands.

"*No,*" Aazuria said, shaking her head. "*I am going to check the labyrinth. She could have gotten lost in any of the intricate channels of caves under the Aleutian Islands.*"

"*Wait, Zuri,*" he signed. He frowned as he moved his thumbs and forefingers, trying to remember all the correct hand formations. "*If I understand correctly, these caves stretch out for hundreds of miles... you can't possibly cover all that ground swimming with your injured shoulder! My great-aunt Sionna sent me to tell you that you have to take it easy, and spend some time resting in the infirmary. She seems like she really knows what she's doing.*"

"*I have rested enough. I must find Corallyn,*" Aazuria insisted, swallowing. She reached up to touch her shoulder gingerly. She felt extreme embarrassment and growing annoyance at the fact that Koraline Kolarevic, the woman who had called herself Atargatis, had managed to stab her in the same location twice. The first time had been with a javelin that had gone clean through her shoulder; Trevain had saved her life by pushing her to the side just in time, or it would have pierced her heart. The second time was in hand-to-hand combat.

"*Your bleeding hasn't even stopped,*" Trevain pointed out, grimacing at her darkened bandages. The blood that had dried on the cloth in the air had not completely washed out in the water. He reached out with his thumb to caress her skin very close to the wound, and he frowned when she winced. "*If this gets...*" He paused, not knowing the signal for 'infected.' He tried to substitute a word. "*If this gets dirty, it could get worse and you could lose your whole arm...*"

"*I will be fine. Sionna gave me a tetanus shot when I*

was stabbed the first time," Aazuria quickly signed to him as she moved through the caves.

He followed her, confused. "*Tetanus?*" he asked, imitating the hand signal she had formed. "*I'm not sure what that is, could you spell it out for me?*"

"*I need to hurry. I am going to pass by the kitchens and collect some basic food to sustain me while I search for her. Can you go to the palace and organize the military to help me search? Your grandmother is drunk, or I would ask you to go to her.*"

Trevain felt nervous as he tried to make sense of her rapid hand motions. "*You want me to organize your military? Why would they listen to me?*"

"*They will. Go at once.*" Aazuria continued swimming through the caves, with long pieces of her dark green dress trailing behind her.

Trevain ignored her command and swam to block her path. He moved his hands in a series of gestures. "*I'm not letting you go off on your own, wounded and emotional. What if you get lost? Rash decisions could make this even worse. Is there a map? Let me come with you.*"

"*I will not get lost,*" she responded, trying to swim around him. "*I have lived here for centuries. I used to play in these caves when I was Corallyn's age.*"

"*Aazuria!*" he responded. "*You're not thinking rationally. We need to weigh our options. What if Coral went back to land? She could be at my house right now. You remember how fond she was of the internet and television.*"

"*This is true,*" Aazuria conceded. Her hands paused for a second in fear. "*Oh, Trevain. I am so worried about her. Could you send Naclana to check and see if she is at your home?*"

Naclana was Aazuria's distant cousin, who served as her messenger. Trevain shook his head. "*I am just as concerned about her safety as you are, but rushing off alone into miles of dark caves isn't going to help the situation.*

Aazuria, come back to the palace and let's find Naclana and tell him together..."

"No. If you will not help me, I shall help myself." Aazuria swam around him, rushing past him in a fraction of a second. All he saw was a blur of green and white. He turned, and immediately swam after her, but he could not catch up for several minutes.

By the time he was close enough to speak to her, she had already arrived at the waterless caves in which food was prepared. He was surprised by the true extent of her athleticism, and her tolerance for pain. He could not believe that she could move at all with her injured shoulder. He entered the room after her and climbed the carved stairs just in time to see the cooks saluting and bowing to her.

"I need basic provisions for a trek into the caves. In a watertight bag."

"Yes, Princess Aazuria."

"My youngest sister Corallyn is missing. Can you please pass my orders to the castle guard to dispatch a search party? Also, if you could tell Naclana..."

"Aazuria," Trevain interrupted. "Please. You need to think twice about this."

"Listen, Trevain," she said, turning upon him with a hard look in her eyes. "This is not up for discussion. My sister could be..."

"Princess!" shouted a male voice.

Aazuria was surprised and turned to see her cousin entering the room, dripping wet. "Naclana. Just the person I wanted to see..."

"Corallyn has been abducted," Naclana gasped, as he tried to catch his breath.

Aazuria stared at him for a moment, blankly.

Trevain felt fleeting disbelief. He almost wanted to smile as though it were some sort of joke, but he could see that the messenger was serious. Naclana had always given him the creeps, and now he imagined that he knew why. The man's very presence was a harbinger of danger and disaster. It was painted permanently in the shadows of his grave, heavy expression.

"We just received a ransom note," Naclana said, straightening his posture and giving a half-hearted version of the appropriate salute to his cousin. "From the Clan of Zalcan."

Murmurs of horror rose up from the kitchen staff. Trevain moved to his fiancé's side, and wrapped his arms around her. Aazuria felt the urge to lean against him for support and shut her eyes tightly, but she could not do this with everyone watching. She could not do this at all. The moment she allowed herself to show her weakness, even to herself, it would overcome her and she would lose her composure. She knew that if she had been paying closer attention to Corallyn's whereabouts after the battle, this would not have happened.

"What do they want?" Trevain asked Naclana. "They aim to exchange her for something?"

Aazuria twitched, moving suddenly out of her frozen state. "That's right. A ransom. All is not lost. Anything they want—I will give it to them."

Naclana cleared his throat. "The note was written in Corallyn's blood. Would you like me to read it, Princess?" When Aazuria nodded. He reached into his vest and withdrew a metal cylinder. He uncorked it and pulled out the heavy paper. The demands had been penned in elegant crimson calligraphy.

When the women on the kitchen staff began to cry, Aazuria lifted her hand, and tried to speak soothingly. "It is just meant to scare us. Do not worry—whatever is requested shall be given. She shall be returned safely. Whatever price is stipulated shall be paid."

Naclana hated his job. He cleared his throat again before reading:

"Dear Administrators of Adlivun..."

Aazuria did not realize that she was clenching Trevain's hand tightly, or that her palms had become very sweaty. Administrators! The person writing the note had been exceptionally sadistic if they had chosen to bleed her sister for such long, unnecessary wording. Every syllable had caused Corallyn anguish. Every syllable ignited vengeful anger within Aazuria.

Naclana swallowed before he continued reading:

"Fine weather for this time of year in Alaska, is it not?"

"Vachlan!" Aazuria shouted, ripping herself away from Trevain to drive her knuckles into the solid rock wall of the kitchen. "Only he! Only he would…"

"Shhhh," Trevain said, catching Aazuria's small wrist and gently rubbing it to soothe her. He could feel that all of her tendons and muscles had grown extremely taut with her rage. He knew that the rest of the note did not matter; Aazuria would not let this man live. If she ever found the opportunity (and he knew that she would seek it relentlessly) she would gut this man, as she had gutted his predecessor, Atargatis.

Unless, of course, Trevain got his own hands on him first. Trevain had never killed before, but as he imagined Vachlan using an inkwell of young Corallyn's blood to write this note, he suddenly knew that he was capable of it. Corallyn was *his* sister too.

Naclana struggled to keep his own voice even as he read the note. "Deliver my wife to me at Zimovia by noon Sunday, or I will drain every drop of blood coursing through the veins of this lovely little girl. I will then proceed to write volumes of vicious letters to General Ramaris with my new ink. She will know that little Corallyn Vellamo's death is on her hands. I shall continue in this fashion of persuasion until you are ultimately persuaded. With Immeasurable Sincerity, Vachlan Suchos."

There was a silence in the room. The temperature of the atmosphere seemed to have quite suddenly fallen by several degrees. The only movement was the blood dripping from Aazuria's knuckles. The gentle gurgling noise of a stew beginning to boil along with the sizzling of a dish which was ready to be pulled from the stone oven interrupted the silence.

"So he wants Visola?" Aazuria asked in a poisonous whisper. "Over my breathless body."

Chapter 5: Goddess of Zimovia

After hearing the terms of the ransom note, Visola nodded thoughtfully. "Volumes of vicious letters? Oh, my. Well, that's progress. At least we'd be communicating."

"Focus, Visola. What is wrong with you? This is Corallyn's life which hangs in the balance. "

"Her life doesn't hang in the balance, because we are going to pay the ransom," Visola said with a shrug. "His request was reasonable."

"What is reasonable about this?" Aazuria said angrily. "He is requesting *you*."

"He only asked for one person in exchange for another person," Visola explained. "He could have used Corallyn as leverage for a lot more."

"He could not have requested anyone or anything of greater value to me. Sedna knows what he will do to you!"

"I guess I will pack my bags and find out," Visola said in a tone of voice which was a notch too cheerful. She forced a halfhearted smile. "I only have until noon Sunday, so I had better leave now and take a fast boat."

"You are *not* going anywhere," Sionna told her sister firmly. "We are going to find another way to do this, right Aazuria?"

"Right." Aazuria sat down suddenly and drew in a deep intake of air. "We have Queen Amabie here, so together we will brainstorm and find a way to work around Vachlan's demands."

"There is no way around his demands," Visola said with a frown. "I know him. I know that he always covers all his bases, and he always gets what he wants. He has never lost a battle."

"Neither have you!" Sionna reminded her.

"I learned a great deal from him. My father and my uncles were great warriors, but I learned more about war from Vachlan than I did from all the men in my family combined. "

"You mean you learned about the dishonorable aspects of war from him," Aazuria said. "The Ramaris men taught you how to fight with principles, and Vachlan taught you how to win at all costs."

"It doesn't matter," Visola said. "This is about Corallyn and ensuring her safety. I don't believe Vachlan would ever harm a child, anyway."

"What are you talking about? Are we even talking about the same man? He abandoned you when you were pregnant, Visola. He has no conscience!" Sionna spat. "He doesn't discriminate about whether it's an unborn child, an infant, or an adult he's harming."

"Ladies, we need to determine our course of action." Queen Amabie frowned, tapping her fingers on the hilt of her katana. "It is possible that the entire first wave of attack which we were so pleased with ourselves about conquering was just a decoy—all along, the plan could have been to abduct Corallyn and use her as leverage against us. Do we know where the enemy is stationed? I recommend the use of brute force."

"Zimovia," Aazuria answered with a grimace. "It is the site of an old settlement of ours in Southeastern Alaska. There is a large, intricate group of islands, straits, and fjords called the Alexander Archipelago. Much of it is covered in ice, but not this particular region. The specific caves he has chosen, the ones under the Zimovia Islets, are almost impossible to successfully attack."

"She's right," Visola said. "The Clan of Zalcan would not have given us that information unless they had established an excellent defense. Zimovia is fantastic. It's probably one of the most defensible undersea areas in the world, at least in my opinion. That's why I'm mentally drop-kicking myself for showing it to Vachlan all those years ago. Talk about shooting myself in the foot."

"Are the caves spacious enough to host a sizeable army?" Queen Amabie asked.

"Yes," Aazuria answered. "It would be *beyond* foolhardy to attack them there. Yet we must find a way."

"Even if we could successfully attack them, there would be no guarantee we could recover Corallyn alive. In all likeliness, they would kill her out of spite once they realized they were losing," Visola said.

"But we have to try," Sionna said. "We have to send out reconnaissance now to try and estimate their numbers and learn about the way they are stationed…"

"That's useless," Visola said. "Any reconnaissance we send into Zimovia Strait will not return."

Aazuria nodded. "They have the advantage of terrain there. Once we swim into that strait, we could be instantly surrounded with no room to retreat, no room to advance. I wish that he would have positioned himself anywhere else!"

"He knew that it was my favorite place," Visola said softly. "It was where we held our honeymoon."

Everyone in the room was quiet for a moment, until Sionna spoke. "Your two-hundred-year wedding anniversary is coming up soon, isn't it?"

"That's right, sis. Thanks for remembering. It's this Sunday," Visola said. She tried to hide her cracking voice by clearing her throat. "At noon. Vachlan is rather poetic, isn't he?"

When no one responded, Visola feebly tried to crack another joke. "What's the traditional gift for the two-hundred-year milestone again? I forget." She snapped her fingers as if trying to remember. "Tin, copper, pearls, silver, oh! Murdering your spouse?"

"Brute force it is," Aazuria said, slamming her dagger down onto the table carved from ice. "We are going to attack the Clan of Zalcan. I will not tolerate my family and my friends being threatened."

"If we were to lead our forces in one massive strike," Queen Amabie mused, "all of your warriors and my own... Adlivun would be exposed. This could just be a ploy to lead the armies away from Adlivun. There could be no one at all in Zimovia."

"What about your home, Queen Amabie?" Visola asked with concern. "Are you comfortable having so many of your warriors here? Aren't you worried about your kingdom being undefended?"

Amabie shook her head. "They will not even be able to find my home. As you know, after Zalcan's offensive against us in the 50s, we had to abandon Yonaguni completely. I am pleased to say that the place we now call home is far superior to our previous situation."

"I would love to hear all about it," Visola said with a sentimental smile. She ignored Aazuria's glare which unmistakably accused her of changing the subject.

"It is called Shiretoko," Amabie said. "It means 'the end of the Earth' and it is nothing short of paradise. The area is very secluded, and it has always been considered consecrated by both land and sea-dwellers alike. Many of our waters are naturally warmed by volcanic origins, very similar to your own hot springs. The native Ainu called it *kamui wakka*, the water of the gods. You will visit us soon, Visola, and see it for yourself."

"I hope that I get that chance, Queen Amabie," Visola said softly. "Yonagumi was extraordinary. I can hardly imagine a better place!"

"You need not imagine, my friend," Amabie said, gesturing to the stately room in which they sat. "Just look around and you will behold the incomparable splendor of your own home."

"You Japanese just can't take a compliment without giving one in return, can you?" Visola said with a grin.

"Why are you being so flippant about this?" Sionna scolded. "Viso, we need your help in planning an attack. Aazuria has declared war, and you must be the one to organize it."

"Nope. There won't be any war. It's not even up for discussion," Visola told her sister with a casual wave of her hand. "I'm going to surrender myself. So you'd better bake me a delicious cake and give me lots of hugs in the next day or two."

"I forbid it," Aazuria said firmly. "You cannot move against me in this situation. We must act together."

"I know Zimovia better than anyone," Visola said. She locked eyes with her friend, trying to communicate in her unyielding gaze that this was her decision to make. "I know how to do the right thing."

"The right thing is not sacrificing yourself!" Aazuria shouted. "We need to discuss this and find a less emotional and hasty solution."

"Hasty?" Visola asked, scrunching up her nose. "Today is Wednesday. We only have four days until Sunday. That's hardly enough time to make a complex plan of action, and even less time to take action, including travel time. Why don't you respect my opinion? Why don't you think that I am informed?"

"I know you are informed," Aazuria said softly.

"I know every inch of that place," Visola said. "I practically lived there. I was practically worshipped there! Once, I met a small clan of Haida people on the shores of that strait…"

"I remember," Sionna said with a small smile. "They thought that you were some kind of special creature when you rose out of the water wearing a green dress and no coat. They were all bundled up in fur. It was the dead of winter. I told you not to reveal yourself to them, but you said that they were starving and you could help."

"That was back when the rules stated that as long as the

natives had no writing system, it wasn't against the rules to reveal ourselves to them," Visola added. "They couldn't do any real damage in exposing us without written records of the events."

Queen Amabie nodded. "I have had experiences like that in Japan. There has been some written record of my existence. Luckily, it is mostly considered nonsense."

"A little infamy never hurt anyone," Sionna said with a smile. "These people thought my sister was magical... like some kind of the Lady of the Lake."

"Yes. Except instead of Excalibur I used my unicorn trident to show them a new fishing technique, and where specifically to go to find the most fish. They called me the Goddess of Zimovia," Visola said in fond remembrance. "Doesn't it seem fitting that it should be the place where I did a good deed where I should die?"

"You are not going to die," Aazuira said, in disbelief. "Quit discussing fond memories and let us focus on the matter at hand; we have a battle to plan." Aazuria lifted her dagger and pulled the decorative cloth off the table they sat around. She began to carve a map into the ice with the tip of her dagger. "This is Zimovia Strait. We probably will not be able to access it by land, since it is surrounded by mountainous terrain and thick virgin forest. There were no roads, and hardly any trails, although things may have changed in recent years. Here are the two main access points by water, and this is the location of the Islets. Am I right, Sionna?"

Sionna nodded, but Visola hit her in the shoulder. "Stop it, all of you!" she removed her own sword from her hip and ruined the drawing of the strait. "Aazuria, please stop planning this 'battle.' There isn't going to be any combat. I'm going to follow the instructions in the ransom note and give myself up."

"No." Aazuria said firmly. "Are you not the one who always advocates force instead of diplomacy? Listen, Visola.

Appeasement never works. If we surrender you, what will he want next? Your twin sister, so he can collect them all and have the whole set?"

Visola cursed softly. "Dammit, Zuri. Why are you being so stubborn about this? Corallyn's your goddamned sister!"

"Forget the blood ties," Sionna said, reaching out to place a hand on her sister's arm. "Be reasonable, sweetie. In Adlivun's traditional government policy, we are all sisters. We are all equal. Therefore, you are Aazuria's sister too, and just as much as I do, she doesn't want you to get hurt."

"Just as I don't want Corallyn to get hurt," Visola said, frowning. "Stop ganging up on me. You are all making this much more complicated than it needs to be."

"I agree," Aazuria said, standing up. "I lead Adlivun, and Queen Amabie leads her people. On Saturday night I will be launching an attack on Zimovia. Are you with me, Queen Amabie?"

"Absolutely, my dear. Our armies shall amalgamate and launch an attack of unprecedented force. I have many excellent officers and military strategists. My *karō* will meet with your colonels to plan our maneuvers."

"None of your *karō* are well-informed of modern technologies," Visola argued. "They won't be able to plan how to use the rifles and..."

"That is correct, Visola. That is why you should be leading this operative. Our chances of success are incalculably greater with your guidance." Queen Amabie smiled at her friend. "Do I have your support?"

Visola sat quietly for a moment before slowly shaking her head. "No."

"I see." Queen Amabie moved to Aazuria's side and gave a small bow of respect. "Princess Aazuria, will you escort me to my quarters?"

"Of course," Aazuria said, returning the bow. The two women walked across the carpet to leave the dry room, exiting downwards into the submerged corridor.

Queen Amabie began swimming through the elaborately carved ice-hallways, and Aazuria followed her. Aazuria was surprised at the older woman's strength and agility. She hoped that she would be in such excellent health when she was nearing a thousand years of age. There were many guards posted throughout the hallways of the castle, but when they reached a stretch without any, Queen Amabie paused to look around. She gestured for Aazuria to come closer, and she began moving her hands while keeping them close to her body, in the sign language equivalent of a whisper.

"I am not sure that Visola is emotionally composed at the moment," Queen Amabie signed quickly. *"She did not say this explicitly, but I believe that she wishes for her own death. Her decision-making is severely compromised with respect to any situation involving Vachlan."*

"You think..." Aazuria trailed off, a bit taken aback. She closed her eyes for a moment before her hands began to move again. *"Is it possible that she is using this situation as an excuse to place herself in harm's way?"*

"I believe that she is very tired. I do not think she wishes to fight anymore. I think she personally wants to surrender."

"No," Aazuria signed, *"no, how can you say this? She was only just reunited with her daughter after all this time. Her spirits should be lifted..."*

"It was too late. She was already broken."

"I understand," Aazuria signed. *"Thank you for telling me this, Queen Amabie. I will not allow any harm to come to Visola. I promise you that I will protect her from herself."*

"I am sure that once we have killed her husband, she will no longer be depressed."

"The sooner the better. Let us not delay—I have plenty of energy reserved just for Vachlan."

"Your shoulder is wounded, dear. You should let me

have the honor of fileting his flesh from his bones."

"By all means, Queen Amabie. You may do that while I remove all four of his lungs, one at a time."

Chapter 6: Ring of Fire

A snakelike rope of smoke rose from the secluded volcano.

There was hardly any wind, and the sea was unusually calm. The line of smoke was almost perfectly vertical, and the shores of the island were almost perfectly silent. With her hands calmly clasped behind her, Aazuria glared at the dark narrow coil. It was the type of thing you could not help staring at for a moment.

"I bet this really screws with the Alaskan geologists."

Trevain's voice startled her out of her reverie. She turned to look at him, and tried to interpret his cryptic expression. She realized that he must be experiencing a massive culture shock. She attempted to give him a warm smile, but only succeeding in slightly elongating the grim line which her lips were set in.

"We send our enemies to the sky," she explained. She lifted her hand hesitantly and moved her fingers as if grasping a chunk of air. "When we cremate our own deceased, we scatter them in the waves to keep them close to us. We swim immersed in them. We inhale our ancestors with every breath—they are part of us. Those who intended us harm are not given the same honor."

Trevain nodded. "It makes sense. That's the opposite of our mythology in which the sky is good and the underworld is bad."

"Good and bad does not matter much," Aazuria said softly. "It is more a matter of 'near and far.' Not that why we do this is important. It is all wrong, anyway." She turned away from the smoke, looking out to the sea. "Our enemies just rain back down on us, even after they have been banished to the sky. We inhale them too. We ingest them. The world is all so connected that it is impossible to escape any one aspect of it, whether dead or living."

He studied her forlorn gaze. "What do you want to escape, Aazuria?"

"Myself." She turned and began walking back towards the shore. She wrapped her arms around herself although she was not cold.

He frowned as he followed her, easily keeping up with her moderate pace. "What do you mean?"

She continued strolling, remaining silent for a moment before answering. "It just seems sometimes like nothing matters in the big picture. The life and death of our loved ones seems monumental to us, but to the world the difference is worth a few puffs of smoke." She stopped wandering and looked at the water pensively. "My father is frozen solid in a brick of ice. Yet the repercussions of his actions are surrounding me and suffocating me as if he were still here. So, I am some great heroine. So, I have made some great difference!" She grimaced. "People are still dying. I almost wish Papa were still here to clean up his own mess. I could remain hiding in a quiet corner, unheard and unknown. I would not be responsible."

Trevain observed her guarded countenance. She did not express very much emotion facially, but he was learning to understand her better. He was beginning to realize that every word she spoke was carefully chosen, and completely earnest. Although she often appeared cool and collected, he could feel that beneath this aloof surface was great gravity.

"You are thinking about Corallyn, aren't you?" he asked, reaching out to touch her dark hair. She had only been in the sunlight for a few hours, but her hair had already darkened to its inky-black state. He felt somehow closer to her when her visage was tanned; it was how she had appeared when he had first come to know her.

"I do not know if it is worth it," Aazuria admitted.

"Launching a full-throttle attack on Zimovia just to rescue Corallyn? It is exactly what Vachlan expects us to do. So many people will be injured on both sides. There will be more mass cremations... if Vachlan is even respectful enough to properly cremate the bodies of my people."

"You can't abandon her either," Trevain said quietly. "She's just a little girl."

Aazuria nodded, noticing that although he now had knowledge of Corallyn's true age, he still felt fatherly and protective towards her. "I love my sister, but I know that her life is not worth more than the lives of hundreds of my people." Aazuria frowned. "The truth is that Visola is right. She is always right. It was somewhat fair of him to request one person in exchange for one person, but I cannot let her go. Visola is too precious. Do you understand that? Is it selfish of me? Am I too immature to be a leader?"

"I hardly know my grandmother, but the idea of using her as a human sacrifice doesn't really appeal to me either." He placed his hands in his pockets as he observed Aazuria's features. "As far as I understand, there is no one better qualified than you are to lead your people. I only have experience running a crew of a dozen men, which is nothing compared to your kingdom, but I know that sometimes even the right decisions feel wrong."

Aazuria pulled her cloak closer around herself. "I wish I could know what Elandria would do. I wish I could speak with her, but she cannot know that Corallyn has been abducted. She is fighting for her own life and it would kill her. Literally kill her."

"I would really like to reassure you that things are going to be okay," Trevain said quietly, "but I have no clue in hell what is going to happen."

"None of us do."

"In my whole life I've never had to deal with as much death as in the past few months," he said. "I can only hope that the worst of it is over."

"It has only just begun," Aazuria said. She turned to look at him curiously. "Can you not feel it? You have a keen intuition about dangers in the water. Do you not dread what you feel is coming? Do you not anticipate enough dead bodies to fill a few more of these volcanoes?"

He swallowed. "This world is completely new to me. Just because I feel a certain way…"

"Have you ever been wrong?" she asked him.

He hesitated before shaking his head.

"Vachlan was not always one of ours. He was not born in Adlivun," Aazuria said. "He and my father had some kind of twisted connection. You can take the man out of the European seas, but you cannot take the European seas out of the man. My father was a conqueror at heart, although he chose to live peacefully alongside the Aleutian people. Vachlan, however… as bad as my father was, Vachlan is ten times worse."

"This is a rather shocking thing to learn about my grandfather. So far, everything I've learned about my mother's family has been so pleasantly surprising. I'm a little bit thrown." He frowned. "I almost wish that I had never learned about him, because it makes me think that I must be capable of the same things. I wonder how my grandmother fell in love with him…"

"He is a heartless sociopath. Yet he is so intelligent! So charming that you wish to believe him. He plays on your inherent belief that people are good," Aazuria said. "Do not consider it as any reflection upon yourself that you are related to this man. I spent hundreds of years wondering if I was like my father, and believing ill of myself for every similarity I had with him. I would even feel disgusted with myself when I saw that I was standing with the same posture as he would, with my hands clasped behind my back. I must believe that I am capable of more compassion than he was in order to get through each day."

"From what I have heard of your father, I don't think

you should worry that you are like him," Trevain said. "I know you're upset about arguing with my grandmother, but…"

"Never mind it," Aazuria said suddenly. "It is not important. If I am going to defeat Vachlan I will have to think like him. I know I need to get inside his mind, but it is such a dark place that I cannot handle being there. What can be his reasoning for requesting Visola? I fear his ultimate intentions. I will have to be ruthless. I will have to be stronger than I ever have been. "

"I'll be right there at your side. I'll do anything I can to help," Trevain said.

Aazuria nodded gratefully. "I will need you. Our numbers are not great. Adlivun has been weakened by my father. Year after year, we have been weakened. We have hardly any men, and only a trifling handful of elite forces comprised mostly of women. There is a very high probability that I will lose. I will need to think of a contingency plan—I may have to move my people all to Shiretoko."

"You could bring them to Alaska, temporarily," Trevain suggested. "I could surely afford to purchase enough property to house them all, or at least rent out some hotels…"

Aazuria shook her head. "They belong in the water. It will be damaging to many of them if they must experience life on land." She closed her eyes. "Good Sedna. How can I even think when Corallyn is in peril? My mind is so scattered, Trevain. I just cannot focus. I do not know what to do. All I can think about clearly is what I would like to do to Vachlan for harming my sister."

"I want a piece of this guy too," Trevain admitted. "I know that he's not directly responsible for killing my crew members, but he was closely associated with Atargatis. I have already transferred all the rage I felt towards her for hurting you and murdering my men onto Vachlan. Is that bad?"

"No. One must fight fire with water, correct? There is rage in water, but it is a constant, consuming, and unpredictable rage. Not a short lived spurt." Her eyes locked with his. "Emotion can be a powerful motivator, but in most people it is too diffused and weak. If you channel all your energy and feeling to a single point, anything is possible." Aazuria reached out and brushed a few strands of his gray hair behind his ear. She managed an adoring smile. "Focusing your righteous rage is never a negative thing. I wish I could do it right now."

Trevain was reminded by her smile that she loved him. He still found it difficult to believe. Although his life had gone through great upheaval and his new world was falling apart around him, having Aazuria made everything bearable. He reached out and cupped her face with his hands before leaning forward to press his lips against hers. When they kissed, he felt tremors of warmth run through him, and he felt such contentment that he would not have cared if the volcano really had erupted at that moment.

He gently removed his lips from hers, and smiled at her darkened eyes. He could not say which of her colorings he preferred; her surface complexion was comforting and earthly, while her submerged countenance was challenging and ethereal. Her azure eyes dared him to be more than he was, and to learn more than he had ever dreamed of knowing. Both were Aazuria, and both were strangely natural and familiar to him. Many women wore their different personas like hats throughout the day; they were businesswomen, mothers, and lovers from hour to hour. A changing skin tone was hardly as significant as those essential changes in character, yet its newness still startled him.

Her fluctuating phenotype seemed to parallel the see-saw dynamic of their relationship. Trevain was the dominant partner above the surface, providing Aazuria and her sisters with access to his mansion, vehicle, and financial resources.

In the ocean, their roles reversed and she became the wealthy provider of luxurious lodging, food, healthcare, and protection. Both of them were used to being the responsible, authoritative ones in their respective environments, yet they were both able to sacrifice that control and defer to the other when necessary. Despite a few hiccups early in their relationship, their implicit mutual trust made the transitions from his world to hers relatively seamless. He imagined that switching back would be just as easy.

As long as they were together, he was fairly confident that no changes, however titanic they might be, could ever faze him again. Trevain's eyes fell upon the smoke behind Aazuria, and he was momentarily distracted from his thoughts. The mock eruption was beautiful in an exotic and morbid way.

"If people see this, are they really going to believe it's a volcano?" he asked.

Aazuria shrugged. "There are plenty of small eruptions that people hardly notice. Even these days, with all of your new machines. Some areas are just so secluded, and some eruptions are so small." She gestured behind her to the volcano. "It is realistic."

"Even without any seismic activity?" Trevain asked skeptically.

"There is always seismic activity here." Aazuria forced a small smile. "This is the ring of fire, after all."

Chapter 7: Violin or Clarinet

Gingerly and afraid, Aazuria extended her arms.

Elandria moved forward within the warm, salty mineral water and hugged Aazuria around the waist rather aggressively, to assert that she was feeling better. She gave the older woman a reassuring smile before pulling away to converse with her hands.

"Sionna told me everything. I am so happy that you were able to defeat Atargatis. I must admit that when she shot me I spent my last seconds of consciousness fearing the worst for you. I cried tears of joy to learn that you were alive and well. Poor Corallyn. She was so distraught about the whole situation. How is she? Why has she not come to visit me?"

Aazuria reached out and gently touched Elandria's long white braid which floated in the water. The water was dark, but the tapetum lucidum in her eyes allowed her to take in enough light to make out her sister's face and figure. She swallowed before responding. She hated to lie to her noble sister who had always been completely honest with everyone.

"Corallyn is doing well. She will come visit you soon."

"Thank heavens," Elandria signed. She smiled, moving a hand down to clutch her chest. The arrow had gone through her back and pierced her heart. It had taken a strained combination of modern medicine and traditional healing methods to save her. *"I have been so concerned about Corallyn's state of mind. I wish I could speak with her. Imagine learning that your mother is alive only to lose her straightaway!"*

Aazuria did not know exactly how to respond. She nodded slowly before moving her hands. *"I am sure that Coral will be just fine. The most upsetting thing to her in this whole mess was that you were injured. Now that you are recovering, her spirits will improve."*

"I hope so," Elandria signed. *"Please let her know that I will be perfectly fine. I will return to the castle once Sionna allows it."*

"I will tell her," Aazuria said, almost cringing as she formed the lies with her hands.

Elandria immediately picked up on her discomfort. *"What is wrong? Aazuria, why are you being dishonest with me?"*

"I... have to go," Aazuria said. She swam to the edge of the hot spring and lifted herself out quickly, in such a swift motion that Elandria could not protest. Aazuria frowned to see Naclana standing there, with his eyes downcast. A gallon of dread socked her in the gut.

"Naclana, what's wrong?" she asked anxiously.

Elandria was carefully lifting herself out of her healing pod as her sister spoke, and she had to take a moment to adjust to breathing the air. Usually, the transition was more or less seamless, but she had been instructed not to leave the water at all until her health was less delicate. She had even been restricted to taking her (unusually thoroughly cooked and mostly mushy) meals underwater. Breathing the air felt like hyperventilating in comparison with breathing water. The way that the lungs extracted oxygen from the air was a very different, rapid process. It was like overdosing on sugar for an instantaneous burst of energy instead of slowly digesting complex carbohydrates. Elandria's body was overwhelmed, and she had to exert a great effort in concealing this. Through her dizziness, she read the expression on Naclana's face.

Naclana noticed her movement and he paused before speaking. "Princess Aazuria, you will have to come with me to receive my news. Visola is waiting in the garden."

Aazuria understood that he was suggesting that Elandria should not be present to hear whatever information he carried. She nodded and turned back to her sister. "Elandria, you need to stay in the water. I will be back shortly, okay?"

Elandria understood Naclana's meaning as well, and her heartbeat immediately began to quicken. The strain on the newly-mended organ caused each beat to actually send sharp pain through her chest. She could acutely feel how challenging it was for her heart muscles to send the blood circulating through her body, and how difficult it was to deal with the massive influx of unnecessary oxygen. She admirably battled the urge to place her hand on her chest.

Instead Elandria pulled herself completely out of the water and approached her sister and the messenger. Her legs threatened to buckle as the world spun around her, but she willed them steady. *"No,"* she signed. *"If it involves Coral, then I need to be there."*

"You should not leave the hot springs, Elandria. You are still healing. Sionna would kill us all. You heard her orders…"

"Why are you treating me like an infant?" Elandria furiously signed. *"I need to know, Aazuria. Show me the minimum measure of respect!"*

Aazuria hesitated, glancing at Naclana briefly for advice. His eyes were wide, and his lips parted as though he was about to protest, but no sound emerged. She gave him a stern, knowing look, requesting for him to speak up against Elandria coming along to make her look less like the bad guy. He did not utter a sound. She shook her head with impatience.

"Fine. Come on then." Aazuria went to her sister's side, and offered her an arm for support. The two girls slowly followed Naclana through the corridors of the infirmary until they reached a room not too far away. The garden was a dimly-lit space which was carpeted with various forms of mushrooms. A small trickle of a waterfall adorned the Southern wall. Many medicinal remedies were nursed and harvested from the damp soil and rocks.

Elandria smiled at the sight of the beautiful room, and the fragrant scent of growth which reached her nostrils. She squeezed Aazuria's hand thankfully before freeing her hands to speak in signage. *"The walk has been good for me. Thank you for allowing me to come along. I want to be at your side whether the news is positive or negative."*

Aazuria nodded, reaching out to embrace her sister again, and holding on tightly for a moment longer than she had intended to. "Whatever happens, Elandria, promise me you will stay calm. For the sake of your health. We must be unemotional."

Elandria nodded. When her older sister pulled away from her, she lifted her hands to her thick white braid and began to toy with it nervously. The two women walked forward, into the room where three members of the Ramaris family were waiting for them, spanning three generations. It was not uncommon in submerged settlements like Adlivun to have many more than three generations of family together at once.

Trevain, his mother Alcyone, and his grandmother Visola all sat near the waterfall quietly chatting. There were several guards in the room, since Visola had made a point of beefing up the security since Corallyn's abduction. Elandria noticed this and her anxiety intensified.

"Is this all of us?" Visola asked impatiently. "Naclana, I'm a very busy woman."

"This will do," Naclana said, fidgeting. "I'm just not too sure that Elandria should be here."

"Please continue, Cousin," Elandria signed. Naclana was not technically her cousin since he was a distant relative of Aazuria's mother, whom she did not share, but technicalities like this did not matter to Elandria. She showed kindness and warmth to all.

"Alright," Naclana said, clearing his throat. "As we all know, Corallyn has been missing for several days now."

Elandria's head snapped around to look at Aazuria. *"I did not know this,"* she signed with a startled look in her eyes.

"I did not wish to upset you," Aazuria said softly. "Please understand."

"You have never lied to me, Aazuria," Elandria said. *"If you start lying to those who are closest to you, it is the first sign of your strength truly unraveling. You are this nation's exemplar! What is to stop the bonds which hold Adlivun together from becoming weak and completely disintegrating?"*

Aazuria pressed her lips together tightly and nodded. *"I am sorry, Elandria. I should not have lied."*

"Take it easy on her, Elan," Visola said, giving the quiet, stern-faced girl a forced smile. *"Aazuria has a lot on her plate right now, and she is worried sick about Corallyn, and blaming herself for allowing the abduction to happen in the first place. We're all on the same team here, so let's not turn against each other."*

Elandria nodded. She very much wanted to sit down and put her head in her hands, but instead she looked to Naclana. *"Please proceed with delivering your news."*

Naclana made a signal to one of the guards in the room, who bowed and exited. "A small case was found floating outside the castle today. It... it contained a message from Vachlan."

"Another letter?" Trevain asked with a frown. "I'm not sure that I want my mother to hear the types of letters that Vachlan writes."

"Young man, I am not as feeble as I appear to be," Alcyone said, placing a hand on her son's knee reassuringly.

"I'm not saying that you're weak, mom. It's just that the last letter really upset me, and I don't want you to..."

"This is worse," Naclana said gruffly. "I almost want to

ask all the ladies to leave the room, but I know that will just make you all even angrier with me."

"Damn straight, Naclana," Visola said, frowning. "So tell me what's going on, and stop pussyfooting around the problem. We all know that Vachlan is a douchebag. Get on with it. I'm expecting the worst here, and the longer you stall, the worse crap I imagine."

The guard returned into the room, holding a small, oblong waterproof case which looked like it contained a violin or clarinet. Naclana frowned and took it from him. "Fine. As you command." He gritted his teeth before flipping the latch and opening the case. It was not a musical instrument which rested against the black velvet lining of the box.

It was a child's severed arm.

Alcyone dragged in a ragged gasp of air. Everyone else remained stunned and silent. Elandria's fingers clutched her braid so tightly that the pattern of her hair was causing imprints on her palms. Aazuria stood unblinking as she stared at the small limb.

Visola was the first to speak. "Is it hers? Have you been able to confirm that it's Corallyn's arm?"

"No," Naclana said. "We haven't done any testing yet..."

"It's her arm," Trevain said slowly. He had risen to his feet to closely examine the small fingernails which were painted in a bright orangey-pink hue. His face was contorted, and it took a visible effort for him to speak. "I bought her that nail polish a few weeks ago. We chose it because of her name. Coral Catalyst."

"Since when has a man's judgment of color been precise enough to identify anything?" Visola argued. "Most straight men I know can't tell the difference between green and blue. It could be any..."

"It is her arm," Aazuria said softly. She reached out and slipped her fingers under the cold flesh, and lifted the small arm from the case. "At least it is *only* her arm. She has not lost her life. As long as she was given medical attention, she will be fine. Right? She can survive without an arm. She could still be alive. Right? Naclana?"

"There's more," he responded quietly.

"Tell me," Aazuria demanded. "Tell me everything you know."

"Not more news," he said, choking on the words. "There are more body parts."

"Which parts?" Aazuria asked, her voice rising in desperation. "Fingers and toes, that type of thing? Good Sedna, even an ear? Parts she does not need?"

Naclana sunk his top teeth into his bottom lip. He was unable to respond.

"Naclana!" Aazuria shouted. The man slightly recoiled from the tone of her voice, and was unable to respond.

"If you please, Princess," said the young guard behind Naclana, a dark-skinned woman clad in heavy armor. She stepped forward and bowed before speaking. "Throughout the last few hours we found several more cases containing all the parts of your sister's body. Among them were her limbs, head, and torso."

The only sound in the room was Alcyone's muffled sob.

"The message was written directly into her skin," the young guard continued hesitantly. "A different word is engraved in every body part."

Aazuria stared down at the arm she held, rotating it to see the word carved into the tiny wrist. Her awareness of anything happening around her dwindled as she stared down blankly at the symbol. She did not notice that a few steps away, Elandria was clutching her chest and fighting a massive bout of nausea and pain. Her heart was beating erratically and quickly, and she was unable to catch her breath. The pain in her chest was spreading and there was a pounding in her head. She felt faint, and although she knew that if she focused she could probably fight her body's inclination to shut itself down, she could not conceive of any good reason to even bother trying to do this.

"Thank you for telling me, Naclana," Elandria signed, closing her eyes. Her knees buckled beneath her, and she began to collapse.

Trevain gathered his senses just quickly enough to catch the falling woman. He held Elandria against him and stared up at Naclana with rage on his face. "Did you have to make a fucking PowerPoint presentation about it, man? Jesus. I despise you."

"Power..." Naclana's brow furrowed in confusion, but Trevain was already leaving the room with Elandria in his arms, depriving him of an explanation. He looked at the Captain's broad retreating back in confusion, as two of the guards in the room left to escort him. He knew that the words were meant to be insulting, regardless of the details of what they meant.

"Mama," Alcyone said brokenly, reaching out toward Visola for support.

"It's okay, baby," Visola said, quickly moving to embrace her elderly daughter. Alcyone's frail body shook with sobs, and Visola held her, realizing that her daughter weighed barely ninety pounds. She was greatly weakened from her time spent on land, and even more weakened by the loneliness of the psychiatric facility she had lived in.

"I can't... I just can't," Alcyone was whispering. "I need to lie down."

"Sure, sweetie, let's get you to bed," Visola said, kissing her daughter's wrinkled forehead, which was covered with wisps of thin gray hair. "I'll be right back, Zuri." She looked pointedly at the guards. "Watch over the princess."

When Visola had taken Alcyone out of the room, carefully supporting her mother around the shoulders, only Aazuria remained with Naclana and the other guards. She had not moved from the spot where she had stood as rigid as a statue since she had learned that her sister had been killed. Murdered and mutilated. Her hands holding Corallyn's small arm were stiff—it was as though she herself were being infected with empathetic rigor mortis.

"Princess Aazuria," Naclana said softly. "I'm so sorry about your sister."

Her cousin's voice drew her out of her trance, and she stared at him, disbelieving. She was suddenly startled by the fact that everyone had left the room. Where was Trevain? Where was Elandria? It seemed like the whole world was tinted in dark purple. Was she still standing? She was not aware of her feet. How had her body remained upright? Why were her cheeks dry? Had she not been crying? She vaguely remembered Elandria collapsing. She remembered Alcyone crying. None of the emotions had been hers. None of the reactions had been hers.

She felt nothing. She squeezed on Corallyn's ashen flesh, trying to convince herself that it was real. This was really happening. She tried to feel pain or hurt—that would be the normal thing.

"Princess Aazuria?" Naclana asked, with worry in his voice. He was disturbed by her silent stillness. His voice pierced into her consciousness again.

"Damn you!" Aazuria whispered sharply to her cousin, lifting her eyes to meet his. She tried to force fake emotion into her voice. "Are you out of your mind? Elandria just had heart surgery!" She reached out and carefully returned Corallyn's severed arm to the case. Aazuria wondered why she was not even sad; she was just hollow. She could not blame the messenger for this. "I am sorry, Naclana. I just wish you had not allowed Elandria to know!"

"With all due respect and more, Princess," Naclana said, bowing deeply in apology. "News like this would have made Elandria swoon whether or not she was at full health." It was no secret in Adlivun that the bond between Corallyn and Elandria had been as deep as between the closest of mother and daughter. From the time that Corallyn had been brought to them by their father, King Kyrosed Vellamo, Elandria had taken care of the young girl as though she was her own child.

"Are you calling my sister weak?" Aazuria asked harshly. "I know she is not your blood relation, but that gives you no right to…"

"That isn't fair!" Naclana said with a frown. "She demanded to be present, and you permitted it."

"I did not know you wished to show me body parts!" Aazuria said. "You can be firm when it suits you, Naclana. You should have been firm here. If I lose my other sister too, I will consider it your fault."

He bowed deeply in respect, apology, and acceptance of this judgment. "Do you want to know all the words which were carved into Corallyn's skin?"

"Of course," Aazuria said. "Let us wait for the others to return." Her eyes fell onto the female guard who had been the one to actually break the news of Corallyn's death. She had the appearance of a fourteen-year-old, and she had probably reached her full height. It was impossible to gauge her true age. From her armor, she was evidently a moderate-ranking military official. "What is your name?" Aazuria asked her.

"Lieutenant Namaka," she answered, with a bow.

Aazuria studied the woman's dark eyes and strong features, and tried to remember where she knew her from. She had likely been a migrant from some distant settlement, probably Bimini. "Lieutenant Namaka," Aazuria said with authority. "I will need you to maintain a close watch on Visola from now on. It was her husband who did this to my sister, and I have a hunch that she is about to do something senseless to retaliate. She is the hot-blooded type. Are you capable of guarding her closely?"

Namaka saluted across her chest with enthusiasm. "Yes, Princess Aazuria. I always have and always will."

Aazuria might have wondered about the girl's unusual gusto, and considered how teenagers were always so thrilled to be given an important task. She might have grieved that Corallyn would never get a chance to reach even Namaka's stage of bodily development, and she might have heard Corallyn's voice in her head wishing, like she frequently had, that she would grow breasts sooner rather than later. All these thoughts were interrupted when she was distracted by Trevain reentering the room. She immediately turned to him, with concern about Elandria at the tip of her tongue, but he was already answering her unspoken question.

"She's in a healing pod and the doctors are looking after her," he said, as he approached her. "She should be fine."

"Thank you," Aazuria told him with relief. "Thank you for seeing to her, Trevain."

"Nonsense," he said. "Elandria took care of me when I was ill."

"She always takes care of everyone," Aazuria said. She turned back to gaze at the limb in the box.

"Rocket launchers," Visola said as she entered the room. The echoing of her heavy footsteps made it sound like a giantess was approaching. She gritted her teeth together, as a growl was emitted from deep in her throat. "I am going to kill them all. With rocket launchers."

"We do not possess rocket launchers," Aazuria said.

"O, ye of little faith!" Visola responded. She placed her hands on her hips, and turned to Trevain with a raised red eyebrow. Although her voice carried a somewhat light tone, there was a new, predatory and almost reptilian hue glinting in her green eyes. "After all this time, she still doubts me and my capacity for vengeance."

"What are we going to do, Grandma?" Trevain asked quietly.

"We're going to give Vachlan exactly what he wants," Visola answered. "He must have known somehow that we had decided to attack him instead of exchanging me for Corallyn. That means he has eyes and ears on the inside. A mole. It's either someone extremely new to Adlivun who is masquerading as one of us, or an old ally of his from back when he lived here. I need to find this person."

"Before you decide what you plan on doing, you need to know the message…"

"Probably more threats and bravado," Visola said angrily.

"What language is that written in?" Trevain asked, pointing at the symbol on Corallyn's arm. "What does it mean?"

"Much like our sign language, we have a universal undersea writing system," Aazuria explained. "It is extremely old—it dates back thousands of years to the first undersea civilization. I believe I am babbling this history lesson to avoid facing the matter at hand, and I will just get to the point. The symbol means 'Surrender' and the little arrow at the bottom right corner indicates that it is a command."

"I see," Trevain said, nodding to pretend he understood. In some part of his mind the information was registering, and he was forming a favorable opinion of the concise writing system, but in all the parts he could currently access, all he could think about was what Corallyn had suffered.

Naclana sighed. "The rest of the message on the other body parts demands that we 'Surrender Visola ASAP or Adlivun will be razed.'"

"Then it's decided," Visola said. "I'm going."

"No. Without you we will lose for certain. We do not have anyone else who can lead the army. No one has the knowledge and experience…"

"Sure, there are tons of folks who can lead. Plus Queen Amabie is here."

"Our troops need you, Viso. I need you. Name one other person who could take your place."

"Trevain will do it," Visola said with a shrug.

"Me?" Trevain asked. "No way. I'm the least qualified out of everyone..."

"True, little grandson." She reached out and pinched his cheek. "For now you are unqualified, but it won't be that way for long."

Aazuria was glaring at both of them. "I will not sacrifice your life, Visola. That is not how bargaining with me works. I am not going to make it so easy—if he thinks that sending me my murdered sister is going to grant him permission to murder my friend, he is mistaken."

"Do you think I don't know this man?"

"Obviously you did not know him well enough before you swam down the aisle with him."

"You gave me your blessing," Visola said angrily. "I know one thing: he won't stop until he gets what he wants."

"We do not have enough evidence to judge his level of determination," Aazuria said. "What he usually wants is you, and you are pitifully easy to get."

Visola's mouth sputtered as she tried to yell five words at once. "Wha— "

"Whoa, whoa, whoa!" Trevain said, raising his hands and stepping between the two women. "Ladies, calm down."

"She started it," Visola mumbled.

"Yeah, she did," Trevain said, turning to his fiancée. "Zuri, maybe this isn't my place... but don't you always say that have you implicit trust in my grandma's opinion? I hardly know her, but I have seen enough to trust her. Everyone in Adlivun speaks highly of General Ramaris. Maybe you should consider her words, and let her go."

"Thanks, Trevain," Visola said with surprise. "Wow, you actually stood up for me. I'm blown away."

"If I can help in any way," he offered, "if you need a fast boat..."

"No," Aazuria said, holding up her hand. "We will go before a carefully chosen council and decide this together.

This conversation is closed and no action will be taken without a consensus."

Visola put both of her hands in her hair with exasperation. "You and Queen Amabie will control the consensus!"

"A council sounds like a good idea," Trevain said.

Naclana cleared his throat, reminding them that he was still in the room. Their heads snapped to look at him. "I hate to have to ask this: would you like to see the other symbols?" Naclana asked.

"Is that really necessary?" Trevain asked.

"It's necessary," Visola said.

Aazuria imagined Corallyn's head severed from her body with a symbol carved into her forehead. She still felt nothing. She supposed that she would not feel anything again until Vachlan had paid for this. "I will look at them," she said.

Trevain's eyes fixated on an unusual breed of mushroom.

Chapter 8: Desperate and Convenient

In a dark, submerged room of the glacier, a small figure was quietly huddled as she hovered within a decorative dome of ice. In the bedchambers of the palace which were underwater, many chose to rest in these hollowed out spherical beds. This well-padded and extremely comfortable furniture was traditional to Adlivun. Mermaids of other clans and those who dwelled above often commented on how nonsensical these globular enclosures seemed at first, but after relenting and spending a night in them every doubter hastily converted. Many even declared that they had experienced the most restful sleep of their lives.

With arms wrapped around her knees, and blankets wrapped around her shoulders, Alcyone did not want to leave the comfort of her ornate waterbed. She had dearly missed this luxury in the decades spent on hard flat beds on land; after a time she had gotten used so to them that she had almost forgotten. She felt safe in her orb, the way she used to feel as a child. She could close her eyes as she floated, her arthritic bones gently supported by the water, and feel at peace with herself. It was almost as though she had never wasted away on land, almost as though her body had not deteriorated very close to the point of being dust. She was not even two centuries old. She was only one-ninety-seven, but she looked more ancient than Queen Amabie who was nine-eighty-seven.

So then, when she had all but accepted herself as dead, when she had taught herself to never look into mirrors to avoid seeing glimpses of her own corpse staring back at her, how was she still breathing while Corallyn no longer was?

She was so distracted in her misery that she did not notice the movement in her room until someone was standing right outside of her bed. She lifted her eyes to see her youngest son with an unusually serious expression on his face.

"Are you ready yet, mom?" Callder signed.

Alcyone was briefly surprised at how quickly Callder had picked up enough sign language to converse. Death did not make the everyday chores of the living disappear, and it seemed that Callder and Trevain had been keeping up with their classes.

"How could I ever have been ready for this?" she responded. Her body was so sluggish that she felt too tired even to move her hands in speech.

"Are you coming to your friend's funeral?" Callder asked.

Alcyone pulled her blankets around her tighter. Corallyn had been the person she had been closest to outside of her family. It disturbed her that the young girl had never gotten the chance to grow up, and never would. Corallyn had lived for almost a century, but there were so many stages of life she would never experience. Alcyone leaned weakly against the concave wall of her bed.

"I only just found her again. We didn't even get a chance to catch up on the last sixty years…"

Callder tried to follow the motions of his mother's hands, but he could not understand all of the words and phrases. He could, however, see the despondent look on the old woman's face. He had not spent much time around Alcyone for the greater part of his life during which she had been locked away, but it surprised him how sensitive he was to her every emotion. Perhaps it was latent memory which was bubbling to the surface which helped him to know her, or some kind of innate familial understanding. Then again, he had always been good with women.

"Are you going to get dressed, mom?" Callder signed.

"Want me to grab some clothes for you?"

Alcyone shook her head in refusal, but Callder moved to her closet anyway. He slid open the ice doors, and looked with confusion at the carved shelves of floating fabrics. He reached out and selected a dark colored dress. He was unable to see its precise color since his eyes were not well-accustomed to the dark. He returned to his mother and held out the dress for her examination.

"Issh tdhiss…" He had opened his mouth and begun to speak, but he quickly remembered that he could not understand the deformed sound of his own voice underwater. The largest complication about needing to use sign language was that he could not hold objects while speaking, or multitask as much as he normally did with his hands. Many of the sea-dwellers could read the motions of each other's lips, but he was not comfortable enough to do this yet. He laid the dress out on his mother's bed, and used his hands. *"Is this good, mom? Do you like this dress?"*

Alcyone looked down at the garment blankly. She shook her head.

Callder nodded and picked it up, returning to the closet to select another. When she refused a second dress, he repeated this half a dozen times before he began to grow impatient. *"Mom, you have to help me out. What do you want?"*

"I want Corallyn to not be cut up into six different pieces," Alcyone responded.

Callder sighed, causing a visible stream of swirling water and bubbles to leave his mouth. This momentarily startled him. Sighing underwater was like exhaling on a cold winter's night, and seeing one's own breath visible in a pale puff of vapor against the dark night sky. The world was so new, yet so natural.

He found himself leaning against the opening of the dome-bed, and feeling quite helpless. When he had initially woken up from his injury, and first laid eyes on his mother, it had taken him some time to recognize her. Once he had some concept of what was going on, he thought that it meant the end of his problems. Every person always retains some hope that someday their estranged family will find its way back together, and when that happens, everything will be okay again. Callder had instantly resolved to himself to quit his drinking and get his life together the moment he saw his mother's smiling face.

Now, he was no longer sure.

"What kind of dress should I get?" he tried asking Alcyone again. *"Why is this one bad?"*

She had not stopped staring at the dress on the bed. *"It always seems to happen this way, doesn't it? One moment you're planning a wedding, and the next you're choosing what to wear for a funeral."* Alcyone tore her eyes away from the dark fabric and looked up at her son. *"Do you remember when your dad died?"*

Callder swallowed and nodded. He did not want to bring up those memories. His brother had asked him to bring his mom to the funeral, but he did not think he could stand to see her like this. He did not want to force her to get out of bed, and he did not want to seem annoying and pushy. She was hurting.

"I'll leave this dress with you, mom," he signed. *"I will come back soon and see if you're ready."*

When Callder had exited the room, Alcyone reached out with one hand to grasp the fabric. Her other hand still held the blankets tightly around her small body. She soon discovered that her fingers were shaking too much to pick up the material. This debilitating tremor had not been as pronounced since she had come to live underwater, but now it seemed to be back with full force. Alcyone took a deep breath of water as she released her blankets and tried to use both hands to pick up the dress. She succeeded in bringing the fabric a few inches higher before she lost motor control again, and her anxiety began. The dress floated in the water, blatantly accusing her of being powerless.

As she tried to control her shaking hands, she wondered whether it would have been better to remain in the psychiatric facility. She had missed her mother and her sons, and the Vellamo family, but she felt like she was cursed. As soon as she was reunited with them, awful things started happening when they had lived for so long happily without her.

Was she a boon or a burden in her children's lives?

The dress was not appropriate. She needed another, but the closet was too far away, and even if she could find the energy to swim over there, her hands would be shaking too much to dress herself. Even if she could dress herself, she did not know if she could find the energy to make it to the funeral. It was a private ceremony, and it was not being held too far away, but she did not think she could withhold her tears in front of her friends and family. She could not bear to look at Aazuria's unreadable expression, and know that although the princess appeared unmoved, she was surely anguished by the loss of her sister.

Alcyone felt the water stirring around her, and she felt a pair of strong arms being wrapped around her. She saw a flash of long red hair, and she knew that it was her mother. Visola hugged Alcyone and kissed her cheek affectionately.

"I'm sorry that I haven't gotten dressed yet. I wasn't feeling well, mama." Even forming simple words was challenging for Alcyone's shaking hands. Visola noticed this. She gave her elderly daughter a kind smile.

"I know, dear."

Visola reached out and squeezed Alcyone's hand gently. Alcyone was surprised by the sudden infusion of strength which this gave her. She looked down through the dark, and saw that her mother's hands were badly damaged. There was a tiny cloud of blood surrounding Visola's knuckles. Alcyone gasped and released her mother's hands to speak with her own.

"Mama, what happened to you?"

"Got mad about a little girl in a box. Blamed bedroom wall. Broke fingers on rock-solid ice."

Alcyone frowned deeply. *"Mama, I don't want to scold you, but..."*

"I can still speak perfectly in sign language, so no real damage is done." Visola wiggled her fingers to demonstrate. *"We all have our ways of coping. It just made me so sick to my stomach that Vachlan did that to Corallyn."* Visola paused, staring at a fixed point. *"I know that he changed. I know that he did horrible things since he left me. I just never thought... I never really believed..."*

"That he was pure evil?" Alcyone signed with disgust. *"And that man is my father. Is he even human?"*

"He's British."

Alcyone smiled. *"Mama, your British jokes stopped being funny in 1914."*

Visola clasped her hands together, and forced herself to be cheerful and to appreciate the moment before speaking. *"Most mothers would be devastated at the insinuation of being uncool and obsolete. I'm just happy that my little girl has returned home to call me names. More motherly-insults, please, Alcie."*

"You're old-school, mama. So passé and... fogyish. Definitely yesterday's news." Alcyone grinned.

"Oh, you kids these days," Visola said, smiling. *"You think you know it all! When I was your age, I had to swim everywhere because the boats were crap! In the winter, with no clothes and no shoes."*

Alcyone laughed. *"I like this; it makes me feel younger too."*

Visola peered through the dark into her daughter's eyes before growing suddenly serious again.

"Can you keep a secret, baby?"

"Of course, mama. What is it?"

"I have decided that I'm going to see your dad, kiddo."

Alcyone felt as though she had been struck. *"Mama, no! What if he hurts you?"*

"It's okay. We used to have a safety word for that. It was Albuquerque."

"That's not what I meant. What if he really, really hurts you?"

"I expect that he will, Alcie. Better he hurt me than chopping up little girls."

Alcyone stared at her mother for a moment, seeking comprehension. *"Aazuria will never allow it,"* she finally responded.

"Yes, that's why it's a secret. I'm not telling her."

"You're choosing to betray Adlivun for my father? How can you do this? Aazuria is more our family than Vachlan—she looked into an audience of men and was somehow able to pick out my son. She saved my life. She just lost her sister, and she couldn't bear to lose you too. I couldn't bear it, mama."

"Alcyone, my star. You know how you meet someone, one person in your entire life who really gets under your skin?" Visola paused to give her daughter a sad smile. *"Your dad's face has never stopped haunting my dreams. Please understand that I have to do this. I'm going to sneak away during the funeral."*

Alcyone knew that she could not disobey her mother's wishes. She trusted her. *"I understand, mama. I felt that way about John. The boys' father, John Murphy. Isn't that a boring, common name? It's so American."* She nodded, blinking away nostalgia. *"I couldn't tell him my name was Alcyone, so I said Alice. For a moment in time, I forgot everything and became that person. Alice Murphy, a fisherman's wife. We were just regular ol' John and Alice..."*

"I wish I could have been there at your wedding," Visola signed.

"It was nothing special. I had no friends or family on land, and I knew no one. It was a marriage of desperate

convenience—I needed John to take care of me."

"Love is often both desperate and convenient," Visola responded. She picked up the dress which was laid out on the bed, and began to undo the clasps on it. She reached out and gently began to peel the layers of blankets away from her daughter. *"Here, let me help you get into this."*

Visola helped her daughter to slip out of her nightgown and into the green dress that Callder had chosen. Alcyone felt embarrassed that her shaking hands were so incapable that her mother's broken fingers were doing what she could not.

"I was supposed to take care of you in your old age," Alcyone said as Visola adjusted the gown. *"This is all wrong. It's all reversed. You already took care of me once."*

"Maybe your father will beat me until I'm crippled and you'll still get a chance to take care of me."

"Mama! That isn't reassuring."

"Sorry, sweetheart," Visola said with a smile. *"Truth is that I'm the luckiest mother ever to have enough strength to take care of my daughter twice. I wouldn't trade this for anything."*

Alcyone looked at her mother solemnly for a moment before speaking in a pleading voice. *"Don't go, mama. We have been separated for so long. Now after just a few weeks together..."*

"I must, Alcie. Trust me on this. Will you help me? Sometime after midnight, pretend like you just discovered I've gone missing. Tell them to hold off on their attack, okay? Do anything you can to stop them from attacking Zimovia. They won't be successful."

"What if they won't listen to me?

"They will. Here, stand up sweetie, let me look at you."

Visola helped her daughter up, and Alcyone's hands hung loosely at her sides. *"Mama, don't you care about Zuri? She lost her father and Corallyn. If something happens to you, she's going to lose her mind."*

"No, she won't. She's got Trevain to help her through.

He's the perfect devoted boy-toy."

"Boy-toy!" Alcyone protested, uncomfortable with her son being called this, but then she saw that her mother was smiling. Leave it to Visola to entice a smile out of her even as they prepared for the funeral of her childhood friend.

"You know, mama, I spent so many years regretting ever leaving Adlivun. Now, after what happened to Corallyn, I'm beginning to think that it was for the best. I experienced so many different aspects of life. I have my two boys. Even if I died now, or even if I had died in that asylum... I would have left some mark on the world in my sons. They would carry on something of me in them long after I was gone. What has Corallyn left behind? Nothing."

"I know how you feel, Alcie." Visola looked at her daughter lovingly. *"I feel the same way about you. If I never did anything good in the world, if I never achieved anything at all, my life still couldn't have been meaningless because of you. I have tried so hard to hate your dad with a vengeance, but how could I? He gave me you."*

"Anyone can pop out sperm. It doesn't make him a good person, and you should not allow nostalgia and paternity to stand in your way of fighting this war."

"Sweetie, I said I couldn't hate him as much as I would like to. Doesn't mean I'm not going to kill him dead as a doornail!" Visola smiled, and then frowned. *"What the hell is a doornail? Anyway, Corallyn did leave something behind. Memories. We have her in our memories, and I'll never forget that crazy kid."*

Alcyone nodded. *"I love you mama. Please be careful,"* she signed, before reaching out and hugging Visola tightly.

"I love you too, baby," Visola said, returning the hug with gentle fierceness. She hoped that it would not be the last time she held her daughter. *"Let's go honor Corallyn."*

Alcyone smiled, and began to swim out of the room. She had forgotten how much easier it was to move in water than on land, and she was thrilled that she did not need her mother's help to move her legs. She felt somehow stronger once she was engaged in the familiar motion of swimming.

When the two women emerged from the room, they were startled by guards rushing through the corridors, swimming past them in a flurry. Visola frowned, sensing that something was wrong. She reached out and drew her daughter closer to her, and swam upwards through the tunnels. The cathedral where the funeral was being held was in a dry room, so it was closer to sea level than the bedchambers. Underwater, tunnels did not need to be perfectly horizontal, and could be positioned at every angle, or even be completely vertical. Visola now navigated one of these vertical hallways, before reaching the intersecting corridor and swimming to the cathedral.

When she entered the room, the first thing she became aware of was the way that Aazuria was shouting orders to guards. Trevain had his head in his hands, and Elandria looked terrified. Queen Amabie had her arms crossed across her chest, and Callder was pacing back and forth restlessly. No one was paying attention to the urn which contained Corallyn's cremated ashes. Something important was disrupting the private ceremony.

"What's going on?" Visola asked with puzzlement, as she wiped her wet bangs out of her eyes. "I was only gone for a few minutes."

Aazuria turned to look at Visola and her daughter. She did not hesitate or break it to them gently; there was no time. "No one can find Sionna," she said bitterly.

Visola swallowed. She turned to make brief eye contact with her daughter, and saw Alcyone's worried expression. She looked at Queen Amabie, and saw pity and fear in the woman's eyes. This was serious. Everyone was assuming the worst.

"Have you asked the infirmary staff?" Alcyone questioned.

"Of course," Aazuria said with a scowl. "She has been

missing since around the time we found Corallyn's body. We were so distracted by the body parts that we did not realize this."

"It's not possible," Visola said softly. "I pumped up security over a hundred percent after they took Corallyn. I even have the Ningyo warriors standing watch. We're so heavily guarded that not even the tiniest stray fish can break into Adlivun."

"Well, evidently someone did," Queen Amabie said.

"There's a note," Naclana said, as he burst into the room.

"What does he want?" Aazuria asked. "Tell me at once. Summarize."

Naclana lifted his shoulders helplessly. "The same thing he's been requesting all along; Visola."

Aazuria exchanged a look with Trevain before turning to gaze at Queen Amabie. Visola walked into the center of the room, and put her hands on her hips.

"We can't sit on our asses and wait any longer. It's obviously not working. We need to change things up." Visola spoke with great forcefulness. "Here's what's going to happen: I'm going. While I'm gone, Trevain and Aazuria must get married and go through the coronation. It will be good for Adlivun to have a King and Queen again," Visola said. "You will stop preparing to attack Zimovia at once, and place all our troops in a defensive position. Do you all understand me? Bolster our defenses."

Aazuria found herself nodding, even though she did not agree with this strategy. At the moment, Visola was too determined. Arguing with her would be futile.

"Trevain will serve as a figurehead commander for our forces," Visola continued. "I know this seems like a strange decision. Aazuria could do it, but she has a reputation of being a bit soft when it comes to the military. They'll walk all over her. Trevain has an aura of newness about him—the lost son of Adlivun returning home after fifty years. The only thing better than a general leading the forces is a king."

"Grandma, I don't think I can…"

"You will. I'm deputizing you, Trevain," she told him, conclusively. "You ran a ship—you know how to be in charge. Consider it a promotion from being Captain. I saw your library. I leafed through your books on naval warfare. You have all the knowledge you need to do this."

"Theory and practice are two very different…"

"Even if you were not my grandson, and even if you were not marrying the princess, I would still ask you to be the Admiral of our fleet. We need your modern perspective in our navy. I shot you in the arm. Atargatis blew your boat up, and you're still standing. You're tough, grandson. You can inspire this country. Zuri will help you make decisions, and Queen Amabie will be here until things settle down. You won't be alone."

Trevain shook his head. "I really don't…"

"It's not up for discussion," Visola said. "I'm going to get my sister back. There is no way that I'm letting her come back in pieces like Corallyn did."

Aazuria stared at her friend for a moment before beginning to nod slowly. She realized that reasoning with her was impossible. "Okay. I understand, Viso. You have to do what you have to do. I support your decision—I appreciate that you're willing to sacrifice yourself to save your sister."

"Thanks, Zuri." Visola bowed slightly from the waist. "I knew you would understand."

"Please be safe, Visola," Aazuria said softly. The princess extended her arms to her friend, and Visola walked forward to embrace her. At the last second, Aazuria shifted her weight and slammed the back of her hand into Visola's head. It happened so fast that Alcyone barely had time to shriek. The general started falling to the floor, but Aazuria caught her around the waist and gently lowered her.

"Forgive me, my friend," Aazuria said tenderly, looking down at Visola's closed eyelids. She turned to the others in the room. "I hate to do this, but I must forfeit Sionna." She saw in the surprised and incredulous expressions that someone was about to argue with her and she violently gestured to Corallyn's urn. "I have lost my sister too, but there is no way in any dimension of hell that I am going to let Visola make a martyr of herself on some wild goose chase. Her foolish recklessness is endearing, but this situation calls for patience; and we all know that patience has never been Visola's strong suit. Am I right?"

"I agree with your decision, Princess Aazuria," Queen Amabie said, saluting Aazuria and inclining her head ever so slightly. "To protect those we love, we must sometimes use great force."

Alcyone nodded too as she stared at Visola's unconscious body. "Thank you, Aazuria. You have saved my mother's life."

"Visola's life was hers to give," Elandria interjected with hesitating hands. *"She deserved the freedom to sacrifice herself if it was her wish! Would you not have done the same for me, Aazuria?"*

Aazuria cast her eyes downward and could not respond. She felt a pang of remorse as she looked at Visola's peaceful expression as she lay on the floor, her red hair spread out all around her.

"This dude is my grandfather, right?" Callder asked. "I just don't understand how he can do this shit."

Alcyone moved across the room to sit beside her youngest son, and she slipped her arm around him comfortingly. Meanwhile, Trevain was crouching down over his grandmother, and shaking his head.

"She may have seemed crazy to you, Aazuria, but I really believe she knew what she was doing," he said crossly. "You told me what a brilliant strategist she is, and what an amazing general. So, why don't you trust her?"

"Visola is a protector by nature. In the past, she has thrown her body in front of me like a meat-shield. She would happily die for Sionna without thinking twice. I trust Visola with everything, and everyone, except for herself. She just thinks of herself as… as just a tool," Aazuria said.

"That is correct, my dear. General Ramaris did tell me that she considered her body to little more than a weapon," Queen Amabie affirmed. "When a friend is in such a self-destructive despair, it becomes our duty to restrain them."

"If she had any self-respect then she would not have married Vachlan in the first place," Aazuria said venomously. She looked up at her cousin who was still holding the note he had never gotten a chance to read. "Naclana, see to it that Visola is imprisoned in comfortable quarters."

"Yes, Princess Aazuria."

Chapter 9: Tell me Something Good

Trevain rubbed circles into his aching temples. This meeting was not going well.

Aliens. He was sitting around a table with Aazuria and Queen Amabie and the heads of their military, and he felt a bit like he had been abducted by aliens. Superior, honorable female aliens who expected him to learn their language in record time, and lead an attack on another alien race. They expected him to be their hero; their knight in shining armor. He felt like he was melting under the heat of the pressure, which felt like several thousand degrees kelvin.

One of Adlivun's high-ranking officials, a woman named Mardöll was speaking about the pros and cons of the different types of terrain from which they could launch their attack. Trevain was having difficulty keeping up with her fast moving fingers. Although the meeting was being held in a dry room, the universal sign language was necessary to bridge the language barrier with the Japanese. He was trying to focus, but he kept getting distracted, his thoughts spiraling off into every possible direction other than the one in which they needed to travel.

"Can you explain that last part again, Major Mardöll?" he asked. When she nodded and began to sign, he tried to focus. Greek might have been easier to understand at the moment. He wished he could be like his brother, who was also present at the meeting for some strange reason. Callder had dozed off beside him discreetly—he was one of those strange people who could sleep with their eyes open. Trevain had given up on hitting his brother to keep him awake.

"I see," Trevain signed when Mardöll had finished explaining. He did not see. He could not stop thinking about his grandmother. He wished that Visola was here to make her lewd and inappropriate jokes, to smile and wink at him in her good-natured way, and to put everyone at utter ease about the situation with her carefree charm, yet serious, intense comportment. When she said she was going to accomplish something—even if it was ridiculous-sounding, and she said it with a giggle and a glimmer of mirth in her eye, he had no doubt whatsoever that she would somehow succeed.

How could someone be so happy-go-lucky and yet so stern and resolute at the same time?

Trevain had never felt so trusting toward anyone else he had ever known; he had never been so compelled to depend on the expertise of someone other than himself. He knew that he was beyond fortunate to have met Visola. Not many men got a chance to meet their grandmother for the first time at the age of fifty, and no man *anywhere* had a grandmother like his. She was outrageous, yet so noble.

She did not deserve to be in prison.

"You are complicating things, Major Mardöll," said a woman named Geira who was another respected army official. Trevain could not remember her rank. *"The decision is not a difficult one. We train our warriors in the water, and so do the Ningyo. We must approach them from the north, directly through the channel."*

"And where do you think the Clan of Zalcan trains their warriors?" a Japanese warrior named Chikasui asked, raising his eyebrows and wiggling them at Geira.

It bothered Trevain enormously that everyone at the meeting was ignoring the fact that Sionna had been captured. They were writing her off as dead. He wanted to hold on to some small hope that his great-aunt would survive, but all of these experienced aquatic-military-professionals seemed to believe that hope was counterproductive. He realized that Chikasui-with-the-annoying-eyebrows was still speaking.

"They are famous for wrestling with sharks as children, are they not? They wear countless strands of necklaces with shark-tooth-beads to boast of their battles. They consider themselves the kings of the oceans. I say that we approach from land. It puts us closer to the precise location where they are stationed, and it may garner us the element of surprise."

"It also places us in immediate danger, with an exhausted army. I do not think attacking over land is a good strategy," signed Mizugiwa, a younger and slightly more timid Ningyo official.

"That is because you are afraid of the land. Incompetent child. It is your fault we lost Yonaguni!" an older man named Kishibe responded spitefully. Trevain began to rub his temples again. It had been hours. They were not getting anywhere. Visola could have correctly figured out in thirty minutes what it was taking two nations days to agree upon—he was fairly certain that the leaders of both nations would have agreed upon this, if not anything else.

"Boys, boys, be calm," Queen Amabie signed, before raising a hand to quiet them. *"Do not blame one another for that which was beyond our control. We may have lost Yonaguni, but we did not lose our lives."*

"Indeed. We must look to the past without emotion to remember our mistakes and learn from them," Chikasui signed. *"We cannot allow the Clan of Zalcan to win again. Because of them, we were forced to abandon our home and flee like frightened animals. We cannot let them cause further harm to our allies. The warriors of Adlivun came to us in our time of need, and this is how we repay them? Let us work together and focus."*

"I lost my son at Yonaguni." Kishibe scowled at the other men. *"I am more dedicated to this than any of you! For me this is a personal mission of vengeance. What greater cause is there than vengeance? I say we march over land to attack."*

"I agree," Aazuria signed, "about vengeance, but not about the land. We cannot expect to surprise the enemy since we know that they might have a spy among us. What we can do is position our forces correctly, where they will be strongest and most comfortable: in the water."

"Thank you, Princess Aazuria," said Mizugiwa. "Do you see this Kishibe? Women have more sense than you."

"Gentlemen! Are you karō or are you bickering schoolboys?" Queen Amabie shook her head disapprovingly. "Do you really enjoy disgracing an old woman in a foreign kingdom? In the home of our friends?"

"My deepest apologies, Queen Amabie," Chikasui began, bowing until his forehead touched the table's surface.

"Please excuse me," Trevain signed, as he abruptly stood up. He turned to leave the table and exit the room, ignoring all the correct etiquette of paying respects to the two queens. He was sick of it all. Aazuria looked after him curiously, and also excused herself to follow him.

"Are you alright?" she asked him when they were outside of the room and in a dry area. "Why did you leave?"

"It's useless. We can't decide on anything," he complained. "This is a mess."

"I know," she whispered. "Worst of all is that someone in that room could be leaking information to Vachlan. How can we plan an attack when there might be a traitor among us?"

"We need my grandma."

Aazuria sighed. "She is not emotionally ready for this."

Trevain suddenly reached out to grasp her shoulders. "Come back to land with me, Zuri. Just until this blows over. We'll bring our family along—Elandria and Callder, my mother and grandmother. We can live in peace. We don't have to fight this senseless war. These are your father's leftovers. You don't have to die because of this."

Aazuria reached up and removed his hands from her shoulders and slowly backed away from him. "If you want to go back to land, then so be it. If you want to take your family, or my sister, then ask them. If they agree, then so be it. I belong here."

"Aazuria, look…"

"No, you look! When Atargatis first began attacking us, I was scared and confused. I did not know who was terrorizing these waters or why. My first instinct was to run. I ran away to land, and that is how I met you." She bit her lip. "I have spent my entire life blaming my father for everything. After he was gone, when Adlivun needed me to step up and take the reins, I could not do it. I was petrified. I did not want to fully accept my new responsibilities. That is why I was going around having everyone call me 'Princess' for months after my father's death; I was just so paralyzed with fear and unable to move forward." She paused in her ranting to take a moment to compose herself.

"Trevain, the moment that I saw my little sister's arm in that box, this became personal. Something changed in me. Before that moment, the Clan of Zalcan had been attacking King Kyrosed Vellamo's daughter. A six-hundred-year-old child! Now, they're about to *be* attacked by Queen Aazuria Vellamo, and I am not going to fail. I will not allow myself to slumber peacefully until I have carved some symbols of my own into Vachlan's flesh." She crossed her arms over her chest. "I understand that this is not your world, and if you wish to leave and return to safety, so be it. We are not married yet and nothing holds you here. You should go, and you should go now."

"I don't want to leave you, Zuri. I just wanted to offer another option. The same way you worried about my grandmother, I worry about you. Don't you think I can see how stressed you are?" Trevain asked. He moved closer to her and lowered his voice. "I'm getting a little jealous of how closely you cling to that rifle all the time. I think you snuggle with it more than you do with me at night."

Aazuria could not resist a small smile. She reached out

and touched his elbow. "Thank you for being such a trooper. Having you is making this impossible situation slightly more bearable. I would be losing my mind without your support."

"You're way stronger than I am," he told her seriously. "I *did* lose my mind when I thought Callder was dead, and there weren't even any body parts involved. It wasn't like Callder was any great loss to the world, either."

"Do not say that," Aazuria scolded him softly.

"It's true. Corallyn was a bright, curious girl. She was a good kid."

Aazuria bit her lip, nodding slowly. "We must go back to the meeting."

Trevain took his fiancée's hand, and was leaning in to give her a light kiss when they were both startled by a noise. When they saw who was approaching them, they both gripped each other's hands a bit more tightly.

"I do not think I can handle more bad news, Naclana," Aazuria said with a frown. "Please, tell me something good."

"Princess Aazuria," he said, saluting. "I am just a messenger. Guards have captured a suspicious looking figure creeping around the eastern shore of the glacier. She could be one of Vachlan's scouts or spies."

"That might be good news," Aazuria said, releasing her death grip on Trevain's metacarpals. "Excellent work. Bring her to us."

"I'm not sure if I can. She is wearing some kind of strange armor, with a large apparatus hooked up to her body," Naclana explained. "I didn't want to bring her into Adlivun in case they were explosives. It might be some kind of kamikaze attack."

"What did the apparatus look like?" Trevain asked.

"There were two massive cylinders on her back," Naclana described, with gestures. "There were tubes going into her helmet, and a pipe here, by her mouth. There were giant things on her feet, like fins."

"It's a scuba-diving suit," Trevain said, nodding. "It's

fine. Bring her into the room where the meeting is being held."

"Yes, Captain Murphy," said Naclana, turning to fulfill this command. As he took his first step, he hesitated for a moment, feeling a bit awkward about taking orders from someone other than Aazuria. His hesitation was only momentary, however, and in the next moment he had disappeared.

"Look at you!" Aazuria said, gently punching Trevain in his abdomen. "Giving orders already."

"My grandma told me to," Trevain said, smiling and taking her arm. "Let's get back to the meeting room."

They made their way to the room, and once they were there, Aazuria allowed Trevain to explain what was happening to the others, while she pulled the rifle off her back and pointed it at the room's entryway. Before many minutes had passed, two guards were dragging a struggling woman into the room. Aazuria aimed her rifle at the woman's chest, holding the gun firmly.

"On your knees, fiend!" Queen Amabie commanded. "Who sent you? You would be wise to talk now, and avoid the permanent scarring from horrible torture."

The woman in the pink and black scuba suit recoiled in surprise, and would have stumbled backwards if two strong guards had not been holding her fast. They pushed her to the ground, and she found herself on her knees. She raised her hands in the air, as one usually does when at gunpoint.

"What the hell," the woman muttered, but her voice was muffled by her scuba mask.

"Unmask her," Aazuria said. She stared at the light sandy-brown tresses which peeked out from under the helmet curiously. The guards roughly reached down to do as they had been commanded, with much protest and cursing from the woman. When her face was revealed, Aazuria's eyes widened. The taut contours of her arms which rigidly held the rifle began to soften as she exhaled.

"Fisherwoman," Aazuria said in greeting, as she lowered the rifle.

"Sea-wench?" The woman on her knees peered closely at Aazuria. "So you really are a mermaid."

"Of sorts."

"Jesus, that's a big gun."

"Brynne Ambrose," Trevain said in wonder. "What the heck are you doing here?"

"Captain Murphy!" Brynne said, a huge smile spreading over her face. She immediately launched herself at him, hugging him violently. "I knew you were alive. I knew it! You're a jackass for making me worry about you. I have been searching for weeks."

Trevain returned the hug, but noticed that Brynne's sudden movement had caused every Ningyo warrior in the room to draw his sword and approach them quickly. "It's okay," he told them, holding up his hand to reassure them. "She's my co-worker." He immediately felt silly for using that modern-sounding description in front of a bunch of ancient undersea samurai. Luckily, most of them did not understand English. Queen Amabie immediately translated what he had said, and the skeptical men lowered their swords.

"Trevain, did you know this place was down here?" Brynne asked with amazement. "It's like an ice hotel on steroids."

Callder, who had been peacefully sleeping through most of the meeting, had woken up for the exciting part involving guns and knives. When the scuba mask had been removed to reveal Brynne's face, he remained frozen for a moment. He did not quite know what he should say to her, and if he should approach her at all. When she threw herself at his brother, however, he found himself rising to his feet and approaching them.

"Get off my woman," Callder complained, as he physically separated the two. "That's enough."

"Callder?" Brynne whispered. "But you're dead."

"Only legally," Callder explained, with a cheeky wink. "Not sexually."

Brynne reached out and slapped him in the face before she began to sob.

"I'm sorry! I'm sorry!" Callder said, lifting his hands in much the way Brynne had when there had been a gun pointed at her. "I know, we broke up years ago, that was very inappropriate, you're going to sue me for workplace harassment, etcetera…"

Brynne reached out and grabbed Callder's shirt and pulled him towards her for a ferocious French kiss that lasted several seconds and made everyone in the room very uncomfortable. Queen Amabie and Aazuria shared an amused look. Brynne abruptly released Callder and turned toward Trevain.

"You. Why would you let everyone think that you and Callder were both dead? Do you know how miserable I was? I'm an emotional overeater, and I swear I have gained about ten pounds because of you two! It went straight to my hips."

"At least six pounds for me, right?" Callder asked. He was looking at her hips, which were swathed in the tight spandex-like material of the scuba suit. He could not see the extra pounds, although it might be because she normally wore baggy sweatpants which concealed her figure.

Brynne ignored him and continued reprimanding Trevain. "Did you know I'm a multi-millionaire? Why the hell did you leave everything to me? They read your will. Are you fucking insane?"

Trevain grinned. "Well, who else was I going to leave it to? I don't have any pets."

"I already have fricking reporters asking me for interviews," Brynne informed him. "It's disgusting. They're saying I was involved with you. If we include the settlement for *The Fishin' Magician*, I'll become one of the richest women in America."

"I told him we should get a new boat and name it the *Master Bai...*"

"Shut up, Callder, the grown-ups are talking. *Sole heir*, Trevain? What the hell?"

"Just relax, Brynne. I made that will years ago," Trevain explained. "Can you imagine if I'd left Callder any money? He'd blow it all in a week and he'd end up begging on the streets."

"No way!" Callder protested. "Why do you think so low of me? It would take me at least *a month* to spend all of *your* money, and then I would probably become a gigolo."

Brynne and Trevain shared a look before Trevain cleared his throat and said, "I rest my case."

The Japanese men burst out laughing, with a few seconds of delay when Queen Amabie had finished translating the last word that Callder had spoken.

Aazuria approached the three land-dwellers with a smile. "Perhaps you three should head back home to Alaska. Trevain, it seems you need to go and take care of your affairs on land. I guess you have to explain to them that you are still alive and reclaim your assets."

"Yeah, I should make a quick trip," Trevain said. A visual came to his mind of the mail piling up in his mailbox. It was a silly, mundane thing to think of when he was now in the middle of a war. His new life was in danger of collapse but he could not erase all the minutiae in his mind, the nagging little reminders of things which used to be really important.

"I would like to stay here, and remain dead," Callder said. "I was never very good at life on land... and my mom is down here. I feel like this is where I need to be right now."

"Can I stay too, Aazuria?" Brynne asked. She reached out to grab Callder's hand to explain herself, although this was not necessary.

"Of course," Aazuria responded, "but you may encounter difficulties since you cannot breathe underwater.

Many rooms are dry, like this one, but there are also many dark, submerged areas."

"No problem. I've got night vision goggles and a scuba suit," she said with a wink. She hesitated. "Just... are there toilets? Or do you guys just go... anywhere?"

Aazuria's eyes widened and her voice rose. "What kind of uncivilized barbarians do you think we are? Of course there are toilets! Good Sedna!"

"Okay, relax! It's not like I've been in an underwater ice-palace before. Keep your shirt on, girlfriend. Do you have internet access too?"

"No."

"I can't live for long without the internet. Maybe I'll find a way to get you hooked up." She turned back to Callder. "You wanna show me around, big boy?"

Callder smiled and began pulling Brynne to the door. He called out over his shoulder. "Can you imagine that all I had to do to get the girl was die? Who knew?"

Aazuria shook her head. She lifted her hands to speak to everyone in the room. *"I am deeply sorry for the interruption. Shall we return to our proceedings?"*

Chapter 10: Doubt my Stylishness

She felt like there was a piping-hot firebrand stuck inside her ear. She reached up to try and remove it and found, to her annoyance, that there was no iron poker to grasp. This was perplexing. Visola strained with the palpable effort of opening her eyes and focusing her vision. The first thing which registered in her mind was perfectly spaced vertical rails. She blinked rapidly, somewhat incredulous.

"Seriously?" she murmured to herself. "Prison?"

Her head was throbbing. There was a ringing in her ears like the sound of an oncoming train. She tried to push herself off the ground and stand, but she was too wobbly to stay upright. She groaned. *Aazuria obviously isn't used to knocking her friends unconscious,* Visola thought to herself. *She used too much force. Someone with a softer cranium would have been irreversibly brain damaged right about now. Amateur.*

Visola noticed that there was only one guard watching her; a dark-skinned young woman. She frowned. This was somewhat insulting. Did Aazuria and Queen Amabie really think that one regular girl and a few metal bars would be enough to restrain her? Unless the chick was some kind of deity (and Visola noticed a small pimple on her adolescent cheek, so that was unlikely) and the bars were laced with high voltage, then she was fairly certain she could outwit this girl and win her freedom. All that she needed was to get the girl within an arm's length to grab her.

However, she might need to regain her balance and coordination first. Did she have time to wait for recovery? She looked at her wrist, where of course, there was no watch.

Just a simple gold bracelet she had worn forever. She stared at the bracelet for a second, remembering when it had been given to her by King Kyrosed Vellamo along with her job. She had worn it more proudly than an engineer wore his ring.

Pushing the memory away, she began to assess her captor. The young woman seemed tough and focused. Visola wondered what her reflexes were like. Feeling around on the ground near to her, Visola found a small rock. She tossed the rock at the far wall, on the other side of the woman, to see if the woman would fully turn toward the sound. The young woman did not move from where she stood, but a muscle in her jaw twitched. She seemed to be ready and aware of everything around her, although she looked frozen solid.

Visola tried to stand once more, and began slowly pacing in her cell, while holding the bars for support. She saw that the guard's eyes were following her, even though the rest of her body did not move a millimeter. Damn, but this little girl was disciplined! Visola was impressed. Of course, Aazuria had assigned one of the best warriors to watch her. Could anything less be expected of the princess? Yet Visola knew that good reflexes and training did not mean that a person was intelligent and capable of sound decision-making. She leaned against the bars, with a large yawn.

"How long was I out?" Visola asked, thinking that once she started up a nice chit-chat, the girl would be pliable.

The guard did not respond. Visola wanted to curse. This was not going to be easy.

"It must have been a long time," Visola said. "Did I miss any developments?"

The guard still did not respond. Impressive. Visola slid back down onto the prison floor, sitting on her thighs with her calves folded out to either side. It was a desperate yet somewhat cute posture. She chewed her lip thoughtfully. There must be some excellent strategy she could use to get out of this situation. She just needed to figure it out. There must be some kind of original and complex manipulation which would be effective.

"I need to pee."

"There's a cup in there."

"I don't see any toilet paper."

"Just shake and drip-dry."

Visola pouted. "Gosh, you're mean." She began to draw geometric patterns in the dirt of the cell floor. "When I get out of here, I am going to demote you. Maybe you'll be kitchen staff, or a sanitation worker."

"I do appreciate the culinary arts," the girl said with a shrug.

Visola squinted, trying to recognize her captor. The girl was not a descendant of one of the ancient, Nordic warrior families of Adlivun like Holma and Geira. Her skin was much more tanned than the average Alaskan mermaid, and there was an unusual accent in the girl's voice. Most of Adlivun's people had strange accents since King Kyrosed had changed their national language to English from Russian. Before the brief Russian phase, they had spoken the Aleut language and mingled among the Aleutian people in Alaska. Hundreds of years before that, before they had migrated to the Bering Sea from Europe, they had spoken Old Norse. This confusing mix of languages caused a mix of interesting accents depending on age. The youngest might have no accent at all and only know English, while the oldest struggled with a thick mingling of residual taints from forgotten languages.

Then there were the migrations. Adlivun had taken in great numbers from other undersea settlements in their respective times of political unrest. There were those from Japan, from the Bermuda Triangle, small Mayan settlements, and of course, from Australia. Visola assumed that her prison guard had been displaced from one of these places; probably the Caribbean.

"Where are you from?" Visola asked her guard. "The Bimini Wall?"

The guard's eyes drifted towards Visola, but she did not respond.

"My husband, Vachlan, destroyed the Bimini Empire. Now he's trying to do the same thing here—and I'm in prison because I wanted to stop him. Do you think that's fair?"

"You're in prison for your own protection," the young girl responded. "Orders of the princess."

"Oh, Sedna," Visola muttered, rising to her feet. "Get me a messenger. Get me Naclana! I've got a few choice words for Zuri. Tacky! Tell her that this is tacky! Sticking her best friend in jail? How long is she going to wait before she becomes Kyrosed Vellamo? Like father, like daughter! Tell her all that for me, okay?"

"You can tell me yourself," Aazuria said, as she entered the room.

Visola immediately felt a little apologetic. She saw that her friend's pale blue eyes were bloodshot and that there were large bags under them. Aazuria's long albino-white hair, the rare trait of highborn sea-dwellers of old, was usually perfectly styled and garnished with pearls. Now, it was pulled up into a disorganized bun, with loose tendrils sticking out of it messily. Visola was not sure how long she had been out for, and how much had transpired in that time, but she knew that Aazuria was unwell. She could tell at a glance that her friend had not been sleeping, and she wanted to reach out and give her a hug and apologize for her mean words.

"You look like a crack whore," Visola said instead.

"Thanks."

"You tacky bitch. How could you do this to me?"

"I cannot let Vachlan have you," Aazuria said quietly.

"It's too late. You have to let me go. He has my sister. Sionna is worth ten of me."

"That is not true."

"I'm the one with the concussion. Is there something wrong with *your* brain?" Visola asked, walking forward until her nose poked through the bars and her forehead was pressed up against them. "Sio is a weirdo whose idea of a naughty weekend is creeping into a library and photocopying modern medical journals. She helps people. In all of the waters of the world, who knows more about mermaid anatomy than she does? Adlivun can't afford to lose her."

"I know that Sionna is brilliant," Aazuria said, "but I will not sacrifice you."

"I want to sacrifice myself," Visola insisted.

"You may give up on that idea now, my friend," Aazuria told her. "I am launching an attack on Zimovia tonight."

"Hey, Zuri," Visola said with a smirk.

"Yes?"

"Check your blind-spot."

Visola reached out and grabbed Aazuria's wounded shoulder and pulled her against the bars. Aazuria cried out at the pain of Visola's tight grip, and did not notice that her friend was stealing her knife from the sheath at her hip. In an instant, Visola had spun Aazuria around so that her back was against the bars. She held her shoulder firmly with one hand, and pressed Aazuria's own knife against her milky-white throat.

Visola winked at the guard, who had been unable to stop this. "Give me the keys and the Princess doesn't get her neck sliced open."

"Do not give her the keys," Aazuria told the guard. "She is bluffing. She would never hurt me."

"I don't know about that, sweetie," Visola said pressing the knife deeper into Aazuria's throat. She released her tight grip on her friend's wounded shoulder, and slipped her arm instead around Aazuria's waist. She tightened her grip, around the smaller woman's abdomen, forcing the air out of

Aazuria's lungs and pinning her against the prison bars. "You knocked me over the head and put me in prison, didn't you? I think that changes our relationship a little bit."

Although Visola was much taller and more heavily muscled than Aazuria, the princess did not show any fear. "You know that I did so for your own safety. I expect that you respect my surprising use of force and you understand my actions," Aazuria said, completely unfazed by the knife against her throat.

"That may be true," Visola said in a low tone, close to Aazuria's ear, "but I'm also mightily pissed off. Very much in the mood for slitting throats… maybe with some candlelight and soft music in the background. Hey, guard lady, can you hum a romantic tune as I sever Aazuria's jugular?"

Aazuria sighed, wiggling with discomfort. "This is not convincing, Visola."

"Then you grossly overestimate my sanity. Due to the fact that I am a maniacal psychopath, my momentary anger at you is effortlessly overpowering centuries of adoration." Visola gestured to the guard with her chin. "Hey, you over there. Haven't you heard stories about the bloodthirsty and irrational General Visola Ramaris?"

The young guard nodded, with a visible amount of anxiety on her face.

"Well, little Oatmeal Cookie, how would you like to witness a spectacular assassination?" Visola gave her an enchanting smile. "I know how to slit a throat so that it makes a little mini-fountain for a few seconds. My daddy taught me when I was a little girl. You see, I've killed so many people. Hundreds of people—I've lost count really. As with anything one does frequently, you develop a taste for it, a knack for it, and ultimately a style. Style is the most important thing… do you doubt my stylishness?"

"No," the guard said, shaking her head and swallowing fearfully. "No, I think you're really stylish."

"Dear Sedna," Aazuria groaned. "She is playing you, Lieutenant. Do not listen to her. She means me no harm."

"Is that so? Check this out, Apple Strudel." Visola winked at the young guard before digging her knife into Aazuria's neck.

"Just ignore her antics," Aazuria was telling the guard. "She is not actually going to... ow!"

Visola cut into her friend's neck until blood began to drip in two rivulets down the pale throat of the princess. Aazuria found herself suddenly standing very still and breathing very evenly as she felt the pain and pressure at her neck. She felt a quiver of uncertainty run through her as she felt the warm wetness of her own blood dripping down her neck. Her lips slightly parted in surprise at the volume of the fast-moving streams which were already trickling down over her breasts. "Viso," she whispered.

In a clear and even voice, with unwavering eye contact, Visola declared her intentions to the guard. "I'm going to slice deeper and deeper with this knife until I cut right through Princess Aazuria Vellamo's throat unless you open my cell right now."

Aazuria felt a small tremor of fear in her gut. The tone in Visola's voice was deadly; she had never heard her friend speak like this. "Visola," she whispered hoarsely against the blade pressing on her larynx. "This is high treason."

"Ha! I'm the treacherous one? You knocked me out and put me in the dungeons like a common delinquent! You let my sister get abducted because you wouldn't let me follow Vachlan's demands! You obviously didn't care about your own sister enough to take the right actions to save her, but guess what?" Visola's furious voice had become a hiss. "I'm not a pussy like you, Aazuria. I won't let Sio be cut up into pieces, even if it means killing you to save her."

Aazuria closed her eyes tightly, feeling tears prick at them for the first time since Corallyn's death. "How can you say all this, Viso? It is not that I did not care about my sister.

I loved Coral. I just valued your life more than hers! I could not let anything happen to you, Viso. I just couldn't."

The young guard finally succumbed to her confusion and opened the door of the cell with nervous, fumbling hands. Visola removed the dagger from Aazuria's throat, and released her. Aazuria crumpled to a heap on the floor, sobbing. Visola exited the cell and knelt beside her friend.

"I know, Zuri. I know," she said, tightly hugging the princess.

"I screwed up," Aazuria said, through her tears. "I acted with personal interests. I let emotion cloud my judgment. How could I have known he would do that? How can I know what he will do to you? It's impossible," she said. "I do not want Sio to get hurt, but I will not lose *you.*"

"The right thing to do in this situation is to throw me to the wolves."

"I can't!"

"I know. That's why I'm making your decision for you. Love you, Zuri." She pulled away, and slammed the hilt of Aazuria's own knife into her friend's head. Aazuria crumpled to the floor as Visola rose to her feet.

Visola moved over to the stunned guard, and grabbed the key from her. "Go into the cell," she ordered. The frightened guard did not hesitate to comply. Visola stooped down to grasp Aazuria, and gently dragged her friend behind the bars as well, laying her out on the ground.

Visola turned to the guard. "What is your name?"

"Namaka," the girl answered timidly.

Visola grabbed Aazuria's dress and tore a strip off, handing it to the guard. "Namaka, press this against her neck to stop the bleeding." The young woman complied as Visola observed her features. "You're from Bimini, aren't you?" Visola asked with a frown. The girl nodded, and Visola glared at her. "I am the only one who can stop Vachlan, and I need to do this alone. Do you understand me?"

Namaka nodded. "I understand, General Ramaris."

Visola chewed on her lip for a moment, before holding up her wrist. "I have not removed this bracelet in five centuries." She reached down and fiddled with the clasp. "Zuri selected you to watch over me for a reason. Now I'm appointing you to watch over her. You will answer to my grandson. Keep an eye on him as well. Do not allow them a single unguarded moment —but give them the illusion of having plenty of privacy." Visola fastened the bracelet around the young girl's wrist.

"You are now her private guard. Take care of her for me," Visola commanded. "Do not even leave her side. Especially don't let her come after me."

Upon seeing the girl nod again, Visola reached out and touched her shoulder. "You've done a good job here, Namaka. Now it's up to you to keep the princess safe."

"I will try my best, General Ramaris," Namaka said, giving Visola the salute of honor. "Good luck."

"Thanks, kid. I'm gonna need it."

Chapter 11: Sunday, February 23rd

Her two-hundredth wedding anniversary was as good of a day to die on as any other.

This was her manner of thinking as she stealthily navigated through a pitch black cave, her footsteps making no sound whatsoever. Her crazy, whimsical plan which would never, in a million years be successful was to sneak down into the bowels of the Zimovia Islets through the secret passages that she knew quite well. She would steal her sister, who was hopefully bound and unharmed in the exact spot from which she emerged, as well as unguarded—or at least, lightly guarded by a few of Zalcan's warriors of whom Visola would easily dispose. Then Visola would melodramatically hug Sionna and escape with her sister back through the tunnels into the dead of the night. They would escape through the forests to where Visola had stashed her fast boat, and make it home in time to have herbal tea with their friends in the evening. She visualized nursing a comforting cup of chamomile, while Sionna had either ginger or peppermint.

This slapdash plan could conceivably work, Visola reasoned. Stranger things had happened. Fortune was a fickle thing. There might even be several resplendent rainbows, cauldrons of gold, and baskets of fresh seasonal fruit magically waiting for them in the boat upon their escape from Zimovia. (In her gung-ho zest for adventure and rebellion, Visola had forgotten to pack a lunch.) If life suddenly decided to become all fairytale-like, all of these things would surely happen and more. The fruit would be dipped in chocolate or topped with whipped cream, and there would be an excellent dessert wine for accompaniment. Her stomach growled. She quickly calculated the probability of this happening to precisely negative nine-thousand percent. These were delightfully encouraging odds.

Visola had already encountered two roadblocks in her path. Literally; two of the secret passages that she knew led down into the submerged caverns of Zimovia had been naturally barricaded with the passage of time. It would take hours to uncover all the dirt, fallen trees, growing trees, and networks of roots that had covered and changed the areas she used to know so well. It was rather disarming and disconcerting to see that the foliage and landscape of Zimovia had changed so greatly since she had last been there.

How could the earth have changed so much while she remained exactly the same?

Certain paths and landmarks were emblazoned so strongly on her memory that it made her feel extremely out of touch with reality to see that the images did not match the silhouettes of her mind's eye. It was a strange kind of nostalgia, which almost physically pained her. She had to admit that it was not the place which she was remembering, but the keen experience of beholding the place with the person she loved. She could recall walking hand in hand with Vachlan through these forests so vividly that it almost felt as if his hand was still in hers. Visola did not intend for this thought to bring a small, peaceful smile to her lips, but she was completely alone in the dark, and about to die, so it did.

She remembered worrying that he would not see the same beauty in the place as she did. She remembered worrying that her own vision was tainted by the fact that her father had brought her here to train for blissful years on end when she was a child. They had mostly stayed underwater, but occasionally she and her sister would sneak up to explore the land through their various secret tunnels. Yes, it was theirs; she had never felt like she *owned* a place more than the Zimovia Islets. It had been her private, cherished gem until she had chosen to share it with Vachlan.

"We could go anywhere in the world for our honeymoon, and you choose to go there?" he had asked with mild surprise in his tone.

She had nodded, a bit embarrassed. "If you would prefer to have grand exploits somewhere we have never been, we can do that instead..."

"The most sacred places are often close to home," he had answered. *"We can explore at any time, and we will have plenty of time to do so. Let us go to the place you treasure the most."*

He had made love to her there, fashioning Zimovia to be even more beautiful to her for a fleeting time. Alcyone had almost certainly been conceived there. Then, with his unexpected and sudden abandonment, Visola had found herself wandering this island heavily pregnant and at the cusp of insanity for years. Most of the mermaids in Adlivun chose to spend the durations of their pregnancies exclusively on land to accelerate the process of gestation. However, many of the members of the royal families and aristocracy chose to remain underwater to elongate the gestation of their unborn children, just it did to their own lifespans. They believed that this resulted in healthier, more capable offspring, but it took great mental and physical stamina for a woman to be able to sustain such an extended pregnancy. Especially alone.

Perhaps the saddest part was that she had truly believed that Vachlan would return.

During that phase of her life, she had been surprisingly weak. Far too weak to be a mother. She could not believe that her husband had left her, and she had lived in denial until she was consumed by fantasy. It had taken great efforts from her sister and Aazuria to pull her out of delirium. When she was finally able to move past it, she had needed to cast all memory of Vachlan from her mind in order to function.

She did not often allow herself to remember, but since it was possibly her final night among the living, she figured that she might as well face her darkest memories. She might as well face the fact that the reason they were her darkest memories was because they were ultimately the happiest ones which she had no chance of ever experiencing again. They were the joyous moments which had become so tainted and sour that she could not bear to revisit them.

Visola had reached the third passage on her list, which was accessible from the bottom of a sizable pond. A tunnel extended downward from the seabed in something of a natural staircase. As she navigated the dark passage which had not been used in decades, she disturbed and frightened much of the reclusive sea-life who had made it their home.

As she descended, she began to wonder exactly what she would say to her husband when she saw him. It would have to be adequately flippant and aloof. Her face would have to be completely expressionless. *"Hey, Studmuffin. Here I am. A lot of trouble you went through for a booty call,"* she practiced with her hands. Her brow immediately creased. *No, I will not address him like that*, she scolded herself mentally.

She recognized this indecision and hesitant practicing of speeches as nervousness. It had been a long time since she had felt so apprehensive about meeting someone. It had nothing to do with the fact that Vachlan was sitting on an army of unknown multitudes. (Death and torture did not terrify her as much as they should have, and she indifferently acknowledged that many would chalk this up to some kind of mental illness. She merely considered it a peculiar personality quirk. Everyone was different, after all.) No, it had everything to do with the fact that Vachlan was Vachlan.

No other man could put irritating winged insects in her stomach the way that he could.

She had always known that he would be her undoing. Now, it seemed, she was approaching the moment of her undoing and all she could really do was determine the most stylish way to extinguish her candle. She would clutch fast to her style until her last breath, and when her style was gone, beneath it would be her honor. She began to experiment once more with the best sign language greeting. Maybe something cool, modern, and American sounding. Her brows creased with the effort. *"Hey, Swordfish. Heard you been killin' a lot of people. How's that workin' for ya?"* She shook her head angrily at herself. *"Mornin', Alligator. Sorry about Atargatis, your bed-buddy. I accidentally killed her. Oopsie."* That would not do either.

Visola was fairly confident that this route offered her at least the element of surprise. Not that anything could ever surprise the brilliant strategist that was her husband. He thought of every possible outcome to every scenario. He was a genius. Her hopes were not high, nor were they moderate, nor were they even palpable. She could not plan ahead, or consider the future. She had to take each rung of the proverbial ladder at the pace of one agonizing step at a time.

Here was a rung. She found herself quite suddenly out in the open, in a well-lit underwater area. There were people here. Mostly men. Heavily armored men who snarled when they caught sight of her and recognized her colors. She wondered if they were expecting her, and if they would guide her to Vachlan without a fight. A second later, when they began to slowly advance in a warlike pattern, her question was answered.

And the adrenaline started.

She quickly did an assessment of how many there were, and it was just over a dozen. They had been caught off-guard, or at least they gave her the distinct impression that this was the case. She observed the way they moved, and she smiled. This was not going to be a big deal. It might be a bit time consuming and wasteful of energy (she cursed inwardly again for neglecting to bring snacks) but they were not elite warriors by any means. Her father had pitted her against groups like these when she was a pre-teen, and they had not gotten any more difficult to defeat.

Besides, today was one of those days on which she rather felt like being a one-woman-army. She often had days like these, but there was usually no opportunity to act on the feeling. She knew she should appreciate the circumstances. Visola did not reach onto her back to access one of the two rifles which hung there. One of the swords on her hip would be enough. Visola hacked away at her attackers with ease, almost as though on an automated setting, and she found it somewhat therapeutic. While she did this, she continued to consider what she should say to Vachlan. That was far more taxing than wiping the floor with a few ill-trained lackeys.

It occurred to her that she might never get as far as speaking with Vachlan himself. Perhaps she would encounter a few expertly-trained minions, or greater numbers of ill-trained ones who would wear her down until she was exhausted. Either way, she was not sure if it would be a relief or a disappointment to avoid encountering her husband at all. It did not *really* matter if she saw him or not—she was here to recover Sionna.

She was positive that he would make that task impossible to achieve without going directly through him. Visola's mind travelled to a video game which Corallyn had tried to show her on their brief stint on land. There had been layers of increasing difficulty one needed to defeat in order to recapture a stolen princess.

"This is ridiculous, Corallyn," Visola had griped. *"Playing this two-dimensional game isn't going to teach you anything about military strategy."*

"That's not what it's about!" Corallyn had argued. *"It's supposed to be fun. You get to go through all these dangerous quests without actually ever being in danger."*

"How is that supposed to be thrilling for someone who is accustomed to actual peril?" Visola had asked.

Now, as she recalled Corallyn's adorable dedication to

that silly videogame, and the young girl's laughter and celebration of every little virtual success, Visola felt nauseated. She would never have a chance to tell Corallyn that her video game actually *was* incredibly fun, and she had just been acting like a stuck up bitch because it was what she did best. These thoughts gave her a little burst of anger and she channeled it into her fighting technique, disposing of her next three enemies with particularly painful and gruesome methods.

These men were like ants! Why would Vachlan, who knew the level of her skill, have such poorly trained men guarding his camp? Either her presence really was not expected, or she was just in the outskirts of the camp, and would have to fight her way to the center. Possibly for several hours. She opened her mouth to give a loud and frustrated scream of exasperation.

Although the noise was somewhat muffled by the water around her, the scream seemed to intimidate the men around her as if it were a battle cry, and this made her chuckle, which further intimidated them. She shoved her sword into the chest of a man nearby, and leaving it there, used her free hands to speak in sign language to the remaining warriors.

"I need to sneeze," she told them. She held up a hand, as if indicating to them that they should wait to resume the battle until after she had sneezed, and she acted as if the sneeze was building up. *"Aaahhh... ahh...."* Visola could not believe that the warriors were actually waiting. Deep inside, she was cracking up. Who had trained these men? *"Choo!"* Finishing the sneeze, she pulled a handkerchief out of her Kevlar armor and began to daintily dab her nose, and the men finally began to see that she was mocking them. They sneered and dove forward to attack her.

She pulled her sword out of the floating enemy she had used like an impromptu umbrella-stand, and she went back to work at hacking apart the inexperienced little boys belonging to the Clan of Zalcan. Every time she felt a little bit guilty about wounding or dismembering a fresh-faced young warrior, she just thought of Corallyn and Sionna, and her guilt faded. She felt justified. When the first dozen men were incapacitated, Visola began to swim through the catacombs. She wondered where Sionna was being held, and if she could possibly find her. It occurred to her that if she had more people with her, backup of any sort, they might have stood a chance. She had not expected the defenses to be so sparse. After less than a minute of solitude, she came upon another group. This gathering was slightly larger than the first.

Her mind drifted once more to Corallyn's video game, and she almost expected these men to be a precise degree more difficult than the first. It was a harder level now, right? Her character, having gained experience from defeating the last group, was supposed to have developed more health or *mana* points. Sadly, the process of learning and growing in the real world was not as immediate or as measurable as it was in the virtual world. The concept of *mana,* or spiritual energy, was one which she was extremely familiar with. The corresponding word used throughout all Inuit lands was *inua*, and the Japanese word for it was *ki*. Both concepts were paramount to battle, and often cited as the true determinant of who would be the victor in any match.

Although intangible, *inua* was believed to be present in all things, such as water and air, and in all plants and creatures. It was part of the reason that breathing water was considered to be sacred with contrast to breathing air—there was more *inua* in the water. Visola was not a very spiritual person, but she did believe that there was more to every fight than merely strength, skill, and intelligence. There was some kind of magic that she could not describe or understand; she became suddenly aware of its existence within her when she was pitted against an opponent, and whether it was called *inua* or anything else, she knew only that it was important.

As long as she had water to breathe, and particularly big fish to fry, she did not think that her *inua* could be depleted.

It was the drive that kept her body going when its physical energy was low. She had learned something from Corallyn's silly game. The simple visual representation of life force as two distinct types of health actually aided her focus and gave her a new way to process the battle. It also gave her new thoughts with which to occupy and soothe her mind to make her less intimidated by the dozens of men who had just caught sight of her.

Visola felt guilty for wasting time with the goofy sneeze, and any part of the fight which resembled having fun. This was not the *fun* type of battle. She had to get to her sister. This time, Visola did pull the rifle off her back, and prepared to systematically dispatch of the next group of men. When she began to fire, she was careful and swift with her marksmanship, for she did not want to allow the crowd to get close enough to swarm around her. Even as she shot her enemies, she thought about Vachlan. Would she have to fight him too? In hand-to-hand combat, or with firepower? She remembered his skill and speed. She remembered that he had usually won their mock sparring matches, but much had happened since then. Visola was much less soft. This would be different.

She was no longer an inexperienced neophyte; she was a seasoned warrior. Thanks in part to Vachlan himself. While Visola had been mushy, malleable clay when they had first met, the unbearable heat of his betrayal had baked her into a hardened masterpiece of sculpture. She was stronger now, and more resilient than she ever had been. Her courage was approaching fearlessness. She had even gone against Aazuria. She shot the final man in this group who was able to move.

Once all the men were either killed or too wounded to be a threat, she stared at them with disappointment. In Corallyn's games, after one killed an enemy, they sometimes dropped an item which could be of use. While this might have been intended by the creators of the games as a metaphor, here on the battlefield it was a reality that one simply needed *stuff*. There were plenty of weapons for Visola to plunder, but nothing of higher quality than her own. *What I wouldn't give for a protein bar right about now,* she thought to herself. She considered rummaging through the armor of the men for scraps of food, but this would have made her feel like a vulture. She was not in Zimovia for the protein bars. She was there for her sister, and she could ignore her growling stomach until she reached her goal.

If she had been patient she *would* have hunted for a snack, and she *would* have crawled into a secluded nook for a nap to refresh her energy after the long journey. Those would have been the wise things to do. However, Visola was so wired by the stimulation of the fight, and so intoxicated by the forward momentum of making progress, that she was incapable of stopping. If she stopped, she feared she would not be able to access the surreal grit and determination she felt again.

She began navigating through the tunnels again, trying desperately to access the mental map that she had created years ago. She had an excellent sense of direction, but it became difficult when all caves looked exactly the same. Occasionally she would come across pockets of more guards and warriors. She wondered why they were so clumped together instead of being spread out all around. It gave her time to rest between bouts of battle. It was like the occasional all-out sprint instead of a constant, tedious marathon. This was perfect not only for Visola's personality, but for her physiology.

At some point, she became conscious of the fact that she was running out of ammunition and energy. She had not known she would need to do this much fighting; she had anticipated that her enemy was expecting her presence, since he had gone to such great lengths to summon her. She switched to super-efficient mode, which consisted of making as few motions as possible, and disabling her opponents quickly, with the least calorie output. Visola found herself sheathing her larger sword, and using two medium-sized ones to sever spinal cords. This was the pinnacle of efficiency, and even somewhat merciful—if you turned a man into a paraplegic instead of killing him completely, he could still read a book.

It carried on this way for some time, until Visola began to feel bored. The catacombs and connections of caves stretched on for miles and miles, and she could be at this for days! She was yawning while fighting, and struggling to keep her eyelids open. That is why when she rounded a blind corner, and found herself swimming into a very large open space, she was startled by the fact that her enemies were congregated in this area by the hundreds.

She considered feeling her usual strange combination of fear and excitement, but all that she felt was tired. As they noticed her, one by one, she realized that she could not turn around and swim away. They would certainly catch her. She could not rely on her weapons or skill anymore. A dozen at a time by hand was one thing—twenty at a time with the rifles were manageable too. But hundreds of men in one very large, very open space? She sighed and threw her rifles and her larger swords down before throwing her hands up. She would have to talk her way out of this one.

A massive blonde warrior who wore decorative dark armor, replete with endless strands of shark's teeth, beckoned her. She assumed that he was a leader of sorts. These men seemed more civilized than the ones she had met in the caves, and by virtue of that alone she assumed that they were the more highly trained squadron. She could do nothing else but follow the warrior's order and swim forward to meet him.

She very quickly found herself surrounded by all of his men. She sighed deeply, feeling trapped. *If I had a protein bar I could defeat all of you,* she thought to herself glumly. The blonde warrior signaled to his men, and the ones closest to her withdrew their swords from their scabbards and pointed them at her. Several of the sharp tips poked into her green Kevlar armor.

"Explain yourself, intruder," the leader signed.

"Hey, look!" she signed back to the leader. *"You oughtta be a bit more cordial. I'm the guest of honor. I received a handwritten invitation and a gift basket and everything."*

"General Visola Ramaris?" he questioned.

"In the flesh."

"Why did you not say this instead of attacking us?" he asked angrily.

"I didn't attack you! Your untrained barbarians attacked me. I would have explained if I'd had a spare second."

He nodded, his lips set in a grim line. *"Fine. I will go get Vachlan."* He turned and gestured to his men. *"Watch her."*

Visola suddenly felt uncomfortable with all of those eyes on her. She spun around, scanning the hundreds of eyes. If she had felt insulted earlier that Aazuria had only left one person to guard her, she supposed that she should feel flattered now. Strangely, that was not the first emotion that came to mind. She did the first thing which she could think of in order to ease the tension in the atmosphere.

"Hi," she signed, waving at them. She could not resist a smile when a few of them waved back. And why not smile? These men were not the military leaders of the Clan of Zalcan—they were just young men who had been born into the clan of nomadic vagrants. Or perhaps they were employees who had been recruited. They did not make the decisions—they had nothing personal against her. They followed instructions, and as long as their instructions were not to kill her, she was safe. She imagined that these instructions could change at any moment, so she might as well enjoy their company now, while the waters between

them were neutral instead of hostile.

Besides, knowing that in a few minutes she would be reunited with her estranged husband gave her the biggest desire to flirt that she had ever experienced.

"So," she signed to the men coyly, *"fine weather for this time of year in Alaska, isn't it?"*

"You're Vachlan's wife?" one of the men asked. *"Is he fucking insane? If you were my wife I would never leave you."*

"That's really sweet," Visola said, beaming. *"The situation was complicated of course. The main complication was that he was a dick."*

Many of the men in the room chuckled, and a few of them nodded in agreement. Visola felt a bit heartened by this. She received the rush of a stand-up comedian with a captive audience; regardless of the fact that she was literally being held captive at sword-point by her audience. Enemies or no enemies, Visola loved having an audience.

"So what about that Atargatis?" she asked them, raising her eyebrows. *"You guys let an ex-ballerina lead an attack?"*

"Ballet is actually a challenging sport that requires great strength and tolerance of pain," one warrior dropped his sword to respond defensively.

The man beside him rolled his eyes. *"He's just saying that because he had a crush on her."*

"Everyone told Vachlan that we should go in with full force all at once," someone else responded. *"He said 'always test the waters.' I guess he knows best."*

"Atargatis was a nine in the looks department," one man said. *"She had a great rack. Kind of a six as a commander though."*

"Six?" Visola said, scoffing. *"Five-and-a-half at best. All she managed to do was drown a few lousy fishermen and stab some shoulders. I do agree about the boobs, though. Man, I wish I had honkers like those."*

"Your boobs are stunning, General," signed a young man, nodding emphatically.

Visola smiled at him thankfully, and had started to form her flirtatious reply when something whizzed right by her ear. In the next moment, before she could process what had happened, she saw the quarter-sized dark hole in the middle of the forehead of the man who had complimented her. There was shock on the faces of his companions, and all the smiles that had been on their faces disappeared. A dark cloud of blood began to surround the young man as his eyes stared forward, wide open but unseeing.

Visola felt awful. It had just been a little bit of harmless flirting. At least, her flirting was usually harmless. She briefly wondered if it signified unrest in the Clan of Zalcan's camp that they were killing their own men; then she realized that this type of thing would only inspire more discipline in the troops. They had plenty of manpower to spare. Considering the way she had left Adlivun, after knocking her princess unconscious, she was not one to pass judgment on this.

She did not want to turn around to see the beast that had shot the bullet because she knew exactly what she would see. It would be him, but he would be changed in some awful way. His viciousness and spite would appear in his transformed face as great ugliness and scarring. It would be a creature of untold horror; something that children could not look at without bursting into tears. She could feel his eyes boring into the back of her skull. His violating gaze was forcing itself between the strands of her hair and into the skin of her scalp, beyond hair follicles, blood and thick cranium, and into the most tender part of her brain. There, it sprouted razor-blade blossoms which it promptly juggled with inside her head, slicing and dicing away at her grey matter.

Turn around, her frayed cerebellum told her. She refused. She could see his reflection in the fearful faces of the men in front of her. She could see the way that he petrified everyone, and she did not need to see the revolting person that was causing this. *Turn around,* her unprincipled curiosity implored her. She had seen glimpses of him from afar in the battles of the 1950s, but she had not faced him directly. *There is a monstrous phenomenon behind you,* her imagination told her. Her self-degradation had to add, *and you're married to it, sucker.* She had never been a wimp, and she knew that she needed to turn around eventually. *I need a divorce,* the progressive part of her declared. She took a moment to make her face absolutely, utterly expressionless. *Maybe I should think about baseball,* a desperate part of her suggested. *I like baseball,* an honest part of her argued.

Unify yourself! the wisest division of her psyche commanded all the other squabbling subdivisions forcefully. *Be strong, and be calm, and be emotionless. Everything will be okay. You should turn around.* So, knowing that it was the wisest part of herself which advised this, Visola obeyed it. *I am bulletproof,* declared the brave bits. There were quite a few of those. *Only because my clothes are made of Kevlar,* explained the derisive portion. She ignored this last comment, and was able to make herself tranquil and strong before she finally turned around.

Some good all that mental preparation had been. She saw him and knew that she should not have come. Aazuria had been right to lock her up. She silently wished that this was all a nightmare; at any moment she would surely wake up comfortable and protected on the luxurious floor of her prison cell. She held her breath. At any moment now. Really, any moment. Hard floor? Vertical bars? Okay, so never mind—this was real, devastatingly real.

Meeting the scrutiny of his steel-grey eyes made her feel sweltering hot and bitterly cold at the same time. It was a thousandfold more difficult to tolerate the intensity of his gaze when it was penetrating her skull from the front instead of the rear. She felt like her eyes did not offer as much protection as the dense bones of her skull had. He was already piercing beyond her eyeballs to knead her memories with his knuckles, and to dissect her thoughts with his fingernails. She tried to get past the pain in her skull to objectively observe her enemy. His jet-black hair was pulled back into its classic ponytail at the nape of his neck. Had he not changed his hairstyle in all this time? Had he not grown hideous with all the horrible deeds he had done?

It did not seem possible, but he looked exactly the same. Except for his eyes; those vicious grey-blue eyes would have terrified any lesser woman to tears. Visola could not help seeing the blatant resemblance to her daughter in his face. Although Alcyone's coloring was closer to Visola's own, there was still *so much* of Vachlan in her. Seeing this; seeing the glimpses of Alcyone in this man who was little more than a stranger, drew her spirit to him involuntarily. Visola realized that she had to face the terrible truth.

She was not strong enough to face the father of her child.

What woman ever was? For all that he was, and all that he had done, all she saw when she looked at him was her Vachlan. Not only did she feel exactly the same towards him as she always had, but seeing Alcyone reflected in him made her love him a little more. She hated herself for being so demented. She made a mental note to kill herself later to end this incurable dementia.

She noticed that Vachlan's deathly-grey eyes were scanning every square inch of her body. He was probably searching for prominent adverse changes that could have occurred in the last couple centuries, and he was probably disappointed to find none. Her hairstyle had not changed at all either. She still wore it in her signature wildfire-cut. (This meant that when it got so long that it became bothersome, she grabbed a handful and chopped off five to ten inches with whatever sharp item was at hand.) Visola watched as his eyes lingered on her hair and her face. Then he did the unthinkable. He smiled.

She knew she was in great peril. She would feel safer with a knife nestled between her ribs.

"How's my ferocious little Glacier Gladiator?" he asked her fondly. *"I see you met the welcoming party."*

She knew it. She had known it! He always began with a charming witticism to throw his opponent off their game. Luckily she had mentally prepared for this banter, and her retort was at the tip of her fingers. What was it again? What had she decided on? Something about a booty call and an alligator. Oh, she would call him such affectionate names that he would be completely confused and disoriented! If only she could remember exactly what she had planned.

"Release my sister," she found herself demanding.

"Visola! Beloved wife, no greeting for me after all this time? Why should I let Sionna go?"

"I am here, like you requested. It is fair."

"Since when do I care about what is fair? Since when do you care?"

Visola licked her lips, although it was a futile motion underwater. Her lips were obviously already moistened, but the pressure of her tongue caressing them made her feel as though she were preparing for something. She was.

Visola pulled her small tanto-knife from its concealed sheath at her side. She would never surrender *all* of her weapons. She spoke with one hand, and mouthed the words as she positioned the blade. *"If I do not have evidence of Sionna's safety within ten seconds, I will commit hara-kiri and deprive you of all the fun you could have with torturing me. Do you really want to be a widower? It would mean that when you were bedding dozens of strange women you wouldn't be doing anything wrong, and that might take some of the thrill out of it."*

"Your wit, darling! How I've missed it." Vachlan's small smile widened even as Visola placed the dagger against her lower abdomen. He had always appreciated that she was capable of humor in the bleakest of situations.

"*Come now. You are too much of a wimp to disembowel yourself, Visola,*" he told her impatiently. "*You know that I hold all the cards. I have no reason to give up your sister. Quit being dramatic. Killing yourself, or at least threatening to do so, won't buy her freedom.*"

"*No, but it will save me from having to look at your ugly face,*" she said with a smug smile. Sionna was off the table. He would not return her sister to her. She had ventured all this way for nothing. Sionna was lost.

More importantly, he had insulted her honor by calling her a wimp, and he had also called her dramatic; no one got away with speaking to her like that. She needed to find a way to punish him that would result in instant gratification for her. Now that she was here, surrounded by the enemy, Vachlan was smiling because he was about to do Sedna-knows-what with her—whatever he had planned would surely be disgraceful. It seemed that he did not remember the one crucial element about her personality: challenging her, or saying that she was not capable of doing something was her easiest, most effective source of motivation for doing that same thing. He really did not believe she was serious!

She was. She would much rather die by her own hands instantly now than slowly by his. It was time to make a stylish statement. Pushing her armor down out of the way, Visola gritted her teeth and sliced the dagger across her stomach, from left-to-right. With her free hand, she reached down into her stomach and yanked out a handful of her own guts. Searing pain shot through her body, and for a moment it felt like she had taken some new designer drug. If she had been on land she might have fallen, but the water kept her buoyant. The satisfaction was intense. She fought to stay conscious against the dizzy, blinding pain. She wanted to laugh, but she knew this would contort the muscles in her abdomen and that would not be fun.

Why did she feel more secure with her guts in her hand? It had something to do with power, she imagined, but she was in too much agony to think coherently. Everyone around her was too shocked to take any kind of action. It was not every day that a pretty girl flashed you with her internal organs; this was way better than pay-per-view!

A kernel of wisdom came to Visola and reminded her that this might not kill her. Usually when one was performing seppuku, a good buddy would be around to finish the job with a beheading. She decided to improvise. She generated a few last internal thoughts about the people whom she loved; she sent an apology to her sister for being unable to save her, and an apology to Aazuria for disobeying her. She sent love to her daughter and her grandsons. Feeling satisfied with these absolving thoughts, she slammed her dagger between her ribs instead, aiming for a major artery. Suicide was a thing which had to be done right, and she was very serious about this. There was a gurgle in her throat, and she felt the consistency of a different liquid congesting her lungs. She knew that if anyone deserved to drown in their own blood, she certainly did. This was final.

She did feel safer with a knife nestled between her ribs.

None of the dozens of men who were witness to her action could deny that this was honorable. Perhaps they would tell stories about it later to their wives and children. This thought made Visola smile. Gone, but not forgotten, thanks to her dramatic gesture. *I spent too much time around Queen Amabie,* Visola thought to herself. *Seppuku isn't supposed to be reflexive. Well, I think she'd be proud of me.*

The look in Vachlan's eyes was extremely rewarding. At least she would die knowing that she could still surprise him. She could still deprive him of that which he wished to possess. She could beat him by exerting what little control was hers in this situation, by destroying that which he wished to destroy. Visola had preserved the sanctity of her self in being the one to cause its end.

She lifted her hand from the hilt of the knife, and dropped her intestines with the other hand. She used her last bit of energy to form the only facetious, glib quip which came to mind:

"Happy Anniversary, Submarine Cowboy."

She realized as she signed the words that she should have given her final phrase a few more seconds more of careful thought. It could have been so much more humorous, and so much more sardonic, if only she possessed a few more seconds of life in which to deliberate. Maybe she could have even included some alliteration or assonance. Visola was usually so clever and original with her usage of condescending pet names, but the pressure of the situation had placed a serious damper on her creativity, and she could not help feeling the slightest twinge of disappointment.

Although looking at Vachlan (who was moving toward her with a frown on his handsome face) definitely made her welcome and embrace her fast-impending death, the incomplete feeling of not having chosen the perfectly patronizing pet-name gave her the slightest yearning for life. Oh, the mortifying and ludicrous monikers she could have mustered if only her aim was a little less true and her strike a little less steadfast!

Nevertheless, Vachlan seemed deeply unhappy with her state of rapid expiration. This was reward enough for her. As her world darkened, she dimly wondered if anyone had ever successfully denied her husband his kicks like this before.

Chapter 12: A Game of Chess

New Holland, 1797

The solid gold chess pieces were heavy enough to play with underwater; they did not float around like the cheap pieces of wood that children often recovered from shipwrecks. There were few greater joys for a sea-dwelling child than to explore a shipwreck with their playmates, searching for treasure. Occasionally, they would even come across skeletons or decaying bodies, and they would run screaming from the ship in horror. Shipwrecks were hands-down the best places to tell ghost-stories.

At this moment, the *Tizheruk* was anchored in the harbor, floating above the water, and she was not yet wrecked. Hopefully she would not be wrecked anytime soon, for there was a long journey home. To the delegation from Adlivun, a shipwreck would be inconvenient and annoying, but not particularly dangerous. They could just board one of the other boats in the fleet or swim the rest of the way.

Slim fingers picked up a queen and hovered over the board. After a moment's hesitation, the queen violently descended, knocking over a rook. "There. I know what you were planning," Visola said, giving her opponent a look of superiority. "Now what's this about a new advisor?"

"It is none of your concern, child."

"Yes, it is. Uncle Sigarr has always been your advisor, Father Kyrosed. He served your father before you. I know you two had a disagreement before we left Adlivun…"

"Sigarr is old and senile," Kyrosed said, stretching back in his chair as he studied the chessboard. The two were killing time while Aazuria entertained the Yawkyawk leaders in another part of the ship. "Contrary to what your uncle thinks, the world has changed since the Magna Carta was signed, and he refuses to change along with it."

Visola frowned at these untrue accusations. Kyrosed was a hypocrite. The document he mentioned was one meant to limit the power of kings, and he did not seem to acknowledge that this might be necessary underwater as much as it was on land. "Are you going to demote my uncle?"

"Demote?" Kyrosed laughed. "No. I have already ordered him into exile."

Visola paused. She did not know why she was surprised by this. She looked down at her hands, which sat in her lap, and clenched them into fists. She thought to herself that she had not even gotten a chance to say goodbye. Realizing that her thoughts had been in Russian, she quickly rephrased the same thoughts in English. Her fingernails dug painfully into her closed palm. "Who shall take his place? Who else is qualified? Uncle Sigarr was irreplaceable."

"A new advisor will be joining us soon, someone with respectable European lineage. He is arriving on a ship from Calcutta. I think you will find him to be a brilliant warrior. He has fascinating ideas, and he is going to help us assimilate the Yawkyawk people."

"King Kyrosed, the Yawkyawk are never going to agree to be assimilated," Visola said.

"That is why we are going to convince them, Colonel Ramaris."

"Princess Aazuria has been telling you that it would be impossible for years; these people love this southern continent. New Holland is their home. We cannot displace them to *Alyeska* so easily."

"Why are you listening to my daughter's humanitarian drivel?" he asked. He moved a bishop three spaces diagonally. "You and I both know that we need to inflate our numbers and grow our empire. We will instill fear in the

Yawkyawk. We will generate a mass migration."

She looked down at the chessboard, trying to conceal her frustration. "Since Queen Undina died... since you returned from Russia, you have been a changed man, King Kyrosed."

"With good reason. I met people there of great insight, and they foresee great changes in the future of the world. This young man who will join us; he is a visionary who will not only fill your uncle's shoes, but innovate entirely new kinds of footwear."

"Wonderful," Visola said. She moved a pawn one space forward. "Just keep him away from my feet. I like my shoes."

"I will introduce you two when he gets here. He's quite remarkable. Those British..."

"Of course!" Visola said with a groan. "Is this some new obsession of yours, Father Kyrosed? First you insist that all of Adlivun has to speak English, and then you import strange men to fill important positions..."

"The English have conquered the land."

"They certainly have not," Visola said, rolling her eyes. "They do not have *Alyeska*. They may have claimed part of New Holland, and begun shipping prisoners here, but there is still so much..."

"You are so young, child," King Kyrosed said with a small smile. "They will soon have all of this land and much more."

"They do not have any influence over us, or any other part of the submerged world. It stands to reason that they never will."

"No, but they present an excellent model for the way we should govern ourselves and our neighbors in our world. Adlivun could be the underwater counterpart of Britain if we position ourselves correctly."

He moved his queen five spaces horizontally. Visola sighed, preparing herself for another one of the King's speeches. She watched the chessboard while he ranted, and tried to drown him out.

"Yonaguni is like France. Like us, they are an undersea superpower. We will never own them, and it would be foolish to try. More can be gained from mutual respect than from squabbling with the Ningyo."

Visola tried to conceal a small smile. What he meant to say was that the Japanese could destroy them. Although Queen Amabie was older than the Arctic leader, she could easily take King Kyrosed in a fight. Visola would bet money on it and enjoy watching. Why had he moved his queen there? Her knight could take it. Was he trying to draw her knight away from that section of the board? Or had he genuinely overlooked something?

"What about Bimini?" she asked as she cautiously moved her rook instead. She took his knight. "What is your analogy for them?"

"They are like Russia, maybe," Kyrosed said, as he moved his bishop. "We could take Bimini if we wanted to."

"We could *not* take Bimini," Visola said. "Must we speak in English, King Kyrosed? Even here in private? It gives me a headache to constantly have to think about the conjugations."

"Yes, Colonel Ramaris," the king answered as he looked at her sternly. "We have to get used to it. Also, you must remember to call me Father Kyrosed in front of the Yawkyawk. It makes me seem kinder."

She looked down at the chessboard in disgust. She already had a father. "So what did you offer to pay this man?"

"He and I had a connection. I offered him anything he wanted."

"And what did he want?" she asked him.

"Oh, just the usual. Gold, mostly," Kyrosed said. He looked at Visola knowingly. "He also has a thing for redheads."

"Excellent." She laughed and stretched her arms. "Because there are no redheads from here to Europe. What are you really paying him with?"

"He is not only interested in material payment. He and I share a common vision for underwater world domination. He is a very rare man." Kyrosed moved his knight before winking at Visola. "Also, he likes his redheads feisty."

"Good Sedna!" Visola said, nearly tipping over the chessboard. "I am one of your chief military officials. If my father knew that you said things like this, he would be very displeased. How can you treat me like currency?"

"If you would agree to lie down with me, then I might treat you with a bit more favoritism," Kyrosed said, moving his queen. "Check."

"You're disgusting," Visola said, before looking down at the chessboard. She was so disturbed by the mental image of sleeping with this man whom she so despised that she did not take enough time to choose where to move her king. She moved it one space backwards in retreat.

"You should consider being with me, Visola. We could have great fun together. I hear I am extremely skilled with my tongue." Kyrosed leaned forward and smiled at her lustfully. "Check."

"King Kyrosed!" Visola rose to her feet, slamming her hand on the table and making the pieces all jump. "We have had this conversation countless times. If you mention it again, I'm going to take my sister and go to Yonaguni," Visola told him. "Queen Amabie would treat me much better than this."

"Bullshit. You would never leave Aazuria. You have been her protector since you two were children, and you are far too attached."

"But do I love her more than I hate you?" Visola said with a sneer.

"That is no way to speak to your king, Colonel Ramaris. You're in check, by the way," Kyrosed said with a smile. "You forget that I know you. You hate learning new languages and your Japanese is poor."

"I would manage."

"I have contacts in Japan. I would send them to kill you if you ever left Adlivun."

"Who?" Visola demanded.

"For one, Kishibe."

"I have heard of him. He is a ruffian with a drinking problem. He could never kill me."

"Kishibe is a great warrior. If he can't manage to kill you, there's always the more vulnerable Sionna."

"Don't you dare bring my sister into any of this! If anything ever happens to her, and I even suspect you are responsible, I will castrate you!"

"Curb your insolent tongue, child! Show some respect to your superiors, and move your damned king out of check!"

Visola clamped her mouth shut, seething with anger. She looked down to the chessboard, her eyes blurry with emotion. It suddenly occurred to her that Kyrosed was provoking her so he could win the game. That would be just like him. She sat down again, and tried to decide what to do with her king. She noticed that she could still take his queen with her knight, and she did so.

"Excellent move," Kyrosed said. He moved his bishop to take her knight. "Be calm, Visola. When we return to Adlivun I will raise your salary. You and Sionna and your father will be very wealthy."

"What about Uncle Sigarr? Will you end his exile and let him return?"

"No."

Visola sighed. She ran a hand through her hair before moving her rook. She had been bored in her quarters, and had petitioned the king for a game of chess, but now she regretted it. Loneliness was better than the maddening intensity of his company.

"You know, my new advisor mentioned to me that he fancies having twin redheads. Together," Kyrosed told her, as he moved his bishop again. "Check."

Visola swallowed her angry retort. She looked down at the chessboard, considering whether to fight or surrender. She moved her rook. "This goes against tradition, King Kyrosed. The Ramaris and Vellamo families have been close for millennia. My ancestors have died for your house, and yours have died for mine. You should not treat my Uncle this way."

"The world is changing rapidly, and so must we. Checkmate."

Visola was glad that the never-ending game was finally over. She rose and marched to the door, yearning to be away from Kyrosed's aura of slime.

Chapter 13: Sort of Alive

Visola followed the young dark-haired girl through the halls of the ship. They had returned from visiting with the Yawkyawk leaders and spending several days in their territory. Even though it was not as luxurious as Adlivun, and even the ship was more comfortable, Visola had enjoyed their stay immensely. She regretted having to return to Kyrosed.

"Papa!" Aazuria called as she entered the room. Visola followed behind her twelve-year-old body with a deep scowl.

"My darling daughter!" Kyrosed Vellamo exclaimed, opening his arms in a gesture of welcome. "How was your mission in Arnhem Land?"

Aazuria gave her father a demure smile and a deep curtsey. "It was enlightening. Papa, I fear I cannot condone your plans to absorb the Yawkyawk. Their way of life has been unchanged for thousands of years. I have never seen so many people so happy and content with themselves and their environment. The relationship between the sea-dwellers and the land-dwellers is intricate."

When Aazuria paused to gather her thoughts, King Kyrosed turned to glance at Visola. He rolled his eyes skyward, indicating that he did not care about his daughter's opinion. They had travelled with a small campaign from Adlivun after communicating through emissaries for years. His intent was clear, and he would not leave until he achieved his objective. He began nodding to appear attentive when he realized that his daughter had begun speaking again.

"The land-dwelling people consider the Yawkyawk to be spiritual guides of some sort. They believe that the water has magical properties with respect to fertility, and they believe you can become pregnant by just going near to the water."

"That's fascinating," King Kyrosed remarked, but Visola could see that he really believed it was dumb.

"What actually happens is even more interesting. The natives go on these 'fertility quests' where they lie by the water, and smoke a certain herb. They go days without eating, hoping for a water spirit to appear to bless them with a child. The Yawkyawk mermen come out of the water and make love to the land-women, but they believe that they are only spirits in a dream. They imagine all kinds of fanciful beasts and creatures, and tell the most outlandish stories about the origin of their children. One woman told me that her son was given to her by a creature called a *muldjewangk*, and that is why he is such a fearsome warrior."

"That's all very well, Aazuria," Kyrosed responded, with a frown, "but I don't see what it has to do with us. We need to bring these people home with us."

"Papa, we cannot," she said quietly. "They are set in their ways—it will ruin all of their beautiful beliefs and fantasies."

"Aazuria, my dear, we left the Nordic seas when they became uninhabitable. Now the Yawkyawk must leave the seas of New Holland if they wish to survive. This land is being colonized as we speak, and the natives are being subjugated just as they have been everywhere else. Why can you not see that?"

"Why would you send me to learn about them if you were just going to overrule and disregard any advice I gave to you?" Aazuria asked angrily.

"I sent you to learn about how to make them see things our way."

"You sent me because I look like a young, innocent, pretty girl, and you wanted to use me to try and control them," Aazuria corrected. "Well, I will not do it. Adlivun does not need for you to increase its population by importing slaves. So if you want to lie to them and tell them life will be better for them in frozen *Alyeska* than in the land they love, you may do it yourself, Papa."

"I intend to do just that," he told her.

Aazuria turned and marched out of the room. Visola smiled, and moved to follow her when Kyrosed stopped her.

"Colonel Ramaris!" he called sharply.

"Yes, Father Kyrosed?"

"It is essential that you keep Aazuria indoors tonight. Do not allow her to leave the ship. I will be running errands on land, and I need to trust you with her safety," he said. "Is this understood?"

"Yes, of course, Father Kyrosed."

"Very well. Go after her and do not let her out of your sight. There are penal colonies here, and that means there could be prisoners and convicts anywhere. Both of you must stay on the boat."

Visola saluted the king, and left the room. She walked through the halls of the ship, heading for Aazuria's cabin. She knocked on the door, and receiving no answer, she opened the door and entered. Aazuria was lying on her back on her bed, and staring up at the ceiling.

"I am so upset, Viso," she said quietly.

"I know," Visola said, closing the door and moving over to sit on Aazuria's bed. "That man makes me angrier by the day."

"There is nothing I can do," Aazuria said, "except dance at the billabong."

"What?"

"There will be a party tonight—a beach party at a lake. Will you please come with me, Viso?"

"Father Kyrosed says that we are to stay on the ship tonight," Visola told her.

"Since when do you listen to him?" Aazuria asked, turning to face her friend. "I do not care what he wants."

"I am not really in the mood, Zuri."

"Do not be a spoilsport. There will be dancing. You must come with me; you know how I love dancing!"

"Personally, I can live without it."

"You would not let me go on my own and be unprotected in a dangerous land, would you?"

"Of course not, but I have instructions to keep you from going out at all. He seemed serious."

Aazuria looked thoughtful for a moment. "I guess you don't want to see all of those half-naked, well-muscled, exotic men indigenous to the Southern Continent. There is always the next trip."

Visola sighed.

*   *   *

"A pipe for the princess?"

"No, thank you," Aazuria signed politely to the older woman who was offering.

"What exactly is that?" Visola asked, studying the curiously shaped pipes and containers of herbs.

"It is some kind of hallucinogen. Rather similar to opium, I believe."

"Why don't we try it, Zuri?" Visola asked with a grin. "I mean, when next are we going to be in New Holland?"

"Substances that distort reality are the same all over the planet, but reality is not."

"Spoken like someone who has never tried a good substance."

"I cannot!" Aazuria whispered. "Papa would be so disappointed."

"And he'd be cheerful if he knew you were dancing on the beach with naked men?"

"He should not have insisted that I learn to dance if he was never going to permit me to do so." Aazuria said, with a small smile. "Besides, I know you will not tell him."

"What makes you so sure?"

"He is already cross with you. You do not wish to let him know that you are betraying his trust and letting me

129

gallivant instead of keeping me under lock and key."

"You never 'gallivant,' Aazuria," Visola said with a roll of her eyes. "I bet you're here with some secret ulterior motive. Cultural observation? Or something altruistic."

"I am here to dance to the sound of the drums in the light of the full moon," Aazuria declared. "Will you join me?"

"Dancing is not really my thing."

"Oh, how I wish Elandria had come! She could have enjoyed singing with the musicians."

"I think Elandria's type of singing is a bit more refined than this, Zuri."

"It might be healthy to forsake precision for one night for the pursuit of pleasure."

"Go on then, you little hedonist," Visola joked.

Aazuria smiled at her friend, and ran out to the beach where the land-dwellers and sea-dwellers were both dancing around an enormous, raging bonfire. There was no other place on earth where the two cultures blended together so effortlessly. Here, the land-dwellers did not fear or suspect the sea-dwellers of being evil or somehow against them. They considered them benevolent spirits. While the two peoples lived in their separate worlds for most of their lives, once a month they would come together to dance.

The drums were strangely affecting.

Aazuria's tiny ankles seemed to be constantly spinning around each other as her bare feet swirled and pounded the sand. Visola's eyes narrowed in a considerable effort to keep up with the swiftness of the girl's lithe twelve-year old body.

When Aazuria threw her arms up to the moon, and laughed as she spun around, Visola realized just how much her friend had needed this. She had needed a moment's release from the constant pressure and insidious plotting of her father. Aazuria could not be as innocent and oblivious to Kyrosed's downward spiral of morality as she seemed. In fact, she was probably more troubled by her father's increasing depravities than anyone.

Many rumors had been circulating in Adlivun about the reason that Aazuria's younger sister Elandria had recently developed nervous conditions. Aazuria had been tight-lipped about the situation, even around Visola, but everyone was saying that Kyrosed Vellamo had forced himself upon his younger daughter. It made sense to Visola, although she had no concrete evidence, for she could think of no other reason that Elandria would have locked herself up inside of the castle, refusing to see anyone. The girl had not spoken in years, and she seemed to be trying her best to make herself disappear. Murmurs of "Poor Elandria" were often heard throughout Adlivun, but never around Aazuria who grew upset and insisted to everyone that her sister was perfectly fine.

Now Visola could see everything clearly in the way that Aazuria danced. Sometimes the princess politely allowed the Yawkyawk men to pick her up by the waist and spin her around in the air—they were fascinated with the foreigner. She interacted graciously among the women, and even joined hands with the children, moving joyously with them. The firelight played on her face and skin like the warm hues of a painting. All of this was lovely, but in the moments that Aazuria was alone, Visola could see the sadness in her friend's eyes. This sadness was always there, but now it was suddenly defined and outlined. She was trying her best to dance it away, and with any luck, she might succeed. It was a fine strategy.

It occurred to Visola that there was nothing more powerful than the rhythmic sound of those drums, and the enchanting flicker of the bonfire. There was no way that two people could dance on that warm beach together in the nighttime and still remain enemies. It was peaceful. The sounds of people chattering in a strange tongue, the music, and the quiet waves on the beach were all hauntingly peaceful.

That is why Visola did not dance; she was not a peaceful person. In another life, she might have liked to be. She might have liked to be less tense and querulous, but it was her job to be on guard. This is why her hand flew to the hilt of her dagger when a shuffling noise was heard very close to her. Visola turned and saw the old woman who had previously been selling drugs.

"Would you like to know your future, violent one?" the woman asked.

Visola's lips cracked a smirk at being called this. She briefly wondered how the old woman knew that she was violent, but then she figured that Aazuria had said something.

"I do not have anything to pay you with," Visola responded apologetically.

"You do not need to pay me," the woman responded, seating herself beside Visola comfortably. *"On the night of the full moon we give each other gifts. It can be very healing to give gifts to another person. Consider this fortune a blessing from a stranger."*

"Alright," Visola signed, feeling a small amount of healthy curiosity. *"What do you have to tell me?"*

"Let me look into your lungs," the woman said, and her hand darted out to collide with Visola's breastbone. Visola was surprised by the speed and force of the old woman's motion, but she did not protest. She was sure that the drug-peddling clairvoyant was relatively harmless.

"You will be killed by the man you love," the woman said after a minute. She looked up at Visola as if she was greatly startled by what she had seen.

Visola's eyebrows rose. She waited to see if the woman would explain herself, but no explanation came. *"What do you mean? I have never been in love. There have been men... but no one of importance."*

"Hush, I need to read your lungs," the woman signed before her hands shot out again and grabbed Visola's ribcage. Her fingers traveled upwards and generously groped

the undersides of her breasts.

"Well, this is weird and uncomfortable," Visola said out loud to no one in particular, knowing quite well that the woman could not understand English.

"*Right now, you are elsewhere,*" the woman told her, with a confused look. "*You are far away, and you are dying. You are surrounded by flowers. Can you not smell them?*"

Visola sniffed the air. There was nothing except the smell wafting over from men smoking pipes. It seemed to her that this woman was deeply under the influence of whatever substance she was peddling. "*I seem sort of alive to me. I could be wrong.*"

The old woman rubbed her nose in frustration. "*I need more information. Tell me, which stars are calling out your name?*"

Visola understood this question. She looked up at the sky, and noticed for the first time since they had arrived in New Holland that she did not recognize much. She felt a sudden wave of dizziness as the stars seemed to blur and move in her vision. It might be that the smoke from the people near to her was influencing her senses.

"*I do not know these constellations very well,*" Visola told the woman. "*I am from very far north, and most of the stars are different there.*"

"*It is not knowing, it is feeling. Listen to what they say!*"

Visola sighed, and glanced over to make sure that Aazuria was still fine. Seeing that all was well, she stared back up at the sky, figuring she had little else to do to kill the time. She scanned the dark foreign skies thoughtfully. "*Those ones.*"

"Ah. I see. You are firebird masquerading as mermaid."

Visola frowned at this cryptic diagnosis.

"*You are marvelous at flying, violent one. You are marvelous in both air and flame, but this is not the time or place."*

"I do not understand..."

"You must swim deeper now than you ever have before."

"Right now?" Visola asked, in a joking tone. *"I'll get a headache."*

The woman held up her hand as if to indicate that she had something important to say. Her body began to shake, and her irises rolled back until only the whites of her eyeballs were visible. Her hands moved quickly in sign language as she trembled.

"Go deeper; in order to survive, you must. Hope is shallow—you dip your toes in it all the time. Submerge yourself until you find fortitude. Swim deep enough to taste prudence in the salt. Breach the murky waters of valor." The woman's vacant eyes suddenly locked on Visola with a vicious temper. *"You do all this, yet you reach your limit when surrounded by truth! It crushes you, it crushes your bones. The pressure is too heavy, and the darkness too obscure. It is also cold. You cannot go any further. You have never gone beneath the truth. You cannot navigate the endless fathoms of forgiveness."*

Visola remained silent and unblinking for several seconds. Was it some kind of poem? Was the old woman reciting from memory? The words struck a chord in her, although she did not understand them. She chewed thoughtfully on her lip as she spoke with her hands. *"Are you telling me I must forgive someone? I have never forgiven anyone in my life."*

"If you want to survive, you must."

"Where are you getting all this?"

"I have no idea what it means or from whence it came," the old woman responded with a smile. *"I hope you liked your gift."*

Visola sighed as she watched Aazuria dance around the fire. *"Yes. I think I need that pipe now."*

Chapter 14: Firebird and Falcon

Visola puffed lazily on the pipe. She smiled a half-lidded smile as she yawned and stretched out in the sand. She could see that Aazuria was tossing around a silver ball in a giant fountain of blood. Sometimes the princess even juggled two or three balls. Visola had not known that her friend could juggle. When she grew bored with watching the circus animals splash around in the fountain of blood behind Aazuria, she turned her eyes to the sky, which was quieter. She sighed peacefully as she tried to listen for anything the stars might be trying to tell her.

One star tried to whisper, but it was too far away, and Visola told it to speak up. It agreed, and said it would also come closer. The star left the sky and began to travel toward her. As it came closer, growing larger and larger, she realized that it was not a star at all, but a great phoenix. The bird's body was made of red and gold flame, and it approached at an alarmingly rapid rate. The contrast of the bright red flames against the dark night sky was striking and terrifying.

The bird seemed to take a breath as its cavernous eyes widened; it let out a huge screech as it expelled fire from its lungs in a massive river of lava. Visola gasped, and tried to get out of the way. She found that she was attached to the ground by her wrist. She tugged and tugged, but she could not get free and the lava was heading straight for her.

Suddenly, she felt the light fluttering of wings across her face. A dark shape materialized between Visola and the stream of lava, protecting her from the onslaught. She saw the silhouette of giant black wings against the fire. When the heat of the flames became too much to bear, she found herself instinctively closing her eyes and burying her face into the sand, and she tasted the grittiness of it. She felt so helpless to be unable to run or fight. She should not have smoked the pipe; she would not have allowed someone to tie her down to the ground if she had been at full alertness.

The dark bird which had saved her from the fire now flew to her side and encircled her with a warm dark wing. The feathers were soft as they caressed her shoulder and cheek, and she relaxed against the bird.

"I need to take you somewhere safe," the bird told her.

"Thank you," she said softly. "I was so scared. I could not move. I was defenseless. That has never happened to me before."

"It happens to all of us sometimes."

"Why was the phoenix upset with me? What if it returns to burn me to cinders?"

"We will be long gone before it returns."

"I wish I could go, but I am latched to the ground. I tried to run already."

"I could carry you if you're out of sorts. You could climb atop my back."

"You will not be able to lift me," she whispered, clutching her left wrist. "There's a heavy metal chain. I cannot remove it. Will you please help me take it off? It weighs a ton."

"Certainly, good lady. What a fine piece of work it is."

"It's a just an awful ball and chain. Please take it off!" she pleaded.

"It seems to be welded on."

"I was afraid of that," she said softly. "I will never be able to move. Not unless you chop my hand off. Will you see if there's an axe nearby and please chop my hand off?"

"I don't think that's a very good idea."

"Then I am lost."

"I will save you. If you hold on to me tightly, I will fly away into the sky, and we shall be free."

She squinted. "Who are you?"

"Falcon of the Seas."

"Falcon." Visola nodded. "I should have known. You are such a noble bird. Far better than eagles."

"Thank you, good lady."

"Are there falcons this far south?"

"I am not from around here."

"Of course not. Where are you from?"

"Dreamland."

"Ahhhh. I have never traveled there," she said, reaching out to stroke his breast. "Your feathers are so dark. Soft as black silk. I would have guessed that you were a raven, but they are so sneaky; I do not like them very much. Would you like to sit on my arm?" Visola extended her limb so that the bird could alight on its perch.

The great bird testily reached out with one of its talons and circled Visola's arm around the elbow. Then he withdrew. "I'm afraid that my claws will leave ugly scratches in your smooth skin. You need to wear a special glove for this."

Visola smiled. "My skin is actually a lot tougher than you might think, but you're the most considerate bird whom I have ever had the pleasure of meeting."

"I am not a bird, Visola. I am a man."

"What?" she asked, frowning. "Then why do you have a sharp beak and massive claws?"

"That story is too long to tell."

She reached out and felt his claws, wrapping her fists around his talons. "Did an evil sorceress cast a spell on you to change you into a winged creature? That is horrible! Unless you like it better? Do you like it better? If so, I wish I could be a bird, like you."

"No, good lady. It is better to be a human being."

"I am not totally a human being, you know," she said in a low tone. She lifted her hand and began to make lazy swimming motions. "I am a fish. A human-fish. Are you going to eat me, Falcon?"

"I promise I will not eat you. You're safe." The bird seemed to have a twinkle in his eye. "I prefer earthworms, personally. Fish give me indigestion."

Visola was quiet for a moment as she combed her fingers through the dark feathers of the bird. "Falcon, is there a way I could change you back to being a human being? I want to break the curse the sorceress cast on you."

"I do not think so. I have been trying to break the curse for a hundred years. I have flown all over the world, and I still cannot find the answer."

"I heard that most curses can be broken with a kiss," Visola said. "May I try, Falcon?"

"This particular curse was cast by a remarkably advanced sorceress. I do not think that a simple kiss will work this time."

Visola ran both of her hands along the pointed beak of the bird. "There's no harm in trying." She leaned forward and pressed her lips against the falcon's beak. It was hard and cool to the touch. She had never kissed a beak before, and it felt somewhat odd. "Is it working?" she asked, pulling away.

"No. I'm afraid not," the bird said, somewhat disappointed. "I could hardly feel your soft lips through the hardness of my beak. I suppose I've cracked so many seeds open with it that it's numb to sensation. I must be a lost cause."

"Do not say that!" Visola scolded. "You saved me from the phoenix and I have to repay you. If there's a way to break this enchantment, I promise I will find it." She reached out and slipped her arms under the dark, heavy wings of the falcon, nestling against his warm breast. She nuzzled his feathers contentedly. "Do not be disheartened. I am a great warrior. If there's a dragon to slay, I will slay it for you. Easy as apple pie."

"There are no dragons," the falcon said. "There is only

time."

"Time," she murmured. "I cannot defeat time."

"None of us can."

"Poor Falcon," she said. "It must have been a great villainess who cursed you. Your wings are so very heavy. Do they get tired from flying all day?"

"They do," he answered gruffly. The tips of his wings were caressing her lower back.

She inhaled deeply. "You do smell like a man." She reached up and ran her hand over the curve of his head. "Close your eyes," she told him. When he did, she pressed her lips against his eyelid. Feeling how smooth it was, she began to place more kisses along his cheek. It felt more like skin than feathers, and she let her tongue dart out to press against his cheek. It tasted like sweat.

"You taste like a man too," she said, pulling away in surprise. When he opened his eyes, the two stared at each other for a moment. Visola was spellbound in his gaze. "Your eyes are so round and dark. Behind them there is an intense anger, like that of a man, but no man I have ever met."

"That is only because we had not met."

"Now that we have met, I want you to stay with me. You must be my falcon. I will take you everywhere—you will come home to Adlivun with me, won't you?"

"I will be your Falcon if you will be my Firebird."

"Are you going to ask the sorceress to change me into a phoenix?" Visola asked with worry. "I have some issues with my temper, and I do not want to breathe fire onto my sister and scorch her."

He smiled, reaching out and tangling his talons in her hair. "You are already a firebird. Look at this wild, red mane of yours. It's inhuman."

"I already told you that I am not human," Visola said, closing her eyes as she wrapped her arms around the bird's neck. She was conscious of a strange swaying motion that led her to believe that the bird was carrying her. She did not remember being picked up, but she felt abnormally safe.

"That's right. You're a humanfish. A mermaid."

"No. Not really," Visola said as she nestled against him. "I'm just a warrior. The king says 'fight' and I fight. I'm the little horse on the chessboard, and I leap over everything if he wants me to, and he still treats me badly."

"That's the way kings are," the falcon said. "You can't let them do that."

"The Japanese king is so nice. I should go to live with them, but I can't leave Zuri."

"Is that your husband?"

"No! Princess Aazuria. I am her bodyguard. I was guarding her before the phoenix came, and now the whole world is on fire."

"She is safe, I promise you that. I just need to take you somewhere safe."

"I have never been safe. Have you ever been safe?"

The swaying motion stopped, and the falcon's sharp eyes pierced into her. His pointed beak carried a serious expression. "No," he answered, "and whenever I thought I was safe, it turned out that I really wasn't."

The swaying motion began again. "Be safe with me," Visola pleaded.

"I wish I could be," he answered. "I am taking you somewhere now that is supposed to be safe, but I'm not too sure. One can't be too sure."

Visola closed her eyes, and she almost fell asleep. The swaying was lulling. When the motion stopped again, her eyes shot open, and she saw that the falcon was about to fly away. "No, please don't go!" she begged him. "Why don't you stay and make love to me?"

He hesitated. "I can't," he told her. "I'm just a falcon."

"It's not a huge impediment," she said, reaching for him, and pulling his body against hers. "You are so warm and soft. Make love to me, falcon."

"You should not make love to strange birds, good lady—have you not heard the cautionary tale of what happened to Leda? What if I were the troublesome Zeus, disguised to take advantage of your moment of weakness?"

"That was a swan," she informed him. "I am very particular about my man-birds. Swans and ravens are not to be trusted."

"Neither am I, really."

"I know you're different. You saved my life, Falcon." Visola nuzzled his beak, and smiled almost drunkenly. "Stay with me tonight. You may be a bird, but I can make you feel like a man."

"There is no way I can resist an invitation like that," he told her, before sinking his sharp beak into her neck.

Chapter 15: *Barrel of Piranhas*

When Visola awoke, she realized with a start that she was not alone. The warmth of another body so close to hers had made her sticky and uncomfortable, and she was quite sure that it was not a puppy cuddled up against her back. No, as advertised, it was one of Aazuria's half-naked, well-muscled, exotic men indigenous to the Southern Continent. She groaned, and slammed her elbow backwards into the man's stomach, shoving him away from her with disgust. He hit the floor with a loud crash and an *oof* as the wind was knocked out of him. *At least I have a story to tell Sionna when we get home,* she thought to herself. She snuggled back down happily between the sheets. Then it occurred to her that she was no longer on the beach.

He hit the floor? Visola frowned and opened her eyes. She saw the wooden patterning of her bedroom wall on the ship. This confused her as she had not remembered returning to the boat. She had brought a Yawkyawk man back to the ship? What had she been thinking? What about Aazuria? Visola was reminded of the fact that she should never party, because she always partied too hard. Was it really worth ruining days or weeks of her life over one night of pleasure? Pleasure that she could not even remember, for that matter.

The man she had accidentally shoved off her bed made a grunting noise. She turned over to face him, and propped herself up on her elbow so that she could speak to him in sign language.

"Please leave my room immediately," she told him. Even as she commanded this, she observed his features and physique. He was wearing trousers, but unclothed from the

waist up; she was surprised by her evidently impressive subconscious taste. She kept her face stern, and did not betray that she found his appearance pleasing. *"I was drugged last night, and I apologize for anything I said or did, but I do not remember any of it, and I did not mean any of it. You must leave immediately or I will employ force to remove you from my quarters."*

The man rubbed his head where he had hit it on the floor. "God almighty, are you always this grumpy in the morning?"

"I am *not* gru..." Visola froze. He had spoken in English. With a thick British accent. She noticed his fair skin and precisely groomed black hair which was swept back into a small curled tail. "You are not a Yawkyawk man," she said slowly.

"No," he said, yawning.

"You're Father Kyrosed's new man."

He nodded, closing his eyes and stretching sleepily. "I tried to explain that to you last night, but you were convinced that I was a bird."

"You swine!" she yelled. She pounced on the man, and punched him in the face viciously. "You scoundrel!"

"Now hold on a moment," he said, grabbing her wrists. He was surprised to find that he could not easily subdue her. "You're being a tad judgmental."

Visola straddled him and forced his hands above his head, pinning them there with one hand before punching him in the face again. "I was delirious! I was drugged! I expect you to know better—you are civilized!"

The man realized he had to be fully awake to defend himself, and he managed to wrestle her off him. He pinned her under him and smiled down at her. "Are you saying the Yawkyawk are uncivilized then?"

She slammed her forehead into his and used his moment of surprise to throw him off her. She tackled him again and continued to wrestle for dominance. "They have a different culture than ours. They are more natural and simple. I expect they have different definitions of right and wrong."

"So if I were not an Englishman, I would be off the hook?" he asked as he forced her onto her stomach and locked her arms behind her. "That seems unfair."

She tried to throw her skull backwards to connect with his nose, but he dodged the strike. She tried to writhe with her legs to escape his hold, and failing, she began to repeatedly kick him. "You know better than to take advantage of a situation the way you did!"

He laughed. "You may cease your assault on me. We did not sleep together."

"I woke up beside you!" she shouted, exasperated with the fact that he had actually pinned her down. How was this possible? This was turning out to be a bad morning.

"But nothing more than sleeping happened," he explained, rather calmly in comparison. "You will notice that we both have our clothes on. You were just telling me an interesting story about your fascination with avian creatures. You were rather affectionate."

"I was hallucinating!" Visola said with a deep frown. She continued to struggled, and was surprised when he kept her pinned down with very little effort.

"I know. Drugs are bad for you," he said, "but unbelievably entertaining for me. I do have a great weakness for a good story. I loved the theatre with a passion as a boy."

His earnest manner and lack of retaliation convinced her of his honesty. She abruptly stopped struggling and began to consider the situation. "Let me clarify what appears to be happening to make sure the effect of the hallucinogen has actually worn off," Visola said. "Do you actually have me pinned down?"

"Yes, that is correct. By your fighting skill I would assume this is this not a common occurrence?"

"No. I don't think it has ever happened with someone who wasn't a family member."

When he was quiet for a moment, she looked over her shoulder and saw his suspicious expression. She snarled. "What are you thinking? I come from a family of warriors, and they trained me so well from my birth that I have never been defeated."

"Until now?" he asked with amusement.

"I hardly call this 'defeat.' We weren't being serious, were we?" she asked. "This was just an invigorating morning joust."

He released her with a smile. "I must say, it has been rather invigorating. Next time could you try to refrain from breaking my nose?" he asked.

"I apologize," she said, flipping over and sitting up. She extended her hand to him. "I am Colonel Visola Ramaris."

"Vachlan Suchos, at your service," he responded, shaking her hand firmly.

"Vachlan," she repeated, with a self-deprecating smile. "Not Falcon—Vachlan."

"Please forgive me for the indecency of our meeting. I had an extremely long day yesterday running errands for King Kyrosed, and I had not slept in two days. I was sent to retrieve you and the princess in the wee hours of the morning, and I fear…"

"Is Aazuria safe?" Visola asked with dismay. "I usually guard her so closely, but last night…"

"Her father is upset with her for disobeying his orders. She could have been seriously injured. He has locked her up as punishment."

Visola sighed. "He's always locking her up. I hate to speak ill of your new employer since it's your first day on the job, but you do know that King Kyrosed is a very disturbed man, don't you?

"We all are," Vachlan answered. "People in positions of power are usually just more disturbed."

Visola studied the stranger and could not help feeling relaxed by his calm manner. He seemed intelligent and composed in addition to being very physically skilled. She hated to admit it, but he probably would be an excellent asset to Adlivun. She reminded herself that he was taking her uncle's job, and she should be predisposed to disliking him.

"I must have said and done some embarrassing things last night," Visola said quietly. "Please don't consider that as your true first impression of me."

"On the contrary, good lady—I found you fascinating!" Vachlan said. "I could not stop listening, and I would have liked to grab a pen and paper to scribble down notes about the tales you were telling. You held me spellbound, illustrating your every word with gestures and expressions— it was quite theatrical. You were passionate and warm. I wished I could have continued listening, but I was exhausted from travel. Overall, your birds rather reminded me of the story of Philomela."

Visola's eyebrows knitted together. "You are a strange man, Vachlan Suchos." She rose to her feet and walked over to her bed, sitting on the corner of it comfortably. "Tell me about yourself."

"Yes, Colonel," he said, rising to his feet. "Would you like the whole story or the abridged version?"

"Tell me everything important."

"Everything is important," he said quietly. He began to pace back and forth across the small room as he considered how best to tell his story, and whether he should tell anything at all. Visola observed him vigilantly, analyzing every nuance of his posture, gestures, and expressions. She was searching for one little error, one minute mistake to cling to so that she could nurture a healthy hatred towards the foreigner. She felt a strange combination of disbelief and déjà vu—she was incredulous that this seemingly perfect man had been dumped directly into her bed, and yet she was certain that this had happened before. The collision of these opposing feelings resulted in a frustration-headache, and Visola hoped that she was still just dreaming.

Maybe the man was actually just a bird sitting on her windowsill.

"It was disconcerting when you called me Falcon. My mother used to call me that."

"Is that how this works?" she asked. "Are you going to try to ply me with some tortured-childhood story to get into bed with me again?"

He smiled at her, approaching and placing a his hands on the bed on either side of her. He leaned forward, putting his face very close to hers. She felt slightly intimidated, and wanted to lean back, but she held her ground. She was suddenly conscious of the fact that she had morning-breath. When she had been wrestling with him earlier, she had not noticed, but something had quickly changed in her impression of him. It might have happened when he was able to pin her down, although she hoped she was not that shallow.

"Will it work?" he asked. "If I tell you a stirring story, will you take pity on a tired traveler?"

"I don't know. I haven't heard the story yet."

"Good point. Now I'm thinking of how to embellish it to make it more dramatic."

"You're stalling," she said, as she observed his dark eyes. "You feel uncomfortable facing your past and you're making sex jokes to delay having to speak about it. You intend to distract me altogether."

He pulled away from her abruptly. "That is correct."

"King Kyrosed mentioned that you two had some kind of shared vision. Why did you come here?" Visola asked.

"Do you want me to be candidly honest, or do you prefer the dazzling-seduction version?"

"Both," she answered. "Start with the honest, end with the seduction."

The birdman nodded, taking a moment before he began speaking. "I was born in 1585, to a rather respectable family. I was well-educated, and my mother was a great lady of leisure and wealth. I had dreams of being a playwright, and my skill was praised by many, but how could I compete with that lucky bastard, Shakespeare? It was surely timing that made him so successful. I always said to my friends and family that if I had been born a few years earlier..."

"Are you joking?" Visola asked, with her red eyebrows lifted cynically.

"No. Anyway, I decided that if I could not make it as a writer, I would be a man of action. I would be *the* man of the *most* action. So when I was sixteen I joined a crew and set sail for the new world, and I spent many years exploring exotic lands. Colonel Ramaris, are you listening to me?"

"No. I fell asleep when you said you wanted to be a writer. Dear Sedna, you're boring."

"I immediately followed that by saying I decided to become a man of action instead."

"You couldn't even hold my attention for that long," she said with a yawn. "No wonder you didn't make it as a playwright—although I do think you could have a promising career writing lullabies to make troublesome children fall asleep."

"Please, allow me to continue. Your attention span is dreadful. Where was I? Ah, the Caribbean. I grew very wealthy from exploiting innocent natives—it was the popular thing to do—and soon I owned a merchant ship of my own which I used to transport exotic goods back to Europe. One fateful day, in 1605..."

"One fateful day?" Visola asked mockingly.

"Please stop interrupting me, Colonel," Vachlan said a bit sharply. "As I was saying, *one fateful day,* I was sailing near Bermuda when my ship was caught in a massive storm; a hurricane, in fact. We were wrecked. Everyone drowned. I drowned too." Vachlan paused for dramatic effect. "I was only twenty years old, and I thought my life had come to an end..."

"Goodness. I really hope that you survived. I can't

imagine what happens next." As Visola said this in as monotonous a voice as she could muster, her entertainer grew weary. He sat down on the bed beside her and sent her a discouraged look.

"You are extremely difficult to please," Vachlan said with vexation. "This is the true story of my life, as you requested. Although I may not tell a tale as eloquently as you do, please try to imagine yourself in my situation. Drowning is not an agreeable thing—I held my breath until I thought I had died, and I was terrified."

The story reminded Visola of something she had once known. She squinted, searching her mind and trying to grasp the memory. A fleeting image came to mind of an older, grey-haired man, but she could not recognize him. The memory was gone as soon as it came, and she returned to listening.

"I woke up in chains, inside a walled undersea fortress. I was kept as a slave for years in the kingdom of Bimini until they freed me and gave me a job. I couldn't communicate with them at first, but they taught me sign language and how to fight. It was an amazing time for me."

"Do get on with it. I hope something interesting will happen soon." Visola tried her best to act tough and aloof, but the truth was that she wanted to know every single detail about this man. The mere fact that she was so curious spurred her to act more apathetic and rude. The best way to stop an unwanted attraction was to become repulsive.

"Yes, well..." Vachlan shrugged. "In short, I earned the respect of the royalty of Bimini, and I was permitted to return to England to find my mother. When she saw that I had not aged at all in over a decade, she knew that I had been underwater. This almost disturbed her more than if I had drowned. She was inconsolable as she told me her story. My mother had been the princess of Ker-ys, an underwater city near France, until her own siblings had tried to murder her for the throne. She fled to live with friends on land, and was too scared to ever return. She feared that they would try to kill her again." He turned to look at Visola with a wild, yet focused wrath in his eyes. "So I went. I hunted down and killed every last member of my family who had ever threatened my mother, and then I invited her to return to Ker-ys and live there with me. I preferred the underwater life, you see." Just as quickly as his eyes had begun to show dark emotion, it dissolved back into light confidence. "Careful, Colonel, you're beginning to look interested."

Visola inwardly cursed. It was as though he knew that she had been trying to repel him with her callousness. "I admit that it's surprising that a pretty boy like you has any balls."

"But I do, good lady. I have been told that I have the testicles of dragons."

She did not know why this phrase made her feel a little flushed around her neck. She hoped that it was not visible. Visola glanced down at his pants skeptically, almost expecting to see coconut-sized spheres in his trousers.

"Figuratively," Vachlan explained, clearing his throat to indicate that she should stop examining his groin.

"What happened then?" Visola asked, without averting her gaze.

"Ah. Not much more. My mother reined as the queen of Ker-ys after I paved the way for her."

"So Father Kyrosed hired you because you're a spoiled little prince?" she asked.

"He hired me because I *was* a spoiled little prince who made a grave mistake. I missed only one of my mother's enemies, and that person murdered my mother. I grew upset. I could have taken the throne of Ker-ys myself, but instead I traveled to Bimini. I begged the Emperor to let me command a small force of men, and I led them to destroy and enslave all of Ker-ys. That was the first kingdom I thoroughly devastated. Of course, that was in the mid-seventeenth century, and my resume has only grown since then. That is why Kyrosed hired me."

"Oh." Visola did not realize she had been holding her breath. The flush must surely have spread to her cheeks by now. The story was riveting. "So," she said, swallowing. "You had the opportunity to rein over the city of your birth as King, but because of injustice you chose to be a lawless avenger?"

"Now you're romanticizing me," he said.

"The rumors are all about you," Visola said softly. "Everyone gossips about a 'Destroyer of Kingdoms' who ruins everything he touches and leaves carnage in his wake everywhere he goes. It is you."

"Oh, I don't like being called that very much," Vachlan said with a frown. "I was just angry, you see. All the destruction? It was rather therapeutic. You can't keep these kinds of things pent up."

"You're considerably more interesting than you look," Visola remarked.

"I also appreciate irony," Vachlan said. "It gave me a strange kind of pleasure to know that while terrestrial Europe was conquering the Caribbean, the aquatic Caribbean was gaining complete control over almost every undersea settlement in Europe and Africa. I unified the different states of Bimini—I absorbed their Mayan neighbors, and pretty much every undersea tribe in South America. I made them untouchable in only a hundred years."

"Then why did you leave?" she asked. "Weren't you happy with your success?"

"My living arrangement was acceptable. I just didn't feel appreciated, you know? I had a small disagreement with the Emperor one day, and I quit. I decided to seek employment elsewhere. I went back to England, and did a bit of studying. I considered pursuing my writing again—I tried re-releasing some of the works that had not been received well before—maybe I had just been too progressive for the Elizabethan era."

"Really?" Visola asked, her face contorted in amazement at the size of his ego. "You conquered half the globe to expand the reach of the Bimini Empire, and then you decided to go back to being a writer?"

"You are not artistically inclined, are you? You wouldn't understand. Sometimes—hardly ever, but in extremely rare moments—the point of everything is not establishing power, or amassing roomfuls of gold doubloons, or even instigating gratuitous bloodshed. Sometimes, a man just needs to stop—and smell the flowers. He needs to *cultivate* a garden of flowers, and think deep thoughts about who he really is underneath the façade created by the pressures of the world. I just needed to take some time to relax, and reconnect with myself. To rejuvenate my soul, and read a little."

"Cultivate a garden of flowers?" Visola asked slowly and incredulously. "Who *are* you?"

"That is precisely what I needed to find out! Who was I, indeed?" Vachlan asked, holding up his finger as if giving a lecture on the greatest philosophical question. "But as I searched for myself in the libraries, and in the quiet spaces, I began to feel impatient. I began to feel the familiar thirst gnawing at me. I could not pause. I had to keep moving to remain sane; I had to keep fighting. I needed to seek out the loud chaos, tame the wild beasts and wild landscapes. I tried tricking my body by writing on moving vehicles so that I still felt like I was moving somewhere, but it did not work. I could not focus."

Visola could not help feeling drawn to him—she understood this thirst for chaos very well.

"Besides," Vachlan continued, "I saw some of Shakespeare's plays, and I just became consumed with my old jealousy and anger. He had only become more famous since I had left! Death couldn't even kill the bastard. I wrote a sprinkling of plays, but no one wanted to perform them. Damn them all! One play was about a crocodile who loved the scent of jasmine so much that he…"

"No," Visola said, holding up her hand. "Don't get into that now. I'm sure I'll read them later."

"Yes, well, I grew annoyed with England, and I fought against them in the American Revolution. I was somewhat fond of America, and considered starting a new life there, but I missed life underwater. I began to work as a hired mercenary for influential undersea employers—I didn't really need the money, but again, I had to keep moving. I briefly stayed with the Rusalka people in Russia, and that is where I met King Kyrosed Vellamo. He was on a diplomatic visit with his allies, and I had never even heard of Adlivun. He spoke of a close alliance with the Japanese, and plans to conquer a sizeable settlement here in New Holland. I had never been to this part of the world, so it seemed like great fun to me. After making a stopover in India for a quick assassination, here I am! At your service, my lady."

"Oh, please. You're not here to serve me—I am not a wimp like King Kyrosed, and I can do everything which needs to be done myself," Visola said. She crossed her arms and glared at Vachlan. "So, Kyrosed Vellamo hired the 'Destroyer of Kingdoms' to be our very own bedfellow." She glanced down at his bottom which was still planted audaciously on her bed. "Literally. It seems to me he's taking a great risk. You have turned your back on every place you ever called home, and fought against them. What makes Kyrosed think that you will show any semblance of loyalty to us?"

"I have never turned my back on a kingdom or destroyed one without very good reason."

"Fighting against England because you had a bone to pick with Shakespeare?"

"They were going to lose anyway. I needed the exercise."

"The little squabble with the emperor of Bimini?"

"You don't know what the little squabble was about. It

was a matter of principle."

Visola considered this for a moment before shaking her head. "Well, I must say this, Vachlan Suchos: you are the most interesting man I have ever had the horror and honor of waking up beside. After hearing about your life, and your personality, I am convinced that this only happened because I was drugged out of my mind. This is never going to happen again—whatever happened. You are a drifter, and you will likely be here today and gone tomorrow: as your Colonel, my first command will be that you keep your personal life out of your business life. You will stay away from Princess Aazuria, and her sisters in Adlivun. You must also stay away from me and my sister. You are our employee. You are not our friend. Do not give anyone the illusion that you are their friend, as you are evidently incapable of making and maintaining any bonds."

"Understood, Colonel."

"Great. Now, I need to get some armor on, and we will meet with Kyrosed to discuss the plan regarding the Yawkyawk."

"You don't need to get dressed, Colonel. You can stay in bed today."

"Excuse me? How dare you! You intend to discuss the matter without me?"

"The matter is resolved, Colonel. Take a look outside your porthole."

Visola turned and kneeled on her bed as she threw aside the curtain covering her porthole. She could not believe what she saw. She stared for several seconds with her face completely expressionless. The Yawkyawk people were lining up for miles to climb aboard the other ships in the harbor. Visola realized that she was staring in open-mouthed astonishment, and she quickly composed herself before turning to Vachlan.

"How did you do this?" she asked him.

"It is essential to know the way your victim thinks."

Visola noted that he said 'victim' instead of 'enemy' and this quiet confidence sent a strange tremble through her center. He was brutally honest. This was both refreshing and alarming.

"New Holland is very wild and uncivilized, and there are many large and unknown creatures of both land and sea. More importantly, there are even larger *imagined* creatures which haunt the dreams of these people. A few cannonballs convinced them that something called a *bunyip* was attacking them. Now, they're afraid to go into the water. Imagine their gratitude when King Kyrosed offered them sanctuary?"

"A bunyip?" Visola asked in wonder. "That doesn't sound very frightening."

"It would if it was part of thousands of years of oral tradition, and you had looked around for it in the shadows of every coral reef and every cave for your entire existence. It also helped that almost everyone on that beach was drugged. Even *you* thought the cannonballs were some sort of phoenix attacking you."

Visola stared at the Yawkyawks, who had resisted King Kyrosed's pressure for years. They were now willingly heading for the ships en masse, with all of their belongings and children clutched tightly to them. This seemed both absurd and unethical, but she could not help thinking that Vachlan had done her job for her.

"It only took you a few hours," she murmured, gesturing at the mass exodus of the southern mermaid colony, "to accomplish all this."

Vachlan glanced out of the porthole to study his handiwork. "They are a very primitive people compared to the kind I am used to dealing with. I would be disappointed in myself if it took me more than a few hours to devise and implement a strategy."

Visola turned to observe Vachlan closely. "Now, are you going to be the kind of man who makes life easier or harder? It looks like you've done my job for me, but looks can be deceiving. Is all of this going to blow up in my face? I am in a barrel of piranha. You're just a barrel of piranha, aren't you?"

He seemed to understand that these questions were rhetorical. He lifted his shoulders in a casual shrug under her scrutiny.

"Kyrosed Vellamo might be insane, but he is also a genius. You are pure, distilled danger. While it is unsafe to have you among us, we still cannot afford to let someone else have you," Visola said softly. "You're a master of manipulating the mind. You're the greatest weapon we've ever had."

"Thank you, good lady. It is not what I really want to do, but I seem to be skilled at doing it." Vachlan looked at her curiously. "I have spent my life advising kings, but I never have anyone to advise me. It is better to labor at something one loves without ever achieving results, or is it better to pursue that which one can easily achieve success at?"

"I don't know," Visola answered quietly. "I was trained to fight, and it was always what I loved to do. I've never loved anything else, and I can't imagine having to choose. Vachlan—forgive me for asking, but may I see your writing?"

"I burned it all in a heated outburst."

"Oh, forgive me. I was just curious."

"I was kidding," Vachlan said. "My writing is quite personal, Colonel. I thought you said you wanted to keep this professional?"

"I changed my mind."

*   *   *

"Visola?" Aazuria asked, as she cracked open her friend's door. "I snuck away. I'm so sorry about last night. I did not know that Papa would be bombing the beach... are you reading?"

Visola was lying on her stomach and furiously flipping through the pages of a play.

"He's brilliant. His writing is… oh, Zuri, you have to read his writing."

Aazuria frowned. "You—you are actually reading?"

"This is so real. He writes about the things that he actually experienced, and he twists them all up into the perfect shape. When he writes about global domination, I get chills. He could actually do this."

"Have you been crying?" Aazuria asked in shock.

"It's very moving. He seems so lonely."

Aazuria shook her head sadly as she withdrew from the room. "She is lost."

Chapter 16: Sheer Power of Rage

"To kill him by having his ship sucked into a maelstrom?" Visola was saying with excitement. "It was so poetic, and so fitting. He caused so much turmoil in the world, and he seemed finally at peace when he knew a greater force would finally be doing the same to him."

"You understand it!" Vachlan exclaimed. "You actually understand it!"

She smiled at him. The two were sitting cross-legged on her bed and facing each other as they discussed his work. "I need to see this performed," she told him. "We have an underground amphitheater in the caves of Adlivun. Once we get there, we should have this produced."

"Do you think King Kyrosed will let me have a break in work to do something like that?"

"He is very fond of the arts; he is as tyrannical about forcing culture on Adlivun as he is about anything else."

"That's true. When I met him in Russia, he was parading his daughters before the court and showing off their skills. 'See my daughter dance! See my daughter sing! See my daughters play instruments!' The poor girls. He treated them like circus animals."

"He was trying to find them husbands," Visola said with a grimace. "Vachlan, have you heard the story of Sedna?"

"No, but I've heard the word spoken by your people dozens of times. Is she some kind of god?"

"Yes. I can never hear the story without thinking of Aazuria. Would you like to hear it?"

"Certainly," Vachlan said.

Visola smiled. "Long ago, an Inuit king lived with his daughter, Sedna, who refused to marry. Eventually, a hunter came and proposed to take Sedna away and give her a life of luxury in a land over the sea. He offered to pay for her with a great quantity of fish. Sedna did not want to marry this man, but her father was greedy to receive the fish. He sold his daughter, giving her a sleeping potion so that the hunter could easily take her."

"I see that you do not have a very high opinion of King Kyrosed."

"It's even lower than you think," Visola said seriously. "Anyway, the hunter took Sedna to his home, which was a floating island of ice. There, he threw off his human disguise, revealing himself to be an evil raven! Sedna was devastated, but she could not escape. Her life was unpleasant, and she was always hungry and freezing cold. She sent word for her father, crying for him constantly, not knowing that it was he who had sold her. Her father could hear her sorrowful wails on the howling arctic winds, and he felt guilty for what he had done. He decided to load up his kayak, and he paddled for days to the ice kingdom where his daughter was being held captive. When he arrived, Sedna threw her arms around her father, thanking him for coming to her rescue and telling him how the raven had mistreated her. He took her into his kayak, and they set out to sea."

"These human-bird liaisons seem to be a common theme with you."

"Hush, and listen," Visola said with a laugh. "As Sedna and her father were escaping, they saw a black speck in the distance. The raven had discovered that Sedna was missing, and had grown angry. He gathered up his raven friends, and they pursued the boat. They flapped their wings furiously, and whipped up an enormous storm, causing gigantic waves. The kayak that Sedna and her father were on began to sway and lurch around violently. Sedna's father—splendid man that he was—decided to sacrifice his daughter in an attempt to save himself. He screamed out, 'Here is your precious wife! Take her, but do not hurt me!' He grabbed his daughter and tossed her off the side of the boat, into the freezing ocean."

Vachlan frowned deeply. "Do you really think King Kyrosed would do that to any of his daughters?"

"The story gets even worse," Visola said, reaching out and touching Vachlan's hand. "Sedna's body began freezing, and she swam to the boat, holding onto the edge for dear life, and begging her father to save her. Instead, guess what he did? He grabbed his paddle, and he began to pound her fingers. Her hands were so cold and frozen that the tips of her fingers broke off. She still held on, so he continued clobbering her hands until her fingers broke off at the knuckles. When she cried for mercy, and begged her father to take pity, all that he could think about was saving himself from the great storm. He pummeled the paddle into her hands one final time, cutting off her fingers completely, leaving not even stumps where they used to be. Sedna could no longer grip the boat, and she sank down to the bottom of the sea."

"By George! What a nasty bloke."

"The tips of her fingers became whales, and her knuckles became seals. The stumps of her fingers became walruses. Incredibly, Sedna did not drown—no, she was kept alive by the sheer power of her rage. She swore vengeance on her father, and her anger transformed her into the omnipotent goddess of the sea. She loves and protects the beasts born from her fingers. She punishes unkindness with storms and famine, and she rewards kindness with food and warmth."

"You tell an excellent story, even when sober," Vachlan told her with a smile. "I must say that I'm worried about whether I made the right decision in choosing to be employed in Adlivun if that is the kind of person to which you compare your leader."

"I think you should go," Visola told him, handing him

the manuscript of his play. She bit her lip. "Go back to England and be a writer, Vachlan. You are so good at it, and surely if you keep trying, people will notice your work. What is there for you in our frigid ice palace?"

"There are endless new things to learn and discover," he answered. "Not to mention a gorgeous firebird…"

Before Visola could blush, the door to her bedroom flew open.

"I thought I would find you here. I need you both," Kyrosed said with a frown. "I have a predicament; we have run out of boats to transport the Yawkyawk."

*   *   *

"Let those ones stay and multiply. Let them grow in numbers again, and when you feel like a second helping, we can always come back for more."

"Brilliant. It's like farming human beings. I have to congratulate you on excellent work, Vachlan. This is exceptional; no one knows quite how to control and intimidate people like you do." King Kyrosed slapped the other man on the back companionably.

"It's what I do. Besides—when people are innocent it is easier to take advantage of them. They will be obedient subjects; and grateful too, I imagine."

"Yes, they actually think that we're saving them. They think that we are heroes. The only person displeased about this is my daughter. I'm going to give the command for the ships to sail, and go and try to appease her."

When Kyrosed left Vachlan's side to signal the ships, the people left on land, and those in the small boats around the ship began to scream to be taken on board. Their voices could not be understood, but their sign language was desperate. Visola approached Vachlan and stood beside him, as they looked out at the people they were leaving behind.

"Does it feel like a victory to you?" she asked him.

"It doesn't matter much to me." He shrugged. "I'm heartless. I just do what needs to be done."

Visola frowned at him, and was about to respond when they were both distracted by a woman's scream. They could not understand her, but there was a particularly desperate tone in her voice. She was standing in a small boat, and holding up a young child.

"Please," signed the man beside her, who was probably her husband, *"please take our daughter! She is too young to be eaten by the bunyip. Please save our little girl."*

"Christ," Vachlan muttered. He began leaning over to take the child, but Visola grabbed his arm.

"No! What are you doing?" she asked him. "Leave the girl with her family."

"Reality doesn't matter, Colonel Ramaris. What matters is what people believe. They believe that her life will be better with us, so let us give them that happiness." Saying this, Vachlan reached down and took the small child from her mother.

"So who will take care of her now?" Visola asked angrily as she stared at the scared toddler in Vachlan's arms.

"I'm sure there are plenty of women in Adlivun who have lots of motherly instinct to spare. We'll just give her to a good family."

"She had a good family!" Visola said, gesturing to the couple in the boat who were crying, and obviously very distressed. "What about her father?"

"Children don't really need fathers," Vachlan said with a shrug. "I never had one. Trust me, everything will be fine."

"My father is everything to me," Visola said in heated protest. "He taught me how to fight; he spent hundreds of years training me privately. He taught me everything he could. I wouldn't be worth anything if I didn't have that support. You're denying that little girl something more valuable than gold, Vachlan. Something priceless that can never be replaced."

"I'm sorry, Visola. I don't want you to be upset. Forgive me." It was the first time he had called her by her first name. He gently rocked the toddler in his arms. "I will make it up to you. I will make sure the girl has an amazing life in Adlivun. She'll learn and do more than she ever could here in New Holland."

Visola turned away from him, and placed her hands on the railing of the ship. She stared out at the people who had just lost their child, and the dozens of other people who were being left behind while hundreds of their family members and friends had embarked on Adlivun's fleet. Vachlan had brought two ships with him as well, and these were also filled. As the ships pulled away from the harbor, she stared back at the people sadly, realizing that Kyrosed had ripped this realm apart. Could he have done it without Vachlan, the Destroyer of Kingdoms? Now that he had them, what would he do with the people? Would he use them as slaves? Would he treat them as regular citizens? Would they improve life in Adlivun? Life had been comfortable to begin with.

The people were smaller now, and she could just barely make out that they were still waving their arms to the family members they would never see again. She felt sick. The wind tossed her red tresses against her face, and she brushed them away with annoyance. Behind her, she heard Vachlan talking to the little girl, and trying to soothe her tears.

"Don't cry, child. I promise that things will be alright. What's your name?" Vachlan had placed the toddler on the floor, and was speaking in sign language as he also spoke in English. The little girl did not respond, and continued to bawl. Vachlan sighed, asking her again in sign language. *"What is your name?"*

When her tears finally calmed, she answered between her sniffles. "Namaka."

"That's a beautiful name," Vachlan responded.

Visola's head snapped around. "Namaka?" she asked, feeling a chill run through her. She suddenly remembered an ache in her head, and the sight of prison bars. It was so vivid that it replaced the bright sunlight on the ship for a moment. She approached the little girl, and stared at her features. Dark skin, and dark eyes. Chubby little arms, and thick black hair.

"Lieutenant Namaka," she repeated, staring at the toddler as everything clicked into place. "You're his infiltrator. You're the mole. You're the one who betrayed all of us! You're the one who got Corallyn killed, and Sionna captured!"

If she could get rid of the child now, would it change the future? If she could grab little Namaka and toss her off the side of the boat, letting her swim back to her parents, would that fix things? Would a little cruelty to a toddler in the eighteenth century fix a major mess in the twenty-first? Visola crouched to her knees and reached out to grab the little girl, but her hands passed directly through her. Visola herself was no longer solid—her arms were becoming transparent.

"Throw her overboard, Vachlan! Throw her back to her parents!" Visola yelled. No one around her showed any indication of hearing what she had said. Instead, they continued talking to each other and completely ignored her. Vachlan was chatting with little Namaka, who had stopped crying to stare up at him curiously.

"Loyal to him, are you?" Visola shouted at the child. She reached out to grab Namaka by the neck, but her hands were just ghostly wisps of air. "All this time you were in our home, under our noses? Some kind of sleeper agent? I swear to Sedna I won't let this slide! Do you understand what you've done, Namaka? And I gave you my bracelet! I put you in charge of Zuri! If you hurt her, I will come for you. I will find a way to come for you…"

Visola's body was disappearing, and her voice was fading. Although she tried to scream louder at the girl, it was useless. No one could hear her. She could no longer speak, and she could no longer feel her body. An extremely bright light began to surround her. Was she dying? Was all of this some kind of pre-death delusion?

As she looked at the fading vision of Vachlan chatting with Namaka, she felt a wave of nostalgia. She wished she could just return to her fantasy, and continue to experience the months and years of getting to know Vachlan. It had been so nice before everything had fallen apart.

Please let me stay here, she mentally begged the blinding white cosmos, hoping it could hear her thoughts. *Please let me stay in 1797. I'll do anything.* Yet she kept moving through time, or space, or possibly both, away from the moment on the boat. It seemed that she was destined to be elsewhere.

What was the point of remembering and reliving this small, but pivotal event if she could do nothing about it? How could she die before she had gotten the chance to tell Aazuria who the traitor was, and to punish Namaka for her duplicity? As the white light consumed her, she thought of Sedna.

She wished that she too could stay alive against all odds by the sheer power of her rage.

Chapter 17: Goodbye, Terrestrial Dwelling

"Yes, it was a horrible accident," Trevain said into the phone. He had returned to his house to sort out his affairs. "I haven't received the settlement yet, but I'm definitely going to need a new boat."

His fingers toyed with the Ramaris family ring, which Aazuria had returned to him the last time she had been on land. She had been upset, but still too classy to throw it at him. It was this ring that had helped her to discover his heritage. He would return it to her before their wedding ceremony.

"No, I need something bigger," he told the person on the phone. He waited for a moment. "Yes, I realize what it's going to cost. What do you have?" He waited for the response and then shook his head, as though the person on the other line could see this. "No—a lot bigger. I'm thinking battleship-bigger. Even an old discontinued model, or something of the sort."

Trevain smiled when he heard the surprised protest on the other end. "Yes, of course, for fishing. I'll have the necessary modifications made." He waited before delivering his final, very convincing argument. "I lost my whole crew. Those lives can't be replaced. I'm willing to pay a few extra bucks for safety. Do you know how big the ocean is? Exactly. Get me the biggest sturdy old battleship you can find." He returned the phone to the wall.

He tucked Aazuria's ring into his pocket, and began moving through the house. Eventually, he found himself standing in the doorway of the room that had been Corallyn's, and he scanned it with his eyes. It was too soon for Trevain to gather her belongings. He could not deal with the loss yet. Her bed was still a mess. Her diary was lying on the night table at an angle, partly off the table, as though it had only just been cast aside. Her laptop was on her desk, and the light was blinking to indicate that it was still on, just sleeping. He considered collecting her things, and bringing them to Aazuria, but he could not even force himself to take a step forward into the room. He would try again at a later point in the future. He shut the door, and moved down the hallway to where Mr. Fiskel was gathering clothing and personal belongings from Callder's room.

"Thanks for taking care of things while I was gone," Trevain told his old friend.

"I'm just glad that you're alive, Captain Murphy," Mr. Fiskel said with a smile. "I swear I never doubted for a moment that you would survive that wreck. I'm finished with this bag."

Trevain nodded, taking the suitcase from Mr. Fiskel. The two men began to walk across the corridor together, heading for the stairs. "I'll need you to collect the mail about once a week, water the plants, and just do a general check up on the place. Your pay will remain the same, of course."

"That's not necessary, Captain Murphy…"

"Of course it is," Trevain said as they descended the stairs. There were two other suitcases already by the door. "I'll let you know when I return. We can catch up on things then. How is your health, Mr. Fiskel?"

"I'm strong as an ox, Captain Murphy," the old man said with a grin. "How are things with Miss Aazuria?"

"Great," Trevain said, with a touch of sadness in his voice. "We're getting married."

"I'm sorry, Captain, but shouldn't you be more excited to be getting hitched to a gorgeous young gal like Miss Aazuria?"

"I am thrilled, Mr. Fiskel. It's just that a lot has happened recently and she's not her usual self. We were going to have an elaborate wedding, but it turns out that it's going to be rather rushed and practical."

"Why? Did you get her pregnant?"

"No, of course not. Well… I don't think so."

"You dog!" Mr. Fiskel said, clapping Trevain on the back with a laugh.

"I've never been called that before," Trevain said with a smile. "Well, let's get going, Mr. Fiskel. I don't want to keep you away from your family, and I have to get back to mine too. Wow—that's also a new phrase. I'm a family man now."

"Enjoy it while it's enjoyable," Mr. Fiskel recommended.

The two men exited the house, lugging the suitcases with them. Trevain briefly popped back into the house to set the alarm before locking up. After he had set the alarm, he heard his phone ringing.

"Damn," he swore. "I'll just let the answering machine take it."

The two men carried the suitcases to the trunk of Trevain's Range Rover. Trevain found himself looking up at his house with a twinge of nostalgia. *Goodbye, terrestrial dwelling,* he thought to himself. *You were a fine house to live in, but much too lonely.*

*   *   *

Usually, the traditional Adluvian wedding was held in a submerged room, but Brynne could not breathe underwater or understand sign language, so it was modified for her attendance. Elandria and Alcyone were adding last-minute decorating touches to the cozy little room, and stressing about the details as is customary for even the most practical of weddings.

"I'm going to be the best man," Brynne declared, "since Calzone is just a little boy. He can hold the rings or something."

"Why d'you have to be so emasculating?" Callder complained. "You were so nice when you first learned I was alive."

"Yes, but then I remembered why we broke up in the first place," Brynne complained. "Your headlights are out, your wipers are broken, your body is covered in rust..."

"Do not insult the body!" Callder said firmly, gesturing down at himself.

"Your engine is damaged and frankly it costs more to fix you than to buy a new one."

"Brynne, I have changed since I died. Can't you see that? I'm a different man, and you should be marrying me. We've known each other way longer than Trevain and Aazuria..."

"That's how I know you're not good for me. I've always wanted a brand new Mercedes," Brynne said firmly.

"Then you have to stop using me!" Callder told her. "I'm not a sex slave, you succubus!"

Brynne shrugged callously. "Since when do you have self-respect, anyway?"

"Since the world declared me dead!"

"Children!" Alcyone said in frustration. She and Elandria had been doing finishing touches to decorate the room where the wedding would be held. "Can you please stop arguing?"

"I'm sorry, Mrs. Murphy," Brynne said apologetically.

"This is a day for the princess and your brother," Alcyone told them. "Try to behave."

"Sorry, mom," Callder said. "I guess weddings always make you think about your own love life. You can only chase after a girl for so many years before giving up."

"Callder, my boy. Don't give up on Brynne. She's only testing you," Alcyone told him with a smile. "Oh, here's the priestess!"

The priestess was a small woman who was half Aleutian Inuit and half Australian Yawkyawk. She had a deep scowl on her face. "This wedding breaks every tradition of Adlivun!" she exclaimed. "The groom must not see the bride for a week before the wedding. They must have time to carefully reflect upon their choices in solitude. I will not perform the ceremony without having the traditional Week of Airosen!"

"Please understand, Sybil—this is a special circumstance," Alcyone reasoned.

"Marriage is forever. There is no divorce in Adlivun. Sea-dwellers create lifelong bonds of fidelity and love." The priestess looked at Brynne and Callder distastefully. "We are not fickle like those on land."

"I resent that," Brynne said angrily.

"So do I," Alcyone said with a frown.

"Skipping the Week of Airosen curses a union!" the priestess insisted. "Do you really wish for Princess Aazuria to be cursed like her father?"

"Trivial superstitions don't make a marriage," Elandria interjected. *"The individuals entering the union are not going to change who they are in the space of a week. Trevain is a good man, and my sister is a caring woman. They are both leaders. What matters most is the dedication and kindness the husband and wife give each other."*

"If they cannot dedicate a week of reflection to the matter, how dedicated are they?"

Alcyone sighed. "They're in the middle of a war, Sibyl. There is no time for them to sit around and think for a week."

"Cursed," the priestess muttered. "They will be cursed if they rush into this."

"I'm not happy about it either!" Alcyone said angrily. "I wanted something spectacular for my boy. This is horrible. This is like a lame courthouse wedding with a justice of the peace. This is just as boring as the way I married John."

"It is not exactly time to celebrate," Aazuria said, entering with Trevain.

"See this?" the priestess said, gesturing wildly to

Trevain and Aazuria. "They have been with each other before the ceremony. No deliberation, no time to reflect."

"I don't need more time to reflect," Trevain told the woman. "I love Aazuria."

"Is she with child?" the priestess asked, moving over to peer closely at Aazuria's stomach. "Is that the reason for the rush?"

"What? Of course not," Aazuria said. Then she paused. "Well... I do not think so."

"It's irrelevant," Trevain told the priestess.

"Fine," Sybil said, gesturing to the carpet where there were two urns filled with water. "I will need both of you to take your places beside your own pitcher of Sacred Water."

Alcyone whispered to Trevain quietly as he walked by her, "When my mother returns, can we have a real wedding? Promise me?"

"Of course," he told her, kissing her forehead.

When everyone was seated on the carpet, kneeling in the formal *seiza* position in their respective places, the priestess Sibyl began to speak. "There is an urn filled with Sacred Water before the woman, and another before the man. Both of you are required to breathe the water into your lungs, and hold it there for thirty heartbeats. Then you must expel it into the urn—this will infuse the liquid with the *inua* from deep within your body, transforming it into the Sacred Breath." The priestess looked at each of them intently. "Are you both ready?"

When they answered affirmatively, the priestess nodded. "Place both of your hands on the handles of the urn before you." When Trevain and Aazuria had each gripped their urn, Sibyl closed her eyes and spread her arms. "Repeat after me: Into this water I cast a fragment of my *inua*—the best and worst of all that I am. With this water I freely bind my *inua* as I expel the Sacred Breath."

Trevain and Aazuria spoke together. "Into this water I cast a fragment of my *inua*—the best and worst of all that I am. With this water I freely bind my *inua* as I expel the Sacred Breath."

The priestess lifted her hand in command. "Breathe now."

Trevain and Aazuria each gripped their respective urn, and lowered their faces to the liquid. They breathed in the Sacred Water, both feeling a tingle in their throats. They knew that this sensation was from some additive in the water, possibly an herb, but it still gave the centuries-old effect of making them both feel like they had inhaled something magic which scoured and scraped at the insides of their bodies. When thirty heartbeats had passed, they exhaled into the urn. They both felt like they were, in fact, blowing a little bit of their souls out into the water.

They lifted their heads from the water, and looked at each other with solemn smiles.

"Now repeat after me," Sibyl told them. "Please accept my offering of all that I can offer. Please accept all my love and all my strength as your own."

Trevain and Aazuria repeated these words, never taking their eyes away from each other. "Please accept my offering of all that I can offer. Please accept all my love and all my strength as your own."

It might have been a rushed and basic ceremony, but it was just what they had needed. A quiet, spiritual moment which somehow had the power to subdue the deafening pandemonium. Sibyl was asking them to repeat another phrase. "All of my worldly goods are yours, and all of my otherworldly goods are yours as well. I give you myself in the Sacred Breath."

Trevain and Aazuria smiled as they earnestly spoke the words. "All of my worldly goods are yours, and all of my otherworldly goods are yours as well. I give you myself in the Sacred Breath."

Brynne felt herself getting a little teary-eyed, and she reached up to wipe the droplets away from her lashes. She glanced over at Callder, and saw that he was smiling at her. She could not help returning his smile. It was too sweet of a moment to pretend to be made of stone and fury as she usually did.

The priestess looked to Alcyone and Elandria. "Do those with the blood of the betrothed sanction this union?" When Alcyone agreed and Elandria responded affirmatively in sign language, the priestess gave another order. "You may both exchange the urns—carefully now."

When Alcyone moved to take the urn from before her son, her hands were surprisingly steady. She looked at him with vast motherly pride as she switched the position of the urn to before Aazuria. She bowed deeply to the princess before returning to her seat. As she did this, Elandria was lifting the urn from in front of Aazuria. Elandria's quietness gave her the ability to be unusually expressive with her eyes, and Aazuria could clearly see the intensity of her feeling.

It was an unusually quiet and small wedding—Aazuria did not have her parents alive to attend the ceremony, her sister Corallyn, or even her friends and lifelong guardians, the Ramaris sisters. Even Queen Amabie could not attend because she was training with the army and filling the hole in leadership left by Visola. Somehow, all of this did not matter in the moment that Aazuria locked eyes with Elandria—in her sister's face was all of the familial loyalty and love she could have ever needed. It was evident that the younger woman worshipped her sister, and wished her enough happiness for ten kingdoms, and ten lifetimes.

When Elandria swapped the urn with the one Alcyone was carrying, she also gave Trevain a smile of support and trust. She had not the slightest doubt that this man would love her sister as much as she did, and bring only good things into their lives. She could not have wished for a better brother-in-law, and she easily communicated this to him with her eyes.

"Excellent," said Sibyl. "Now, the betrothed must grasp

the urn holding their companion's Sacred Breath. Look at each other and speak the following words with sincerity: I accept and absorb your *inua* into me. I accept the best and worst of all that you are. Your soul will join with mine, and mine will join with yours. We are changed, but unchanging, like the eternal sea."

Trevain and Aazuria reached forward to grasp the exchanged urns, and they repeated the words. "I accept and absorb your *inua* into me. I accept the best and worst of all that you are. Your soul will join with mine, and mine will join with yours. We are changed, but unchanging, like the eternal sea."

"Breathe now, and be married."

The princess and the captain lowered their heads and followed the instructions, allowing their lungs to be inundated with the Sacred Breath of their loved one. The burning sensation was felt once more, as if there was actually a fusion of souls occurring within them. They held the water in their lungs for the required expanse of time before expelling it. They removed their faces from the water, feeling somehow refreshed and transformed. The priestess smiled as she lifted her hands.

"Above us are the stars, and below us are the stones; as time doth pass, remember... like a stone should your love be firm, and like a star should your love be constant. Princess Aazuria Vellamo of Adlivun, and Captain Trevain Murphy of Alaska, I declare you married before the gathered witnesses of men and nature. Be true to each another."

A somber silence followed her declaration. Trevain felt like he was still waiting to be given permission to kiss the bride, but that did not seem to be a part of this ceremony. He really wanted to reach out and touch Aazuria, but he did not want to disturb the dense, divine ambience in the room. Aazuria's chin was lowered slightly, and there was an enchanting blush tinting her pale cheeks. Alcyone was wiping away tears of happiness for her son, and Elandria's hands were clasped together joyfully. Even the initially-cynical priestess seemed immersed in enjoyment of the moment.

Callder had taken Brynne's hand during the ceremony, and now he looked at her with an unsmiling determination that was rarely found on his face.

Chapter 18: Scent of Sarcasm

The afterlife smelled like posies. It was a strange scent. A nose twitched, trying to inhale and make out exactly where the scent was coming from, but it felt that something was blocking it from fully exercising its olfactory abilities. A hand reached up to aid the nose and collided with an unpleasant plastic tube. The tube was impaling the innocent nose, and restricting it from doing what it longed to do. The hand discovered, with great disgust at the tactile quality of the synthetic material, that there were more offending tubes traveling into the mouth. The eyes could take no more of this, and they forced themselves to open. The head lifted off the pillow, so that the eyes could squint as they looked around. To their chagrin, they saw the interior of a hospital room.

Visola was surrounded by hundreds of bouquets of violets of every imaginable color. They seemed to be extremely fresh, and their fragrant scent had been able to reach her through the plastic tubes, and even all the way to her dreams. The sight was charming and pleasing until the recent events came rushing back to her mind. It occurred to her that the flowers were a gesture of ridicule. She reached down to her stomach and felt with her fingertips through the blue-patterned white fabric of her gown. The deep cut had been stitched up and was healing well.

Shit. I'm alive, she thought to herself with disappointment. She let out a soft groan and lowered herself back to the pillow. It was impossible to be in a hospital and not think about Sionna. Everything around her, and every machine and instrument attached to her reminded her of her sister's clever words rushing out in enthusiastic explanation. Why had Vachlan refused to return Sionna? It seemed to her that although he was many things, ruthless among them, he would at least be honest.

Was Sionna even still alive? When she had been making her way down into Zimovia, Visola had been almost sure of her sister's safety. Perhaps she had needed to convince herself in order to move forward through those tunnels and seek her. Now, it all seemed like it had been pointless. Visola stared at the white square tiles of the hospital ceiling. Her twin sister. She had heard stories about twins having some kind of intense connection that led them to instinctively feeling when their sibling was in danger or dying. She tried her best, but she could not find any hint of this knowledge within her. Visola's intuition was faulty; the magic was broken. Sionna could be dead.

She began trying to slowly and carefully remove the tubes from her nose and mouth. She grimaced when an ample amount of blood came along with them. Once this gruesome task was completed, she breathed deeply of the air on her own. The scent of the violets filled her nostrils with a rush. It was too pleasant and fragrant to be meant negatively. What if Aazuria had led the attack on Zimovia and rescued her, and it was Aazuria and Trevain who waited outside the hospital? Heartened by this thought, Visola stretched out and tried to reach one of the bouquets nearest to the bed. There was a note inserted among the flowers.

Violets for my violent one.
Missing you terribly, dear wife. Get better soon!
Love, Vachlan

"No," Visola whispered. She clenched her hand into a fist and pounded it weakly into her mattress. "No, no, no, no!" The mattress winced under the weight of every word.

The profusion of fragrant, lovely flowers was intended

purely as insult. She should have recognized the scent of sarcasm. Visola considered, and began, throwing the flowers across the room, but she paused mid-swing. She did not wish to create a ruckus and draw attention. She needed to slip away unseen before she was forced to be reunited with Vachlan. She looked around the room for materials to use in her escape, and she was angered when she noticed that each bouquet of flowers had a different note attached to it, filled with more mocking wisecracks to abuse her upon her awakening. She growled in frustration. She needed to get away from that place.

There was a telephone in the room, and Visola softly cursed. Everyone was underwater and away from access to any phones. She figured that it was worth a shot to call Trevain's landline, in case his butler might be monitoring the line. She struggled to sit up in bed, and dialed the numbers frantically. She heard it ringing, and bit her lip.

"Hello, you've reached Captain Trevain Murphy. I'm not in at the moment..."

She sighed, and waited for the tone. "Hi, grandson. It's me Visola. I got into Zimovia, but Vachlan wouldn't free my sister like he originally said he would. The bum. Anyway, I tried to kill myself and I just woke up in this hospital in..." Visola looked out the window of the hospital, realizing that she had no idea where she was. Gorgeous snow-covered mountains were visible just beyond a small city. She looked down at the phone, and saw the name of the hospital. "Ketchikan. I'm in a hospital in Ketchikan. I must have been air-lifted here. Please tell Queen Amabie that I'm disappointed with the efficacy of her hara-kiri technique. Regarding launching the attack..." Visola was startled when a nurse entered the room.

"Oh, my! You're awake. I'll run and get your husband."

"No!" Visola shouted after the nurse, but it was too late. She groaned and quickly replaced the receiver. Visola threw her legs off the side of the bed, and began to stand up. The blood rushed to her head, but she battled her dizziness. She discovered that although she had freed herself from the respiratory tubes, there were still needles feeding into her arms and wires connected to her finger. She ripped everything out of her body. Once she did this, an annoying noise began sounding from the machines, and she knew that she would have to move quickly.

Visola went to the window, looked down at the street below. It was only a three story drop. She was not sure if the fall would kill her or not, but whether she landed dead or alive it would be better than facing her husband. She forced the window to slide open. She was disappointed to see what a tiny opening there was, covered by a screen—but she believed it was just barely large enough for her body to fit through. She tried to remove the screen by looking for latches, but to her vexation, it was impossible. She heard footsteps in the hallway, and she began punching the screen until there was a hole. She desperately ripped at the hole. Visola grabbed the ledge above the window and tried to lower herself through the hole, feet first. She had a bit of difficulty getting her hips through, but once they slid through, she was confident that her shoulders would fit. In a few seconds, she had squeezed herself through the window, and she hung from the ledge. All she needed to do was let go.

She exhaled to relax herself, preparing for the impact. She expected that the head trauma would be much more serious than when her head had collided with Aazuria's hand. It might be difficult to walk away from this one so easily. She took another deep breath, feeling her pulse racing. It was mostly suicide, she told herself. If she did happen to live, then that would be the unlucky outcome. She might still fall into Vachlan's hands. She heard noise in the room above, and she knew she needed to let go. So, she did.

Visola's hands opened, releasing the window she had been gripping so tightly that her fingers ached. She felt the sensation of falling, and waited for the impact. She shut her eyes so that she would not see the ground coming, or see the sky leaving. All that she saw was her daughter—not her daughter's face at seventy, or her daughter at seven, but the soul that had remained underneath those faces throughout all of her ages, and would continue to remain. She smiled.

Where was the impact? The fall could not be *this* long. It was not a hospital in a major city, and the height of the building was rather unimpressive. Visola impatiently squinted one eye open. She saw that nothing was moving. She opened both eyes and looked up to see that a hand was around her wrist. Vachlan had caught her from falling. Why had she not felt his hand around her wrist? She must be on a considerably high dose of morphine. She frowned, and used her other hand to try to sink her fingernails into Vachlan's hand to make him let go. Instead of producing this effect, he grabbed her other forearm, and began to reel her back into the window.

"No," she whispered, beginning to struggle. She kicked the wall with her bare feet, trying to build enough momentum to push away from the wall.

"Where do you think you're going?" he demanded.

"Somewhere without sarcastic flowers." She twisted her arms, knowing exactly how to twist her arms to evade the grasp of a stronger opponent, but he was too strong. She pulled her torso up so that she could sink her teeth into his hand, and she bit down on him, ripping into his skin. He did not even flinch or cry out when she tore off a chunk of his flesh with her teeth. She immediately spit it out, letting it fall three stories below.

"Gross. You taste nauseating," she told him as she struggled.

"I believe you used to have a different opinion," he said. He made a forceful heave and managed to get her head and shoulders through the window.

She could feel how weak she was. She could not fight him in her current state. It would have been tough even at full health. No conceivable number of protein bars would help. Vachlan reached down and grabbed her around the waist, and managed to pull the rest of her body through the window in one mighty haul. The two of them flew to the ground, and Visola found herself landing on top of him. She cursed. She was too dizzy to move and she thought she might pass out where she lay. That would be embarrassing.

Vachlan grabbed her and pushed her off him, knocking her to the ground. He moved on top of her to hold her down. "What the hell were you trying to do?" he asked her angrily.

If she had been feeling up to her usual standard of mental alertness, she might have made a joke about switching positions. Instead, she could only focus on getting free. "Hey, Vachlan," she said in a lame, and tired attempt at being suggestive. "I'm totally naked under this hospital gown."

She kicked her knee up into his groin, and followed by shoving both of her elbows into his eyes. She twisted her body and slipped out from under him. She tried to get to her feet, but her legs gave way under her. She cursed and grabbed the hospital bed to pull herself up before running for the door. Not surprisingly, Vachlan beat her to the door and shut it before she could exit.

"You put up a hell of a fight for someone almost-dead," he said to her as he slammed her into the wall beside the door. When he pinned her firmly to the wall with his body, she sighed in defeat. It was a rare moment that she was not in the mood for the challenge of wrestling with someone who vastly outranked her weight class, but this was that moment.

"Why are you trying to kill yourself, Visola?" he asked.

"Why the hell do you care?" she responded, staring at his chin. Visola was six feet tall. Hardly anyone towered over her like Vachlan did. It was still disconcerting, even after all this time.

"I need you alive," he said simply, as he studied the flecks of emerald in her eyes.

"I need my sister alive," she shot back. "I guess we both aren't getting what we want."

Vachlan glared at her, and she tried her best to match the intensity of his gaze, but she had to blink to clear her sight once his two heads began separating into four. She tried to make a private internal joke about how her blurred vision was accurate since he was so two-faced, but her thoughts could hardly form coherently. She closed her eyes for a second, and when she opened them, she was shocked to find that her head had fallen forward to rest against his shoulder. She jerked her head backward, and it collided with the wall sharply. It felt like she had been asleep for half an hour, but in reality it could not have been more than a moment because there was surprise on his face too. She blinked rapidly to keep her eyes open, and she cleared her throat to brush off her mortification.

It was not acceptable in her personal policy to cuddle with the enemy. Not anymore. Her eyelids felt heavy, and her head began to roll forward again. She fought to straighten it. "I'm going to pass out," she told him with a yawn, "but I promise you this—when I wake up, I will succeed in killing myself. I can be very dogged."

He raised a hand to her face, holding her chin firmly between his thumb and forefingers. "What do you want from me, Visola?"

"Nothing," she murmured sleepily. "I just want to get away from you."

"And if I free Sionna?" he asked. He observed as her drooping eyelids shot open.

Visola's heart skipped a beat. Sionna was alive and her freedom was still an option. Before she knew what she was doing, she had placed a hand on his chest, and she was whispering, "Please. Vachlan, please..."

"You must be hallucinating to ask so nicely."

"I always seem to be hallucinating around you," she answered softly.

Before he realized exactly what he was doing, he had released her chin from his vise-grip and was gently brushing a few strands of red hair away from her eyes. He quickly made it seem as though he was only feeling her forehead for fever—and indeed, there was a temperature.

"I'll bring Sionna here so you can have evidence of her safety," he told her before she could slip away. "Then, like I promised, I will let her go home. You will return with me to the camp in Zimovia, and you will stop trying to kill yourself."

She smiled. She knew that he would be fair. Now that she was assured that her sister was going to live, the dark spots were fading. The violets were suddenly sincere. Her head pitched forward again, and when it hit his shoulder this time, she did not have the energy to pull it off. "Thank you," she whispered against his shirt. "Thank you."

She did not even realize that her whole body had begun falling, and that his hands were holding her up. All her strength was gone, and her voice slurred as she spoke. "I don't care about anything as long as Sio's safe."

"You should lie back down, V. You need to get your rest."

Even as he said this, she was already half-asleep on her feet. "So when I'm better you won't feel guilty about torturing me, V?" she mumbled.

"Yes," he answered truthfully.

"Okay."

Chapter 19: The Suicide Sisters

"Mrs. Ramirez? Mrs. Violet Ramirez, can you hear me?"

A bright light was shining into Visola's eye, causing her to blink angrily, and twist her head away from her attacker.

"Mrs. Ramirez, we have…"

"Ramaris," Visola said hoarsely.

"Yes, yes, sorry. My Spanish is horrible. I'm Dr. Chen. I have some questions about your insurance. Also, forgive me for asking, but is your husband your next of kin?"

Visola groaned.

"He's a very nice man. Very concerned about you. There seems to be a small problem with the papers he gave us. The dates are kind of…"

Visola opened one eye to look at the doctor with disdain.

"Well, I'm sure you'll sort everything out if you recover. I mean, when you recover. Oh, I also need to ask; are you aware that you have four lungs?"

"Fuck off," Visola mumbled as she returned to sleep.

*　　　　*　　　　*

When Visola woke again, she felt like she had been dead to the world for several days. The first thing she noticed was that her flowers were gone. The second was that there was a head of thick dark hair resting on a pair of folded muscular arms on the bed near to her thighs. The contrast of the tanned skin and black hair against the white sheets was striking. This confused her. He was sitting on a chair by her bedside, keeping watch over her. Did he still care in some weird and twisted way?

The third thing she noticed was his outfit. He wore modern clothes; a dark grey t-shirt and simple jeans. If it were not for the overdeveloped muscles, he might have passed for a normal Alaskan man, and not an infamous undersea vanquisher. The only reminders of the truth were the plentiful tan lines on his wrists and neck from the strings of shark-tooth-armor that the Clan of Zalcan wore.

She sighed, and wished that he was a simple American man. If only he were as sweet and nonviolent as her grandsons... who were, coincidentally, his grandsons too. That was rather mind boggling—not the fact that the men were related, for it was easy to see the physical resemblance, but the fact that she and Vachlan were grandparents. It seemed like just yesterday they had been kids making love in lagoons. Now they were all grown-up and he was trying to extinguish her family and everyone she held dear. Life moved along so quickly.

Then again, it was the fact that he was so dangerous and capable that had attracted her to him in the first place. If he had been harmless, she never would have taken notice. She never would have been intrigued. She knew that she should be hating him, and feeling regret for making the wrong decisions, but she could not manage to do this when he was sleeping on folded arms at her bedside. All she could do was feebly wonder if he still loved the theatre.

She reached out to touch the tan lines on his wrist, and just barely grazed his skin with her pinky and ring finger before her eyes closed. It occurred to her, as she drifted off, that neither of them wore the rings they had exchanged.

*   *   *

"I don't understand you. Why you would say that to her, knowing how she overreacts? What the hell is wrong with you, Vachlan?"

"Shut your mouth, woman, or I will gag you again."

185

"Sure, right here in the hospital, in front of the nurses. Go ahead."

"I can kill all of these insignificant fools without much effort."

"Then do it. No one's stopping you. I'm not stopping you."

"You couldn't stop me, Sionna."

"Maybe not. What are you trying to prove, brother-in-law?"

Visola's eyelids fluttered open and she sighed. "Shush! You two are giving me a headache. I feel like part of an Italian mafia family."

"Viso," Sionna said, leaving her argument and rushing to her sister's side. "You have an infection. You've been running a high fever, and you're on an antibiotic drip. I'm going to need you to…"

"Relax," Visola said, smiling at her sister. "This is not your hospital. Sio, I am going to need *you* to go home immediately. I need you to…" Visola could not speak in front of Vachlan. What she really wanted to say was Namaka's name, but she could not do this—her personal vendetta was not the most important thing she needed to communicate. Vachlan knew English, sign language, and possibly Russian. She chose the obscure Aleut language, and tried to remember the words she needed. "Instruct them to prepare *ayxaasix̂*…"

"Not another word. No military talk," Vachlan warned. "Keep it brief—if you try to send any messages home, or speak another word I do not understand, Sionna will not leave this room alive."

"That wasn't military talk, it was strictly family business," Sionna lied. "Frankly, I feel uncomfortable going home until I know Viso is better."

"I'll be fine. He brought me flowers," Visola told her.

"Good Sedna, she's delirious," Sionna murmured, feeling her sister's forehead.

"No, I really did bring her flowers," Vachlan said. "I left nasty messages in every single bouquet."

"How charming," Sionna remarked, raising an eyebrow.

"Sio," Visola croaked. "Tell me one thing before you go; did you reveal anything to the Clan?"

"No, of course not."

"Not a thing?" Visola asked, frowning. "Didn't they torture you?"

"They intended to, but I was aware that I was a bargaining chip. I told them that if they touched me, I would just swallow my cyanide pill."

Visola laughed. The movement hurt her insides, but she did not indicate this. "You are just like me! We're the suicide sisters. Did you really have a cyanide pill?"

"Of course not," Sionna said. Upon receiving an angry glare from Vachlan, she decided to explain. "My pill contains a much faster-acting chemical weapon called saxitoxin. It's a thousand times more potent than cyanide. I harvest it myself from butter clams."

"But what if you accidentally swallowed it?" Visola asked with worry.

"I have to crush it between my teeth first," Sionna explained. "The pill is made of thick rubber. You weren't the only one who Papa trained, you know. We just had different types of training."

"You're so much smarter than I am," Visola said with a groan. "I sliced myself open and tried to play cat's cradle with my intestines, and it still didn't kill me."

"You are far too impulsive to carry saxitoxin," Sionna said. "Imagine if you did have one of my capsules? You would have swallowed it, and it would have been final. I'm so overjoyed that you're only extremely injured."

"Aww," Visola crooned, struggling to extend her arms as she made the sentimental sound. "C'mere, Sio."

Sionna wrapped her arms around the injured woman. When she spoke, her voice was heavy with emotion.

"Besides, love. A quiet poison-death would not suit you. You deserve to go out with flamboyant fireworks in the biggest, loudest blaze that ever burned on the earth."

Visola squeezed her twin with all of her strength—which was no longer very much. She was already feeling tired again. "I love you, big sis," Visola said softly. "Now, please, get the hell away from here." Visola usually insisted vehemently that Sionna's one minute of seniority was negligible, and Sionna knew that her sister must be expecting to die if she was acknowledging this marginal youth. Sionna squeezed the injured woman's hand, and gave her a knowing look.

"If something happens to you, I will feel it. Be patient." She leaned forward and pressed a light kiss on her sister's lips before withdrawing from the bed.

"Well, the years have certainly changed you gals," Vachlan remarked with a drawl. "I remember you ripping each other apart so much that I never felt comfortable enough to suggest a ménage à trois."

"You're not my type, Vachlan," Sionna said as she sauntered by him. "I prefer men who improve the surface of the planet."

Vachlan glared after her retreating form as she walked down the hallway.

Visola smiled, readjusting herself on the flat, generic pillows. "She just seems innocent. Really, she's more of a badass than I am! I'm lucky to have her."

"You're lucky I let her live, you mean," Vachlan said as he leaned on the doorframe.

"Yes. Thank you," Visola said sleepily. "She's worth twenty of me. She's so serene and thoughtful."

"Ain't too hard on the eyes either."

Visola knew this was his offhand way of giving her a compliment. She turned away from Vachlan, and pulled the thin blanket around her shoulders. Now that Sionna was safe, there would be no more bargaining or threatening. Now, the unpleasant part would begin, and she would find out why the Clan of Zalcan wanted her. It did not really matter what happened to her from this point on. She was just happy that her actions had resulted in Sionna's freedom. Her tongue toyed with the new item in her mouth, trying to find a comfortable place for it to be stored.

Her sister had given her the saxitoxin capsule.

Chapter 20: Correcting Her Attitude

When Visola woke up again, she was no longer in her hospital room bed. Gone were the white tiled ceilings; they were replaced by the darkness of an abandoned mineshaft. She could feel that her fever had departed, and that her health had vastly improved. She could also feel that there were iron shackles around her wrists and ankles. When she pulled on them, the chains jangled against each other discordantly. Somehow, this was still far more pleasant than finding plastic tubes in her nose.

"You'll have to forgive the accommodations," said a familiar masculine voice echoing off the cave walls. "My employer was becoming impatient, and there is much we need to learn from you."

Turning her face away from the source of the voice, her tongue felt for the security of the tiny rubber capsule concealed in her mouth. Even without the pill, she knew that she would never reveal anything about Adlivun, but it did give her comfort.

"You remember how this works, don't you?" he asked.

Visola wondered why he was being so condescending. She was growing impatient. She almost longed for the mental challenge that torture presented. It had been a good while since she had been on the receiving end. Was this karma? She was curious to learn what karma felt like.

"We're going to begin with the routine procedure of correcting your attitude," he told her. "You will need to answer a few simple questions, truthfully and respectfully. Are you ready?"

She did not respond. Correcting her attitude? Let him

try. She did not even look at him—she knew she could bear any amount of pain, but she would prefer not to witness the emptiness and cruelty on his face.

"I asked if you were ready."

She felt cold metal digging roughly into her neck, followed by a powerful jolt of electricity. It caused her body to convulse, as sharp searing pins and needles ripped through her nerves. Still she did not speak.

"It's time for you to begin cooperating. Let's begin with an easy one. Say my name."

Visola could not believe that he was going to do this to her. He was going to go through every step, just as he would have done to any common prisoner. Did Vachlan not remember teaching her everything he knew about torture? Did he seriously think that he could convince her to adjust her attitude? She would not break. She would not speak. He might as well get right to the point, and get to the seriously maiming and disfiguring bits.

When the next burst of voltage was administered, Visola felt all of her muscles instantly contract and become rigid. It felt like there were fish hooks being driven into her entire body, and she was being dangled from them. This painful tension lasted until the electricity was removed and her muscles relaxed. The saxitoxin pill was tucked away in the corner of her mouth where she would not accidentally bite down on it. She did, however, wish that she had a piece of leather to bite into. It should have been common courtesy for Vachlan to provide one.

"Follow my instructions, Visola. I asked you to say my name."

When she refused to respond, he grabbed her and turned her to face him. Looking into his eyes was much more tortuous than the electricity. She realized that the gun that he had used on her had effectively paralyzed her body, and her muscles all felt like jelly. This could be a problem. Visola had to accept that there was no escape. She was his prisoner, and she could not defeat him. She had not expected that she would be able to—she had only wanted to free her sister. Anything that happened to her now was meaningless. It was still a difficult concept to accept for one who thrived on fighting.

The natural thing to do was to steal a few pages from Elandria's playbook. In fact, she would steal all the pages and write a few of her own. She would never speak to Vachlan again. Not with her voice, and not with her hands. She would withdraw into herself, and become unresponsive. She would not focus on denying him satisfaction—she would focus on self-preservation. She wondered if the two were one and the same.

"I asked you to say my name," he repeated in a deathly whisper. When she did not respond, he grabbed her face and smiled at her. "Last chance, Viso. If you don't be a good girl, you'll never walk again."

She tried to be expressionless, but a cold sweat was beginning to break out on her shoulders. Her pulse was beginning to race. She knew that he was completely serious. She closed her eyes, trying to escape the ghastly look on his face. Had he always been so cruel? *Yes,* part of her answered, *but never toward me.* She felt his fingers release her face, and she heard him shuffling about the room. There was the clinking of metal against metal.

"I am not the monster that the world thinks I am. Not really. I will give you one last chance, Viso—and to be fair, I will ask you a polite question. Polite, because I could ask you anything at all. You know that I could ask you to say my name for days until you cracked, but I respect you too much. I know you're getting bored, so let's get straight to the point."

Vachlan paused, and Visola felt the fabric of her dress being slid up her thighs. She felt something cold against her knee. She wanted to open her eyes, but she had a feeling that seeing whatever he was doing would not help her situation.

"Why were you unfaithful to me?" he asked.

Her eyes shot open at this question. She stared at him in surprise, unable to keep the emotion from her face. She wanted to respond, and she wanted to tell him the truth, but it seemed pointless. He would never believe her. She observed the frightening fact that he was holding a *pickaxe*. He was polishing it with a white cloth, and he had apparently used the same cloth to clean her knee. He was going to smash her kneecap unless she answered.

"Answer the question, dear. If you ever want to walk again." He finished disinfecting the pickaxe, and tossed the cloth aside. He positioned the pickaxe over her knee, and he began practicing his swing. "Why did you cheat on me?"

Visola gritted her teeth together, and stared up at the jagged rocks of the mineshaft. Her eyes narrowed. It did not seem to her like these were questions that interested the Clan of Zalcan. What would his employer say if he knew what Vachlan was doing on the company clock? She felt the metal weapon prodding her leg roughly.

"Visola! Why did you betray me?"

He was going to do it anyway. Whether she responded or not. If she told him the truth, if she told him that she had never been disloyal, he would think that she was saying it to save her legs. She knew that the pain from his lack of faith in her would hurt more than her busted kneecap would. It already did. He believed the worst of her and she could not change his mind. The impossible tragedy of the situation brought a small little smile to her face.

"Why are you smiling? Was it so much fun to hurt me? Answer me, Visola! Why?"

He had been hurt? This distressed her. She had never considered that he had been hurt. She could not look at him without feeling remorse and sadness for this situation which had been out of her control, so she turned away. She wished she could go back in time and find the moment that someone planted these lies in his head. Like Iago. It was a strange moment for *Othello* to pop into her head, but it occurred to her that Vachlan had been manipulated in the exact same way.

"Visola!" Vachlan roared. "Answer me! Why did you fuck Kyrosed Vellamo when you were married to me?"

She gritted her teeth together, silently waiting for the impact of his swing. She almost wanted him to stop these horrible accusations and hurry up with the mutilation. Then it came. Visola saw him swing the axe back over his head, and she instinctively tried to move away from the target location of the strike, but her legs were still too paralyzed from the electricity. She saw it happen as if it was in slow motion, and when the pickaxe smashed into her knee, the pain was blinding.

Visola barely managed to keep from crying out. Her breathing did quicken perceptibly as she gasped. Tears came to her eyes without her permission, and sweat began rolling down her forehead as she struggled with the pain. He was right. She would never walk again. Not that it mattered, because she did not foresee escaping his custody anytime soon. Would she be dragged around like a punching bag wherever he went? For how long would this torture last?

She moved her tongue over to touch the saxitoxin capsule, but she would have felt like a wimp if a smashed kneecap was all she could handle. Her breathing was already calming down, and she was already becoming used to the pain. She was a warrior; it was hardly the first time she had suffered a broken bone. Besides, it was only physical pain anyway.

Vachlan casually swung the axe back over his shoulder, and turned to leave the room.

"Next time, just answer the question," he advised her calmly as he retreated.

Oh, he was good. She allowed her eyes to close, since sleep was the best painkiller she knew, and the only one to which she had access. Strange words randomly drifted through her mind, but she could not remember where she had heard them. *Go deeper; in order to survive, you must.* As long as she did not speak, she could maintain the upper hand. *Hope is shallow—you dip your toes in it all the time.* There was power and poise in silence. She would never be disgraced.

Chapter 21: An Intimate Activity

This was disgraceful. Vachlan was excellent at torture. Everyone always said he had a true gift. Visola was not surprised with his capacity to make her feel pain; she expected him to be impressively creative. What confused her was that he was not attacking her psychologically the way he normally plagued his victims. She knew what he was capable of—and while the pickaxe had been very characteristic of his usual style, (it was his signature to use interesting weapons) she could not help but wonder why he had taken it easy on her for weeks after that incident.

Her leg was in a brace, and she could not even attempt to move it without excruciating pain—but that was the normal state of a prisoner of war. Nothing was special about the fact that while she was almost starving, Vachlan was eating scrumptious meals a few feet away from her, and orating long monologues while he leisurely enjoyed his meals. He really was still fond of the theatre. Nothing was special about the fact that he waited until her stomach was growling loudly, and she felt faint from hunger before he dangled a spoonful of something delicious inches away from her lips, and asked for her to tell him what he needed to know before feeding her.

"Come on, Viso," he would say, "you know that you're going to lose all of your gorgeous muscles unless you have a bite to eat. So how about you tell me exactly how large Adlivun's army is? Precise numbers only, please. No estimates."

Hence, her muscles were shrinking. There were no mirrors in the grimy little mineshaft where she was kept, but she could see when she looked down at herself, that her bones were becoming more and more visible. This was frustrating. Her only comfort was that she had still managed to remain silent throughout these weeks of harassment.

What surprised Visola was that Vachlan had not attempted to rape her yet. Not that it would be an attempt, since she was shackled quite well, and probably weaker than she had been since the age of two or three. No, it was well within his ability, and she was surprised he had not taken advantage of the situation—what was stopping him from torturing her in that manner? Was he saving it for a special occasion, to really crush her spirit? She thought that it might. She thought that desecration of that one thing which had been so special between them might actually break her enough that she took the pill—but she almost wanted the chance to find out how strong she really was. She almost wanted more of a reason to hate him.

"A person's sexuality is deeply connected with their sense of identity," Vachlan had said to her many years ago. This had been his reasoning for why it was always easy to break someone down emotionally by torturing them sexually; man or woman.

She considered this as he now slowly bent back her fingers to break them. *"There are more nerve endings in the hands and the face than in any other part of the body."* He had told her this, as he had caressed her hands and kissed her face while making love to her. *"That's why they are the most sensitive parts to torture with either pain or pleasure."*

Vachlan was an expert at multitasking. He was also an expert at focusing directly on one thing for long periods of time. There was no man like him on the planet, she thought to herself, as he broke another one of her fingers. She gritted her teeth, and watched. She watched as if from a distance. The more he tortured her, the more detached she felt from her body.

It seemed that torture was making her a spiritual woman. Harrowing near-death experiences often did that.

Sometimes the effects were reversed, and sometimes they remained. She wondered what would be left of her after her husband was finished. He took another one of her fingers into his hands, and prepared to break it.

"Just speak, Visola, and I won't break your finger," he said gently. "All you have to do is answer my questions. That's easy as apple pie, isn't it?"

She wanted to smile at the phrase, but she could hardly remember how to move her frozen lips. She had worked so hard at remaining expressionless. She stared at the finger which he held, and she still felt a pang of fear inside of her. Why should she feel fear? Why should she care? Pain was not important. Did this really even matter? She had already broken her fingers herself when she had learned of what he had done to Corallyn. Being here meant that Sionna stayed in one piece. Having this happen to her was the price she paid for Sionna's freedom. So she would pay it without complaint or fuss.

"Do you know how many of my men you killed on your little rampage into Zimovia?" he asked her quietly. "Three hundred and twenty four. How did you manage that?"

The number surprised her. She had not been keeping count. She was sure that at least half of that number were only paralyzed. *Adrenaline,* she thought to herself, although she would not allow herself to speak. *I knew my sister was at the end of those defenses.* Another, more foolish part of her being, the part that she had tried to kill, answered differently. *I wanted to see you,* she thought. *I knew you were waiting for me at the end of those warriors.* She felt a small rush of anger at herself for thinking this.

She was surprised when he released her finger. "Visola... why won't you speak to me? I actually have a special present for you today."

The soft singsong tone of his voice made her swallow the lump in her throat. That was his sickeningly sweet Destroyer-of-Kingdoms-voice. It was the voice that preceded ultimate agony. She weakly reminded herself that she had gone through the pain of childbirth. That had been Vachlan's fault too. Surely nothing he could do would rival the pain of forcing his kid out of her. She shuddered at the memory. It occurred to her that she had never made him pay for that. She knew that it was her own fault. Everything was her fault. *I really should have known better than to marry someone nicknamed 'The Destroyer of Kingdoms' in the first place,* she told herself. *That was a real smart move, Viso.* She tried to move her hands for some reason, and had to fight back the urge to moan when sharp waves of pain overwhelmed her. Broken fingers were very disagreeable.

Vachlan began whistling a tune, and Visola turned to observe his actions. She paled considerably when she saw what he was holding: very large nails. Her eyes widened when she saw that he was disinfecting them. It was never a good sign when he began disinfecting an item. It usually meant the item was about to end up inside her body. *No. No way. He's not really going to...* As she tried to block out the annoyingly jolly tune he was humming, she could not help remembering a recurring nightmare she used to have. She would always wake up writhing in pain, and moaning out loud. It used to be her husband who offered a comforting embrace.

"Shhh, Viso. What's wrong?" Vachlan had asked, shaking her gently. *"Seizure, bedbug, cramp, or nightmare?"*

"I'm sorry," she told him, as she jolted out of her dream. *"It's the same stupid dream. We're in New Holland, and King Kyrosed brings out a massive carved wooden trident. He smiles, and he orders me crucified."*

"Crucified?" Vachlan asked in surprise. *"Don't you need a cross for that?"*

"I don't know."

"If there's a trident, we should make up a new name for it. How about Tridentified? Trixified?"

"Vachlan! It doesn't matter. The worst part is that he orders you to nail me to the wood. Then I scream and beg for you not to do it, but you go ahead and nail me down anyway. Isn't that weird?"

"Sounds kind of kinky. You have the wildest imagination," Vachlan told her. *"Hang on; I'm going to write this down. Maybe I can use it in a play later."*

Why did he have to write everything down? She mentally cursed herself. If only she had known the dangers of telling her husband her nightmares. Why did he have to be the kind of artist that delighted in bringing fiction to life? Well, he could try to break her down in this way, but one element of her nightmare would be very different. Visola would not scream and cry for him to stop. She would be silent and take it like a man.

When he pulled out the expertly carved wooden trident, Visola nearly opened her mouth to say something acerbic. Vachlan was insane. There was no getting around that simple fact any longer. He was completely insane. As he set up the trident-cross, while whistling, she began to fidget in her shackles. She liked shackles. They were comfortable—she did not treasure the idea of being nailed upright for long periods of time. It did not seem like it would be relaxing.

"You know the interesting thing about crucifixion?" Vachlan asked her, as he tested the sturdiness of the trident. "They're not quite sure how exactly it kills you. There are lots of different ways you can die, and it depends on the person, their health, and the way it's performed." He moved over to her and undid her shackles. He grasped her upper arm roughly as he pulled her upright. It was the first time she had stood on her smashed kneecap, and she wanted to lie down again very much. She had no choice in the matter. Vachlan dragged her over to his wooden piece of art. "How would you like to be my very own garden ornament, Visola?"

She looked at where his hand gripped her arm, and felt nauseated at the sight of her emaciated biceps. His hand fully circled her upper arm. This was normally the point at which she would fight, but this sight alone dissuaded her from doing something foolish. She cast her eyes on the ground—she could only wait and endure. If it ever became too much to handle, she had her safety blanket incased in rubber in her mouth. There were moments she felt so hungry that her body almost instinctively yearned to chew down on that capsule, but she maintained enough discipline not to.

Torture often turned a person into an animal fighting for survival, and Visola was determined not to let this happen to her. She had seen it too many times in her victims, and it simply was not attractive. Not that she cared about appearing attractive before her captor. She just cared about her dignity.

Vachlan seemed to notice her arm too, but he still forced her against the trident. He disinfected her right hand thoroughly before lifting it to the wood. He retrieved one of the cleaned nails and a mallet. "One of the ways they say you can die from crucifixion is through suffocating. They say that when your arms are stretched out for too long, your lungs become weak and unable to breathe. Interesting, no?" He saw that Visola's eyes were fixed on the ground, and he forced her chin up with his free hand. "Viso, all you have to do is speak to me, and I'll stop treating you like this. Just tell me what I want to know. Can you do that for me? For old times' sake?"

She fought the urge to spit in his face. She fought the urge to demonstrate any kind of hatred or anger, and she just stared back at him blankly. His grey eyes were still too difficult to behold, and she would much prefer to have the nails driven through her hands. She could not reconcile the man who was mistreating her now with the man who she had experienced such happiness with. She could not try. His eyes bewildered her.

"Just answer the question, Viso. You know the one." He moved his face very close to hers, and for a moment she greatly feared that he might kiss her. It terrified her that somehow, her body still seemed to yearn for his. She remained very still as he examined her face. He frowned. "Are you shaking?"

She had hoped that he would not notice, but yes, she was shaking. It was more of a physiological reaction than a psychological one. At least this is what she intended to believe.

"Why were you unfaithful, Visola?"

She felt the cold sharp edge of the nail against her palm.

"I'm going to ask one more time, and then I'm going to nail you to the trident. Just like in your nightmare. So save yourself a whole lot of pain, and tell me a little story. You were always really good at that," he said. He positioned the mallet on top of the nail. "Why did you have an affair with Kyrosed Vellamo? He told me, you know. He told me himself. Why did you choose him? Why did you go to him? Answer me, Visola! Answer me now!"

She turned to look at her hand, and stared at the nail. She imagined Kyrosed's face, and felt a rush of anger. He had ruined her love. He was the one who had done this to them. How dare he? How dare that man haunt her from beyond the grave? She imagined Kyrosed's forehead where the palm of her hand was.

Vachlan yelled, an unusual sound of pure madness, before slamming the mallet down onto the nail. Visola sucked in a huge gasp of air, but still did not cry out. Imagining Kyrosed's face taking the blow had helped—it had even given her a small amount of pleasure. She was becoming numb to the pain. Many of her fingers were already broken in several places, so what more was a nail through her palm going to accomplish?

"I'm going to get you to speak today, Viso," Vachlan told her. He moved across her body to grab her other arm. "Do you really want to be nailed to this trident? I promise I will free you and let you lie down if you just speak to me. Just tell me what I want to know, and I will be merciful.

Otherwise, you're going to be very uncomfortable for a very long time."

Visola closed her eyes. She could not look at him. Strange words floated across her fuzzy mind again, and she struggled to keep it clear. *Submerge yourself until you find fortitude. Swim deep enough to taste prudence in the salt.* She saw a strange woman's face, and remembered a beach in what was now called Australia.

"Why did you do it, Viso? I loved you."

She could not listen to this. Those words being in past tense killed her more than anything he could have done. He could have crushed her body with a steamroller, and it would not have stung quite so fiercely. She fought back tears, and silently prayed for him to nail her hand to the trident and be done with it. She needed him to leave so that she could have a good cry. One hand was already nailed. It would be silly not to do the other.

"Visola, you have three seconds. Tell me now, or you're going to be crucified."

She counted them in her mind. She actually made it to five seconds before she felt the nail go through her hand. *Mind over matter,* she thought to herself. *They're just tiny puncture wounds. The nails were even disinfected, and that was very sweet of him.* The fact that she had had many nightmares about this very act did not make it any easier on her. It was a fear of hers—being held in this vulnerable position and having nails through her palms. It was her ultimate horror enacted in the flesh.

He was still so painfully theatrical. She was surprised when she felt his hand rest on her cheek for a moment. Without really intending to, she leaned against it, drawing all possible tenderness out of the touch to refresh her spirit. She was becoming dependent on her captor. She was far too attached to him. He was the only human being she had seen for weeks, and she could not help it. Even nailed to a trident, reliving a scene from her very worst nightmares, she still wished that he would make love to her. It would somehow all be better if he would only embrace her with warmth again. His hand lifted from her cheek, and left only coldness in its wake. She could hear him toying with his metal tools, and selecting a new instrument to torture her with.

She sighed, feeling very angry with herself. This man had chopped Corallyn into little bits. How could she still appreciate a moment of tenderness from him?

"Visola," he said angrily. "If you want to keep your eyes closed so much, let me help by blindfolding you." She felt him fastening a piece of fabric around her head. Somehow, she had liked it better when having her eyes closed had been by choice. Vachlan enjoyed screwing with her mind far too much.

"Now let's see. Are there any parts of you which aren't in pain?" Vachlan asked. He placed a hand on her lower abdomen. "Your stomach is probably still sore from when you slashed it open." He slid his hand higher. "You stabbed yourself in the chest too. Then of course, there's my abundant handiwork: the highlights of which include your smashed kneecap, broken fingers and nailed palms. What should come next?" She felt his hands encircle her throat. "How about this? If you won't speak to me, I'll squeeze your voice out of you."

The horror of the nightmare intensified as he strangled her. She felt like she was drowning in darkness, blindfolded and nailed upright. It was the most dreadful experience she had...

"Excuse me, sir?" came a young male voice, interrupting them. "Prince Zalcan has returned."

"Shit," Vachlan swore, releasing Visola's neck. "Watch her, I'll be back." He moved to leave the room. Visola could hear the young guard moving closer.

"Hey, pretty lady," said the guard as he approached. Visola immediately began calculating whether she could stand on her good leg and kick with her damaged leg. No—

the kneecap was too weak to bend. She considered tearing her hands away from the trident. Would the wider part of the nails rip at her hands too much? If she needed her hands, she would rip through the nails. Her head was free. She could still use it to head-butt, and that would... Visola wondered why she was strategizing for a fight all of a sudden. She had given very little serious thought to fighting off Vachlan, and in the beginning she might have stood a meager chance. Was it because she could tell from the sound of the young guard's voice that he was inexperienced, and that she could defeat him even in her current state? Or was it because she somehow felt safe with Vachlan, and would not allow anyone else to torture her?

If a victim could afford to exercise favoritism between captors, should that person really be a victim at all? All of this thinking was giving Visola a headache, and that was one thing she could not afford to have, considering all of the other parts that were aching. She just needed a little bit of relaxing action—a little bit of an ego boost, and a little spurt of fighting juice. This young man who was approaching her, and reaching out to touch her with his fingertips, was almost close enough for her to...

"Hey!" Vachlan yelled at the guard. "I changed my mind. I'll see Zalcan later. You—go get my cot and bring it into this room."

Visola felt a bit of relief that the boy would not have a chance to harm her, laced with the disappointment that she would not have the chance to harm him. Torture was becoming an intimate activity shared between Vachlan and Visola, and she would feel uncomfortable if someone else participated in causing her pain. It was like inviting someone into their bedroom.

"Yes, sir. You'll be sleeping in this room from now on?"

"Who the hell are you to question me?" Vachlan sneered.

"Sorry, sir." When the boy scurried toward the room's exit to carry out his task, he found Vachlan standing in his way and grabbing his shoulder.

"Are you an idiot, boy?" Vachlan asked, roughly shaking the guard. "Why did you go near the prisoner?"

"What do you mean?" he asked. "I wasn't going to hurt her…"

"Hurt *her*? If you had stepped one inch closer to her, she would have killed you!"

"I don't see how that's possible," the boy said.

"You fool! She could smell your weakness. She could smell your stupidity as you underestimated her. Did you not see that muscle in her jaw twitching? She was already prepared to smile as you died."

Visola was surprised at this analysis. It was true—her cheeks had been anticipating pulling the corners of her first smile in weeks. Did Vachlan really know her so well? Did he remember her so well?

The boy frowned, although he did take a step away from Visola. "She's all skin and bones, not to mention crucified."

"Her skin and bones are worth more than you would be on steroids. A real warrior knows how to use their body regardless of its condition. Real power is in the mind, and I haven't been able to make a scratch on her mind. You're worthless. Get out of here and bring my cot."

Chapter 22: Playing Dead

It had been three days since he had nailed her to the trident. He kept her well-hydrated and adequately-fed while he had continued to torture her. He experimented with new techniques now that she was forced to stand on her one good leg. She shifted on the leg uncomfortably as her body grew tired, sometimes allowing her weight to transfer to the injured bones for brief periods just so she could rest. For some unknown reason, Vachlan had begun sleeping on the cot in her room. He had not removed her blindfold, and she relied on her hearing to gauge her surroundings. She could hear his breathing become rhythmic and slow when he slept. She drifted in and out of sleep fretfully, waking up with a start whenever she heard the slightest noise, or drip of water.

Visola had discovered that the more moribund she looked, the less of a beating she got. Vachlan seemed extremely sensitive to her health, so she began playing dead as much as possible. When he believed she was unconscious, or deeply asleep, he paid careful attention to her wounds and kept them clean. He monitored her blood loss, making sure that although she was kept in constant pain there was no danger of actually killing her. He even bathed her and washed her hair. She sometimes imagined that his touch was gentle, and that he was whispering kind words softly when he believed that she was unconscious.

She could not be sure of this. The problem was that she was becoming such an excellent actress that she was not entirely sure whether or not she was really unconscious, half the time. Visola was in so much pain that she could not really tell the difference between drama and reality—she only knew that pretending things were a few notches worse than they really were could save her life in the event that he went too far. She did not know whether any of the kind words she remembered him saying had actually been said. It did not matter, because she needed their comforting effect to remain internally unscathed. She would clutch to fantasies if they kept her strong. Reality blurred with imagination, and she was so often blinking blood out of her eyes with her swollen, sluggish eyelids that she wondered if her vision would permanently be tinted with a ruby film once she could see again. Would it make her more optimistic to see the world through built-in dyed rose-colored glasses? These were the kinds of thoughts which swam through her mind, disturbing her and making her wonder about her own lucidity.

Among those, were the strange phrases she attributed to some old poem or song. *Breach the murky waters of valor.* She could not remember where the words were from, or what they meant, but they came into her mind as they pleased.

Torturing anyone was based on a few simple principles. The ultimate fear that one tried to instill in a victim was the fear of dying. Usually, everyone had a fear of dying. The second element to play with was the victim's attachment to the world. Most people had love for someone, or someone to live for—someone to take care of. Although Visola had plenty of love in her life, she did not feel like her connection with anyone was so strong that it would crush them if she died. Her daughter had lived a whole lifetime without her, and Alcyone had her sons. Aazuria would probably be the most affected, but Trevain would keep her in check and prevent her from going berserk. Trevain seemed like the kind of person who was very down to earth, and could ground those around him. Sionna never felt strong emotions; she thought about things too much, and she probably already expected her sister's death. Sionna had even given her the means. She would understand.

Visola's ability to completely let go of her fear of

dying, and completely let go of her attachment to the world, helped to keep her as sane as possible. Many might have made a case for her sanity being questionable to begin with, and she was sure that this also helped. She had experience with torture, and she knew what to expect.

That is why it startled her, when she was playing dead as usual, and she heard an unfamiliar footstep. She did not move or indicate that she had heard it, and she reminded herself that it could just be another fragment of her imagination. That was until she heard the voice.

"Vachlan, my good man!" said the new voice. Visola was surprised at how feminine it sounded, and for a moment she was not sure whether it was a male or a female. She was preparing to become jealous, and preparing to scratch out some eyes before Vachlan even responded.

"Welcome back, Prince Zalcan. How was your campaign?"

This was Zalcan? Visola wondered in disbelief. Surely not *the* Zalcan Oris who was the leader of the Clan? She was overwhelmed with curiosity to see his face, but as much as she strained, she could not see through the opaque fabric. Was he as small and feminine as he sounded?

"Exhausting," said the prince in response. "My father works me like I'm some sort of pack animal."

"Emperor Zalcan has a lot on his plate. He was just demonstrating his faith in you when he delegated the toughest quadrant of the ocean to you."

"He has great faith in *us*, my brother!" Zalcan said, clapping Vachlan on the back. "You did a splendid job in the Atlantic, especially when you crushed the Rusalka. Father has no doubt that with your guidance I will soon have the Pacific under my thumb."

Visola could almost hear and imagine the feminine man lifting his thumb into the air as he spoke. The Rusalka had been conquered? They had been allies of Adlivun, and there had not even been a request for assistance. They must have fallen so fast that they had not even had time to send a messenger. This was very bad. She felt a drop of blood rolling down her cheek, very close to her nose. She had to struggle to refrain from twitching her nose and revealing that she was awake.

"So this is your prisoner, Vachlan. The wife who betrayed you?"

"She's the one, Prince Zalcan."

"I see. It must have been a real hoot torturing her. I was expecting you to come to me with your report a lot sooner."

"Forgive me. I wanted to make sure I squeezed as much information as possible out of her before giving you my report."

"Has she been very chatty? Very cooperative?"

"Very," Vachlan responded. Visola wanted to frown, curse, and object that this was untrue, but she was worried that it could be considered cooperating.

"Wonderful. Can I play with her?" Zalcan asked, approaching Visola excitedly. The drop of blood was slowly descending and resting just barely on the top of her lip. She had the consuming urge to let her tongue dark out and lick the drop, but she continued playing dead.

"No, you'd better not," Vachlan said quietly. "I really let her have it earlier. She's unconscious."

"You never let me have any fun," Zalcan complained. He reached out, with the thumb that Visola already despised, and roughly wiped the droplet of blood away from the corner of her lips. She fought the urge to sink her teeth into the appendage. It was a precious opportunity to bite off the thumb which intended to oppress the whole Pacific Ocean beneath it, but she let it pass. Taking his thumb would not stop him. She needed to take his head. Then she needed to take his father's head. Visola did not know how she could possibly do it, but she knew that she needed to stop Emperor Zalcan Oris.

The thumb had lingered on her lips for a second too

long before Prince Zalcan withdrew it and turned back to her husband. "So what did you learn from her?" Zalcan asked. "How many men are in Adlivun?"

"I'm afraid it's not good news," Vachlan answered. "They have many more warriors than we expected. They have received reinforcements from the Ningyo... and a group of rebel Rusalka warriors also managed to escape to Adlivun."

Visola kept the surprise away from her face. Was it true? She had only been away for a few weeks, and there had been no Rusalka reinforcements in Adlivun. She had not sent for them, since there had been hardly any communication between the nations in almost a century. Was it possibly that Adlivun's army had received a huge influx of warriors? This idea made her hopeful, but she was still skeptical. Where was Vachlan getting his information—from Namaka? Was it possible that Namaka was feeding him lies?

"Damnation," Prince Zalcan cursed. "Father said this was going to be an easy victory. Do you have a precise number, Vachlan?"

Vachlan seemed to pause before responding. "She hasn't given me a precise figure, but from her descriptions, I gather that there are upwards of fifty thousand warriors protecting the nation."

"Fifty thousand warriors!" Zalcan exclaimed angrily. "Fifty *thousand* warriors?"

In her mind, Visola was making similar shocked noises of incredulity. Vachlan had hardly questioned her about the army at all! His questions had all been personal, and she certainly had not given him a morsel of information about Adlivun. She felt like her head was going to explode with the effort of remaining still and silent. These farfetched words had cut through the hazy cloud which had surrounded her thoughts, and she began to understand what was happening. Vachlan was lying to Prince Zalcan. Vachlan was betraying yet another employer. But why?

"I was not even expecting them to have ten thousand!" Zalcan was shouting in a shrill, girlish voice. "I thought these northern settlements were less populated, Vachlan!"

"I thought so too," Vachlan said quietly. Visola could feel that his eyes were on her. Did he know that she was awake and listening?

"We can't defeat that many!" Zalcan screeched. "No wonder that fool Atargatis failed. But Vachlan, are you sure she's telling the truth? Is this woman's word reliable?"

"She's their general, Prince Zalcan," Vachlan answered firmly. "Besides, look at her. She's crucified. She's completely broken. She'll tell me anything I want for a piece of cheese, like any filthy rat. Don't you trust my work?"

Zalcan began sniggering as he moved closer to Visola. He reached out and poked one of her nailed palms. She did not react. "You did do quite a number on the poor girl." Zalcan ran his hand along Visola's arm, dragging his fingers along her elbow and bicep. He caressed her neck roughly, examining the bruises that Vachlan's hands had left there. "I am disappointed that you didn't save a little bit of fun for me. She's a pretty little thing, no? I would love to hear her scream."

"I am sure you will," Vachlan told the other man quietly, with a strange tone in his voice. "I'll let you know when she's awake sometime, and you can join us."

"Splendid, splendid!" Zalcan said, as he placed both hands on Visola's hips, aggressively groping what little meat she had left on her. She believed that her leg was healed enough to kick him, but she would save it until she had the opportunity to cause more permanent damage. Zalcan was giggling. "Yes, I can see that you did break her down quite well. Excellent work, as always. If we don't have enough men to destroy Adlivun as it stands, I will just send to my father for more. The emperor can surely spare a bit more manpower for his favorite son."

"That's very wise, Prince Zalcan," Vachlan told him.

"You should dispatch a messenger to him at once."

"Why don't you do it for me?" Zalcan asked, without removing his hands from Visola's body. "Go and dispatch a messenger. I will enjoy your wife's lovely body in the meantime. Unconscious or not, she's still warm."

"Don't touch her," Vachlan said in a low voice. Visola held her breath.

"Hey, be nice and share!"

"No," Vachlan said vehemently.

"Why not?" Prince Zalcan whined with surprise.

"Trust me, you don't want to do that," Vachlan said, in a grim tone. "She's still a bleeding mess down there from the last time I raped her."

"Ah, why didn't you just say so? I don't want your damaged goods."

Visola could not believe what she was hearing. Was Vachlan lying to protect her? He had never once raped her. Why would he tell the prince all this? Was he just being possessive?

"Exactly—I thought you deserved more than damaged goods," Vachlan was saying. "She's almost dead, anyway. You can find better."

"If she's so useless, then why waste resources keeping her alive? Dispose of her."

"I believe she has more information to reveal. She could really help to fine-tune our strategy so that we take out Adlivun efficiently."

"Efficiently? I don't care how many men we lose," Prince Zalcan said with a casual shrug. "We know that they have fifty thousand, so I'll just send more than that, and bombard them until we win. Simple. What do we need her for?"

"We need to preserve as much of the army as possible to take the Ningyo," Vachlan told him. "Don't forget—fighting the Japanese is going to be harder than fighting the Alaskans. We've been building this army for a century, and we can't waste it. If we play our cards right, we could destroy Adlivun within the first half of this year, and get the Japanese in the second half. Your father will be so proud of how fast you conquered the Pacific."

"Ah, I see. That sounds ambitious, but if anyone could manage that, it would be you. I'll trust your advice, Mr. Destroyer-of-Kingdoms." Zalcan giggled at the nickname. "I know they don't call you that without good reason."

"Thank you, Prince Zalcan."

"But I have a word of advice for you too. I am still your leader, and you have to listen to me."

"Sure, what is it?"

"Don't keep the prisoner alive for sentimental value. You're stronger than that. You have a history with her, and she's obviously distracting you from your work. If she's told us everything she knows, and she's no longer useful, get rid of her. Just kill the girl."

"She still knows plenty about…"

Zalcan made a disappointed clucking noise with his tongue. "Kill the girl."

"Okay. Sure. I will," Vachlan said, nodding.

"Thanks, brother. I have to run and dispatch those messengers. Enjoy yourself."

When Prince Zalcan left, Visola heard her husband sigh. Several minutes of silence passed, and Visola assumed that Vachlan was lost in thought. She certainly was. It seemed that this was one of the rare extended torture sessions during which the victim would learn more about her enemy. She just did not know how to make sense of it other than to believe that Vachlan was protecting her. She could not understand this, but it was obviously true. He had told the prince all kinds of lies to save her from torture and rape— and he had inflated Adlivun's numbers to stall the attack. Visola swallowed the saliva that had been gathering in her throat.

In an instant, Vachlan had crossed the room, and had

ripped her blindfold off. Even though the mineshaft was dark, her eyes still had to adjust to the light. She opened them slowly, squinting at him.

"You heard all of that, didn't you?" he asked her.

She did not respond.

He sighed. "Well, that's lovely." He began to pace back and forth restlessly, and she allowed her eyes to follow him. His hand lifted to stroke his chin as he took dozens of brooding steps. Visola stared at him curiously, feeling the urge to smile, but restraining her lips. She knew that one should not smile at the person who had recently crucified her. She did not want to seem superior and unintentionally earn more physical torment just because she was amused. Vachlan had, after all, agreed to kill her—and he did not always lie. She was surprised when he suddenly turned to look at her.

He observed her face for a moment. Seeming to have made a decision, he moved to his cot. He dragged the small bed over to where Visola had previously been shackled to the ground, and where her shackles still remained. He returned to where she stood nailed to the trident.

"Here let me take these nails out," he told her. He grabbed a tool, and began to carefully pry the first nail out of the wood. When her hand was free, her arm and body began falling forward. He easily caught her and held her upright by tossing her arm over his shoulder. He began working on the second nail. Once her hands were free, he lifted her and carried her over to his cot. He laid her out carefully. He propped his pillow up under her smashed kneecap to help increase circulation and healing.

Visola had never been so happy to be lying down. Her head rolled back against the cot blissfully. She was looking forward to a deep, restful sleep which her body could use to heal. She felt like she was healing already. A little sigh of contentment escaped her lips, and Vachlan noticed this subtle sound. She barely made any sounds, and he had become very perceptive of her every breath.

"I'm going to pull the nails out of your hands, Viso," he told her softly.

She turned to look at him then, her face no longer as expressionless and hard as she had trained it to be. Although she did not allow herself to smile, she knew that she could not keep the shine from her eyes. She was sure that he understood, as he carefully cleaned her hands and removed the large nails which he had driven through her palms. He occasionally stole a glance at her as he worked on sprinkling turmeric on her hands, applying a healing ointment, and bandaging the wounds. He could see that she trusted him. She trusted him implicitly.

"Viso, I just..." he began to explain, but trailed off into silence. He returned to wrapping the bandages around her hands. By the time he had finished caring for her, she had almost fallen asleep. He reached up and grasped the shackles that would fasten her to the wall. Visola heard the sounds of the chains, and opened her eyes. She saw him hesitate.

She lifted her wrists toward him, giving him better access to fasten the shackles around her wrists. She did not want any more complications to this situation. The prisoner-captive relationship was a simple one; it was much simpler than being husband and wife. He locked her wrists in the shackles, and moved to do the same to her ankles. Visola was glad that he was shackling her, because if he did not, then she would need to try to escape. She was in no condition to escape, but her pride would have forced her to try. When he finished binding her, he moved away. He lay down on the ground, a few feet away from her cot. His back was turned away from her and facing the only entrance to the cave.

Visola suddenly realized why he had ordered a cot brought into this room when he had heard that Prince Zalcan had returned. He had chosen to sleep in these uncomfortable surroundings so that he could be close to her—so that he could defend her against any possible trouble. From the real enemy. He was not her enemy. Was all of this some twisted, convoluted love game? He had been acting a role, like in the theatre. Since his back was turned, she finally allowed herself to smile a little. A little tear of happiness escaped her eye as well. If Vachlan was on her side, then she felt completely safe. She even felt safe from him, for she was certain that he did not mean her any irreversible harm.

"Go to sleep, Viso," he ordered her gruffly. "If you keep staring at me you're going to burn a crater into my back. Stop thinking so damn loudly."

Her smile grew wider. *Goodnight to you too, Vachlan,* she thought to herself. The pleasant thoughts somehow overwhelmed all of her body's aches, and she knew that she would have lovely dreams.

Chapter 23: Only Two Syllables

Undersea coronations were very rare due to the extended lifespans of monarchs. Customarily, the ceremony was a spiritual event, but the focus of this one was revving up the morale of the military. When Aazuria saw the crowns, which had been carried in by the army officials Holma and Geira, she was immediately upset.

"I thought we pawned all of our jewels!" she whispered harshly, turning around and looking for someone to scold. She normally would have scolded her youngest sister, or even Visola—they had been responsible for collecting and pawning the jewels. When she turned around, and neither of them were standing close to her, this made her even more upset. Elandria was there, and she shook her head sadly.

"They pawned small heirlooms and trinkets. You cannot get rid of the priceless crown jewels, Zuri. They have belonged to our family for thousands of years."

"Viso wanted modern weaponry. Do you know how much those emeralds cost? They each weigh about 250 carats if I remember correctly. What do we need them for? Get rid of them. I do not want a damned emerald on my head. I want Corallyn back!"

"Shhhh, you must calm down, dear sister. The ceremony is starting."

"If we did sell them, I would not even know where to get weaponry," Aazuria said with mounting anxiety. "Visola had special black market contacts and I do not..."

"It's okay, Zuri," Trevain said, reaching for her hand and giving it a squeeze. "Money is not a problem. Weapons are not a problem. Boats are not a problem. You have to relax."

"I cannot. I do not think I am ready to become Queen," Aazuria said.

"You are ready. Nothing will change except your title," he responded. "I'm not ready in the least, but I'm just going to hide behind you and hope no one notices me."

This drew a small giggle from Elandria, and both Trevain and Aazuria turned in surprise at hearing her voice. She smiled at them graciously. "I love you both," she said softly, inclining her head in a gentle bow.

It was the first time that Aazuria had heard her sister's voice since she had recovered from her wound. Aazuria knew that it took a great effort for Elandria to overcome her own fears and speak. She smiled at the younger girl with fond tenderness and the highest esteem. Somehow, the rarity of Elandria's speech imbued it with mystical qualities—it could instantly influence one to correct their mistakes before they even made them, or in this instance, instantly warm one's heart and lift their spirits.

Queen Amabie had begun speaking to the citizens of Adlivun who had gathered in the amphitheater. Her own warriors were gathered among them. Aazuria turned her head to listen to the stately Japanese leader, enthralled by her resonating voice and regal gestures. If anyone could give a speech, and if anyone could rile up an army, it was Queen Amabie. Her words were even convincing and reminding Aazuria of her own virtues, and making her feel a little more deserving of the position that was her birthright. The position that she had obtained sooner than necessary through patricide.

Aazuria was beyond thankful that the older woman happened to be in the kingdom for this event. In fact, Queen Amabie had been indispensible in all of the events that had recently transpired, and would continue to be crucial through the culmination of this war. She was the closest thing Aazuria had to a mother-figure, and this was more valuable than the emeralds in the crowns. For a six-hundred-year-old woman, there were not many people to look up to and learn from. There were not many people left who would praise and celebrate her victories like a proud parent would.

Queen Amabie's endorsement of Aazuria as both a political leader and a person gave all the Adluvians even deeper faith in the woman they already loved. When the elaborate crown was placed on Aazuria's head, she could feel the substantial weight of the giant emerald, but it was also strangely comfortable. She could shoulder this gem; she could endure its encumbrance.

"It is not blood alone which makes nobility," Queen Amabie said. "It is the way one fights their battles and the way one handles a crisis that shows true merit. It is actions which reveal discipline of character, and I think you will all agree that Aazuria has performed the noblest deeds of all. Today marks the end of tyranny in Adlivun! Today we celebrate the new reign of a leader devoted to justice! Hail Queen Aazuria! "

"Hail Queen Aazuria!"

When the great cheer arose from the amphitheater, it brought tears to Aazuria's eyes. Even Queen Amabie made a deep bow from the waist, and it was not necessary for Queen Amabie to bow to anyone. Although Aazuria knew that many people had opposed King Kyrosed's regime, when she had performed the act of killing him, she had felt completely alone. She had endured the guilt, the regret, and the sadness of loss without truly facing her actions or speaking to her people about the event. Now that Queen Amabie was bringing up the issue before the gathered audience, and Aazuria could hear their thundering support, she felt completely vindicated.

Accepting a scepter which had been offered to her by Geira, she lifted her head, and stood proudly before her people and her allies, allowing their gratitude and support to wash over her like an invigorating downpour. It did not rain under the sea, and there was no changing weather to interpret, adapt to, or feel anything about, so Aazuria found her blazing storm in the emotions of her people. Being gathered into the coliseum-like space caused all of their sentiments to amplify and reach her with an unspeakable force. These were good acoustics for a sense of renewed kinship and community.

Needless to say, she felt strengthened.

She reached to her side to grasp Trevain's hand, and looked at him lovingly. He smiled at her.

"I thought that this would be silly... but it's actually rather moving," Trevain whispered to her.

"I would like to formally introduce Admiral Trevain Murphy. As many of you know, Queen Aazuria has recently married the grandson of General Visola Ramaris. He has lived his entire life on land, with a successful career as a mariner," Amabie explained to the auditorium, as she gestured to Trevain. "He brings with him a new perspective, new knowledge, and new technology. He vows to help to render this nation and its allies cutting-edge and keep us ahead of our enemies. In addition to his intelligence, he is of impeccable integrity—much unlike Adlivun's previous king. I would like you all to trust in Queen Aazuria's judgment, and welcome King Trevain. Together, they will lead the campaign to defend this kingdom! Together we will vanquish our adversaries!"

The audience cheered for the new king and queen, but the cheer quickly dissipated into a hushed silence. Murmurs rose from the crowd, and people began pointing and whispering. Aazuria and Trevain frowned, and turned around to see what they were looking at.

A solitary woman holding a gigantic sword was casually walking into the center of the arena.

"Y'all didn't invite me?" she said with a playful pout.

"Viso?" Aazuria asked with a gasp. She ran to the edge of the stage, feeling silly when her new crown started to slip off with her swift motion. She reached up to straighten the crown as she called out to her friend. "Viso!"

A roar began to sound from the amphitheater, as everyone witnessed their beloved general returning from the supposed grave. A chant arose among the spectators. Everyone took up the chant and contributed their voices in rumbling unison.

"Gen-er-ral! Ra-ma-ris!"

Everyone in the stadium was stomping their feet in time with the syllables, sounding a massive, reverberating echo against the cave walls. The woman seemed to enjoy the chanting, as she headed for the stage and raised her sword in the air, brandishing it in the air proudly. The cheer became louder.

"Gen-er-ral! Ra-ma-ris!"

It was a heartening display. Aazuria ran to her friend and threw her arms around her. The hug that was returned was not as strong as she expected, and she frowned. She pulled away slightly to look at the woman's face. It was Visola's face, but it was not Visola inside of it. "Sio?" she whispered.

"Shhh," Sionna said, tilting her head downward and speaking close to Aazuria's ear so that the audience could not read her lips. "Look at how energized they are. We don't have to tell them that it's me. We don't have to disappoint them."

"Gen-er-ral! Ra-ma-ris!"

"No one would be disappointed to know that you are alive," Aazuria said quietly. "You have done so much for everyone in this room—you have helped them for centuries with your knowledge of healing."

"Come on, Zuri. Let's give them a little faith. No one would cheer for little old me—besides, 'Doctor' has only two syllables."

Aazuria smiled. "Now that's the type of thing she would have said. How is she?"

"She will be fine," Sionna said softly. She could not tell Aazuria that she had given a suicide pill to her sister. She did not want to be the first to face the wrath of the newly-crowned queen. "She managed to say one word to me in Aleut. She told me to prepare *ayxaasix̂* before Vachlan cut her off."

"Ships?" Aazuria asked. "She wants us to do battle by armada?"

"Then we will prepare the ships," Trevain said, approaching both of the women and putting an arm around each of them. "Good to have you back, Aunt Sio."

"It's good to see you, kid," Sionna said, hitting him on the back with excessive force. "Sorry, I am trying to act like my sister. Ideally, I should grab your ass, but that's a bit too much for me. I think we should prepare the navy, but I want to hold out and wait for some kind of signal from her before we attack. I know it sounds crazy and whimsical, but I really believe she will find a way to give us one."

"That's not crazy," Aazuria said. "We will wait."

"Until then—if it makes them happy, I will become her." Sionna winked and walked to the edge of the stage, smiling and thrusting her sword in the air. "For Adlivun!" she yelled.

While she worked the crowd, in a surprising performance that even made those closest to her wonder whether she really was Sionna, Trevain spoke to Aazuria privately.

"I'm glad this is going to be a boat battle, because I can definitely contribute a little something."

"I will not allow you to come along with us, Trevain," Aazuria told him. "This is going to be war. You forbade me from accompanying you on your little fishing trip when I knew there was danger. This is the same thing, except I know that there will be trouble you have never faced before."

"I'm going to claim a sexist double standard and say that you can't forbid me from coming along because I'm a man." Trevain pointed to the crown on his head. "Also, I've got this shiny new trinket which I believe gives me the authority to insist 'I wanna come' and then, while we travel, to repeatedly ask 'Are we there yet?'"

"You are not coming with me and this is final. Please stop using humor to soften me up so you can get your way."

"Damn, you caught on to that, huh?" Trevain sighed. "Listen, Zuri—grandma gave me responsibilities too. Consider this on-the-job-training. You are my wife now, and I will not let any harm come to you. Besides, not only am I a skilled seafarer, but I know how to fence."

"Trevain, you have great experience governing ships, but what if you end up in the water? Fighting submerged is entirely more difficult, and you need more training. You have the potential, but we need to condition your body over years of exercise, swimming for great lengths and at high speeds. There needs to be a slow transition of moving you from land to sea; we cannot do it all at once."

"I know, Zuri, but you have to let me try. I will rise to the occasion, I promise."

Both of them were startled out of their argument when the crowd began making collectively amused sounds. Aazuria cringed as she watched Sionna grab the nearest unrelated man (who happened to be an older Japanese general) and plant an enthusiastic smooch on his lips. The Ningyo warriors burst into good-natured cheering and laughter, as the Adluvians giggled at the antics of the woman they believed to be Visola.

"Oh, dear," Aazuria remarked. "She is enjoying this."

"I didn't know she was such a stellar actress," Trevain said, obviously impressed.

"It is a tad bit overstated and vulgar, don't you think?"

Queen Amabie approached the couple to add her opinion. "How authentic!"

Chapter 24: *Kill the Girl*

Vachlan could not sleep. He had pretended for several hours, while listening closely to his wife's tranquil breathing. At some point, he had turned to face her, and he was surprised at the content expression on her face. Her shackled hands were folded close to her chest, and there was even something of a smile on her face. He frowned. She had won. She had taken everything that he had thrown at her, and she had not broken. He could not throw anything more, because somehow, torturing her was torturing him much more. He had never experienced this psychological rebound before—she was a perfect mirror. Every injury he caused her was reflected into his own mind and magnified. He was not strong enough to continue doing this.

Three words echoed in Vachlan's consciousness like an annoying tune he could not shake away. *Kill the Girl.* It would not be a difficult task, and he knew that it was necessary; it was time. It was the prudent thing to do. His employer had requested it. *Kill the Girl.* He had dozens of compelling personal and professional reasons to carry out the order.

Just why did she have to look exactly the same? No one had hair as red and wild as fire. It was impossible. Even while she was sleeping, quietly dormant due to her body's need to heal the damage he had inflicted upon her, her hair still announced her indomitable life-force. It was completely unviable for Visola to ever look peaceful, or shy, or anything resembling demure. She had probably been born fierce, maybe wailing out a battle cry and pounding her newborn chest. Even then, covered in placenta and gore, he imagined that she had been gosh-darn pretty. Being covered in blood had never taken away from her beauty. It was a look that not many women could pull off—and not many women ever tried, especially in Elizabethan England. Vachlan found that he had risen to rest on his elbow to better examine her. He also found that he was lifting himself off the ground and moving closer to her.

Just why did she have to smell exactly the same? Her natural scent blanketed him like a familiar place—like a garden he had walked in as a child. He had very much enjoyed strolling through gardens. He observed the gentle curve of her lips, wondering if she could possibly be comfortable when her body was broken in a dozen different ways. Was she really relaxed, and possibly amused?

Yes, she was. It was part of what had made life with her so easy and enjoyable. Nothing fazed her—not really. Even if it did, she quickly overcame it, pushing it down to a place where she could watch her woes from a distance, and deal with them on a higher, unaffected level. People considered her carefree due to the seemingly frivolous way she responded to even the worst of situations, but he knew this was not true. He knew that she felt things as deeply as those who were overwhelmed, but unlike them, she was able to function perfectly under duress.

Just why did her lips have to tempt him so? She was deeply asleep, and perhaps she would hardly notice if he... no. His instructions had been clear. *Kill the girl.* He did possess a tiny slice of respect for his employer. He had *zero* respect for Visola, the woman who had betrayed him! Zero. His head nodded to emphasize the thought. This, of course, was what he had been trying to convince himself for centuries. The truth was that he had more respect for Visola than anyone else who breathed. The *utmost* respect; he held her above anyone who walked the earth or swam the waves. No one lived each day with more honor, and no one held their head with more pride. In protest for her sister's life, he had watched her rip her guts out, and he had loved her a little more.

Her bold defiance only rendered her more endearing. How could it be that she had betrayed him? His Visola—his beloved wife who he knew to possess the most undying, unconditional loyalty possible—how had *she* stooped to do what she had done? There must be some reasonable explanation. All he needed was that explanation, so he could finally forgive her. Had she been threatened? Had she been forced? Had King Kyrosed leveraged her sister's safety over her head, just as Vachlan himself had done? It was no great secret that Sionna was the general's weakness. Anyone with a twin could be easily controlled by virtue of that umbilical attachment.

Why did she refuse to tell him the truth? What horrible secret was she keeping? Did she not know that if the situation had been beyond her control, he would pardon her? He just needed to know. His eyes had not left her lips. They were slightly parted in sleep, and he watched them thirstily, begging for a stray word to escape. He could have stared at her lips forever, just waiting for an accidental crumb. There would eventually be some leak in her resolve, right? She could not maintain complete control of her body at all times, and surely she would make a mistake and utter a word in her sleep. Had she ever spoken in her sleep? He strained the channels of his thought, trying to remember. It had been so long. Usually, they had fallen asleep together once they had exhausted each other. They had always been competitive in every aspect of their lives—who could stay awake the longest? Who could love the longest? Now, apparently, she was being competitive again. She had made the rules of the game inside her head, and as long as she did not speak, she was winning.

It drove him crazy not to hear the sound of her voice. How did she know precisely what would disturb him the most? For he was disturbed. He was angry. The bitch had cheated on him. She had been his whole world. Visola Ramaris had been the one good thing in his entire existence. She was his Firebird; the choice that he had been proudest of making. She was the one woman alive who was not terrified of him, and of the things he had done. Instead, she admired him, and she was intrigued by him. She respected him as much as he respected her. She should have known that her actions would destroy him, and send him back into the dark madness in which he had always existed. She should not have disgraced him! She had made him into his personal laughingstock—had inspired myriad monologues of relentless self-loathing. She had done the unthinkable; she had allowed their *enemy* to lie with her. She should be groveling. She should have spent every minute of these past few weeks groveling. Was she not ashamed or remorseful? She had ruined him, and now she lay there sleeping blissfully with a smile on her face! How dare she not grovel?

He had to end her. She was still unhealthy for him. If he forced himself to remember all the horrible events he had squirreled away to the back of his mind, he would gain the gall to do it. He used to brag about having the testicles of dragons, and he was sure he could find them again. Vachlan closed his eyes in meditation.

The outline of the man that caused all this began to etch itself into his mental canvas. The majestic long white hair and beard, typical of the monarchs of the undersea, began to materialize. The brilliant azure eyes were framed by an abundance of wrinkles from undeserved laughter. Kyrosed Vellamo had been an imposing fellow to look upon, and Vachlan often wished that he had never done so. Even greater was the mistake of listening to the king's honeyed lies, so perfected to a mathematical precision, like the arts he had encouraged his daughters to learn. Those lies had coaxed him halfway across the world.

"When was the last time you were with her?" King *Kyrosed asked.*

Vachlan frowned. "Why do you ask that?"

"I'm sorry. I guess that was too personal. I was just wondering."

The king toyed with the royal ring on his finger in a gesture of mock nervousness. Vachlan glared at the king's hands, and fantasized about chopping those fingers off. Visola had hated Kyrosed Vellamo more than anyone. Yet she had chosen to be with him? How had this happened? Why had this happened?

"You were just wondering about the last time that I slept with my wife?" Vachlan asked.

"Yes... well, it's just..." Kyrosed paused, and seemed to be thinking of how to phrase things most eloquently. His royal shoulders raised in a delicate shrug. "She only recently discovered her pregnancy, and you were away in India for several months, so naturally I wondered..."

"You wondered what?" Vachlan asked, approaching the king. He stared into the man's sickeningly blue eyes. "You wondered what!"

"Nothing. It's nothing."

She had been carrying another man's child. There was no doubt about it. Everyone had been insinuating it. The whispers and looks of pity were too much to bear. With Visola away, leading her own campaign, she was not there to speak with personally. There was only a message she had left with Naclana saying that she wished to meet him in Zimovia. What did she need to tell him?

"Well, you know they've been fighting recently," Naclana said, sipping on his drink.

"Fighting?" Vachlan exclaimed. "Viso and Zuri have been fighting? What on earth would get between those two?"

"King Kyrosed, of course," Naclana said. "I don't really know the details, but I heard his name coming up a lot. Princess Aazuria kept mentioning a matter of honor, and Visola kept saying that she couldn't face the truth..."

His mind had filled in the blanks, twisting everything

into the shape he least wanted to see. Every night he had seen it in his nightmares, over and over: Visola betraying him, Visola laughing at him, Visola taunting him. Now, King Kyrosed stood before him as clear as day. The older man arched his white eyebrows and fixed Vachlan with a smug smile. "Sorry, lad," the king said. "When you have true power, you get used to taking what you want. You don't think about the consequences. You know what I mean, don't you?"

Vachlan shook his head, not wanting to respond out loud to the phantasm of his nemesis.

"Are you afraid that she looks like me?" King Kyrosed asked mockingly. "Is that why you have never seen her? You're only half a man, Vachlan. You ran—you ran like a scared little mouse."

He glared at the ghost. He knew the truth! He had seen it in every inch of Kyrosed's haughty expressions. He had heard the hints in every syllable, in every morpheme, and in every silence. He turned away from Kyrosed's apparition to look back to his wife. Vachlan knew that he would be wise to kill her now. He observed her lying on his cot, completely vulnerable. It was not his style to kill someone when they were at their most vulnerable, but perhaps it would be merciful for Visola to die in her sleep, with the trace of a smile on her face. She would never see it coming, and she would not have a chance to hate him. He would do as Prince Zalcan had ordered. He would kill her.

"That's right," King Kyrosed whispered in his ear. "You always knew it would come to this. We have to punish women when they're unfaithful. Teach them the ultimate lesson and show them who they're dealing with. You and I were never forgiving men, were we?"

When Kyrosed placed a hand on Vachlan's shoulder, he shrugged it off angrily. *I am nothing like you!* His thoughts were racing. He knew that Kyrosed was not really behind him, and he closed his eyes tightly to wish the specter into oblivion.

"Look at her! She's not even remorseful," the king continued. "She thinks she's better than you. She's superior, and the rules don't apply to her. She's a woman, and she can do whatever she likes—she can hurt you if she likes. You brainless clown. Quit delaying and do what needs to be done."

Vachlan found himself reaching for his sword, which lay on a pile of cloth and blankets. When he saw the blankets, he could not help wondering if Visola was cold, and considered covering her with one. The thought happened before he could control it, and with his sword clutched tightly in his hand, he reached for a blanket. He lovingly arranged it over his wife, tucking the corners around her with trembling fingers. He mentally insisted to himself that this was his final humane, sentimental act. He returned both hands to the hilt of his sword.

While torturing her, he had used odd and unconventional instruments, but this was different. She deserved an honorable and swift end. He swallowed, lifting his sword. *She doesn't even deserve that,* King Kyrosed's voice sneered in his mind. *She cuckolded you. Visola doesn't deserve a kind quick end—why don't you wake her up and let her watch? Do it slowly and have some fun?* Vachlan shook his head to clear the voice away. He hated that voice, and had no idea why it would not leave him alone. He would behead Visola, and he would do it cleanly. It would be over, and it would stop haunting him. He could forget her, and forget all hope of forgiving her, and he could live the remaining centuries of his life in peace.

His eyes glazed over as he stared at the sleeping girl. She was completely vulnerable; she trusted him. He had seen it in her eyes when he had removed her blindfold. She knew that he would never let any harm come to her. Not any real harm. This was not true—she was mistaken to have such trust in him. She was mistaken to think that she could allow herself a deep and restful slumber, completely off her guard. Was she off her guard? Visola was never truly vulnerable, was she? He watched her chest slowly expand with her breathing, and he knew that she was; she was utterly defenseless.

He tightened his grip around the hilt of the sword, adjusting it slowly in his hands. He raised his hands to shoulder level. *I need to do this, now. No more stalling. Do I really have the balls to do this?* he asked himself. *No,* part of him answered. *Visola does not deserve this. Whatever happened with Kyrosed—it was not her fault. She is probably so ashamed of it that she cannot speak about the subject. She deserves better.*

No! She betrayed me. Reasons do not matter. Circumstances do not matter. She is remaining silent out of guilt and shame. If it had not been her choice, she would have confessed that she was forced or blackmailed. She betrayed me! She made a joke of me! She ruined our perfect life, our dreams of having a family together... and she knew how badly I wanted a family! She knew how badly I wanted a place to cast my anchor and feel at home. She knew that she was my answer, and my end—the end of my drifting, destructive existence.

We intended to create and nurture life, when all we'd both known was destruction. We wanted to make a change: to be human and happy. She ruined it all! She ruined it all, and this is my long awaited vengeance. So yes, I will now kill General Visola Ramaris. I am bound to her through our marriage, so I accept that with her death, I will slay a part of myself. Nevertheless, it must be done. Forgive me—if there is anyone who has the power or jurisdiction to do so, I ask your forgiveness in advance. My dead mother, or any possible gods who preside... Sedna, the Inuit goddess that Visola so respects. Please, forgive what I'm about to do.

He adjusted his grip once more, turning to stare into the dark silver of the metal. He saw his own grey eyes reflected back in them, distorted and stretched. He closed them briefly, unable to look at himself. He imagined the strike before he delivered it. It was the correct procedure—to think about something carefully and picture doing it several times before following through with the motion. Especially when the decision being made was such a large one. He knew that he did not really have to make the decision. His job was to follow orders, and his orders were to kill the girl. He could empty his mind of conscience, and just allow himself to be the tool guided by another. Yes, that is how he would find the resolve. He would cast aside his personal feelings and become a weapon.

Visola, please forgive me for betraying your trust. You should have known better than to trust me.

As his arms pulled the sword back in the beginning of a swing, images of Visola flashed through his mind. He remembered her laughter, although it had been a considerable fraction of an eternity since he had heard the sound. He remembered her green eyes glistening in the sunlight, her body moving under his as they made love. He remembered her whispered words, her strong hands clinging around his neck. More laughter. He remembered her sternness, and her hard voice reprimanding him. He remembered the gracefulness with which she moved in battle—like liquid flesh. There was no one quite like his wife, and he never felt more triumphant and free than when he was in her company.

The sword quivered for a millisecond in his sturdy, battle-worn hands. How could he kill the most alive person he knew? It was an insult to the world, and an insult to all of nature. Visola's spirit was a masterpiece of creation; he loved the way that it was always in perfect harmony with her body whenever she moved, and the way that she never could subdue it, even when she was trying to remain expressionless and silent. He could never conquer her—he knew that. He could also never destroy her, despite being the Destroyer of

Kingdoms.

Now, he would strike down upon her neck, in one violent, powerful strike. It would sever her head from her body, and her life would pour out in her blood. He would steal her breath, and smother her life, but he could never truly extinguish her flame. She was one kingdom that could never be destroyed. This was the thought which reassured him, and returned the strength to his hands. The words and thoughts dancing through his mind were empty and emotionless. Their purpose had been to prolong the inevitable, but now it was time. Vachlan steadied himself, and looked at his target: her slender neck. He could not look. He did something he had never done before when about to kill. He averted his eyes from his victim. He could not face how dishonorable his impending strike would be. He just had to get this over with.

Vachlan clenched the muscles in his arms, and drew the weapon back for momentum. He exhaled as he swung it downward in a firm, true strike to sever the head of his wife. He closed his eyes tightly and waited for impact. He knew how it would feel, and he braced himself. A feeling of horror coursed through his gut, and he felt an overwhelming bout of nausea. The impact came. His eyes shot open and he froze. He breathed a few staggering breaths. He had expected to feel the force of her life leaving her body through the blade. A clean cut. Skin, flesh, veins, bone, soul. The impact which he felt, however, was completely different from what he had expected. Abrupt. Metal.

Visola ripped her eyes open, feeling pain shoot through her arms as the full force of Vachlan's blow was absorbed by the shackles on her crossed wrists. Having heard the sound of metal whizzing through the air, she had reflexively moved her hands into a blocking position. Dazed, she stared at the clashed metal for several seconds before her eyes followed along the long blade to its wielder. She saw that Vachlan's head was turned away, and she could not register what had happened. Her mind replayed the jarring sound of metal against metal—she felt her clenched fists tightly pressed against her jawbone. She was not even sure that she was completely awake. She had been dreaming deeply only seconds ago, and the dreams still lingered, casting a haze over reality.

When Vachlan turned to look at her, he seemed more surprised than she was. Her stomach sank and she understood what had happened. She felt betrayal wash over her. It drained her strength. She pushed his sword away from her neck, and rubbed her sore wrists. She could not reconcile why this had happened; had she not gone to bed thinking that she could trust him? Had he not shielded her from Zalcan? Of course—because she was *his* special toy to abuse, and he would not allow anyone else to share in his amusement. It had been jealousy! Pure jealousy between competing men, having nothing to do with her whatsoever. It had not been the well-meaning, loving kind of protection.

Why did she feel betrayed? Why had she expected more? He had killed Corallyn. He had brutally dissected Corallyn, like a soulless beast. No, not even a beast! Animals killed to eat or to protect themselves. Only brutes killed for pleasure, and only thugs killed the harmless innocent. Of course he was not on her side! She had been a fool to believe that—thank heavens that her body was not as quick to trust as her mind. Her body had remained apprehensive and on guard, even while her mind had decided to relax. She sent a little prayer of gratitude to her father for training her so well, and for developing her instincts beyond even her own comprehension. She felt a little rush of victory, as though she had passed some great test.

Vachlan stood frozen solid, as a bead of perspiration trickled down the side of his face. As he stared at Visola's expression, hungrily inspecting her animated eyes, the dread that had paralyzed him slowly receded back to its distant corner. He breathed out, without realizing he had been holding it in, and the air came out in a rush, a sigh...

Of relief.

Vachlan tossed his sword aside, and it clattered noisily to the floor. He fell to his knees at Visola's bedside, grasping her shackled, bandaged hands. He could not bear her tormented stare, and he bowed his head, resting his face on her hands. He shut his eyes tightly as clarity came to him in patchwork flickers, and he realized how unhinged his emotions and behavior were. He was losing touch with reality, and he was losing command of his own actions and thoughts. He was filled with regret and despair. He did not even know what he wanted anymore; he did not know what was right and wrong. His whole body trembled with the weight of his emotions, shaking under the force of a sob.

"Viso," he said, his voice breaking. He was sobbing, but it was muffled against her hands. "What have I done to you? God, I don't know what I'm doing."

Visola felt the moisture of his tears sliding over her wrists. They coated the narrow space between her bandages and her shackles. She tried to resist the instant wave of pity and love that afflicted her, but she was powerless at the sight of his suffering. She realized that she was witnessing a phenomenon that no one alive had ever seen. Vachlan never cried. He never felt remorse. Words swam through her mind again. *You reach your limit when surrounded by truth! It crushes you, it crushes your bones. The pressure is too heavy, and the darkness too obscure. It is also cold. You cannot go any further.* Visola blinked the confusing words away, and tried to focus on the even more confusing situation unfolding before her. She watched her husband's shoulders shuddering involuntarily.

Seeing that he was inconsolable naturally aroused her maternal, or perhaps wifely instinct to console him. She slid closer to him on the cot, and touched her head to his. She kissed his temple, and kissed his wet cheek. The moment her skin brushed against his moist warmth, she forgot everything but the desire to be close to him. There was sense and rationality in this touch. Hundreds of years of lost love and longing were kindled in the uncertain connection of her lips against his cheek.

Vachlan's disbelief at Visola's tenderness quickly turned into desperation as he turned his face into hers, pressing his lips against her chin. His tears soaked her skin as they tumbled off his lashes, and he found himself seeking her mouth. He pressed his lips against hers hungrily, pulling her bottom lip into his mouth, and running his tongue over her skin. It had been so long since he had tasted her. His mind seemed to shut down as he lost himself in the passionate pressure, as their clammy lips smashed together. Their kiss was pleading and parched, but quickly being flooded by a monsoon.

There was so much wetness that it was several minutes before Visola realized that she was crying too. She was so transfixed on his mouth that she had been unaware of the potency of her own need, disintegrating her mental fortresses like acid. She awkwardly put her arms around him, trying to untangle herself from the chains. With her kiss, she tried to communicate everything that she had been inhibiting herself from explaining for weeks. *Understand me,* she begged with her touch, and her tears, *please understand me.*

He pulled away from her abruptly. He looked at her tear-streaked face with amazement.

"I'm setting you free," he said, fumbling for the keys at his waistband. He seemed dizzy, lost, and uncomfortable with his surroundings. "You have to get out of here." He moved to unlock her shackles, but she pulled her hands away from him.

"No," she whispered hoarsely. It was the first time she had spoken in weeks, and she was surprised at the sound of her own voice. "No."

"Visola, please," he said brokenly, as he tried to grasp her hands to remove the chains. "You have to get away from me. I can't hurt you anymore."

"It hurts more to be away from you," she said softly. Her tears were blinding her until she could not see, although she furiously tried to blink them away. "If I go, then I'll never see you again."

"I am a curse in your life," he told her as he wrestled her for the handcuffs. She twisted away and put her hands beneath her so that he could not reach them. "Viso, you need to go. Leave Zimovia and never look back. Go *now*."

"I don't want to go," she whispered. A small smile came to her lips. "I can't get very far on this leg anyway. Listen, Vachlan. I would rather stay as your prisoner than live apart from you again. There's nowhere else I'd rather be than right *here*."

Vachlan gently ran his fingers through her tangled red hair. Grasping the back of her head, he pressed his lips against her forehead firmly. It felt strangely to her like a kiss of promise.

"Well, there are many places *I'd* rather be," he said. He stood up, and headed for the door.

"Vachlan, don't go. No!" she called out weakly. "Vachlan!"

He was already gone. Visola bit her lip, pounding her chained wrists into the jagged rock wall beside her. She groaned at the pain in her sore, swollen hands. She hoped that he would return.

Chapter 25: Letter of Resignation

Thick, rough fingers dug into her injured knee, jolting Visola awake. Her first reaction was surprise that Vachlan had begun torturing her again. Then she realized that those thin fingers with sharp fingernails did not feel like Vachlan's hands, and those eerie, shallow gasps did not sound like his breathing—she opened her eyes and lifted her head to view her attacker. It was a strange man whom she did not recognize. He had dark brown skin, and was probably of Indian descent. Visola fixed the man with her most intimidating glare.

"Such pretty green eyes," the Indian man remarked, in the feminine voice Visola had heard before. "Why would he ever put a blindfold on those?"

He tightened his grip, increasing the brutal pressure on her knee, and Visola tried to pull her leg away from him. She looked around for Vachlan, and was alarmed to see that he was still not in the room. Where had he gone? Her first fear was that something had happened to him. Had he been punished or harmed for failing to carry out orders and kill her? Her second fear was that he had abandoned her. The panic which suffused her had plenty of historical evidence to justify flourishing in her chest. Her pulse began to quicken. She had shared a sweet emotional moment with Vachlan. He had considered it a sign of his weakness, and he had gone running.

"Are you looking for your husband?" Prince Zalcan asked, putting his face close to hers. "Vachlan left on important business. He said I could enjoy you as much as I liked."

"Is that so?" Visola asked, recoiling at the heavy stench of whiskey on the man's breath. She realized that she had begun hyperventilating, and she tried to regain her composure. She could outsmart this slip of a boy.

"We haven't been properly introduced," the man said with a sleazy smile. "I am Prince Zalcan Hamnil from the Maldives, heir to the Clan of Zalcan."

"I'm General Visola Ramaris, also known as the woman who's going to kill you."

He laughed, a high pitched and annoying sound, especially at close range. "Have you noticed your handcuffs? I don't think that's likely."

"You don't know me very well," Visola said. "I always make good on my promises. Do you want to know how I would like to kill you? With acid. I would like to drown you in acid—pinching your nose while slowly pouring it into your mouth until you inhaled it, letting it fill your lungs. Can you imagine how it would feel to have acid eating away at your lungs?"

"You have quite the imagination," Zalcan said, with a snigger. "That's never going to happen. Let me tell you what is going to happen—I'm going to pound you raw. Vachlan says you're a great lay, so I'm here to try you."

"Try me?" she asked, stalling for time. "Am I an article of clothing, or a gourmet dish?"

"You're a woman—a scared helpless animal who exists only for my enjoyment."

Visola chuckled. "You really think you're more masculine than I am, Ladybug?"

"You doubt my masculinity?" he whispered as he reached down and began to undo his pants. "Let me demonstrate the extent of my manhood."

"Sure," Visola said with a smile. "Put it in my mouth. My teeth aren't that sharp, I promise." She ran her tongue over her incisors, with a malicious look in her eyes.

"Thank you for the offer, but I don't take orders from

commoners. I will choose exactly where to put my…"

"Listen, Hamnil—may I call you Hamnil?"

"No. You must address me as Prince Zalc... *ow!"*

Visola had used her shackled wrists to deliver a blow to his head. She cursed when it was not strong enough to knock him unconscious.

"That hurt!" he squealed, as he fell away from her cot. He rolled up into a ball on the floor, clutching his head. He whined loudly. "You bitch!"

Visola groaned. "I really doubt that anyone, in any part of the world would consider you masculine. That's perfectly fine and you don't have to prove anything to any…"

"Vachlan said you were broken!"

"He broke my heart once," Visola said, with a melodramatic melancholy. She smiled at her attacker. "Want to hear about it? I'm in the mood for some girl-talk, and maybe if you have any ice cream or chocolate…"

"I have a better idea," the prince said, grabbing a nearby baton, and aiming it at Visola's arm.

Prickly icicles of electricity ran through Visola's body for several seconds when the prince fired the weapon. When he removed it, after what had felt like an eternity, she was vastly weakened. The pulsing contractions of her muscles continued without her permission. Although she fought to regain control of her mobility, her body refused to follow instructions. She knew that her adversary had gained the upper hand. Her eyes rolled to look toward the room's entryway, praying for Vachlan to return. Had he really abandoned her? Had he done this *again?*

"Poor little redhead," Zalcan said with a grin. "All paralyzed and nowhere to go. Want another taste?" He fired the weapon at her again, and again, until Visola was completely incapacitated and blinded. He prodded her with the baton, laughing gleefully. "Where are your smart remarks now? Would you like me to put this in your mouth? I wonder how much it will hurt if I shock your sassy tongue!"

Visola could not even reply to tell him that she truly believed another one of those shocks would kill her. There was a great plummeting feeling in her chest, and she wondered if her heart was failing. As she struggled with the disruption of her body's basic maneuvers, the cot squeaked under her. Zalcan had climbed back on top of her, and was returning to his initial intended undertaking.

"It does take some of the fun out of things now that you are a lifeless doll," he said to her with a frown as he slid her dress up around her waist. "Can you still scream? Please try. I really want to hear you scream as I do this."

Visola tried to fight her dizziness and move her frozen lips. Her tongue felt heavy and awkward, as if she were trying to push a boulder around in her mouth. Her thoughts went hopelessly to Vachlan. *I can't believe he left me here with this man. All because of a kiss? I thought he cared... he acted like he cared. Didn't he? I swear it wasn't my imagination. I should have learned by now not to ever try to interpret a man's actions or his words. They are never good indicators of their thoughts or decisions, because men think much later, long after they have spoken or acted. Damn you, Vachlan!* Visola felt an overwhelming sense of helplessness and despair that was only partly due to her paralysis. *You always leave me when I need you the most.*

"You really are unable to speak!" Zalcan said with a smile. "I didn't realize how powerful the electricity would be. You're totally vulnerable now—it's highly amusing. Vachlan has the best toys lying around, doesn't he? Let's see if the tiles match the tapestries!"

Never in her life had Visola wanted to hurt someone more than when Zalcan began pulling off her panties. He giggled when she was exposed, and commented in delight about how much he liked well-coordinated home furnishings. Visola thought about her husband wretchedly.

"Now you get to feel how much of a man I am," the prince said with a sneer, as he positioned himself over her.

"The way I showed that little bitch Corallyn before I chopped her up."

Visola felt tears come to her eyes, and she emitted a sound that was half-gasp, half-laugh. Vachlan had not killed Corallyn. Vachlan had not been the one who killed Corallyn! This revelation left her in such a bizarre combination of crying and laughing that she seemed hysterical. She had known it all along, deep down. She had known that her husband was good, and not capable of the things that he had been blamed for. He was puppet whose strings were being pulled by others. She felt vindicated to have Vachlan's character somewhat restored in her mind. When she had believed that Vachlan had done wrong, she had believed herself a fool for loving him. Now, she knew that it was not true.

"Vachlan," she managed to whisper, although the word sounded like it was being filtered through molasses. Her tongue had still not regained full functionality, but her vision was returning. So he had not killed Corallyn, but he had allowed it to happen—just as he would not be the one to rape and kill her, but he would allow it to happen. He had abandoned her, but still she only felt love for him.

"So you can speak?" Zalcan said with delight. He slapped Visola in the face. "Don't say *his* name! Say mine, and I want you to scream it for me. Do it!"

When he slapped her again, Visola felt the pressure of something against her gum. There it was—a final, forlorn idea. If she could move her tongue enough to get to the pill, she should be able to crush it with her teeth. She was going to lose this fight, but she did not have to stick around and watch.

What she would have said if she had been in a wisecracking mood was, *Hey Hamnil. How do you feel about necrophilia?* He would have displayed confusion or surprise, and she would have responded, *Well, you're about to find out,* before crushing and swallowing the pill. Then she would

244

have felt at least a millisecond of smugness before she died, and he would have understood her meaning from context.

However, Visola was not in a wisecracking mood; she was feeling rather miserable and broken. So when Zalcan nudged her knees apart with deranged excitement, and when she felt the sickening moisture of his dangling, offensive organ against her thigh, she made her decision. Visola quickly moved her tongue to dislodge the pill from the corner where she kept it, and she positioned it between her molars. *Thank you, Sionna,* she thought to herself as she gripped the rubber capsule. *I hope you can feel when I'm gone—I know you'll take care of everyone. You are worth fifty of me.*

She bit down tentatively on the thick casing of the pill, feeling it give way and testing its flexibility. The moment before Zalcan could defile her, she clenched her jaw and...

Visola froze in surprise as something collided with Zalcan's head, knocking him into the wall. She saw a massive arm reach out and grab Zalcan by the hair, hauling him away from her. She managed to turn her head just enough to see her husband swinging a spiked club with all of his force.

"You little nancy bugger!" Vachlan bellowed. "I was only gone for five minutes, and you..."

Stuttering with incoherent rage, Vachlan continued to bludgeon his employer in the head with his mace until Zalcan's face was a ghastly, bloody mess. The Indian man's body was soon as limp and lifeless as the ground upon which it lay. Zalcan had become one of his well-coordinated room furnishings, for a bloodied corpse went well with a dank, abandoned mineshaft, at least in Visola's opinion. She probably should have cringed at this gruesome sight, but instead she was filled with a wave of deep contentment. Vachlan had not abandoned her.

"Spit it out," Vachlan said, turning toward her and holding out his hand. He must have seen when her tongue had worked to remove the pill from the corner of her mouth. Visola hesitated, but Vachlan was already reaching into her mouth and extracting the pill.

"That's mine," she complained.

"You had this the whole time?" he asked angrily, brandishing the warm rubber capsule in front of her face. Its shape suddenly reminded Visola of a miniature football. Vachlan flung the pill across the room, into a pile of junk. "No wonder your sister kissed you on the mouth. She even gave you a lecture on how to use the damn thing right in front of me. How stupid could I be?"

Vachlan tossed his bloody mace aside. He reached down to pull Visola's dress back over her hips. Once she was decent, he began unlocking her from her chains. He moved quickly, fueled by anger. When her wrists and ankles were free, he pulled her into his arms. He held her against him as protectively as a tiger would guard its young from a predator. Visola closed her eyes and rested against his chest, wondering how he knew that she needed to be held so badly just then. *You didn't abandon me.* The love she felt in his embrace seemed to infuse her muscles and coax them out of paralysis. *You came back for me.* She wanted to thank him out loud, and tell him how thankful she was.

"Nancy bugger?" she asked softly instead, with a light teasing tone in her voice.

Vachlan smiled, and squeezed her shoulder reassuringly, as if he understood what she really had meant to say. "Visola, my darling, how about a little gratitude for saving you from violation?"

"No, I appreciate it, I really do—but couldn't you have said something a little more heroic while saving me?" The truth was that she could not really imagine anything more heroic. She also could not have hoped for more conclusive proof of his allegiance.

"As you well know, during the spontaneous and transient act of passionate murder, it is extremely challenging to think of the ideal words to say. You must forgive me if the first phrases which spring to mind aren't trendy American insults."

Visola squinted an eye open to glance down at the man on the floor. She grimaced. "What do you think Emperor Zalcan is going to say about the modifications you made to his son's face?"

"I hope he'll consider it an eloquent letter of resignation." They smiled at each other. Vachlan laid Visola out on the cot, and began moving around the room. "I need to get you home," he said. He indicated a large waterproof case to her. "I was gathering supplies while you slept."

"You can't," she told him, surprised with how thoughtful he was. He had been planning their escape, even if this situation with Zalcan had not happened. She felt anxiety seize her. "If you go anywhere near Adlivun, they'll kill you."

"I need to take you somewhere safe."

Visola watched his lips move as they spoke those words. Her eyes narrowed as she searched her memory. She was almost sure she had heard him say that exact phrase once before. An overpowering feeling of déjà vu hung in the air; it was strange but comforting. She tried to shake off the intangible sensations and return to reality. Visola needed to compensate for weeks of silent anger.

"Why didn't you tell me that you didn't kill Corallyn?" she asked him furiously. "All this time I believed…"

"What? She was just a child! What kind of a monster do you think I am?" he asked her. He seemed equally upset furious. "Are you insane, Visola? How could you believe I would do something like that?"

"How could *you* believe that I would cheat on you!" she shot back, grabbing and throwing the nearest object she could find at him.

He froze, and the pair of pliers hit him squarely in the chest. He stared at her, unblinking. "You didn't…"

"Of course not!"

He crossed the room and returned to her—she had fallen off the cot in her effort to reach for something to throw at him. He wrapped his arms around her, burying his face in her hair. "God, Viso…"

"Two hundred years. Two hundred years!" she shouted against his chest. "Don't even touch me, you… you fucktard!"

"I'm a… what?"

She pushed him away halfheartedly so that she could punch him in the face wholeheartedly. Her already-broken fingers exploded in pain. "Shit," she cursed, shaking her hand.

"Relax," he told her with a smile, rubbing his jaw. "Once you're better, I promise you can abuse me all you like."

"Don't ever forget that you said that," she said sternly, pointing a bandaged finger at him. She waggled her finger menacingly. "Now what the hell are we going to do?"

"Let's get out of here," he said, taking her hand. "I'm going to get you to Adlivun."

The name of her home had never sounded sweeter to Visola. It was impossible. She shook her head. "Your men will come after us. We won't get very far."

"We'll fight."

"I'm useless. I'll just hold you back," she said, giving him a sad smile. "You have to escape without me."

"I'm not going anywhere without you. Not ever again."

"Romance—how lovely," she said, rolling her eyes. "No time for that. Focus on getting out of here alive."

"I have a plan," he said. "We're both going to make it. There are guards stationed everywhere in Zimovia Strait, except to the west, across the mountains and ice."

"Mountains and ice?"

"It's the only direction from which we couldn't be attacked, so I didn't station guards there. Maybe I was subconsciously leaving an escape route."

"This might surprise you, but I have a broken knee. Can't do mountains."

"It's fine—I can carry you. Maybe I was subconsciously starving you to make you lighter."

Visola saw the twinkle in his eye. She pouted. "Hey! You thought I was fat?"

"It doesn't matter now—I've fixed the problem," he said with a drawl, putting his hands on her bony ribcage. He moved his face close to hers and spoke in a comically sultry voice. "You know how much I like my women anorexic and dying."

She smiled at his sexy sarcasm. "Well then, let's get going—wait! I have a plan too. Let's leave a note. You will have to write it for me."

Vachlan began looking around for a piece of paper before grabbing a fancy pen that was lying nearby. He dipped it into the blood pooling in Zalcan's eye socket, and lifted the pen, poised and ready to write.

She stared at the paper, still curious to see if he would write in the same fancy handwriting of Corallyn's ransom note. She remembered his handwriting, but so much time had passed that she could not be sure. "Prisoner escaped. Gone after her," Visola began narrating. When Vachlan penned the words, she was relieved to see that his handwriting was a messy, manly scrawl. It was not elegant calligraphy. She knew who had written the note. "Will return shortly," she continued narrating. "Load all men up into ships and await my return to command an attack on Adlivun."

Chapter 26: Conversations on Ice

"What does she look like?" Vachlan asked sleepily.

They had escaped from Zimovia, and traveled west for as long as possible before pitching their tent. Visola remained quiet for some time before responding. "I see her every time I look at you."

"With your red hair, I hope?"

"Yes. Well, she used to have red hair when she was a girl."

"Isn't she still a girl? A teenager at most."

"She is a very old woman. Her life is almost over. She has two grown sons."

"What? Wait—this is too much information. Our daughter lived on land? I'm a grandfather?"

"Please, Vachlan. I wished for so long that you would return, and you didn't. Now that we're here, and this is happening… it just all seems so unreal, and far too late."

"Viso…"

"Please. No more questions tonight. It's too bittersweet. I need to rest."

*   *   *

Visola was curled up in her corner of the tiny space. She stared at Vachlan's back as she played with a small knife. Her leg was probably well enough to walk on for a few miles, but she did not think he deserved to know this. No, he would have to keep on carrying her until they reached a city.

"Are you thinking about killing me?" Vachlan asked gruffly. He yawned and stretched, having just awoken.

"Yep," Visola said in a chipper tone as she toyed with spinning the dagger between them. Occasionally it would point west at him, and occasionally it would point east toward her. Occasionally it would point north or south at neither of them. Continuously, when it stopped, she would consider what it meant with respect to fate, and whether fate was guiding her to take action, or to just continue being useless. A voice teased her internally. *You have never gone beneath the truth. You cannot navigate the endless fathoms of forgiveness.* She was reminded of the fact that she had felt somewhat comfortable and safe when Vachlan had been her clear-cut, straightforward enemy, and now that he was showing her tenderness she was becoming increasingly confused.

"So why don't you just do it?"

"Need you to carry me around. Can't move on my own—leg smashed."

"Then once I get you home?"

"Sticking you in an oven and cooking you up with some salt and pepper. Having a scrumptious feast—eating your testicles first."

"You can't cook, Viso."

"That's true," she said. She sighed, reaching up and began to trace patterns in the fabric of the tent. "To be perfectly honest, what I'm actually considering is divorce."

He sat up abruptly, his head hitting the small tent and making it shake. "That's impossible. There's no such thing for sea-dwellers."

"I was wondering if you'd get pissed about it. How delightful; your voice rose a whole decibel in volume."

"How could you even *consider* divorce after all we've been through?"

"You mean after the torture, and more torture, followed by more torture?"

"Viso..."

"Or the whole you never having met your daughter, or

maybe you attacking…"

"You have to stop listing my indiscretions."

"Indiscretions!"

"That was a poor choice of wording…"

"Look, Vachlan. I only said I was considering a divorce. I haven't decided yet. I spent some time on land. Everything moves faster there—even ideas are more progressive. I learned that marriage doesn't have to last forever. It's not the end of the world to make a mistake."

He reached out and took her hand. "Visola, I'm willing to spend the rest of my life proving to you that I wasn't a mistake. Please stop thinking about this now—we are sea-dwellers. We are different people…"

"No, we're not. We're just people. The way we work deep on the inside, and the way we connect with others, or rather, the way that we don't connect with others—it's all the same. On land or sea, people are the same."

"Well, if you do decide that you want a divorce, don't tell me."

"Why not? You will probably have to agree. There will probably be some ceremony or some signing of papers or something."

"No. I will never agree to that. Our marriage ends with death, Visola." He reached out and grabbed her fur-covered shoulder.

She could feel the strength of his grip even through the thick layers. She turned and looked at the large hand on her joint, and she could not deny that even as he smashed her skin and muscle, the pressure was soothing. "You're the one who left," she said softly. "You ended our marriage with absence."

"Now I want to begin it again with presence."

"Don't make a fool of me, Vachlan," she begged. "History repeats itself and people don't change. You know you still have the power to hurt me like no one else on earth ever has, or ever will. I can't go through this again.

"It was King Kyrosed's fault... he convinced me that you and he had..."

"No," she whispered, pushing his hand away from her shoulder. "How could you even believe that? That's absurd, and you know it's absurd. If Kyrosed had ever tried to touch me I could have killed him with my eyes closed—with one finger, or even with one toe..."

"I know, Viso, I know... I was just so in love with you, and the jealousy killed me!"

"Like Othello," Visola said with a sad smile. She reached out and placed her hand on her husband's stomach. "I'm not some weak, trusting girl that you can wreck just because someone planted an idea in your head. I'm the general of an army, and I'm your equal, your match, your counterpart. I could destroy the world for a price just like you, if I was so inclined. I watched everything you did, and I learned from you. I could hurt you too. You know this, don't you?"

When he nodded, she continued. "Then please understand if I need a divorce for the sake of my soul. I am a lot like you, but I don't want to become any more like you. So let me think about this and make my decision."

"I won't allow you to even consider that, Visola," he said, turning to look at her fiercely. He leaned over her, and crushed his lips to hers in a demanding kiss. He allowed the determination in his touch to speak for him for several minutes, as he hungrily kissed her. When he withdrew, he could see that her cheeks were flushed to match her hair and eyebrows. "We are going to be together from now on. Viso. Like we used to be."

She had returned his kiss, but she toiled not to allow the abundance of happy, tingly feelings which had been generated inside of her to cloud her judgment. "I'll let you know what I decide," she told him. Her voice faltered slightly in the giddy, scatterbrained wake of his kiss. "I really think divorce could be a positive thing for both of us."

He ripped himself away from her angrily, and began to pack up their supplies. "Just kill me if you decide that you don't want me anymore. What is there left for me in this world if not for you? What is the point anymore? Do you know how much gold, money, and diamonds I have? Do you know how many safety deposit boxes, in how many banks, in how many different countries? How many identities, how many properties, how many passports, how many…"

"Shh," Visola said, carefully raising herself to a seated position. "Don't be silly. I would never hurt you."

"Then, if you decide you want your divorce, just ask your sister or Aazuria to kill me. I am sure they will do it without a second's hesitation—they will do it before you can even finish nodding to give them permission to do so."

"You're still a barrel of piranhas," she whispered. "You're the love of my life and the father of my child, but you already gnawed all my flesh off once. I don't know about you, but I really hate being eaten alive. I prefer to eat than to be eaten—speaking of which, can you hunt some breakfast, V?"

*   *   *

"Mind if we take a break? We're not being followed," Vachlan said, panting slightly to catch his breath. He readjusted Visola in his arms.

"No, we can't stop. Keep moving, and pick up the pace. You're the one who smashed my knee, so why don't you reflect on your actions while you carry me."

"I guess being a wife is like riding a bicycle."

"Are you implying that I'm nagging? You broke my fucking knee, Vachlan!"

"Sound has been coming out of your mouth for two days and I'm already sick of it. Can you please return to giving me the silent treatment?"

She clamped her lips shut obediently.

"Visola?" he asked, as he continued walking and panting. He looked down at her. "Viso, why aren't you talking? I was just kidding. Please don't give me the silent treatment again."

*   *   *

By the time they had pitched their tent for a second time, they were already familiar enough with each other that they felt like no time had passed since they had last spoken. They really were exactly the same people they had always been.

"Vachlan, tell me something," Visola said with a smile. "It's been bugging me for, like, hundreds of years. The night we met—did you really *not* have sex with me?"

He smiled, and turned to face her. He placed his face very close to hers, allowing the corner of his lips to brush her cheek. "Am I not a gentleman, Visola?" he asked, his breath and voice tickling her ear.

She closed her eyes at the butterfly-like sensation. "That depends. Would a gentleman have broken my kneecap with a pickaxe?"

"I suppose not."

"Would a gentleman have literally crucified me?"

"Well... I sanitized the nails first."

"So we did have sex that night?"

"You've asked me this about a million times. I'm still insulted that you don't remember."

"Are you ever going to tell me?"

"If I told you I would lose my mystery and charisma. You wouldn't find me so enigmatic."

"Vachlan... you conquered half of the world. Twice. Once for the Emperor of Bimini, and now for Emperor Zalcan. I think that pretty much gives you infinite enigmatic-points, so don't worry about that."

"Yes. But conquering half the world—half of the

undersea world—twice, does not equal conquering the whole world," Vachlan said, with a little bit of disappointment.

"Good Sedna, you don't really want to do that, do you?" she asked him, hitting him in the arm.

He gave her a small shrug, and rolled away from her onto his back. "What else is there for me to do? I've already proved that I can't be a successful writer." He stared up at the tent thoughtfully.

"Vachlan," she asked quietly. "You conquered the Rusalka. You could have come at us from both sides. You have access to huge military resources. You could have conquered Adlivun by now, but you didn't. Why did you spare us?"

He sighed, reaching down to take her hand. "I sent the Emperor's forces to go south from Russia and conquer Kerys in France. I convinced them that Adlivun would be easy to take, and that we should focus on expanding into the Atlantic. I have the whole European underworld fighting amongst itself right now to take the focus off Adlivun. I don't even really know why I did that."

"He's calling enough troops to defeat fifty thousand warriors," Visola said. "We can't even defeat the troops currently stationed in Zimovia, and you want to make it harder for us?"

"Time is precious. I wanted to give us time," he said. "I told the Prince that you and Aazuria were the main defense of Adlivun; that together, you two were the reason that it had never fallen. I told him that if we removed one of you, that Adlivun would be defenseless, and that I thought you were a bigger asset because you were the general. I think I really just wanted to get you out of Adlivun in case we really did wage war on it and destroy your home."

Visola listened to him curiously. "You summoned me to protect me?" she asked in confusion. Had he really been on her side all along? She cleared her throat. "But you intended to attack Adlivun all along. Did you... did you make it easier for me to defeat Atargatis? I heard that it was under your authority to throw everything at me at once, but you chose to 'test the waters.' Did you do that on purpose to give me a chance?"

He did not respond.

"Vachlan?"

"I guess I did sabotage her, and I did expect her to fail. I did intend for her to fail." He paused. "Viso, there's something you need to understand. Even if we defeat the troops in Zimovia, and even if we manage to stand after that... it's all futile. Emperor Zalcan's mission isn't to conquer Adlivun. He's trying to conquer the world. He's moving towards having his dominion of the sea recognized by all the major governments on land. It's eventually going to happen. He's going to join the UN, have defense coalitions with the governments..."

Visola frowned. "That's unheard of. That goes against the sea-dweller tenets."

"I know, but it's brilliant. The Emperor wants all of the oceans to be recognized as one country of which he is the leader. He wants Aboriginal rights to all international waters."

"I see," Visola said, "because we're the indigenous population..."

"It will change the economy of the world forever."

"Why do you say that it 'will?' Don't you think we can stop him? We have you now, and you know exactly what's happening."

"I can't stop him. He's been planning this for centuries. He has sea-dwellers stationed on land in the parliaments and senates of all major countries. Emperor Zalcan's got it in the bag."

"So why on earth would you abandon the winning team to join the underdog so late in the game?"

"Why do you think?" he asked her, reaching out and tucking her hair behind her ear.

She looked at him crossly. "Don't take me for a fool, Vachlan. I know that you're not doing this for me. You had a place cemented for yourself in the new world order, and you don't just give that up for some dumb broad from your past..."

"Hey, watch your language! That's my wife you're talking about."

Visola made a face at him. "Tell me; is this part of the game too? You helping me escape? Is this some strategic move planned by you and your emperor?"

"No. I want you."

"Don't exaggerate what I mean to you."

"I'm not. I'll prove that eventually," he insisted. "If you want to know the truth, I do have a plan. I've thought about it, and there is a way we could repel the Clan of Zalcan's forces."

"Tell me. We'll discuss it with Aazuria as soon as we can."

"If she lets me live," Vachlan said with a smile. "My plan capitalizes on one basic truth: Adlivun is in Alaska."

"Well, I suppose that if you want to be technical..."

"No, listen to me Visola. Adlivun is in Alaska. We go to Aazuria, and together we go to the American government. We ask *them* for protection."

"The American government?" Visola asked, with a chuckle. "You're out of your mind. Aazuria will never agree to that. What will they want from us in return?"

"Then we go to Russia. Adlivun used to be in Russia until 1867 before they sold it to the Americans. If that doesn't work, we go to Canada. There is a way, and we will find it."

"Does Canada even have an army?" Visola asked with a frown.

Vachlan shrugged. "I'm not too sure. I think they should."

"Begging," Visola remarked. "So this is what we are

reduced to. You want us to beg the land-dwellers for help."

"It's not begging, it's asking a neighbor for protection. They exploited the Aleutian people above the surface, they exploited the Inuit—they should understand why we remained hidden from him for so long. If they want some kind of... I don't know, official merger, or if they want us to pay for the military support, we'll negotiate all that."

"And then our privacy is gone? Then we become national news? A tourist destination? Farewell sovereignty?"

"I don't know what will happen. It's just a suggestion of the only thing that I think will work. It's the only thing that I think will keep us alive, Viso."

She turned her back on him. Her mind was racing so much that she knew she would be unable to sleep, and her eyes were stretched wide open as though she had been injected with caffeine. It occurred to her that all of Adlivun had been completely innocent to what was happening in the rest of the undersea world, and Vachlan returning home with all of this knowledge was a blessing in disguise.

"What about Namaka?" she asked him.

"You know about her?" he asked in surprise.

"I had a weird dream. I remembered when you took her from her parents in Australia."

"I just used her to check up on you over the years. You know—if you had ever gotten really sick I would have come and taken care of you, or if you had ever gotten serious about another guy I would have come and slit his throat."

"So romantic, sweetie, really," Visola said teasingly. She was glad that her back was turned to him, because she could not resist smiling. When she felt him move closer to her, and cuddle against her back, she stared down at the arm he had wrapped around her stomach. It felt right, but it still felt uncomfortable. She knew she would miss him far too much when his arm was no longer around her. "Tell me one thing."

"Sure," he answered, as he nestled his chin against her

shoulder.

"Did you love Atargatis?"

He paused in his nestling. "What do you know about her?"

"I only know what she told me herself. I want to hear the rest directly from you."

"Atargatis was stupid. She was not a warrior, she was a ballerina."

"If she was so stupid why did you sleep with her?" Visola asked.

"How did you find out about that?"

"She boasted about it to me," Visola said, grinding her teeth together. "She insinuated that you belonged to her."

"Oh, dear God! She really said that? What a foolish landlubber. Koraline Kolarevic—that innocent country bumpkin." Vachlan began to chuckle. Then he began to laugh harder, until his whole torso shook.

"Why are you laughing?" Visola asked, turning toward him incredulously. "Was she lying?"

"No—she and I had a thing. Visola, please tell me you killed the poor girl quickly."

"The words were barely out of her mouth before her life ended. Vachlan! How can you laugh about this? Do you laugh about the death of all of your women?"

"If she was bragging to you and acting like she and I had anything beyond the occasional tryst, then she deserved what she got. She knew what you meant to me."

"Fifty years of occasional trysts?" Visola asked angrily.

"Viso..."

She pushed his arm away from her waist and sat up. "I don't feel like sleeping anymore. Let's keep moving. I'll walk." She unzipped the tent and crawled out of it before shakily raising herself to her feet. She tested bending her knee gently before taking a step. There was pain, but it was manageable.

Vachlan exited the tent, after her. "Don't be silly, V.

You can't walk on that leg. Come back and rest with me."
He sighed. "You know that if Atargatis had meant anything
to me, I would not have sacrificed her life by letting her lead
an attack that was doomed from the start. I sent her to
Adlivun knowing that you would slaughter her."

"I know," she said softly, as she tested her leg, walking
in small circles in the snow. "I shouldn't be upset. I may not
have cheated on you when we were together, but obviously
you were gone for a really long time and in recent years I
stopped caring. I never thought I was going to see you again,
so there were other men. There were lots of other men. Lots
and *lots* of other men! So I have no right to be upset."

"Lots?" he asked, frowning. "Who?"

She smiled sweetly. "You'll know when they come
rubbing it in your face and showing off."

Vachlan sighed, knowing quite well that no one would
be doing such a thing. "Viso, what she and I had together…"

"I don't want to hear about it," she said, as she began
walking away through the snow.

"We were united by hate!" he called after her.

"That makes sense!" she shouted back. "Hate gets me
horny all the time."

"Listen to me, Visola. Stop walking and listen for a
second," Vachlan said, chasing after her and grabbing her
shoulders. "Atargatis hated Kyrosed because he stole her
daughter. I hated Kyrosed because I thought he stole you.
We spent all our time together fantasizing about killing
Kyrosed Vellamo."

"And having sex."

"Yes, there was some of that too."

"Fifty years," Visola repeated. It broke her heart to
think about it. "You spent more time with Atargatis than you
did with me!"

"I didn't love her."

"Obviously your ability to hate is stronger than your
ability to love," Visola said bitterly, as she continued limping

away.

*   *   *

"I can't believe you had me carry you for two days when all this time you could walk," Vachlan said, but he was impressed. He had gone back to pack up their tent and supplies, and he had caught up with Visola rather quickly. The two had been walking together for several hours, although Visola occasionally had to pause to rest. He had alternated between carrying her and letting her try to walk on her own for most of the day.

"You call this walking?" Visola asked with a frown. "I call it hobbling. Shambling, at best."

"Still… I really was worried that I had crippled you."

"Ramaris warrior genes," she said cheerfully. "We heal fast. By the way—that whole 'you'll-never-walk-again' bit? Very terrifying. I took mental notes. I'd give it an eight out of ten."

"Eight? And you could do better?" he said with a scowl.

"Yes. Nine out of ten would be breaking both legs. Ten out of ten would be *not* giving the person immediate medical attention, *no*t putting the leg in a brace, and *not* always remembering to keep it elevated."

"Are you calling me transparent?" he asked.

"No, dear. You're completely mystifying."

They smiled at each other, silently acknowledging that through all of their squabbles they were happy to be together and alone again. Even trudging through the wintry fields of snow and ice felt refreshing. Visola sometimes wondered to herself if they sounded like an 'old married couple.' The thought of being anything resembling normal amused her.

"Look at that," Vachlan said, pointing to the horizon. "It looks like we're close to a city."

"About damned time. I would like to talk to some human beings who aren't you."

"You'll quickly find them overrated."

Visola smiled, but there was a sinking feeling in her chest. "Are we going to split up once we hit the town, Vachlan?"

"What? I told you that I wasn't going to ever leave you again."

"I just needed to hear you say it again," she said softly. "If you repeated that once an hour or so, it would really bolster my mental health."

"Silly Viso," he said with a grin. "I'll make a recording for you, and you can play it on a constant loop."

"If only that would make it more accurate," she murmured. She took another step, and her knee began collapsing.

Vachlan caught her before she could hit the snow. "I promise it's true," he told her, as he began carrying her again. "We just have to decide what we're going to do about the men in Zimovia. They're probably going to follow the directions on your note."

"How many are there?"

"About ten thousand men on two dozen ships."

"Do you think we can convince them to join Adlivun?"

"I don't know. They're employed by Emperor Zalcan, but maybe if we showed an impressive display of force and gave them an ultimatum…"

"Impressive display of force," Visola repeated slowly. "Dammit. Fine, dammit."

"I know their numbers are great…"

"No, that's not the problem. As long as it's a navy battle, defeating them isn't going to be that difficult. I'm just concerned that Aazuria will make me clean up the mess afterwards. Diesel from ships, all the crap in the water…"

"Well, if we inform the American government in the near future, I'm sure we can get them to clean up the mess as well."

"Oh. Really? Then we should totally involve them."

Chapter 27: Aazuria Goes Apeshit

"Where are you going, Calzone?" Brynne called out sleepily. "Come back to bed."

"Why do you call me that?" he asked her sadly. "You're always attacking my manhood."

"I'm not," she told him in a seductive voice. "I call you Calzone because you're warm and tasty."

"And you want some of my gooey, meaty goodness?"

"Yeah," she said with a laugh, "so get your tail back here!"

"I'd love to satisfy you ten more times, dollface, but I have to see a man about a mushroom."

"What the hell, Callder?" she asked angrily, grabbing a pillow and throwing at him. "I thought you stopped doing drugs!"

"I did stop!" he insisted, catching the pillow. "I mean an actual mushroom. Trevain asked me to go to the garden and talk with him man-to-man. I figured that since he's always been there for me, I should start being a better brother sometime…"

"That's sweet, Callder. I think you should be a better brother, I really do. But do you really want to listen to one of Trevain's boring speeches about plants? I mean, seriously—he goes on and on, and how important can a mushroom be?" Brynne pouted, and threw the sheets off her naked body. "Who do you think needs you more right now? Your brother or me?"

Callder cleared his throat. "I guess he can wait."

*   *   *

"Where is he?" Trevain asked, pacing back and forth testily.

"It's fine, love," Aazuria said with a tired smile. She was sitting beside her sister on a rock in the garden, and leaning on Elandria's shoulder. "What did you want to tell us?"

"He should be here," Trevain said, crossing his arms across his chest. "He told me he would be here. This is a family matter, and he's..."

"Trevain, sweetie," Alcyone said softly. "Callder is a free spirit. He loves you, but he needs his freedom to be wild. Just let him be. We're all here."

"What about Aunt Sio?" he asked.

"Aazuria is not well, and she needs to rest," Elandria signed. *"Do not worry so, brother. We have plenty of time to make this decision—time moves slowly here."*

Trevain nodded, giving the two women a small smile before turning to Alcyone. "Mom, you know how I was really into botany?"

"Actually, no, sweetie. I missed all of your adulthood, but I do remember your love for toy soldiers. Fill me in."

Aazuria and Elandria both grinned at the mention of toy soldiers, and a small blush crept into Trevain's cheeks. He cleared his throat. "Well, the last time I was in this garden I noticed this strange purple mushroom, and I looked it up when I got home. It's really fascinating—it's called the violet coral."

"The violet coral?" Aazuria repeated softly.

"Yes—it has elements of both Corallyn's name, and my grandmother's name."

"What are you getting at, son?" Alcyone asked.

"Well, fungi are very special. They grow without sunlight, which is why you can cultivate them down here, so far beneath the surface. Instead, they feed off decaying organic matter. They take something negative—death, and they transform it into something positive. They create life from destruction and turn it into something beautiful."

He looked at Aazuria and gave her a sad smile. "So, if it's a girl, I would like to name her Clavaria, after the genus name of this mushroom. In honor of Corallyn and my grandma."

Aazuria felt a wave of grief wash over her as she looked at him. Even though her thoughts hardly left her murdered sister and captured friend, she still felt additional pain at hearing them mentioned out loud. She felt Elandria placing a hand on her completely flat stomach, and she turned to look at her sister. Elandria smiled, with a light in her eyes.

"It feels like it will be a girl!" she signed when she removed her hand. *"That does tend to the trend in our family. Clavaria is a lovely name—do you not think so, Zuri?"*

Aazuria nodded slowly. "We could call her Vari," she whispered. She turned to Trevain, and launched herself off the rock to embrace her husband. "You are the kindest, most thoughtful man I have ever known."

Trevain held her against him, caressing her back with warmth and empathy in his touch. "I'm just lucky that the men you have known have all been murdering rapists."

Aazuria stifled a small chuckle against his chest. "Too soon," she scolded him.

"For shame. For shame!" Alcyone said, rising to her feet. Everyone turned to look at her in surprise. She glared at her son, wiping tears away from her face. "How can you propose to name your unborn child after her as if she is already dead? She is not! She can do anything! You may not have any faith in your mother, young man, but I have faith in mine!"

"Mom, I did not say that I believed she was..."

Alcyone was already storming out of the garden. She ran into Naclana on her way out, and she pushed past him angrily.

"Forgive me," Naclana began apologizing, but Alcyone had already left. He swallowed as he looked after her retreating form. "Well, it's probably better that she didn't hear this."

"Hear what, Naclana?" Aazuria asked.

"Queen Aazuria," Naclana said, saluting across his chest. "I have news for you, but I don't want to upset you."

"Naclana, I am not in the mood for your dallying."

"Please, when I tell you—dear cousin, please be calm."

Aazuria shared a worried look with Trevain, who gripped her arm tightly. Trevain turned to Naclana, and narrowed his eyes. "Tell it straight, man."

"Yes, King Trevain," Naclana said, bowing. "The general has returned... with her demon husband. They are waiting in the great hall."

Before Trevain could react to this, Aazuria's hand had darted to his waist and stolen his sword from its scabbard. She had crossed the room and ducked under Naclana's arm.

"Aazuria!" Trevain shouted. He turned to Elandria. "Damn! Has she always been so fast?"

Elandria nodded as she began to chase after her sister. Trevain followed close on her heels.

*　　　　*　　　　*

When Aazuria entered the room, her eyes were immediately drawn to Visola's wild red hair, which had recently been a lustrous mass of audacious curls. Now, her hair was limp. It hung against her head flat, frizzy and defeated. Aazuria's eyes darted to the warrior's sunken cheekbones and gaunt face. She saw the bruises on Visola's neck before her eyes traveled further to the withered, wasted limbs. Every visible part of her friend's body was covered in fresh scars. She saw the bandaged hands. Visola had been starved and tortured.

Perhaps in these modern times, even under the surface of the sea, kings, queens, and the aristocracy had close to zero significance. Perhaps the words and decrees which left Aazuria's mouth would have minimal consequences. No one in the throne room felt this way as they awaited Aazuria's judgment with bated breath. Sionna was standing aside, with her arms crossed. The newly-crowned queen gripped her husband's sword tightly in her fist as Trevain and Elandria entered the room behind her.

Aazuria shifted her eyes to the man standing beside her friend. Her face was expressionless.

"Approach me, Vachlan," she whispered.

The man began walking toward her. Although his stride was dignified, there was hesitation on his face. Visola began speaking, pleading words which Aazuria could not hear over the sound of her heart pounding in her ears.

When Vachlan was close enough to strike, Aazuria gazed at him with death in her eyes.

"Kneel," she commanded him. Her chest was rising and falling perceptibly.

Vachlan knew that this would be a very unwise thing to do, but he owed it to Aazuria. He owed it to Visola, and to Adlivun—the nation he had once called home. He lowered his head and dropped to one knee before the queen, saluting her across his chest. His eyes were level with the sword she held, and he could see the veins bulging through her translucent pale skin from how tightly she clutched it.

"It would be futile to order you punished," she said slowly. "No one can even attempt to hurt you as much as you have hurt her."

"I know," he answered quietly.

"But it is my duty to try."

She struck out with her sword, slicing the air until the blade collided with his face, knocking Vachlan off his knees and onto the floor. Aazuria could vaguely hear Visola screaming for her to stop, but she was already standing over

Vachlan and forcing the tip of her sword between his teeth. Her previous strike had resulted in a huge bleeding gash along the side of his handsome face, but it had not been enough to kill him. She was poised to finish the job.

Vachlan moved his tongue against the steel, tasting the freshly-sharpened metal edge garnished with the metallic taste of his own blood. *It is rare that the wine so perfectly accompanies the main dish,* he thought as he swallowed the coppery fluid accumulating in his mouth. *Kind of like a German Pinot Noir.* He looked into the azure eyes of Adlivun's queen and realized that this was no longer the innocent, charitable philanthropist he had known hundreds of years ago. She was hard. He wondered what percentage of the tempered rage behind her eyes he was responsible for generating.

"One reason." Aazuria was demanding. "Give me one convincing reason that I should not thrust my blade directly through your skull."

Visola was at her side, trying to pry the sword away from Aazuria's fingers and begging her for mercy. Aazuria effortlessly shoved her weakened friend aside with one hand before returning both to the hilt of her sword. She gritted her teeth together tightly as her blood pumped through her body at a disconcertingly rapid rate.

It took every effort she could muster to refrain from killing him straightaway. She did not even know why she was procrastinating. "One reason, Vachlan Suchos!"

As the tip of her blade prodded his tonsils, he pondered what reason he should state. He tried to remember what he personally knew of Aazuria, and he tried to remember all of the recent hearsay. What was the one thing she held most dear? Was it love? Was it family? Was it honor? He remembered regarding her as a frigid, do-gooding bitch for most of his existence. She was careful. She did not love easily. What reason would seem the most moving to her?

As her icy, unyielding blue eyes bored into him, he

realized that there was only one thing which could save him. The truth. He began to rummage within his unsorted baggage to discover the true reason his life should be spared. Of course, there were several. He enjoyed breathing, for example. It was hard to think under pressure. He still imagined that he could gain the upper hand and overcome Aazuria in this fight, but that was not the point. He needed her to sanction his existence.

Why? Why did he need this? For Visola? Visola wanted a divorce. Why did he need Aazuria's judgment? He had always been above the law, above the rule of the kings and queens and emperors. He had gone where he wished, and he had taken what he had wanted. When someone had displeased him or insulted him, he had destroyed them without a second thought. Now, he was feeling more guilt than he had ever experienced. He could not accept Visola's pardon, for her judgment was tainted by love. Aazuria was a mostly impartial party who could justly deem whether he deserved his life.

He was not sure that he believed he deserved to keep breathing.

Aazuria lifted the sword from his throat, scraping it callously against his teeth and lips as it exited. "Speak now," she commanded.

Vachlan felt a sudden emptiness in his throat where the sword had been. He moved his tongue around to exercise its liberation, stroking the roof of his mouth awkwardly. He swallowed back the mélange of blood and saliva that had gathered once more. As he tried to straighten to some semblance of poise, he noticed that Visola was kneeling at Aazuria's side and weeping. It occurred to him then that this might truly be his final moment. The two women were the closest of friends, and yet Aazuria was completely ignoring Visola's desires.

Neither was Visola fighting or struggling to save his life. Not because she was physically incapable of defeating the queen, even in her current weakened state, but because she was deferring to Aazuria's decision. Her ultimate loyalty was not to her husband, but to her queen, Vachlan realized, and he admitted to himself that this was rightly so. He had proven through desertion that he was not worthy of any loyalty—especially one as absolute and pure as Visola's.

He swallowed again, but this time his mouth was dry. No one would mourn him. Visola was the person who cared for him most in the world. She was the only person that he had ever considered attaching himself to, and he had failed miserably. He had never really stayed in one place for too long. He had never really had a family to speak of. All his life he had been a nomadic mercenary, and he wondered if he really could fulfill the duties he had promised to so long ago. Maybe he should not have returned to Adlivun.

"Vachlan, if you will not speak, then I will be forced to act."

"Queen Aazuria. Please forgive my transgressions. I need to live so that I may redeem myself as a husband and father," Vachlan found himself saying. "I need you to give me the chance to make things right with Visola."

In one swift and unexpected motion, Aazuria slammed the heel of her foot into the side of Vachlan's head. She tossed her sword at Visola's feet before she crouched down over Vachlan, curling her hand into a fist and driving her knuckles into his jaw.

"You want the chance to make things right with her? You want to heal the wounds you caused?" She scowled at him scornfully. "Are you not eagerly anticipating the moment she opens herself to you, the moment she smiles at you with pure trust? Then when she is vulnerable, you can delight in breaking her down again?" She pulled her hand back close to her body, and repeated the motion, coating her knuckles liberally in his blood. "How are you going to betray her this time, Vachlan?"

She hit him again. "How are you going to betray us all?

We welcomed you into our home once and treated you like family. How did you repay us? You sent an army against us, led by Atargatis. Then you had Corallyn killed. Tell me Vachlan, did you kill her with your bare hands? Did you carve those words into my sister's flesh yourself, or did you order an inferior to do it?"

"He didn't do it," Visola said weakly. "Aazuria, it was all Zalcan..."

"When has this man ever followed orders?" Aazuria asked her friend. "If it was done, he could have stopped it. Am I right, Vachlan? You had complete control of the situation. You could have prevented my sister's death. You could have chosen not to harm Visola to begin with. Am I right?"

"Yes," he answered. He pushed on his teeth with his tongue to check if they had come loose. "Queen Aazuria, I am sorry for everything that was in my control, but there was also a great portion of the situation which was beyond me. You must believe one thing, if you believe anything—if I had not been stalling and sabotaging Zalcan's armies, Adlivun would have been under his control decades ago."

"And this is your justification for torturing my friend?" Aazuria whispered.

"No... that was a personal mistake..."

"Mistake! *Mistake!*" Aazuria shouted. She balled her hands up again into tight, solid fists, and returned to beating him mercilessly.

"Zuri, please!" Visola begged. She turned to Trevain, lifting her hands in shock. "She's gone apeshit!"

"Whoa, take it easy!" Trevain said, reaching out and wrestling Aazuria away from Vachlan. He held her against his chest, wrapping his arms around her to restrain her. "Zuri, were you going to let me meet my grandfather before you put him in a coma?"

"Look at what he did to her!" Aazuria hissed.

"I know, but look at the way she feels about him,"

Trevain said. Indeed, Visola had gone to Vachlan's side and was gingerly touching his jaw. She turned to Trevain angrily.

"Yes, I like him a little!" she shouted. "You don't have to make me sound like some lovesick schoolgirl—I am over ten times your age, young man!"

"Sorry, grandma."

"Jesus, he's our grandson?" Vachlan asked, as he stared at Trevain with amazement. He felt a lump of emotion welling up in his throat—an unfamiliar sensation. Was it possible to feel nostalgia for something you had never had? The two men stared at each other, sizing each other up first as adversaries, and then as relatives. "He's large," Vachlan observed.

"Impressive lineage will do that," Visola said proudly. "I think he's a whole inch bigger than you." When everyone turned to look at her, she frowned and began gesturing wildly at Trevain's stature. "His *height!*"

"My name is Trevain Murphy," the new king said, releasing his wife so that he could reach out and shake his grandfather's hand. Vachlan rose to his feet, wiping blood from his nose and cheek with his sleeve before shaking Trevain's hand. "I want you to know that for my grandmother's sake, I am going to encourage Aazuria to let you live. But if you make a single, tiny misstep, I will finish what she started. I will beat the shit out of you, and I will not stop. Is that understood?"

"It's nice to meet you, Trevain," Vachlan responded.

Trevain gestured to the doorway, where Alcyone quietly stood. "That woman is my mother."

Vachlan looked at the elderly woman, and he saw Visola's striking green eyes staring back at him from under wrinkled eyelids. Her hair was white with age, and she was thin and small. He could see his own facial structure in her cheekbones and nose. It was like looking at an elderly version of Visola, combined with the frailty of his own mother.

"Alcie, baby," Visola was saying tenderly. Vachlan was shocked—he had never heard his brassy wife use such a sweet voice. He felt a sudden wistfulness to go back in time, and see what Visola had been like as a mother. He wondered what he would have been like as a father. Would they have had petty parental arguments? Would Alcyone have looked at him with pride, trust, and happiness instead of the utter revulsion that was on her face at the moment? Vachlan could imagine what a lovely little girl she would have been, and he could hardly maintain his composure. He felt Visola squeeze his hand, and heard that she was still speaking to her daughter. "Would you like to come and meet your dad?"

"Mama," Alcyone said, as tears began sliding down her wrinkled cheeks. "Look at what he did to you. I would rather hang myself than ever acknowledge that man as my father."

"Sweetie..." Visola began, but Alcyone had already left the room. She sighed, and finished her sentence unconvincingly: "I'm perfectly fine."

There was an awkward silence in the room, as everyone looked at each other uncertainly. They were vaguely conscious of the fact that they were supposed to be family members, and that there was supposed to be some solidarity between them. Sionna moved to her sister's side, and began to unwrap the bandages from her hand to examine the wounds.

"I need to get you to the infirmary," Sionna said quietly, "and you need to fucking eat something."

"Always thinking about yourself, Sio. Can't stand being the heavier twin, can you?"

Sionna made a face. "I feel like I'm looking into one of those mirrors in funhouses that make you all stretched and narrow. You were ugly before, but now you're hideous."

Visola smiled, and was about to retort, when Vachlan interrupted. "Sionna—why the hell did you give her a suicide pill?"

"The real question is why didn't she use it? If I was

forced to interact with you for as long as she was, I would have. Her body will heal, but the irreversible psychological trauma from having to exist near you? I expect that my sister will either go into a catatonic hibernation forever, or join some sort of strange religious cult which promises her salvation."

"Oh, Sio," Visola said with a smile. "You're just jealous of my hottie husband. I know you want him. I bet you think about him when you mast..."

Visola was cut off by a firm gesture from Elandria, who had been remaining silent, as usual. *"I am sorry to interrupt, but before we become comfortable with Vachlan's unsavory presence, should we not ask Aazuria whether she really permits this? This man is only constant in his perfidy. He is our enemy, and because of him Corallyn is dead. We cannot possibly accept him hospitably! My opinion is that we should keep him imprisoned at the bare minimum."*

"Always the voice of reason," Vachlan commented. "Without the voice, I mean."

"You intend to live here among us, Vachlan?" Aazuria asked him bitterly.

"With your permission, Queen Aazuria," he responded, bowing to her.

"I know that my father wronged you," she said, "but none of us did, and you should not have taken it out on us."

"I realize that now."

Aazuria shook her head sadly. "Visola has always been there for me. She has always protected me, placed me before herself, and even before her family. She shot her own grandson when she believed he was about to harm me. Why is it that relationships are always so one-sided?" Aazuria questioned. "Why is it that one person is always the benefactor, and the other person benefits? One person is always the protector, and the other is the protected?"

She began advancing on Vachlan. "I do not approve of this model. Certain things should be mutual. Just as Visola has served as my protectress, I will be hers. I do not even care if she approves of my actions. You will be accepted back in to Adlivun on probation. If I see you look at her in a way that is not respectful, I will kill you. If I see you look at another woman in a way that resembles interest, I will kill you. If I hear you speak to your daughter in a rude or controlling way, if I hear you talking down to your grandsons, I will kill you. Do you understand this?"

"Yes," he said quietly. "I'll accept whatever conditions you impose. I know that you are fair, and I don't deserve your trust. I just need the chance to be close to my family—I need to be able to protect them from what's coming."

"Then I guess you want your job back," Aazuria said derisively. "The Destroyer of Kingdoms wants to help us preserve ours. Wonderful. I hope you know what you're getting yourself into, Visola."

Visola shrugged. "Nothing I can't handle. He's like a trained puppy dog, on a leash of platinum-plated guilt." Visola made a gesture of pulling on an imaginary leash which was wrapped around Vachlan's neck. He glowered at her unhappily.

"Very well," Aazuria said, turning to leave the room. Trevain followed her, with a passing backward glance at his grandparents.

"Puppy dog?" Vachlan repeated in dismay.

"It's true," she said with a smile, reaching over to pat him on the head. She scratched him behind the ear. "Say 'woof!'"

"No."

"Vachlan, please excuse my sister's behavior," Elandria said with her hands. *"We have recently learned that Aazuria is carrying a child, and this is certainly skewing her hormones."*

"Holy shit!" Visola exclaimed. "Glad to see they were busy having fun instead of worrying about me being tortured and maimed."

"We believe that she conceived on land, after Atargatis wounded her shoulder. Anyway, I apologize for her being somewhat temperamental."

"Temperamental?" Vachlan asked, gesturing to the bleeding gash across his face. "This is what you call temperamental?"

"Yes," Elandria responded. *"If she had not been softened by her condition, and by the unfortunate fact that the child she carries is your descendant, I am fairly certain she would have been more reasonable and slaughtered you without a hint of qualm or reluctance."*

Vachlan stared at Elandria in surprise. He did not know why, but a small chuckle was fighting its way through his throat. It was hardly a humorous situation, but such vehemence from the innocent girl was unnerving. He glanced at Visola's tired face, and for the first time in as long as he could remember, he felt a sense of belonging and home.

"Glad to be back," he told Elandria with a smile.

She did not return the expression. *"If I were queen I would order you executed,"* she signed.

"Let's make a to-do list," he suggested. "If you ever become queen, I'll remind you of the tasks on your to-do list, and you can order me executed."

"I would not require a reminder," Elandria said before turning and leaving the room. Vachlan shook his head—he had not known it was possible to feel even guiltier until he had seen Elandria's stern countenance.

"Viso," Sionna said softly. "I've been pretending to be you while you were away to keep the army in shape and…"

"You've been doing *what?* No way! How's that been?"

"Rather enjoyable and enlightening actually. I didn't know it was possible to act like such a whore and be respected even more in spite of and perhaps because of it. I want your job. Anyway, when you were in the hospital you managed to say one word before the cocksucker cut you off…"

"Hey!" Vachlan complained, but Sionna continued as if he had not spoken.

"...and I knew you'd be back, and I knew that when you returned, I would have to have every ship in our fleet prepared and ready for your command." Sionna saluted her sister. "Just say the word, and I'll launch them wherever you like."

Visola was rendered speechless. "I never knew you had so much faith in me."

"Of course I do. I believe I have been learning to understand you better through imitation. You're a complex woman, sis. I think I finally realize why you curse so much. It's fricking fun. The looks on everyone's faces—it's kind of empowering."

Visola grinned. "Well, I won't be up to full power for a while. You can be me any day you like. Actually, I need you to be me today. Can you make a quick pit stop on land to meet with my weapons supplier?"

"Sure thing, Viso"

"Great. Oh, and before you go—can you throw Lieutenant Namaka into the most uncomfortable cell you can find? And rip my bracelet off her slimy, traitorous wrist. Thanks, Sio!"

Chapter 28: Battle by Armada

"This attack is not just an attack," Vachlan said. "It's a preemptive plan of defense. We have larger concerns than just getting rid of the enemies stationed in Zimovia. We have to begin implementing a long-term strategy."

"Can we really trust him?" Trevain asked Visola quietly.

"Yes," she answered as Aazuria simultaneously said, "No."

"Here's what we'll do," Vachlan said, ignoring the women. "When this battle is over, we don't cremate the bodies like we usually do. We inform the American government. We explain that we were attacked."

"This goes against every tradition we have," Aazuria said.

Vachlan frowned at her. "Would you rather be traditional or alive, Queen Aazuria?"

"I like the idea," Brynne chimed in. "Trevain's shipwreck was widely publicized. It made the news nationally, and it's still under investigation. If Trevain comes forward, and demonstrates that he can breathe underwater, and claims that this was an international attack on his boat… that makes lots of dead U.S. citizens who are already casualties of this war. It will seem crazy at first, but once we can convince everyone, the public will jump at the chance to blame someone for these tragedies."

"I like her," Vachlan said immediately. "She's the girlfriend of my younger grandson? Callder—marry her, kid."

"I'm trying," Callder responded with a helpless shrug.

"Later on, after this is over, we'll talk privately," Vachlan said. "I have many excellent tips on forcing women to do exactly what you want."

"Hey, that sounds great!" Callder said cheerfully. He elbowed his brother in the side. "Having a notorious grandpa is awesome."

"Don't you enter a room alone with that man, Callder," Trevain warned.

"Sedna save me," Visola said, placing the palm of her bandaged hand against her forehead. "Let's get back to the matter at hand, boys."

"This decision cannot be taken lightly," Queen Amabie said. "It is not only Adlivun that will be affected if the American government is involved. It will trouble my home too."

"Trouble your home?" Vachlan asked. "With all due respect, Queen Amabie, you may have one of the best-trained armies in the undersea, but you won't be able to stand against the numbers of the Clan. Trust me when I say that Shiretoko is next on Emperor Zalcan's radar."

"Shiretoko?" Amabie asked. "How do you know the name of my home? Visola, did you tell him…" When she saw that Visola was shaking her head sadly, Amabie sighed. "Of course, you would not have. So it's true. They have not given up on destroying me."

"I'm sorry for my participation in the attack on Yonaguni in the 50s," Vachlan said slowly.

"You're sorry? You're sorry for displacing thousands of innocent people from their ancestral home?" Queen Amabie's face grew very dark. "If you had not been among them, they never would have succeeded. I blame you, and you alone, for the greatest dishonor of my life. If it were not for Visola, I would have killed you then, and I would kill you now." She shook her head. "I cannot fight alongside this man. I am leaving, and taking my army with me."

"Queen Amabie…" Visola said in surprise.

"I am sorry, Visola. Although I love you, and I am thankful for your safety, I must consider Shiretoko. You have chosen your husband over your dear ones." Amabie paused, and elegantly saluted Visola across her chest. It was evident from the sadness in her motion that this was a farewell. "I understand and respect your decision, but I fear I can no longer be counted among your friends."

Visola stared in speechless panic as the proud queen walked away. "Queen Amabie!" she called out, but the woman did not turn around. Visola closed her eyes. "Damn—I can never gain something without losing everything I had before."

"Not everything," Aazuria said softly, moving to Visola and putting her arms around her. Aazuria whispered against her friend's ear in a low undertone which the men could not hear. "Viso—given a strategic choice between your husband and the whole Japanese army... I would have gone with Vachlan too."

"Zuri!" Visola squeezed her friend back so tightly that Aazuria felt the bones in her back crack, causing the queen to laugh in surprise. "Thank you, Zuri. Thank you, thank you."

"I said strategic choice," Aazuria whispered again, smiling at the difference between a hug from Visola and her sister. She kept her voice low. "Given a personal, emotional choice, Vachlan will surely break your heart, but Queen Amabie never would. Are you willing to take the risk on Vachlan just to save our skin?"

"Yes," Visola answered earnestly. "Yes, I have to."

Aazuria nodded, pulling away, and smiling at her friend with understanding.

"We don't have to do battle now," Vachlan said sympathetically as he observed the embrace of the women. He could not hear what they were whispering about but he was sure that it was something suspicious about him. "We could just alert the government before the battle instead of after—I know that neither Viso nor Zuri are in any condition to…"

Both women turned on him angrily. Aazuria was about to scold him for referring to her in the familiar way he used to, but Visola spoke first.

"One last battle," she told him. "I need one final, good old-fashioned battle by armada before the modern armies take over my job and make me obsolete. Besides, this is personal."

*   *   *

"I have never laid eyes on something more gorgeous in my entire existence."

This was Trevain's reverent reaction to seeing the *Tizheruk* in all its glory. The trusty old ship had been restored and updated, and looked even better than it had in 1797. When people around him began to clear their throats to suggest that he had made a great verbal misstep, he quickly corrected himself. "Except for my lovely wife, of course."

Aazuria could not help feeling a blossom of pride in her chest at the sight of the old ship. She glanced at her husband with a smile. "That is fine. I also consider the boat more attractive than you."

Visola had just joined them, and she was having a similar reaction. "My baby," Visola said, lifting her hands to reach up to the ship in awe. She looked as if she were about to sing it a serenade. "My dear, sweet baby."

"Okay, now I'm getting jealous," Alcyone remarked. "Mama, I don't think you were as excited about reuniting with me as you are…"

"Shhh, I need a moment here," Visola whispered, as if she had walked into a cathedral of worship her lifted hands remained in the air for almost a minute before they fell to her sides. "Look at the old gal! Vachlan and I fought so many battles on that boat."

"Australia, India, South America," he added. "The best

part was that it had…"

"Bronze cannons," Vachlan and Visola said in unison, as they stared at the ship wistfully.

Everyone around them exchanged looks and raised eyebrows at their behavior.

"I am going to get Katie," Visola announced.

"Who's Katie?" Vachlan asked.

"A rocket-launcher. A kick-ass Russian weapon called 'Katyusha' which we can load up onto the ship. I've also got some handheld rocket launchers. I really just want to blow stuff up, you know?"

"I know, darling," Vachlan said with a smile.

"I bought a new boat too," Trevain told them. "It should be in the harbor at Soldotna by now. I'll swing by and grab it and join you guys on the way to Zimovia."

"I call Trevain's boat!" Brynne said cheerfully. "It's just going to be like old times, out on the sea with my captain."

"Except we'll be killing people instead of catching crabs," Trevain pointed out.

"Either way, something dies," Brynne said with a shrug. "This way feels better because frankly the poor little crabs didn't deserve it!"

"You sure you want to do this, Brynne?" Callder asked nervously.

"Hey—I used to be a navy woman, but why would I want to be a marine when I could make so much more money working with the sexy Murphy brothers?" She gave Callder a smile. "Besides—these sons of bitches killed my friends. Doughlas, Edwin, Leander, the Wade brothers, Ujarak, and Arnav. Even you nearly died, Callder. Let's give it to them."

"While I appreciate how enthusiastic you land-dwellers are about this, I understand that you really aren't experienced with this type of battle. I would recommend remaining in Adlivun," Vachlan said, staring at his grandsons in particular.

"I have been steering ships for my entire life," Trevain said.

"These are war vessels, son, not fishing boats. The principles are different."

Brynne smiled, and hit Trevain on the back. "Where we come from, on land, they call Captain Murphy by all kinds of nicknames. Whether he's 'The Crab Tycoon' or 'The King of the Sea' everyone knows that he was born for the water. Don't doubt him, bud."

Vachlan frowned. "I wasn't born yesterday. I was actually born in 1585. I've known fishermen who thought they could be marines and it never…"

"Visola named him as Admiral of the Fleet," Aazuria reminded them all. "He's in charge of the navy."

"That's right. This is my job now," Trevain said. "What's your job again, Vachlan?"

"I'm an advisor," the older man said.

"Interesting," Trevain said. "If I understand correctly, you helped Zalcan conquer the world for decades, and then when he became too strong and set his sights on Adlivun, you began to sabotage him, and now you're fighting against him?"

"Yes," Vachlan said glumly. "I suppose so."

"Interesting job description," Trevain said. "Where can I find a job like that? Sea-monster.com?"

When only Brynne and Callder laughed, and everyone else just looked at him with puzzlement, Trevain groaned. "It's a joke. I'll explain what the internet is later. Let's do this."

Everyone began moving around and heading in different directions, but Aazuria grabbed Vachlan's arm. "I'm going to command my own ship," she told him, "but I want you to promise me something."

"Sure, Queen Aazuria," he said with a frown, as he gave her the salute. "What is it?"

"Forget that queen garbage—I know it means nothing to you." She fixed him with an intent gaze. "Promise me as a friend, Vachlan. A very long time ago, we used to be friends."

"I remember."

"Take care of Visola out there," Aazuria said. "We're heading into battle, and anything could happen to any of us. If something happens to me, I need to be secure in the knowledge that you will be good to her."

He nodded and saluted her again. "I give you my word, Zuri—as a friend."

*   *   *

"I can't believe you did this to us, Vachlan," said the blonde warrior with a frown. They had invited him aboard the *Tizheruk* to discuss the terms of his surrender.

"Believe it. I need you to give the orders to your men, and inform them of the change in plans."

"There are ten ships behind me," said the blonde warrior angrily. "You know how strong we are. There are another ten ships at the other end of the strait. You're outnumbered. Why should we surrender to you?"

"My wife will demonstrate," Vachlan answered. He gestured to Visola, who was awaiting his signal on a nearby ship. Visola smiled at the men, giving them a small wave. She signaled another ship close to her before she flipped a switch on the massive weapon she was standing rather close to—her 'Katie' rocket launcher. She had already aimed, and now she began firing a barrage of multiple rockets. Another one of Adlivun's boats followed her lead. Two of the enemy ships were thoroughly bombarded, and the men on them were engulfed in flame as the destroyed boats began sinking within seconds. Visola grinned triumphantly and blew a kiss at the men.

Vachlan watched her handiwork with satisfaction.

"Eight ships," he said. "There are now eight ships behind you, but we can easily correct that."

The warrior observed the weapon with surprise, and cleared his throat nervously. "Well, then I guess we'll be joining you, my friend."

"Welcome to Adlivun's army. We'll offer your men better pay, and better benefits than Emperor Zalcan did. Also, the whole nation is basically comprised of women, so the men will enjoy mingling."

"Mingling, huh? Well, I trust you, Vachlan, sir."

"Don't worry, you'll like the place."

*   *   *

"Aazuria, we have to attack," Trevain said. "They're coming at us, and it's us or them."

"No—we should hold our fire," the queen responded. "We can convince them to join us without harming them."

"Vachlan said that we needed to show an 'impressive display of force' or they wouldn't consider joining us."

"They don't have a leader. They don't have any guidance at the moment. Surely something can be arranged."

"Sea-wench, you need to get it together," Brynne said angrily. "We came here, on the Capt—er, Admiral's nice shiny new ship, with all this firepower, and it would be foolish not to deploy…"

"Ladies, you'll have to excuse me," Trevain said, with a smile. "I have a plan which is perfect common ground between Brynne's thirst for blood and Aazuria's call for peace."

Trevain began walking down the length of the ship, and Aazuria looked after him with worry.

Brynne placed her hand on Aazuria's shoulder. "Hey, relax! Why don't you trust him?"

"I trust him," Aazuria responded, "but I'm just worried for his safety. This is all new to him."

"The true test of a man is his ability to adapt. There's no one like Trevain Murphy—he has all of the knowledge and abilities that a modern man possibly could have, and yet a sort of old-fashioned chivalry. He's a lion on land, he's a fish in the water, and..." Brynne glanced behind Aazuria with a small smile on her face. "I think you'll find he's even rather comfortable in the air. Like a hawk. Don't worry about him so much! He will be fine—just let him take care of you."

Aazuria nodded. "Thanks, Fisherwoman."

Brynne grinned at her. "I wouldn't work for anyone else in Alaska. Trevain was the only captain who had a healthy respect for women, and there was no doubt in his mind that I could do anything a man could do. He's the perfect package. You got lucky, girlfriend."

"So why didn't *you* marry him?" Aazuria asked. "Why didn't you pursue him?"

"I don't know, exactly," Brynne said with a shrug. "I just see him as this perfect big brother. I need my men to be more flawed and human so that I constantly feel superior and comfortable with them. Callder's my man—I feel like there's room for improvement and growth, you know? Trevain is just too good for me. Sometimes I wonder if he's even real."

Aazuria smiled at this. She often wondered the same thing. The conversation of the women was interrupted by a loud noise, as the engines of the small plane on the ship roared to life.

"Now the fun begins!" Brynne yelled.

Aazuria watched in awe as Trevain piloted the small plane down the runway of the ship, and began coasting in the air around the boat. "He can fly that thing?" she asked softly, in an awed voice.

"Up here in the frozen north, it's kind of a necessary skill!" Brynne shouted. "The only difference is that he has to figure out how to fire the bombs, but we went over the controls together last night and it should be fine!"

"Good Sedna," Aazuria whispered. Her heart felt like it had jumped into her throat as she watched Trevain navigated the plane directly towards the enemy ships. He fired a line of bombs directly beside one of the ships, just allowing the firepower to graze the side of the ship and cause it to violently sway in the waves.

"See?" Brynne said, hitting Aazuria in the arm. "He's scaring the crap out of them, and demonstrating how easily he *could* destroy them, without actually harming them."

"An impressive display of force," Aazuria murmured, quoting Vachlan. She stared at the bombing plane, marveling at how easy this seemed. "The world truly has changed since I was a girl."

"Do you really think so?" Brynne asked. "Or have the toys just gotten bigger?"

Aazuria considered this before turning to glance at her new friend. "You are far too insightful to be a fisherwoman."

Brynne winked, and returned to the controls of the ship, to order the giant machine steered directly towards the ships of the enemy forces. They could see that there was chaos and commotion aboard the ships of the Clan of Zalcan. Without proper leadership, they could not stand against the onslaught of firepower from the sky. It was not long before white flags were being hastily raised.

Chapter 29: Week of Airosen

Aazuria slowly pulled a hairbrush through her long silver hair. She stared thoughtfully at her reflection, basking in the luxury of this moment. For the first time in months, she was not sleeping in heavy armor with her hand on a rifle. Instead, she just wore her simple malachite-green silk dress, fastened over one shoulder. Her scar from the battle with Atargatis had almost fully healed, and it was hardly visible. She no longer felt weakened and ill by the beginning of her pregnancy—although her stomach had not begun showing yet, she was very conscious and excited about the changes she imagined she could feel in her body.

It was silly, but she was currently sequestered away in a location a few miles west of Adlivun for her Week of Airosen. She did not feel that it was truly necessary, but she had agreed to follow the ancient tradition for Alcyone's sake. Trevain and Aazuria had promised Alcyone that they would have a proper wedding ceremony once the war was over. With the seized enemy forces being assimilated into Adlivun's army, and with the nation's future looking brighter than it had before, it certainly felt like time for celebrating. Brynne had also finally agreed to marry Callder, and no one was happier than Alcyone was at the prospect of a double wedding. Both of her sons would be meeting this milestone together, in her beloved home—she had come a long way from being trapped in a tiny room in a psychiatric facility.

Aazuria had never imagined that it would be possible to come out of a massive war having gained more than she had lost. She could not help feeling pride and warmth at the way everything had worked out. She could not go as far as to call it 'happiness' since the thought of Corallyn's fate still brought darkness to the forefront of her mind. The damaged relations with the Japanese were another sore point, but Queen Amabie herself had always said that every victory was bittersweet. Aazuria could only wish her friends safety and prosperity, and send these pleasant thoughts in the direction of Shiretoko.

All of Adlivun was pleased with the addition of thousands of seasoned sea-warriors who were already terrified and extremely respectful of Vachlan. The warriors themselves had been skeptical and nervous at first, but they had quickly grown to see the merits of employment and life in Adlivun compared with their life under Zalcan. Sionna hoped that with time, the men would come to view Adlivun with something resembling loyalty and nationalism. Visola had been spending time in the infirmary, and she was healing well, and would soon be taking her job back from her sister. Sionna was having far too much fun playing the general.

There was still much work to do, but now there was also the optimistic sense which could only be earned by accomplishing a great task; the sense that all other tasks could be accomplished, however daunting. Aazuria placed her hairbrush down on the vanity carved from ice. She smiled at her reflection, and stood up slowly. She looked around the small room that she had been occupying alone for several days. It had never occurred to her that the Week of Airosen could be so dreary. She had taken several modern novels into the room with her, including recommendations from both Brynne and Trevain. She had about a dozen decades of literature to catch up on—but even reading could not shake the boredom of staying in one place for far too long, and being separated from her friends and family.

She moved to the carpet, and lowered herself to a seated position. She considered trying to meditate again. It was supposed to be the purpose of the Week of Airosen—quiet, peace, and reflection. Blocking out the noise of the outside world was supposed to facilitate meditation in order to reconnect with oneself. To learn what one truly wanted. The image of Trevain's face came into Aazuria's mind, and she felt a small smile settle easily on her lips.

"I like the idea," Trevain said. *"It sounds like an interesting mental challenge. I'm sure there's a reason our ancestors began the tradition."*

She gladly noted his use of the word 'our,' and his increasing acceptance and comfort with his sea-dwelling lineage. "I love that you are so willing to embrace our customs."

"I already spent years making my decision," Brynne *said with a frown. "I don't really see what one more week is going to accomplish."*

"Yeah—can me and Brynne skip this whole thing? I don't want to give her a chance to change her mind," Callder said nervously.

"No, you guys have to go along with it—when in Adlivun!" Trevain smiled. "If only people on land took the time to sit in peace and quiet for a week to carefully decide whether they really wanted to get married, I'm sure our divorce rates would fall."

"People don't have the time," Brynne said. *"A week is more precious on land than it is here, and hardly anyone can afford to stop their lives for a week."*

"But they can afford to go on their honeymoons after the wedding. Why can't they just take the time to reflect a little before?" Trevain asked.

Aazuria had laughed. "Technically, we are already married, Trevain. Technically, I am already pregnant. It's not like we took the time to carefully decide either! Whether on land or sea, life is short. A week is precious time that I would rather spend with you than away from you."

Now she sighed, in agreement with herself. She longed to see her husband's face, and to reach out and touch him. She longed to speak with him. Perhaps the point of the Week of Airosen was to make the betrothed couple understand loneliness, and truly feel the hollow space, the barren emptiness of utter isolation. Perhaps it was intended to make a person understand the constant yearning to be near to their loved one. If this was the point, then it was working.

Did understanding loneliness make a married couple appreciate each other more? If it did, surely just one week would not be enough loneliness to make the couple appreciate each other for the rest of their lives—were regular doses of hiatus necessary? Aazuria was sure that she would never have any kind of issue with appreciating Trevain, but she could not help wondering about the general population, and about all of the failed and ruined marriages. Would a simple week have been enough to change all of those lives for the better? Or was there some other crucial element in their personalities which had caused the failure?

Aazuria wondered about Visola—she had been separated from her husband for an impossibly long amount of time due to an unfortunate misunderstanding. Due to the lies and plotting of another person. The truth was that Visola and Vachlan had never had any real, serious arguments or disagreements between themselves—all of the damage had been inflicted upon them from the outside world. Since Vachlan had returned to Adlivun, Aazuria could see in the way that the two interacted that absolutely nothing had changed in the way the felt about each other. They still looked at each other with the same secret smiles, and the same warlike passion. Nevertheless, Visola was distrustful and cautious, and tried to limit the time she spent around her husband. She stayed away from him unless there was a professional situation that required their communication. Would they ever recover from this?

Smiling to herself, Aazuria admitted that she hoped they would. She knew they would recover once Visola overcame her own stubbornness. Everything was falling into a comfortable rhythm now that the larger threat of danger had passed. Of course, there was still some planning and anxiety about the future, but things were peaceful enough that the Ramaris sisters could squabble at length about the tiny, trivial details of Aazuria's wedding. It had been an exquisite indulgence to listen to the twins quarreling about something insignificant again—nothing was more relaxing.

"Sleeves are classier," Sionna said firmly.

"Zuri will look better without sleeves!" Visola had insisted.

"No, we need them," Alcyone argued. *"There must be sleeves made of lace!"*

Visola scoffed. *"Baby, you're just not fashionable. Sleeveless is sexy."*

"Aazuria doesn't need to be sexy! She's a queen! She needs to be stately!"

"They're my arms," Aazuria pointed out. *"Doesn't anyone care what my arms think?"*

"No!" Alcyone and Visola shouted in unison.

"Okay, everyone, please calm down!" Sionna yelled. *"Now, as the matriarch of the Ramaris family, I will mediate this..."*

"What? You're the matriarch?" Visola said, deeply offended. *"I'm the one with the children and grandchildren!"*

"Yes, but I'm still older than you," Sionna argued.

"By one minute!" Visola screamed.

"Yes, and that's a minute more wisdom and understanding of the world that I possess..."

"We were conceived at precisely the same time! You're Miss Biology—you're the one who always tells me that we were once the exact same cell!"

"I think we might need a monarch to perform this mediation instead of a matriarch," Aazuria said with amusement.

Aazuria missed her friends, but she knew that the isolation was necessary. She was sure that she would learn something by the end of this mini-vacation. So far, the greatest conclusion she had achieved was just a strong impression that everything was going to be okay. The war had been won, and the hard part was over. She felt like she could relax and laugh, and maybe even shed tears of release and relief.

"What a beautiful bride."

This voice snapped Aazuria out of her thoughts. Someone was standing in the shadows of the doorway, and their face was concealed by a hood. The voice sent a shiver through her, and she quickly rose to her feet.

"Who are you?" Aazuria demanded firmly. She had not been expecting another human being for days. This was against tradition, and she felt a bit annoyed at having her solitude interrupted.

The person walked forward, emitting a small, self-satisfied giggle. The moment Aazuria heard the odd noise, she knew that she was in danger. She looked around the room quickly, searching for some sort of weapon. Her eyes went to her hairbrush, and to her books. She frowned as her fingers clenched in longing for a firearm or a blade.

"You know, Queen Aazuria, hundreds of years ago, my father sent an emissary to your father. He requested your hand in marriage—to me. You were given an opportunity to tie your future to mine, and to form an alliance between our peoples."

Aazuria frowned, as she stepped backwards, crouching down into a battle stance. "I prefer not to agree to marry men when I possess no empirical evidence of their existence."

"Cheeky, aren't you? I wasn't told that you were so cheeky—I heard that you were quite the frigid bitch." The man threw his hood off, revealing a face which was covered in a monstrous mass of pink scar tissue. "What do you think of my visage?"

Aazuria gasped at the sight, recalling the story of Visola's escape. "Vachlan said that he…"

"That's right," the man said as he advanced on Aazuria. "Vachlan really screwed up this time."

"Do not come any closer!" Aazuria ordered. "I will finish what he started, I swear it."

Prince Zalcan giggled. "Are all you Adluvian woman so feisty? I think everything happens for the best. Vachlan wouldn't let me have Visola, but I think you're much prettier. How would you like to go on a little trip with me?"

"I am not going anywhere," Aazuria hissed. "I don't know how you found me, but…"

"Just shut your mouth!" Zalcan shouted, pulling a mace from his robes. He pointed the weapon directly at Aazuria's face. "You will come with me willingly, or I will make your face resemble mine! We'll make a pretty pair, won't we?"

Aazuria thought of her unborn child. She knew she had to fight. *If Visola was in this position she would not be as scared as I am right now,* Aazuria thought to herself. She made a mental note. *If I live through this, I vow that I will learn to fight as well as Visola.*

"You are the man who killed my little sister," Aazuria said softly, staring beyond his disfigured face and examining his even more disfigured soul.

"That would be me—Prince Zalcan Hamnil in the flesh."

Aazuria dove at him, grabbing his wrist to keep the mace away from her, and shoving her elbow into his damaged face. The man screamed, for his skin had not completely healed yet. He lashed out, striking Aazuria in the abdomen.

Gasping, Aazuria stumbled back, fearful for her daughter. The moment of fearful hesitation cost her greatly, because Zalcan used that instant to tackle her to the ground.

He laughed at the expression on her face. "You're coming with me, pretty lady."

"I will never come willingly," Aazuria said, spitting into his face and struggling.

"I expected that," he told her with a grin. He quickly reached into his robe, and retrieved a white rag. "That's why I've got this crazy little thing called chloroform."

Chapter 30: Better than Othello

Visola relaxed, completely nude in the healing springs, submerged in the warm water up to her shoulders. A few unusually large meals, a few stiff drinks, and a few invigorating training sessions had lifted her spirits and improved her physical condition greatly. Sionna said that she was eventually going to recover full mobility in her knee. The sisters did not tell Vachlan this, of course—they led him to believe that he had caused irreparable damage which would cause Visola chronic pain. They both kept very serious expressions on their faces as they scolded him for what he had done, but Visola imagined that he could see the smiles in their eyes.

She heard a noise in the room and she opened her eyes. Seeing the same man from her thoughts, she smiled. "Hey, husband. Caused any trouble lately?"

"I just got back from Namaka's trial," Vachlan said. "They let her off the hook—which is good, because she didn't do anything wrong. She hardly told me anything."

"She's completely off the hook?" Visola asked with a frown. "Oh—Zuri wasn't at the trial. She's still having her Week of Airosen. Very important business, you know; that whole concept of thinking for a whole week before getting married."

"So I've heard," Vachlan said with a smirk. "It's too bad that Queen Aazuria is already married, and already expecting a child. That Airosen thing is just procedural, isn't it?"

"Procedural! No, it's still really important. Although, I do admit that perhaps the standard week isn't long enough for everyone." Visola smiled as she closed her eyes and leaned back against the smooth rock. "I could have done with a few years of Airosen. Maybe a lifetime of Airosen."

"Oh? A little regretful, are you?"

"A little bit," she said sweetly, "but I do think I could change my mind if you came over here and gave me a shoulder rub."

He moved across the room and seated himself very close behind her, slipping his legs into the water on either side of her. He reached down and obediently began to knead her shoulders.

"Mmm, that's good," Visola murmured. "As your general, I sentence you to the penance of giving me unlimited massages for the rest of my life."

"I thought penance was supposed to be punishment," he said as he squeezed her upper arms.

"Isn't it?" she asked, letting her head roll back to rest in his lap. She stared up at him with a smile. "It's taxing, physical labor."

"Touching you could never be taxing."

"Mmm," she responded, closing her eyes in enjoyment. She slipped one of her arms around his leg. He moved his fingers to just below her collarbones where he began kneading her pectoral muscles. His fingers twitched, yearning to continue lower to graze her breasts which remained just under the surface of the water. He restrained himself from doing this, but the thoughts were causing him to be aroused. Visola was resting her head in his lap, so she could easily tell. A wicked smile came to her lips, as she repositioned her head, nuzzling his lap in the process.

"Visola," he groaned in protest.

"Hmm?" she murmured innocently.

"You're in an unusually touchy-feely mood. You must be drunk," he concluded.

"Of course I'm drunk. Do you think I'd be allowing you to touch me otherwise?"

He abruptly stopped massaging her and moved away from the hot spring. He stood up and crossed his arms as he stared down at her angrily. "I'm sorry, Viso! I'm sorry. I don't know what else to say. Do you even want me to be here in Adlivun? Do you even want me to…"

"Husbunny," she said teasingly, as she turned around and reached for his ankle. "Come back here."

"I'm serious," he said, crouching down to stare at her. "I know I screwed up, but I need to know… will you ever forgive me for doubting your character? Will you ever forgive me for hurting you?"

"It's all cool," she said with a relaxed smile. "Othello killed Desdemona even though she didn't really cheat on him. The difference is that Othello was a nice guy to begin with. You were always a creep. And you didn't actually kill me dead, so maybe that means you're better than Othello."

"God, I fucking hate Shakespeare," Vachlan said bitterly.

"I know, sweetie. I know." Visola folded her arms on the rock, and rested her chin on them. She sighed. "Truth is, I can forgive you for just about everything. So what if you were feeling a little pissed off because of some misinformation and you went on a massive killing spree to let off some steam? Who's to say that I wouldn't have done the same thing?"

He watched as she lifted her fingers to move dripping wet red locks away from her face, and he raised an eyebrow suspiciously. It was never that easy with Visola. She looked up at him, and her green eyes were hard and awful.

"But getting me pregnant and leaving me alone with my daughter?" She shook her head, and spoke quietly. "Not that. I'll never forgive that."

He nodded, reaching out to stroke her cheek. "I understand, Viso." He rose to his feet, and began moving out of the room.

"Wait!" she called out with a frown. When he turned

back to look at her, she sharply asked, "Where are you going?"

He shrugged. "I'm not sure. I didn't want to bother you."

"Don't be ridiculous," Visola said, rolling her eyes. "Come back here! You broke my body, so it's your job to fix it. Shoulders—shoulders!"

He smiled. "You're not really drunk, are you?"

"Do you remember how high my tolerance is? It would take more gold than there is in this kingdom to get me drunk!" she boasted. When he returned to his seat, and began massaging her back again, she rested her head on his knee. When she spoke again, the cheerful tone had gone from her voice, and she was serious. "Vachlan, there is a way I might be able to forgive you."

"You're going to make me do a silly dance, aren't you?"

"No!" she said with a laugh. She turned around and grabbed his shirt, pulling him into the water with her. Putting her arms around his neck, Visola stared into his eyes solemnly. "I'm being serious for once. Do you want to hear my super-serious decision?"

"Yes, please," he said softly. The look in her eyes was so deep and intense that it completely distracted him from the fact that her naked body was pressed against him. Well, almost completely.

"Okay. Here it is. Vachlan, if you stay with me, and if you spend more time being here with me than you have spent away, then I will forgive you—absolutely and unquestionably."

He smiled. She drove a hard bargain, but it was fair. He wrapped his arms around her waist. "I will," he promised. "Just watch me. Two hundred years of devoted husbanding coming right up."

"Sure," she said, snorting. "It will never happen."

"Bet you twenty bucks."

She smiled, and hit him. "You're on." Then she bit her lip thoughtfully. "Wait, American dollars, right? I wonder what will happen to the American economy in two hundred years. We'd better bet in gold."

"I love you, Visola."

Her eyes widened. She laughed and hugged him around the neck, burying her face against his neck to hide her blush of pleasure. It seemed that everything was sorting itself out. She could hardly believe how lucky she was, to have her husband back and to have all of their misconceptions cleared up. "You're the greatest weapon I've ever had," she whispered. Vachlan knew that this was the highest declaration of love she was capable of uttering. Of course, utterance aside, there were other ways in which Visola could much more eloquently express her love.

He began running his hands up and down her lower back. "Since the grandchildren are all getting married, should we renew our vows too? It's too bad we missed celebrating our two-hundredth wedding anniversary. We could have had a nice picnic."

"Meh," Visola muttered. She felt a small jolt of joy at being relaxed enough to experiment with new language again. There was something so communicative about that simple sound: *meh*. It was an emotion and an attitude all in one. In her opinion, it was much superior to the plebian *duh*. It was positively philosophical. It was the compression of "come what may" and "I'm above all of this" and "bring it on" into a single syllable.

"What does that mean?" he asked her.

She smiled at him. "It means that we don't need to do that. How about this: if we make it to three or four hundred years of marriage, and you're still around, maybe we can have pie."

"I like pie," he said, letting his hands slip down over her bottom.

Visola paused, glancing over her shoulder down at his

hands. She glanced back up. "If we make it to our five hundredth anniversary, maybe we can have sex again."

He pulled her against him abruptly, forcing her body against his so that she could feel his heat through his clothing. She was forced to tilt her head back to look up at him. "Do you really intend to punish me for that long, Visola?" he said in a mockingly mournful voice.

"I intend to punish you forever," she said earnestly. She was really trying to keep the smile away from her lips. She was really trying to keep the tingles out of her spine.

"I don't think you can resist me for as long as you think," Vachlan said, as he reached down and grasped her thigh, pulling her good leg up around him. He leaned down and pressed his lips against her ear, taking her earlobe between his lips and gently nibbling on her skin.

She swallowed at this intimate position. She had missed him. She had missed him more than she could possibly explain, or ever admit. For every unit of happiness, there was an equal unit of fear which told her that the happiness would not last. This fear made the moment all the sweeter for its rarity. Part of her wanted to cry with happiness, but she was cool-Visola. She struggled with the greatest determination possible just to appear casual. She could not let him know that she was affected. She could not simply tell him that she also loved him, and that being in his arms again was her dream coming true. She was way too tough to stoop to the level of cliché.

"I resisted your torture," she told him, stubbornly jutting out her chin. "What makes you think that I can't resist your seduction?"

"I know you, darling," he said softly, kissing the corner of her cheek and nose. He seemed to know that he would have been kissing away a tear if her pride had not been too great to allow it to fall. "I know that you intend to give me your body and pretend that it means nothing to you. You think you can keep your heart tucked away somewhere secret, out of my grasp. It won't do. I will have all of you again."

"Well," she said, a bit choked up, "I guess we'll see about that in a couple hundred years, won't we?"

"In five hundred years we will both be old and decrepit," he said. He leaned down and pressed his lips against hers, letting his warm tongue dart into her mouth. Visola felt some kind of winged insect fluttering around in her stomach as Vachlan pulled away to whisper, "I want to be with my wife in five minutes."

Visola frowned. "Five minutes?" She was a bit disappointed. She had expected him to say that he wanted her desperately *now*. That was the type of thing he would have said when they were younger. There was nothing romantic about five minutes. "So what am I supposed to do in that time?" she asked with annoyance. "Are you giving me a head start to run away, screaming 'rape' through the infirmary halls?"

He reached down and pulled his shirt off, revealing his muscled chest. "Foreplay, of course."

"Oh," Visola said. She tried to keep the blush away from her cheeks, but the combination of his proximity, his confident words, and the mesmerizing sight of him was too overpowering. She groaned and looked at the ceiling for help, before muttering, "I'm going to regret this."

He used the opportunity to rain kisses across her exposed neck. "I give you my word as an Englishman that you will not."

"That's worth something," she said with a laugh. She hit him in the shoulder. "Vachlan, can you please stop wasting our five minutes and get to work?"

"You change your mind rather quickly, don't you?" he asked, as he circled her waist with his hands and began to tug her underwater.

"Shut up and show me what you learned in the twentieth century."

ABOUT THE AUTHOR

Nadia Scrieva was born in 1988 in Toronto, Canada. She studied English and Anthropology, graduating with an Honors B.A. from the University of Toronto in 2011. She likes knives. Writing has been the most meaningful part of her life since she was a child.

Nadia loves receiving feedback from readers, so do not hesitate to contact her with any of your comments, questions, ideas, or just to say hello.

www.NadiaScrieva.com

CPSIA information can be obtained
at www.ICGtesting.com
Printed in the USA
LVHW111259040221
678375LV00025B/118